Sweet,
Soft,
Plenty
Rhythm

*
*
*

Sweet, Soft, Plenty Rhythm

*
*
*

Laura
Warrell

 PANTHEON BOOKS * NEW YORK

LIBRARY OF CONGRESS CATALOGING-IN-PUBLICATION DATA
Name: Warrell, Laura, author.
Title: Sweet, soft, plenty rhythm: a novel / Laura Warrell.
Description: First edition. New York: Pantheon Books, 2022.
Identifiers: LCCN 2021055170 (print) | LCCN 2021055171 (ebook) |
ISBN 9780593316443 (hardcover) | ISBN 9780593316450 (ebook) |
ISBN 9780375715396 (open market)
Subjects: LCSH: Jazz musicians—Fiction. Man-woman relationships—Fiction. Fathers and daughters—Fiction.
LCGFT: Novels.
Classification: LCC PS3623.A864375 S64 2022 (print) |
LCC PS3623.A864375 (ebook) | DDC 813/.6—dc23
LC record available at https://lccn.loc.gov/2021055170
LC ebook record available at https://lccn.loc.gov/2021055171

www.pantheonbooks.com

Jacket art by Alexandria Coe
Jacket design by Linda Huang

Printed in the United States of America

First Edition

2 4 6 8 9 7 5 3 1

For my mother

Jazz music is to be played sweet, soft, plenty rhythm.

—JELLY ROLL MORTON

The chicks didn't live with that horn.

—LOUIS ARMSTRONG

Sweet,
Soft,
Plenty
Rhythm

*
*
*

Intro

*

Circus

The girl may have been the end for him. The end's beginning, like the bend of a road too slight to notice where it leads. She could have happened to him a day later or a day before, but she was there on that day, in that moment, just hours after Circus Palmer turned forty, a predictable time for a certain kind of end to come, and just seconds after Maggie slid her hand from his wrist and with her lips parted just enough to slip his finger through if he'd wanted, whispered, "I have something to tell you."

Outstretched on a chaise longue beside the hotel pool, Circus watched from a distance as the girl—in her mid-twenties, he figured—did cartwheels alone on the beach, her linen skirt falling open to bare the smooth plane of her hips and the slide of her calves sloping up to her toes. She lured his eyes away from Maggie, who was lying in another chaise longue beside him. All afternoon Maggie had been acting strangely, staring at nothing and losing the thread of conversations. This wasn't Maggie. Circus figured whatever it was she had to say wasn't anything he wanted to hear, so he let his attention be taken by the girl doing flips back and forth across the sand. When she landed on her feet, her hair lashed across her back like a whip, her shoulders lifted and hands spread beneath the melon sunset as if she carried it on her fingertips. Hips, calves, toes, shoulders, hands, she circled in the air again.

"I wasn't going to say anything." Maggie hummed, the sound not fully making its way to him, not quite breaking through his focus. "But I thought you should know."

If she were any other woman, he would have told her to come to the point. But this was Maggie, so he waited, a sense of dread needling in his gut. Chewing at the inside of his cheek—always his mouth needed something to do—he concentrated on the melody the girl made inside his head as he tapped a nervous rhythm on his knee.

"Listen to what I'm telling you." The push in Maggie's voice, major-keyed and salty, brought Circus back to the cabana, back to the Wild Turkey warm in his glass and Maggie beside him. Her lips were pursed as she stroked her long neck and watched the night begin to fall, possibly without noticing the girl, possibly trying not to.

Six days earlier, after not seeing each other for weeks, they'd arrived in Miami and hastily made their way to the hotel in order to get into a bed together. They'd paid extra for a room with a round marble bathtub where they could spend mornings sipping champagne before heading out to the city to visit Little Havana markets and smoke cigars. On the nights Circus played in the horn section of his friend's band—the reason they'd made the trip—Maggie went into the city on her own, dancing in salsa bars and kicking drummers off their kits so she could play. And when he wasn't gigging, they found hole-in-the-wall clubs where they could jam onstage with the band. Other players would recognize Maggie on occasion, asking what it was like to drum behind jazz greats and rock stars, and she'd tell stories about filled stadiums and rowdy tour buses, letting them craft fantasies around her. Usually Circus liked being the storyteller in a room, but watching Maggie hold court gave him a charge. That morning she'd sung

"Happy Birthday" to him playing a ukulele while wearing her bikini bottoms and a birthday hat. He'd laughed and lusted and wished they'd never have to leave the room.

But now this.

He'd come to Miami to draw a clean line between his first forty years and his next, and he'd invited Maggie because she was the only female in his life who knew how to be easy. He didn't love traveling with women. A woman in the room meant ending the night back at the hotel where she was waiting.

"Sorry, baby." He stroked her knee. "I'm listening."

The air was slick with heat, the sky in full dusk. A breeze stuck in the palm trees clung stubbornly to coconuts instead of drifting down to cool him. As Maggie sipped a Manhattan, Circus felt crowded in a way he never had with her before.

"The sun's going down." He finished his drink and looked around for the server to bring another. "Why isn't it getting cooler?"

A barman came with a bottle of bourbon from the other side of the deck, and Circus listened to the soft burble of the pour. Beside him, Maggie hiked up her dress to let the breeze reach across her brown thighs. He couldn't stop himself from looking. To him, she'd always seemed designed rather than birthed, her body lean with crisp angles and slight curves. Circus resented her then for knowing how to steal his gaze from whatever spot on the horizon it had settled on, and he squirmed, sensing the tie lodged somewhere deep inside where he didn't have access, the tie that attached him to her over three years—loosely, but attached nonetheless.

After the barman went away, he said, "I remember when I was a little tyke, me and my buddies did the math to see how old we'd be in 1999. Thought we'd be flying around in spaceships by then. Now here we are, 2013." He looked over at Maggie, who didn't seem to be listening. "Time, man."

She answered only, "Light me a cigarette."

Circus reached into his pants on the cement, pulled two Marlboros from the pack, lit them, and handed one to Maggie. He liked watching her smoke—the moist spread of her lips and the way she always let the tip of the cigarette linger at her mouth before she took a hit.

"I was late." Casually, she ashed the cigarette into the air. "So I took the test."

He let out a hard breath he didn't know had been stuck in his throat and waited for her to smile, to laugh, to do something to let him know she was joking. "I don't believe it."

"Believe, sugar."

"We're careful."

"Only sometimes."

"You sure it's mine?"

The corner of her mouth lifted. "Nice try."

"I'll be damned." Circus opened his legs wider across the chaise. "We're like a couple teenagers."

A chuckle tapered out of Maggie's mouth with a velvety line of smoke. "I didn't think it could happen. Not with the number of years I got on me."

"Baby, you're not of this world. Who knows the miracles that body can do." He took her hand, kissed the inside of her wrist, and linked his fingers through hers. "I got you, darlin'. We'll take care of things when we get back to Boston."

She ashed the cigarette again, winced.

"Right?"

The cigarette smoking between Maggie's fingers and the liquor in her glass reassured him momentarily, but then he noticed the edge in her gaze.

"Maggie, come on," he said.

"I'm thinking."

"What's there to think about?"

"Don't talk to me like I'm a fool."

"You know nothing good could come of this. Shit, I already got a kid barely talks to me."

"Koko would talk to you plenty if you saw her once in a while."

"Jesus, Maggie, don't ask me to do something I'm no good at."

"I didn't ask you for a damn thing."

Circus's body seized as if everything keeping him alive had shut down at once. He tried to stay calm but felt like a cage was rising around him. He imagined climbing back through the moments of the day and settling into the space where he didn't know so it wasn't yet true, where she hadn't yet told him so he was still free.

"Don't do this to me," he said. "Everything's about to happen, you know this. I got Peacock Evans trying to set me up with that producer in New York so I gotta be ready, gotta focus. Man, just talking about it's giving me the jitters."

On the other side of the pool, a woman glanced up, letting her opened book fall to her chest to watch them. He was used to being watched with Maggie. They were loud and beautiful together.

Circus lowered his voice. "You got everything you could want in your world. You want some kid messing that up? You gonna let some kid get in the way of me finally having what I want? Don't mess with what we got. You're brilliant and kinky and don't need jack from anybody. You're my wildcat, Mags. Don't get soft on me."

When Maggie turned her eyes, Circus knew he had the choice to take back what he'd said or let it widen between them. Maggie rose from the chair, her body blocking his sun. He braced himself, his hand sweating around his glass. Maggie's tall frame towered over him, holding him down. Even his clothes seemed to pull at their seams.

"Say something else," she said.

He took a defiant sip of his bourbon. "You're no mother."

Maggie collected her bag and stormed across the deck, back inside the hotel. He was surprised to feel a twinge of regret at her walking away, but a swig of bourbon took care of that. It was the dread that stayed in his gut and grew solid, so that the only relief came from down the beach where the girl was pinwheeling through the air.

* * *

It was the going he liked, liked the unclasping of links, liked getting to whatever was waiting at the other end of his leaving. It was this that pulled him toward the girl, dangled in front of him by either a generous or a mischievous fate. She seemed a promise of good things, good things welcoming and soft, as she stood on the beach and lined her lips with shimmery gloss. Circus loved those first moments when a woman didn't know he was watching and he could linger inside the strain of his body trying to resist. But he didn't linger long this time. The dread pushed him away from the terrace, away from the hotel and away from Maggie until he was slipping on his pants, grabbing his trumpet case from the ground and sprinting down the beach.

The lamps lining the boardwalk lit up as the sky started to deepen on its way to black. Circus made his way through the families lugging floats and coolers back from the beach, the couples strolling arm in arm. Once he hit the sand, he plucked a seashell from the ground, easing up beside the girl. He held the shell up to the waning sun, studying it in hopes of making her curious. She finished another cartwheel and sat hunched over her knees, peering up at him through the part of her hair.

"Wanna make a wish?" He held out the shell for her to see.

She shook her head, a skittish glint in her eye.

"Why's that?"

"I only make wishes on birthday candles. They're the only wishes that come true."

"Suit yourself." He kissed the shell and gently lobbed it into the waves.

"What'd you wish for?"

"You know I can't tell you that." Circus kicked a rock from beneath his shoe. "Where'd you learn to toss yourself around like that?"

Her gaze flickered up the beach toward the cabana where he'd just been sitting beside Maggie. The corner of her mouth quaked into a half-smile, and he wondered whether she understood what had brought him to her.

"I got two left feet," he said. "Even onstage, I can't move with that kind of grace."

"Onstage?" The girl slid her wrap from the beach and tied it around her waist, rising to her feet. "You don't look like an actor."

"What's an actor look like?"

"Handsome." She fondled the wrap's tassels in the knot at her hip. "Young."

Circus took a step closer to her, enjoying the tease.

"Do you tell jokes?" she asked.

"Music, doll." He tapped the trumpet case in his hand. "Why? You like jokes?"

She nodded.

"Tell me a joke then."

The girl reached into her beach bag and pulled out a brush, picking loose strands from the bristles before running it through her hair. Circus took the time that her eyes weren't on him to study the angles of her face—the hewn nose and cheekbones, the pretty point of her chin. He could tell by the coy way she carried herself that she had already begun to understand what those angles could do to a man and was trying to figure out how to handle it.

"A guy with amnesia goes into a bar." She eyed him as she ran the brush through her hair. "He sees a beautiful lady and asks, 'Do I come here often?'"

"'Do I come here often?'" He grinned. "That's a good one."

Something shimmered on the ground, so he poked through the sand and pulled out a piece of sea glass. He handed it to her. "Matches your eyes."

The girl fingered the glass, a smile quivering on her lips. He could smell her now. The oily sweat of her skin beneath brine from an earlier swim, mint chewing gum, and the faint scent of vanilla. "They call me Circus," he said.

"I'm Luz."

He heard the accent. Cuban, he guessed. "Well, Luz, what is it you're doing out here all by your lonesome?"

"I cook in this hotel," she answered, her voice like the pluck of a guitar string out of tune. He couldn't decide whether he liked it. "I always come to the beach after my shift ends."

"Silly, them hiding you in the kitchen." Circus glanced toward the hotel to make sure Maggie hadn't come back. When he turned to the girl, she had her phone in hand, scrolling.

"Am I boring you?" he asked.

She shook her head.

"Promise nothing's more interesting in that phone than what's standing in front of you."

"I don't believe you really wished for anything," she said. "I think you were only pretending."

"What's it matter? You don't believe in wishes anyway." He took another step toward her. "Listen, an hour from now, I got a gig down the beach at Tres Gatos. I wished you'd take me some- where to eat and come with me to the show after."

"Why would I?"

"Oh, you should, doll. I'm good company."

Luz slid her phone into the band of her skirt, turned, and started walking. "What kind of music do you play?"

Circus followed. "Jazz. You ever listen to jazz?"

She shook her head.

"Something else you should do. Sweetens the soul." He stopped walking and lit a cigarette, letting his silence signal his impa- tience, letting it turn her back around.

She asked, "How do I know you're a nice person?"

"I reckon you don't."

"What do I get if I go?"

"Come by and I'll show you, doll. Take a risk."

She yanked at the knot. "Where do you want me to take you to eat?"

"Anywhere. Doesn't matter. Bring me someplace you like to

go." He took another glance at the hotel and a shiver passed through him. "Just get me away from here."

* * *

That night there was no Maggie and nothing growing in her belly. There was nothing except Circus's body and breath. He played and forgot. Horn at his lips, buzzing. Sugary sound rising in the air, the notes skipped from the trumpet's bell as he led the brass section through "Oye Como Va." And in every direction were women, always. At the edge of every stage on every night he played, they were like flowers in the dim rooms where Circus— manly and thick, with a mess of black hair and playful shadows in his eyes—blew his horn. He tipped his cap to a redhead at the bar, then ran his gaze down the row of bodies at the edge of the stage, landing on Luz perched on a stool. They'd shared two plates of pasta at the hotel restaurant, Luz going on about young women things—an argument with a girlfriend and a television show she liked about ballerinas—in a way that usually would have irritated him but today offered a welcome distraction. Circus was grateful then that Maggie had always known to leave him alone on the nights he played. If ever there was a night to leave him be, he figured, it was this one. When the girl smiled up at him, he brought the trumpet back to his lips and let out a blare. She hopped off the stool, laced her hands behind her back, swung her hips.

"It sounds sweet when you play," she said when he joined her at the bar after the set.

"Maybe because I was imagining you sitting here." He ran his thumb across her chin. "That's how you sound to me. Or maybe that's what I sound like when you're around."

The half-smile returned as she pulled away. "I want something to drink."

"I was thinking we could head elsewhere."

Luz slapped her fists against the bar to get the barkeep's attention, then ordered a tequila sunrise. She shimmied her shoulders to the Bootsy Collins tune that was playing.

"Did you know there are clouds in the sky with alcohol in them?" she asked.

"That doesn't sound right."

"It's true," she said. "I read all about it. Big clouds drifting through the sky. They're far from Earth, we can't go up and drink from them. Maybe the stars are having a party."

"I'm sure it ain't the kind of alcohol you're thinking of."

The barkeep placed the cocktail in front of the girl, and she stirred instead of sipped it.

"Drink up quick now," Circus said.

"Why rush?" She slurped, cringing as a flicker of embarrassment blinked in her eyes.

His nerves gnawed at him like the moment before a fight went down in a club or a noise sounded off behind him late in the night on a street he'd never walked.

"Where are you from?" she asked.

He glanced at the grenadine bleeding through the orange in her glass and gently pushed it closer to her. "Kentucky."

"That's not what I mean."

He knew what she was wondering. Everyone always asked. He had African and Shawnee blood from his father, English and Native Hawaiian from his mother. Italian somewhere along the line. Circus didn't know what else. When he toured Europe in college, women thought he was from the Islands, though they never said which ones. No one ever knew what to make of him, and he came to like the lack of definition, the trick of it. It meant he could be anything.

"Or nothing," Maggie had once teased.

"Or everything," he'd replied.

"Are you Brazilian?" Luz sipped her drink through the stirring straw. "You could be."

She took an imperceptible sip of the cocktail and told him

about a man she'd met from São Paulo who was big and dark like he was. Circus let her believe he was Brazilian because she seemed to think it linked them somehow.

"So?" He spun his empty shot glass on the bar. "Where you taking me?"

"Why do you want to leave so bad? I like it here."

"I was thinking you might show me more of your fine town and see where we end up."

Luz settled onto a stool, filling his empty glass with olives from a ramekin on the bar and popping them into her mouth like candies. "Tell me something I don't know about you."

There was something twitchy about the girl, troubled, like she was moving against a rhythm he couldn't follow. She kept touching his elbow and shoulder, kept bumping him with her hip. He liked looking at her, the way her black hair swooped over her eyes and graced the small of her back. He decided he liked her voice, off key as it was and snapping. There was a loose tempo inside it, an undercurrent of sound struggling to find pitch. He liked hearing it the way he liked hearing an orchestra warm up. "Why don't you go first?"

She stirred her finger in the olives and thought about it. "My favorite birds are robins."

"Okay," he said. "What else?"

"I'm afraid of snakes."

"That's just bein' wise."

She stopped to watch the barman pour a margarita into a glass. "Where do you live?"

Circus pulled a pack of cigarettes from his back pocket and yanked a toothpick from inside the plastic sleeve. "Boston."

"Is it nice?"

Chewing his nerves into the pick, he answered, "Depends what you're looking for."

She draped his arm over her shoulder. "Bring me there."

Luz had a faraway look in her eye, a wistfulness he never liked watching women disappear into. He lured her back by tucking a loose strand of hair behind her ear. "We're in February, doll, that's still winter in Boston. It's cold right now."

She held an olive between her fingertips, stared at it, thinking. "Cold's not so bad."

Circus looked around to see what else was happening in the club. The bandleader was chatting up a blonde in one corner of the room. In the other, the redhead from earlier in the night stirred her martini. She noticed the girl beside him, sneered, and turned her back.

When he faced Luz again, she slid a fat olive between her lips, rolling it across her tongue, then tilted her head back to swallow. Circus watched.

"I know what you want," she said, giving the redhead a glance.

"Do you?"

"A bad girl. You think I'm bad?"

Circus was confused suddenly and liked it. She glanced at his mouth, slipped the toothpick from it, and pressed her lips against his. Circus's mouth filled with her—mint chewing gum, stale tequila, an unruly tongue and spit and teeth, but the lack of elegance made him wonder what her body might do. She sat on the barstool, legs swinging and gaze holding him at a tantalizing distance.

"I got a rule, sister." Circus ran a finger over her mouth. "No woman under twenty-five. So before this goes any further, how old are you?"

"Twenty-four. Can't you change the rule for me?"

He leaned down for another kiss but stopped when the club door opened behind her and Maggie stepped inside. In a red dress, she was a spark in the darkness, a stoplight's flare burning a hole in the night. She lingered at the door searching the room for him.

Circus grabbed his trumpet case from the floor and the girl by the elbow and led her out the club's back entrance. The phone buzzed in his pocket. Maggie. He turned off the ringer and snapped on the tiny metronome he kept clipped to his keychain to let the rhythmic tick calm him.

"Circus?" Luz nibbled at her thumbnail. "What's happening?"

He pulled a cigarette from his pocket, lit it, and took a drag.

"Are you in trouble?"

For an instant, he fell in love with the simplicity in her eyes. "Is there somewhere we can go?" He eased her away from the door. "You live around here?"

Luz took a step back, folding her arms over her chest like a child unsure how to protect herself. All at once, he regretted speaking to the girl, regretted bringing her to the club, regretted the thundering mass of his body next to hers that now seemed so small. She was so young. Reaching into his pocket, he offered her two twenty-dollar bills.

"Go inside and call a taxi," he said.

Luz tsked at the money. "I can just call my brother."

She pulled her phone from the band of her skirt and dialed, glancing up at him briefly as if the last few hours hadn't happened and he was only a stranger on her path. He thought to give the girl a kiss on the cheek but realized how pointless the gesture would be. She was already forgetting him as she made her way back into the club.

And so he sprinted through the parking lot toward the water, letting the black sky cover him. Walking alone down the beach toward his hotel, Circus listened to the Atlantic's wet murmur against the shore and the smooth press of his heels against the sand. The scent of the sea and the fresh salt air reminded him he was in a new place, disconnected from the rest of life. But then he was thinking of Maggie. He turned on his phone to see if she'd called and wondered what it was in him that hoped she had. He wondered, too, what it was that resented her as soon as he discovered two missed calls, what it was that made him feel choked.

The first time he'd seen her, standing in the middle of a friend's garden party, she seemed mythic, like sculpture. Circus couldn't stop watching. Everything about Maggie seemed to crackle like lightning—her percussive laugh, her smile, her gait. There was nothing familiar about her, yet as soon as they spoke, everything was easy. For three years, he went to her whenever he needed that sense of recognition and whenever she called in need of whatever she got from him. He'd never thought about how long it would last or how it would end. Until tonight.

Circus planted himself on the beach, lost in the gentle passage of the wind that seemed to move through him. He wanted his horn. Nothing calmed him like its sound. Rinsing his hands in the ocean's salty waters, he opened the case, licked his lips, brought the brass to them, and blew. He played one of the salsa tunes from the night but slowed the rhythm and let the morose, tottering melody fill the air, swaying between minor notes and major. He blew, and the tightness in his body loosened as he gave the song to the sea, to Luz back at the bar, and to Maggie wherever she was.

When he finished, the air held the sound, the wail of the trumpet ringing where the waves met the shore. Circus wished the whole night had happened differently. He saw himself back at the club, dropping the trumpet from his lips, stepping off the stage, and finding himself a spot in the back of the room where he could nurse a glass of bourbon until the sun came up and he knew what to do about himself.

Circus continued to the hotel. The air was loose around him, the wind running its cool fingers through his hair. He found his rental car in the lot and took the bottle of whiskey he'd kept beneath the passenger seat. Sitting on the hood, he took a swig, gazing up at the endless sky, without walls, without corners, and beneath it, found calm. But then thoughts of Maggie came, Maggie wriggling beside him in the sheets of the bed after she'd woken up that morning and later swung her hips as she traipsed through the room humming music. He was desperate for her and knew he should have gone back to the hotel after the gig. As he thought of her, something in him began to crack, something seeping and wet and wounded, and an old terror rose in his chest.

Circus looked up when a flicker of light caught his attention. Maggie walked out onto the terrace five floors above, the breeze lifting the hem of her nightgown. He followed her gaze out to sea where the water was dancing, the waves sighing against the sand. Maggie was near, the crack was closing. The way the moon cast its glow against the railings of the terrace made it appear as if she were contained and just out of reach. He loved her entirely then and imagined a child in her arms, his child, and there was something comforting and erotic about it. He watched her and loved her but knew with each step he took to the room where she waited, his love would fade, and by the time he got to the door, it would have drained completely.

Circus clicked open the lock of the car, laying his trumpet in the back seat and covering it carefully with a blanket. Sliding into the driver's seat, he had one last glance at Maggie and sped out of the lot. The guilt swelled against his ribcage until he drove far enough away to sense its silent pop. He lit a cigarette and found a jazz station on the radio, settling in for the next couple days. The drive north would be long.

Ready, the Heart

*

Koko

"Does it hurt?"

The drag of the sewing needle's point across Koko's forearm left two tiny dots of blood and a sting, so she couldn't tell which of the girls clustered around her on the school bleachers had asked the question. Koko glanced at the other freshman who'd gone first after Natalie De Luca and Kima Brooks asked who wanted their ears pierced or skin tattooed. The girl held a napkin over the freshly engraved miniature heart on the inside of her wrist, her lips parted as if she were secretly taking breaths from the chilled winter day to keep herself from being sick.

"It should hurt," Natalie said, the tip of her tongue curled against her top lip. She sat two planks up on the bleachers, her long legs crossed at the knees. Teeth chattering against the cold, she rubbed at her bare thighs, goose pimpled under the hem of her down coat. "So does it?"

Koko barely recognized the whispery sound of Natalie's voice because Natalie, who'd been Koko's best friend in the neighborhood until the older girl's legs lengthened and breasts swelled three summers before, hadn't asked her a question in years.

"No way," Koko answered.

Straddled on the plank beside Koko, Kima lowered the point of the needle into the flame of her pink Bic lighter. "Where do you want it?"

Koko ran her finger over the inside of her arm beneath her elbow joint. "There. I guess."

A yowl came from the track field yards away, where a group of boys were having a snowball fight, and all the girls on the bleachers turned to look. The captain of the basketball team—the Tower, everyone called him—swept flecks of snow from his jacket with his giant bony hands, cursing whoever had thrown the snowball. Koko watched him bend to the ground to craft another ball with the same precision and care her art teacher shaped molds of clay.

"What color you want it to be?" Kima asked.

The tip of Kima's needle blackened against the flame. Koko bristled, imagining its drag across her arm, though a part of her wanted to feel it again, to see the white scratch of the needle on her dry brown skin, to feel the cut and watch the blood. She wanted the other girls to see.

"How are you gonna color it in?" Koko asked.

"Permanent marker." Kima snapped a wad of gum Koko didn't know she'd been chewing. "The color stays because of the slit."

Millicent, one of the older girls, rolled a collection of permanent markers between her palms, and Koko listened to the strange crack of plastic. She had wondered all year how anyone with an old lady name like Millicent could be as popular as this girl was. But Millicent wore blue jeans that hung low on the angles of her womanly hips, and she had an accent all the boys made fun of, though Koko could tell they liked the sound.

"Why don't you put, like, a gust of wind since your name is Bree?" Millicent stopped sorting through the markers and tilted her head. "You know, Bree like breeze."

"That one's Bree," Natalie said, nodding toward the blonde freshman with the heart tattoo. "This one's named Koko. But if we're letting her hang around, which I haven't decided if we are yet, she needs a new name. 'Koko' sounds like a puppy."

Rolling her eyes, Millicent dropped the markers onto the plank. "I can't keep these little freshman girls straight."

Koko caught an aqua blue marker before it rolled to the ground as Millicent fluffed her hair, then bounced off the bleachers and headed toward the boys. The back-and-forth swing of her hips embarrassed Koko as if somehow the sight were too grown-up for her, like dirty movies or high heels. The boys flocked around Millicent, but only the Tower was taller than she was, and the two seemed to gravitate toward each other in a way that made Koko imagine they were dancing. She noticed that Bree, the other freshman, who now held a lump of snow over the fresh wound on her wrist, was watching, too.

"What do you want the design to be?" Kima asked.

"Maybe a butterfly?" one of the girls suggested. "Kima draws good butterflies."

"Get a bulldog," said another girl, drawing a black diamond on the back of her hand. "Then you'll never forget going to school here."

Kima spat her gum to the ground. "That's something I want to forget. Class of 2013, girl, this is the year I'm set free."

"Maybe she should get the Tower," Natalie said. "She stares at him enough."

Koko felt the soft kick of Natalie's foot against her back. When Koko turned, she hoped a look would pass between them that would tell her Natalie remembered the years they used to run through the neighborhood in their pajamas and make costumes out of their mothers' jewelry. Instead, Natalie blew a sarcastic kiss through her lips, slick with a purple lipstick she said was called Lilac Kitten.

"Circus," Koko said louder than she'd meant. "I want it to say Circus."

Kima arched an eyebrow. "You like clowns or something?"

"Circus is her dad." Natalie slid her phone from her pocket, thumbing at the keys. "She's obsessed with him."

"No, I'm not," Koko mumbled.

The other girls snickered as if cued by the roll of Natalie's eyes. Bree looked up at Koko with a thin smile, her lips caught on the wires of her braces.

"Whatever," Kima said, making another pass of the needle through the flame.

A giddy shriek sounded from the field, and all the girls turned just as Millicent latched her fingers through the belt loops of the Tower's blue jeans and followed him across the snow-covered grass.

"Are they fucking?" one of the girls asked.

"Obviously," Natalie said without looking up from her phone. "Millicent fucks everyone. Why do you think the boys love her?"

The Tower ran faster than Millicent could with her hands attached to him, so she tripped, which Koko thought mean until she realized the fall was meant to give him a reason to help her to her feet. Koko watched them cross the field, noting how the older girl had a way of putting all the prettiest parts of herself just out of reach of the Tower's touch when she moved around him—the corners of her hips, her mouth, the flipped ends of her long black hair. Koko tried to see herself slinking around the boy the way Millicent did, but knew she didn't have that kind of magic, not like Millicent, or Natalie.

They were both tall and raven-haired and delicately built. Even the other girls on the bleachers, including boyish Kima with her sleek frame and straightened hair, were lovely the way Koko knew girls were supposed to be. Their hair fluttered when the wind blew through it, unlike the bun of bristly curls knotted at the back of Koko's head. Their faces were made up of squares and triangles, unlike Koko's rounded nose and cheeks. They looked like girls in shampoo commercials, she thought, while Koko was sturdy and small, thick-thighed and busty. Sometimes Koko saw a pretty girl when she looked at herself in the mirror, and she knew she had something because men in the streets stopped to whistle. But at school, she felt ugly—her eyebrows too bushy, her lips too plump, her brown skin too blotched.

"Would you do it with Tower, Nat?" asked the girl coloring the diamond on her hand.

Natalie looked up, the glint in her eye a tease at the younger girls. "I'd blow him."

The girls laughed or agreed, and Natalie smiled to herself, Koko understood, because she liked imagining doing it. Koko, who'd never been kissed or touched by a boy, let her gaze fall from the Tower's face to his shoulders to his knees, briefly gracing the lump in his blue jeans. She'd seen naked boys, but only hidden under the blankets of her bed, where she watched videos on her phone before falling asleep at night. As the Tower gripped Millicent by the wrists and pulled her to her feet, Koko quivered against the same sensations she felt under her blankets. Readiness, fear, and a light tickle between her legs.

"My boyfriend would die if I did that to another guy." Natalie fixed her hair in the camera on her phone. "Older guys get wicked jealous."

"The boyfriend we've never seen," Kima said under her breath.

The younger girls glanced at each other as if expecting a fight, except for Bree who seemed as in the dark as Koko on the matter. Unruffled, Natalie took a quick scroll of her phone, turning it so the girls could see the photo on the screen of a white male torso, chest slim and hairless, his slanted purplish thing in his grip.

Koko turned her head before the picture could stick, but she wasn't fast enough. She didn't know which of the feelings in her body to allow—exhilaration, confusion, embarrassment, alarm—so she rolled her sleeve further up her arm in preparation for the tattoo as the other girls fought over the phone to have a closer look.

Natalie let out a cackle that sounded wild and sinful. "He sends me a dick pic whenever he wants me to come blow him. It's like the bat signal. Usually he gives me jewelry to thank me when I'm done, so it's a win-win." She stared at the screen, lying back on the plank of the bleachers as if falling onto the cushions of her sofa at home. "Just looking at this picture makes me want him in my mouth."

"Gross," Bree said, then gasped as if speaking were a mistake.

"Don't knock it till you try it," Natalie said.

"Why do you like it?" Bree asked.

Natalie unspooled her lipstick, smothering her mouth in violet. "I have all the power."

Koko turned her gaze back to the Tower, wondering what he looked like when he let his pants fall to his ankles, wondering if he ever made noises like the ones she heard the men in the videos make when women put their mouths and hands on them. The Tower was grinning at Millicent like he loved her, and Koko's heart hurt because she wanted to be looked at that way. As Millicent jumped onto the Tower's back and let him carry her across the field, Koko wondered what Natalie meant by power and if it made the older girls more exceptional than the younger ones. If it somehow made them prettier.

"Someone's thirsty," Natalie said, poking the pink tip of her tongue through her purple lips that reminded Koko of a bruise. "Do you want to have little Tower babies?"

"Hardly," she answered.

Natalie went on about the Tower and Koko's make-believe babies, speculating on whether they'd be tall or short, athletic or lazy. The other girls laughed, but Koko wasn't bothered. Even though she thought the Tower was cute, and even though she had once kissed her rolled fist imagining his mouth, she was no longer thinking about him because her truer love was making his way across the track field. Mr. O'Rourke, the English teacher, waved his hand at the girls while beside him the school guidance counselor, Mrs. Washington, stumbled through the snow in heeled boots.

"I should go," Koko said, certain she knew why the teachers were coming and not wanting the other girls around to see.

"What about your tattoo?" Kima asked.

"Can I get it tomorrow?"

"We're not doing them tomorrow," Natalie said.

Just then Mr. O'Rourke called Koko's name. All the girls turned their heads.

"My God," said the girl with the diamond on her hand. "That's who I want babies with."

Kima hid the lighter and needle in the backpack between her feet as Mr. O'Rourke waved again, his wide mouth revealing a toothy grin. He'd always reminded Koko of a tree, with his lanky limbs knotted at the knuckles and knees, the way he loomed over her desk when he asked questions. Koko also thought of caricatures she'd watched drawn at birthday parties because his jawline was an inch too big, his nose bumpy and his brown hair a shaggy mop. "Goofy," her mother had once called him after a parent-teacher conference. Still, he mesmerized Koko whenever she sat in his classroom or saw him in the halls, and she knew other girls felt the same.

"Your babies would have giant heads," Natalie said and returned to her phone.

Mr. O'Rourke clapped his gloved hands together and said something to Mrs. Washington that made her laugh.

"How's everyone doing this afternoon?" Mrs. Washington asked when the teachers arrived. All the girls mumbled an answer. "Pretty chilly to be outside, isn't it?"

"They're tough," said Mr. O'Rourke, beaming at Koko.

"Maybe we should find some clubs for you all to join," the guidance counselor went on. "There's better things to do with your after-school time than loafing on the bleachers."

"We're bonding," said one of the girls.

"Bonding's good," said Mr. O'Rourke in the bouncy way he said everything. "I hope you're bonding over the Lucille Clifton poems we talked about this morning. I bet that's what you're doing. Am I right?"

All the girls tittered except for Natalie, which seemed to bother Mr. O'Rourke. Koko could tell how much he liked making everyone around him smile. It was one of the things she loved most about him.

"Natalie," he asked, "you didn't like the Lucille Clifton poems this morning?"

She didn't answer at first and continued scrolling through her phone.

"Only the 'Dark Moses' one with the guy's rod twisting like a serpent," she said without looking at him.

"We didn't read that one," he said to Mrs. Washington as his cheeks reddened. "That's not one of the poems I assigned."

Mrs. Washington nodded, though she didn't seem to understand.

"Koko," she said, taking a step forward. "Are you busy, dear? We'd like to get your two cents about something."

The other girls looked at Koko like she was in trouble. She grabbed her backpack and followed the teachers across the field, answering vaguely when they asked about her classes and grades, whether she had plans for spring break.

When they stepped inside the school building, Mrs. Washington stomped the snow from her boots, and the sound echoed in the empty halls.

"Koko, dear," she started, "do you have any idea why we want to talk to you?"

Koko knew but shook her head. The two teachers glanced at each other like actors playing schoolteachers on a television show. Mr. O'Rourke flicked his head in the direction of his classroom, so Koko followed them down the hall, taking her favorite seat at the side of the room near the window. Mr. O'Rourke sat behind his desk and started flipping his fountain pen between his thumb and forefinger while Mrs. Washington opened one of the accordion files she'd been carrying.

"We found something of yours," the counselor said.

From one of the sleeves of the file, she pulled out Koko's journal, on which she'd plastered Day of the Dead stickers and drawn roses and slinky cats. For two days, Koko had been waiting for Mr. O'Rourke to come to her with the journal, which she'd planted on a bookshelf in his room two days before, knowing Mr. O'Rourke cleaned the room himself because he was too kindhearted to leave it to the janitors.

"Did I do something wrong?" Koko asked.

Mr. O'Rourke scooted to the edge of his chair. "Of course not."

"We just have some . . . concerns about some of the things we read in your notebook," Mrs. Washington said. "We weren't trying to invade your privacy reading it. We just needed to see who the book belonged to."

"What are you concerned about?" Koko asked.

Mrs. Washington sat on a corner of Mr. O'Rourke's desk. "A couple of the poems you've written. They're lovely, Koko. You're a talented girl. We're just concerned about the content. Whether what you're describing in them is real or imagined. You understand?"

Koko had never liked the way Mrs. Washington spoke to everyone like they were little kids. It wasn't Mrs. Washington she'd wanted to talk to anyway.

"I'm not comfortable," Koko said.

The teachers glanced at each other again.

"Maybe I should leave you two alone," said Mr. O'Rourke.

"No," Koko said, her hands clenched beneath the desk, "I'm not comfortable talking to Mrs. Washington."

The counselor recoiled. "Why not, honey?"

Koko ran her hands over the surface of the journal, picking at the edge of one of the stickers as she tried to come up with an answer that would make sense. "Mrs. Washington isn't a poet. She won't be able to understand my poems."

"It's not the craft we want to talk to you about, Koko," she answered.

Koko pressed the edge of the sticker firmly against the cardboard cover. "I prefer talking to Mr. O'Rourke."

Mrs. Washington nodded, collected her accordion files, and left the room. After a prickly silence, Mr. O'Rourke stirred a bowl of paper clips on his desk with his fingers, took one, and bent it around his thumb.

"Are you having a good year?" he asked.

"I guess."

"What's your favorite class?"

She shrugged, embarrassed to say "English" now that they were alone. "Not math."

"Yeah." He chuckled. "I was never very good at math either. Tell you a secret?"

She nodded.

"I didn't even make it to algebra in high school. Too much of a knucklehead, I guess."

Koko fidgeted inside the strange sensation that came over her body, as if her leg had fallen asleep but the tickle were moving all over. She had never been alone with him, had never been alone with any boy she loved.

"How many books do you have in there?" she asked, nodding toward the tiny alcove attached to the classroom that Mr. O'Rourke had turned into a library.

He glanced over his shoulder. "You know, I haven't counted. A hundred? Two hundred? Like I said, I'm bad with numbers."

"Can I go in?" she asked, her stomach fluttering like it did when she daydreamed during class about Mr. O'Rourke leading her into the library, shutting the door, and kissing her.

"Koko, I think we should talk about your poems." He came around the desk and sat in the seat beside her. "May I?"

She shrugged, taking in the soapy scent of his aftershave. He took the journal and opened it to the first page, sliding his hand across the words she'd written purposely days before in hopes that he would read them and worry, that this very moment between them would come.

"It's a beautiful poem," he said, scanning the lines. "But when I read it, I feared . . ."

His voice trailed off, and he bit at his bottom lip, nervous, it seemed, about how to handle things. When he looked toward the door, Koko imagined he was wishing Mrs. Washington would return. She would know what to do.

"What's wrong with the poem?" Koko asked.

Mr. O'Rourke kept his eyes on the page. He swallowed, and his Adam's apple bounced. "Koko, are you . . . is this person . . ."

He struggled, and for a moment Koko was sorry for lying.

"Is what you wrote in the poem true?" he asked. "Your stepfather . . . he uses . . . are there substances in your house?"

For days, Koko had imagined this moment but hadn't expected Mr. O'Rourke to bumble so awkwardly through it. The point of writing the poem had only been to stand out from the sea of faces he looked at every day. How easy it would be to tell him now that the poem was made up or was about a girl she could pretend to know, then seize their moment together and move it in a sweeter direction. But for some reason, Koko didn't want to do that. He was struggling. He was struggling over her, and she'd made it happen. She wanted more.

"Yeah," she answered.

Mr. O'Rourke fell against the back of the chair, letting out a long breath he seemed to have been holding in. He paged through the journal absently, not reading or even looking at the poems. "Mrs. Washington should handle this, Koko. She knows the proper channels, okay, the protocol. There's a protocol. Why don't you want to talk to her?"

Because I love you, she imagined saying. Instead she asked, "What's to talk about?"

Mr. O'Rourke got up and paced the room, his hands in his pockets. He stood in front of a Walt Whitman poster as if he were getting some kind of guidance.

"I think I'm supposed to report this," he said.

"What? Why?"

"Are you in any danger? I think I'm supposed to ask. Are you?"

Koko grabbed the journal and shoved it into her backpack. Her voice seemed stuck in her throat, cracked and sticky like she remembered feeling once when she had the flu.

"I'm sorry," he said. "This is new for me."

"Don't tell anyone. There's nothing to tell."

He sat on the edge of his desk the way he always did when he was about to say something serious. Something else Koko loved.

"It's all right," he said. "I won't say anything about this, not today. Go home. Think about it. I'll do the same, and we'll talk again tomorrow. Is that okay?"

She nodded, eager to get out of the room.

"Good, good." He put on a smile. "Tomorrow we'll see what happens."

* * *

Koko climbed onto the city bus, rushing to the back for a seat, then huddling beneath her coat. She imagined herself in Mr. O'Rourke's library the next day. She would tell him she'd made up the poem but hadn't wanted to confess because he seemed so affected. She imagined him letting out the long breath he'd been holding in, saw him pat her knee, saw the relief in his eyes. He would ask to see her poems again, then open her journal to his favorite one, praising her images and metaphors. They would meet every day after, at first to talk about her poems. Soon they'd meet because they wanted to. Then Koko saw him in a different daydream. They were sitting in his library, where each day she would talk about an invented stepfather shooting up in the bathroom until the day she could say the man left. By then, Mr. O'Rourke would love her.

When Koko walked up the back steps of her porch, she noticed her mother's car parked in the driveway. The dusting of snow on its surface meant she hadn't driven it that day. Unlatching the lock, Koko stepped through the door into the kitchen. The lights were out, the room quiet except for the drip from a leaky faucet down the hall in the bathroom. Her mother sat at the dining table, stretched across two wooden chairs, cradled by them, as she slumped against the chair's rails like a doll.

"You didn't go to work." Koko closed the door, slipping out of her boots and coat.

Her mother opened her eyes. Moments passed. The faucet in the bathroom dripped.

"I couldn't," she said.

The cigarette between her fingers had almost burned to its end, though the ashes had yet to fall. Koko tapped them into her own hand to keep them from dropping onto her mother's nightgown, the color of apricot and cream.

Patting the ashes into the sink, Koko asked, "Am I making dinner again?"

Her mother lifted herself in the chair, gazing up at Koko with dulled eyes, her upturned nose and soft bow of a mouth pinched. As a little girl, Koko used to tell people her mother—tall, slender, golden, with shimmering blonde hair—was Cinderella, though now she looked like a Cinderella who'd been scrubbing floors, her skin washed out and hair in tangles.

"I can't," she answered.

Koko opened the refrigerator, looking over the cartons and packages past their sell-by dates. "Macaroni salad or tuna casserole?"

"Tuna."

Koko pulled out the casserole pan along with a pot of sweet potatoes that had spoiled.

"What time is it?" her mother asked.

Koko tossed the potatoes down the garbage disposal, tapping the ashes from her mother's cigarette again as she passed. "Almost five."

With a groan, her mother got up and stretched. "I'm going to watch television."

"You want a drink?"

"My daughter shouldn't be making me drinks."

"Do you?"

"I don't have any more vodka."

Opening a cupboard, Koko found a bottle of cabernet and poured a glass. Her mother looked at it like she was doubting whether to take it. Then she did. "How was school, sweet girl?"

Koko settled against the counter, watching as her mother drank the wine as if every sip pained her. "This is a long one, Ma. I thought you were feeling better."

"I'm just having an off day." She cracked a smile, and for a second, Koko saw Cinderella at the ball.

"You said the same thing last week. Are you seeing that doctor again?"

"He didn't know what he was talking about. It's just a longer spell than usual. It'll pass."

"There are pills, you know."

Her mother stamped out her cigarette in the sink. "I asked about school."

Koko watched her push the crushed tip of the cigarette through the gray smudge of ashes as if she were painting the inside of the sink.

"This girl got in trouble for making up a poem in English class," Koko said.

"What kind of poem?"

"She lied about some guy doing drugs in her house."

"What's the point of that?"

"There's a boy she likes."

Her mother caught her own reflection in the window above the sink and combed her bangs with her fingers. "That's not a good reason."

From a bag in the junk drawer, Koko scooped a handful of raspberry candies left from Christmas. "I guess she thought if this boy knew bad things happened to her, he'd like her, too."

"What's likable about bad things happening to people?"

"I don't know. Maybe he'd feel sorry for her."

"Well, that's dumb." Her mother took two candies out of Koko's hand. "The last thing you want a man to feel is sorry for you."

"What should she do?" Koko asked. "I told the girl she should tell her teacher the truth. Don't you think?"

Her mother finished chewing the first candy and popped the second into her mouth, her gaze growing emptier as she sucked and crunched. When she spoke again, the words seemed to drain out of her. "I don't know, Ko. I'm not the one to ask about making someone love you."

"I meant, what she should do not to get in trouble."

Her mother looked out the window at a squirrel twitching its tail in the trees. "It's so cold out there. Where do they go to stay warm?"

"I think they make dens in the trunks."

"I wish I had a den."

Her mother disappeared into the living room so Koko took the bag of candies and went upstairs to her bedroom. She did her math homework and struggled through a chapter of her biology textbook. Nearly two hours later, her phone chimed on the bed-side table. A text message from her mother.

Is it time to eat yet? she'd typed.

Koko stuck out her tongue at the phone and placed it on her chest at the spot where she imagined her heart beating. She pictured a hand placed there, but not Mr. O'Rourke's. She saw her father's hand. He'd laid it there, she imagined, to comfort her. He'd been coming to mind lately, and Koko didn't know why. He'd moved out five years before, after she and her mother ran into him with a woman at a Market Basket in Somerville when he was supposed to be playing a gig in the Berkshires. At first, he visited a lot, but in the last few years, he'd come by only once or twice a year, phoned every so often. Koko couldn't remember the last time. Not that his leaving changed much. Circus had barely come home during the decade he'd lived with them in the duplex.

Still, she thought of him more now than in the years he'd been around.

I'm starved came another text from her mother.

Koko turned off the ringer and lay back on her bed, playing out scenes on the blank ceiling. Mr. O'Rourke in his library, sitting on the floor across from her, elbows balanced on his knees and hands linked between them as he listened to her. She watched him laugh, nod, then scrunch his mouth the way he did when someone told him a sad story. She imagined him patting her knee and running his hands down the inside of her thighs.

Shivering, Koko switched out the lights and stared out the window into the dusky sky. She rolled her tongue in her mouth and imagined him kissing her. But she couldn't see herself. She saw Mr. O'Rourke, saw his hands and shoulders. She could even smell him. She could see the books on the library shelves and the pattern of the braided rug on the floor. She could see her clothes. She couldn't see herself.

* * *

The next morning Koko took an earlier train to school, hoping to run into Mr. O'Rourke before his classroom filled. But when she arrived outside his door and peeked through the tiny glass window at its top, she saw him at his desk wiping tears from his eyes. He pressed the bridge of his nose between his fingers, shuddering against a deep cry.

Koko backed away from the door. At the other end of the hall, the principal strolled by, waving as he passed.

"Good to see you so early, Miss P," he said. "That's the kind of get-up-and-go I like."

She waved back, keeping quiet so Mr. O'Rourke wouldn't hear. She started down the hall toward the library, where she hoped she could disappear among the shelves until the first bell rang. But just then Mr. O'Rourke's door creaked open, and he stepped into the hallway.

"Koko?" His face was red and softly bloated.

"Oh," she said, "I was just going to the library to get some books for my history paper."

A tear glistened in Mr. O'Rourke's eye. "What's the paper about?"

Koko swallowed. "The Aztecs?"

He nodded, his jaw clenched.

"Are you okay?"

"Just allergies." He showed her the tissue in his hand, pressed it against his wet eyes.

"Well, I was also coming to see you," she said. "About the poem."

"Of course." He twisted the doorknob back and forth like a nervous boy. "Come in."

She followed him inside, and he gently closed the door behind her. Koko slid back into her favorite seat by the window as he leaned against the edge of his desk.

"So," she started, "you're right. I should talk to Mrs. Washington. That's what I'm going to do. I don't want to make you uncomfortable."

"Don't worry about me. I just want what's best for you and whatever situation you're in. You understand that?"

She nodded while at the same time coming up with a story to tell Mrs. Washington to get her off her back.

"Is everything"—Mr. O'Rourke shook his head side to side— "okay at home?"

"Yeah." Beneath the desk, Koko dug her thumbnail into her palm. "I just made it sound worse than it is. For poetry. Like you said. Art has to have more drama than life, right?"

"I guess I did say that." Mr. O'Rourke grinned again, and his upper lip quaked. "I'm glad. And I'm glad you're talking to Mrs. Washington. She knows how to help."

He looked past her out the window, and his gaze grew hollow. Without the stepfather to talk about, Koko realized there was nothing left to say. The poem had gotten her into the room. Now she needed to figure out how to stay.

"Do you like teaching?" she asked.

"Sure," he answered, spinning the wooden apple he kept on his desk. "Sure I do. There are lots of good things about it."

"What's not good about it?"

He chuckled. "The paperwork. My bosses have lots of forms they need me to fill out."

"They probably don't want to lose you," Koko said. "Everyone loves you."

Mr. O'Rourke seemed to want to smile but didn't seem able. He kicked his foot in the air toward her. "What about you? Are you liking high school?"

"Sometimes. But I miss middle school."

"Why's that?"

"People liked me better."

"I understand," he said. "I had the same problem."

"You?"

"Yeah me." He folded his arms and poked at the point of his elbow. "Do you have any idea what you want to do when you get out of here?"

"Not really. What do you think I should do?"

"You could be a baker," he said with an airy smile. "I remember those amazing oatmeal cookies you brought in for Thanksgiving. Or did your mom make them?"

"My mom doesn't do those kinds of things much lately."

"Work keeps her busy?" he asked. "What's she do?"

"I'm not sure. Something about raising money at a kids' school. My dad's a musician, though. He's on his way back from Miami now. He was there playing with a salsa band. He'll probably bring me something," she said, knowing he wouldn't. "He plays all kinds of music."

"Oh, yes, I think you've told me before."

"He plays trumpet." Koko lifted in her seat. "He almost got to play with Dizzy Gillespie when he was sixteen."

"You know Dizzy Gillespie?"

"I know he must be amazing to almost play with my dad."

Mr. O'Rourke was looking at her again and smiling. "Do you play music?"

"I take piano lessons to make my mom happy, but I don't really practice."

"You should, Koko."

"I don't want my dad to get mad at me."

"Why would he get mad at you?"

"What if I'm good?"

The smile loosened on Mr. O'Rourke's lips, and the sadness came back to his eyes. Spinning the wooden apple, he said, "I know going from middle school to high school can be confusing but . . . I just . . ." He picked up the apple, held it firmly in his grip. "You're a good girl, Koko. You study, you read. Those are good things. I know there are kids around here who seem to have it all figured out, but . . . I don't know if I should say these things. Just . . . just pick your friends carefully. Will you do that? No matter how you see other girls acting, you should know there's nothing wrong with being a good kid."

Before Koko could come up with a response, the morning bell rang. She excused herself, then made her way out of the room, where the hallways were already filling. An entire school day lay ahead of her, but all Koko wanted was to sit with Mr. O'Rourke, to talk to him and watch him fiddle with the wooden apple. She wondered what inside him hurt and if there was something she could do about it.

"What did you guys talk about?" Bree, the blonde freshman from the day before, had sneaked up behind her at her locker. Koko noticed the bandage wrapped around the girl's wrist where Kima had etched the miniature heart.

"Infected. I'm grounded for a week." She gave Koko a nudge. "So? Tell me."

"Nothing," she answered. "I asked him about my grades."

Bree glanced at Mr. O'Rourke's door as if hatching a plan of her own. "I live on Oak, so I drive past school all the time after my family's shrink appointment. O'Rourke stays late, like, all the time. I see him getting into his cute little Honda, and I keep promising myself I'll come back, y'know, and like, talk to him. But I always chicken out."

"He's easy to talk to."

Bree shook her head. "What would I say? I'm not brave like you."

She went on about the argument her parents had the week before in their therapist's office, and Koko listened, happy to feel she was finally making a real friend, until her attention was drawn by Natalie and Millicent strutting down the hall. They moved like models, and everyone stepped aside to make way for them. They wore tight off-the-shoulder tops—Natalie's ivory white, Millicent's lemon yellow—and pale blue jeans. Millicent's bone-straight black hair tumbled from beneath a Red Sox cap, while Natalie's hung in a single braid down the slope of her back. The girls laughed at a joke only they shared, though Koko could tell they sensed all eyes were on them. When they passed, Natalie waggled her tongue between her parted lips, coated with her Lilac Kitten lipstick.

"I heard she got her lips done over the summer," Bree said.

"Her family doesn't have money like that."

"They don't have five hundred dollars? She works at Pizza Hut, doesn't she? She could make that in, like, a weekend."

"I never knew anyone who did that."

"Everyone does it back in L.A." Bree examined the split ends of her hair. "I'd get my fucking nose done if my mom would let me."

As Natalie and Millicent made their way down the hall, Koko wondered how they knew to walk like that, to laugh with their necks perfectly arched, to flip their hair at the right second. The giddiness Koko had felt after leaving Mr. O'Rourke's room wilted inside her as she felt shoved back into her own clunky body again, a bulk she wished she could climb out of. In the trail the older girls left behind, Koko was still a kid.

"I don't feel good," she said.

"Really?" Bree pressed her hand against Koko's forehead. "You seem okay."

"I should go home," she said, just as the Tower came up behind Natalie and Millicent to kiss both of their bare shoulders. "I want to go home."

* * *

The driveway stood empty, which meant her mother had gone to work. Koko had the house to herself so she kicked off her boots and coat, leaving them on the floor. In the kitchen, she saw the light blinking on the answering machine and played the message.

"Ms. Palmer," said the guidance counselor on the other end of the line. "We didn't see Koko in homeroom today. Please check in as soon as possible."

Koko erased the message before splitting open a bag of potato chips and grabbing three cans of soda, even though she was allowed to drink only one per day. In the living room, she plopped onto the sofa and kicked up her feet, skimming the channels on television. Nerves still worried at her belly, though she understood they weren't there because she was skipping school or snacking when she wasn't allowed. It was thoughts of Mr. O'Rourke, of Natalie and Millicent, of swarms of students parting in the hallways.

On television, Koko watched a chef pull the limbs from a batch of crawfish and toss them into a frying pan, stirring them later into something called an étouffée. She watched an old movie about girls in a pizza parlor that starred an actress she knew her mother loved. At noon, she made herself a grilled-cheese sandwich with extra slices of Swiss, dipping every bite into a pool of mustard. She watched two episodes of a show about men digging through abandoned storage lockers before she fell asleep. When she woke an hour later, she heard a man on the television say, "You can be the change."

Koko turned up the volume.

"You think you have nothing." The man, in a silver suit that shimmered under the studio lights, looked directly into the camera. *"But everything begins with nothing. Nothing makes something. Nothing makes everything."*

Koko shifted position so she could see him better.

"See yourself doing what you want," the man went on. *"That's what makes it happen."*

"It's that easy?" asked the hostess sitting beside him.

"Nothing is easier."

Koko switched off the television, casting the room in a ripe silence. She whipped off the blanket that she'd pulled from the back of the sofa in her sleep and went upstairs to her bedroom. She opened her closet and tore from their hangers every dress, blouse, pair of pants, and skirt she didn't think Natalie, Millicent, or Kima would wear. Minutes later most of her clothes were on the floor. A loose white top hung alone at the back of her closet, and Koko put it on, sliding the sleeves down so her shoulders were bare. From her dresser, she took a pair of jeans her mother wouldn't let her wear because they fit too tightly, ripped a hole in the knee with a ballpoint pen, and slipped into them. The only baseball cap she owned had Mickey Mouse on its front, but she wore it anyway. When the cap didn't fit over her thick curls, she went to her mother's bathroom to look for a hair dryer and hot iron. Leaning over the tub, she wet her hair, then blew it dry, burning herself twice as she flattened her hair.

Placing the cap back on her head, Koko studied herself in the mirror above the counter. With her middle fingers, she pressed in the edges of her nostrils to see what her nose would look like if she had the money to thin it, sucked in her cheeks to see how sharp the bones beneath were, and pouted her lips, trying to find the shape of Natalie's violet mouth. On a tray in a corner of the counter, she found a tiny pot of concealer, which she slathered onto her face. The pale pinkish cream was too light for Koko's complexion, but she liked how smooth it made her skin look. She swept blush onto her cheeks, thickened her lashes with mascara, and moistened her mouth with a berry lipstick called Kiss Kiss Kiss. Then she gazed at herself, mesmerized by the unfamiliar girl staring back at her.

She had half an hour before the school day finished. Koko scoured the kitchen for what she needed to make oatmeal cookies and found only one egg when the recipe called for two, so she decided to halve it. During the fifteen minutes she waited for them to bake, she went back to her mother's room to try on jewelry and perfume, choosing a strand of turquoise beads and a spritz that smelled like flowers.

The cookies packed into a Christmas tin, Koko made her way to the bus stop, arriving just as one pulled away from the curb. The next came twenty-five minutes later. It was Friday. The school day had ended more than an hour before. There were no drama club rehearsals, no sports team practices or games, no meetings that she knew of. But she hoped Bree was right, that Mr. O'Rourke always stayed late and she would find him there.

The school parking lot was mostly empty by the time Koko arrived. A few skater kids hung out near the front door, one of them smoking a cigarette, which made her think none of the teachers were around. She sneaked through a side door so they wouldn't see her and tiptoed through the halls, the silence slightly chilling without the laughter and conversation and footsteps and slamming metal lockers that usually filled the halls and gave Koko an odd comfort, as if she were part of this place even if she still felt alone there. But as she got closer to Mr. O'Rourke's classroom, she sensed energy. He was in there, she knew it.

Koko turned the corner, and as she did, the lock on Mr. O'Rourke's door unlatched. The door creaked open, and Natalie De Luca stepped through it into the hall. Calmly, she picked her backpack off the floor and started down the corridor toward Koko without yet seeing her. Koko noticed the braid in her hair was an unraveled mess. The violet lipstick had faded from her mouth and smeared at the edges.

Natalie glanced up. She saw Koko and stopped walking. Her eyes widened as if she'd been caught stealing something, but then she retrieved her calm. She scanned Koko's white top and jeans, the Mickey Mouse cap, and her mouth stained pink.

"What's in the box?" Natalie asked.

Koko felt dizzy, as if she had taken one too many spins on a merry-go-round. "Cookies."

Natalie slid her arms into the straps of her backpack, unfastening her braid so that her long hair fell across her shoulders. It was then that Koko noticed the earrings dangling from her earlobes. She hadn't been wearing them that morning.

Natalie nodded toward the cookie tin. "I'm sure he'll love them," she said and disappeared down the hall.

Koko didn't look back to watch Natalie go. She stood in the empty hallway, eyes following the pattern in the Christmas tin. Green and white lines like candy cane twists. She took a step forward and looked through the window at the top of Mr. O'Rourke's door. She'd never noticed the tiny curtain he'd nailed above it, drawn now, though Koko could see past a lifted edge. He was leaning against the doorframe of his library. Shirt untucked. Gaze fixed to the floor. Behind him, a pillow Koko had never seen before lay on the ground.

Koko placed the tin of cookies by the door and crept back down the hall before she started to cry or throw up. Around the corner, a janitor sloshed his mop in a bucket and winked as she passed.

"Puttin' in overtime," he said. "You must be goin' places, girl."

Koko pushed through the front doors of the school and rushed outside as if she'd been chased. She had to catch her breath even though she hadn't been running. The skater kids had gone. A cigarette she figured they'd left behind still burned on the concrete, and she stamped it out to give herself something to do. She knew how to get home but felt lost. She'd left the house with a full belly but suddenly needed desperately to eat. She wished Bree was already a good friend so she could go over and tell her what she had seen, so that Bree could help her figure out if what she thought was happening was really happening.

Koko started down the footpath toward the street where the bus would come in a few minutes. She waited behind a tree, out of sight of the school in case Mr. O'Rourke walked out of the building to his Honda parked in the lot. A cold breeze drifted down the street and blew something into her eye. When she rubbed it, she saw the black mascara smudged on her fingers like ash. She wiped her face into her shirt, rubbing hard at her rouged cheeks and painted mouth. The makeup left a strange splotch in the white cloth like a mistake she'd made in art class. Like a person who only seemed to be there.

In

the

Pocket

*

Maggie

Slender stalks of lavender rose from glass vases in the corners of the hotel room while the bed, piled high with silk pillows, stood surrounded by trays of chocolate, plates of figs, and crystal bowls full of blackberries and plums. In the center of the bed sat the velvet box Maggie recognized from the first two times Tip Badgett had proposed, its lid open to reveal the sapphire engagement ring Tip had inherited from his grandmother.

"Mr. Badgett has you scheduled for our sea salt and honey soak." The young porter uncorked a bottle of champagne and poured her a glass. "Then you'll have a choice of our caviar or hot stone massage."

Aching from the cold, cramped train ride she'd taken from Boston to New York, Maggie stretched across the mattress, gaze fixed on the sapphire's angles clasping the light. "Why don't you pour yourself a glass?"

"Ma'am?"

Maggie pushed a plate toward him, charmed when he turned up his nose at the figs. He had sleepy eyes, swagger, a politeness she could tell wasn't real but that made her want to play with him.

"What's your name?"

"Kamar, ma'am."

"Stop calling me ma'am, you make me feel old," she said. "Don't you get hungry wheeling around everyone's dinner all night?"

"Eating and drinking's not allowed, least not till my shift ends."

Maggie slid a truffle into her mouth. "You like working here?"

"It's all right. I worked in worse hotels."

"What's the strangest thing you found in someone's room?"

He clicked his tongue and gave it a thought. "Found a set of teeth once. Not here, another hotel. They were yellow, and I remember wondering why you would buy some fake teeth and not make sure they were shiny and white. One of the housekeepers, she had a collection of things people forgot in their rooms. Shoes, keys, like, bottles of perfume. Some weeks she got enough to do her Christmas shopping. People always leave important things behind. It happens so much, you get to thinking it's intentional."

Maggie let her gaze linger on his mouth and the tight curls of his hair. He was young and solid, and she wanted to flirt but also recognized how absurd the desire was when Tip was on his way and her belly still cramped with the trouble she had yet to deal with.

Kamar nodded toward the velvet box. "Congratulations."

"Tip does this sometimes." She held the ring up to the light. "I don't let it get to me."

"Looks to me like he means it."

Maggie's nerves shook as she realized he might be right. Tip was a man she'd known long and well. He'd brought her on his first tour almost two decades ago and brought her on every tour after because he always wanted her behind him on her drums. Once or twice a year he'd fly her to him so he could sleep beside someone he wanted to see the next morning. There were phone calls, too, sometimes whispered calls when someone else was in his bed. The two times he'd proposed came after Maggie had performed the kind of drum solo that started riots, though he knew full well Maggie Swan wasn't the marrying kind. But there was something more deliberate about this setup, and his voice had taken on an earnest pitch when he'd called the week before asking her to play the night's gig.

"I'm at your service per Mr. Badgett's request," Kamar said. "Need anything else?"

"The moon, sugar." Maggie snapped the velvet box closed. "I'll take the moon."

Kamar giggled like a boy, and she could tell he was trying to concentrate on her eyes instead of her lean neck and collarbone, instead of sliding further down.

"Speak of the devil," she said when her phone rang and Tip's name flashed on the screen.

Kamar bowed his head and quietly excused himself.

"You tricked me," Maggie teased when she answered.

"No," Tip said. "I'm wooing you. Even remembered your favorite flower."

The peppery heat of his voice set her astir, and she thought back to her last visit to his place in Malibu—poolside, her knees warming under the California sun. Tip had lifted himself from the water, droplets trickling across the panther tattoo etched onto his brown stomach. Then he curled himself around her and sang to her until night fell.

"It does smell delicious in here," she told him, stretching across the bed. "You too scared to propose in person?"

"I didn't want you making a decision quick like you've done before. I want you to relax into it."

"Sugar, we only see each other every once in a while. What makes you think we have enough to build a marriage on?"

"What we have doesn't need constant attention. Don't you need some love in your life?"

"You have a world full of women who would kill to spend the night with you."

"I said love."

A wave like seasickness welled up from her belly, so she sipped from the bottle of sparkling water, hoping the bubbles would calm it. "What time's the gig?"

"Reception starts at eight, we go on around eleven."

"Aren't you beyond playing some rich girl's wedding?"

"Not when her daddy pays half a million dollars for me to sing for twenty minutes."

Maggie pushed the window ajar so she could smell the winter, sweet and cold. Across the way, Central Park muffled the city's noise in its bevy of snow-covered trees. "I need to get on my drums. They're a fresh splash of water to the face, and I need waking up. My hands are tingling, Tip. I want to hear that boom-bosh-boom-boom-bosh."

"I'll have someone find you a set. Whatever Maggie wants, Maggie gets." Tip made a kissing sound. "We just pulled out of JFK. I'm on my way to you, girl. Get ready for me."

Maggie crawled into bed with her clothes on. Limbs tired, stomach sick, muscles of her breasts bulging as if bruised. She pressed her fingers against her belly and imagined the embryo thickening inside but found it impossible to believe anything was really there. A child at forty. Such nonsense. So far, there had been no connection to the seed that had embedded itself in her womb six weeks ago, which made it easier to forget the two appointments she'd missed to do away with it. She knew she was meant to feel something—an instinctive rush, a plumping of the soul—but she could only imagine the seed as little more than a clot on a strand of tissue.

No one knew about what was growing in her belly except for her sister and Circus Palmer, whom Maggie resented now as her stomach took a spin. What she hadn't expected when she started sleeping with him was the growing into each other, the swift evolution from strangers who shared a bed to companions who seemed to have come into the world having already learned to care for each other. She didn't believe she needed him nor he her, but she had a sense that they'd somehow become fundamental components of each other's lives, and there was an unexpected satisfaction in this for Maggie, a woman who had always flinched at any signs of continuity in her days and nights. What she'd expected when she told Circus their news was one of his grainy chuckles and a roll of his eyes. They would finish their vacation and loosely link thumbs on the plane ride home, then she would go off on her own to take care of things. Instead, he'd ignored her calls in the two weeks since Miami, and she was learning for the first time what it was to be something Circus wanted to avoid. As if she were one of the women too foolish to understand the space he required, as if he'd forgotten she needed more room to move than he did. This was a slip-up, not hers but theirs.

Maggie pulled the sheets around her body, watching through the windows as the full moon started to pool in the sky, and in its light, she noticed the windows were dirty. On the other side of the glass, not inside the room but out, the panes were caked with tree pollen from a previous spring, with grains of earth and dust. But there was a handprint in the dirt, high up in the corner of the window where the light of the moon seemed to blister against the palm of the open hand. Maggie wondered who had left the print there and how whoever it was had had the opportunity to reach these windows on one of the hotel's top floors but had chosen not to clean them.

* * *

She had fallen in and out of a nap before Kamar knocked on her door, offering to bring her to a set of drums. He led her through the corridor and up several flights on the elevator to the rooftop bar he said wasn't opening for a few hours so she could play. The drums stood on a small stage, their silver rims gleaming beneath the light. Maggie sat down and took hold of the sticks. At her back, a window framed Central Park under a new dusting of snow, and as she scanned the white treetops, she realized how much time had passed since she'd lived in New York or played for an audience. She missed the city and missed being on the road. Though she'd needed these four years in Boston with her mother as she fought the cancer that would finally take her, Maggie missed the conversations she had on the road with strangers in hotels and airports, missed the shock of different climates, the noise of unfamiliar accents and languages she couldn't decipher, the odd things people did around her because she and the band inhabited a space that had nothing to do with the routine of their lives. She missed the news stories in small towns, the entrées on local restaurant menus, the way every concert hall had its own unique smell. Most of all, she missed those great stretches of silence and inaction as she traveled with the band between cities, the rhythm she'd played that night continuing to drum in her body as all those things worked to dismantle her, then put her back together.

There was no place for a child in this. The fact that a seed had planted itself inside such resistant soil seemed to Maggie an absurd joke. What she'd always supposed came with children was a mix of boredom and fear—of mistakes, of poorly chosen words, of stepping on things, like toys, fingers, bones, flattening what was important and fragile. A child was clatter, tears, mess, shit. Unsatisfiable hunger. She hadn't the time or interest, which made her wonder why she kept finding reasons not to put an end to this.

"You want me to leave?" Kamar interrupted her thoughts.

"Whatever you want, sugar. I'll forget you're here anyway."

Maggie kicked the pedal so the bass drum boomed, locking it to the pulse she sensed in the center of her chest. She started in on a groove from Tip's most popular song, the one he would lead with that night, though she shifted the meter to a dancehall beat, popping her shoulders to the sound. The groove, buried deep in her muscle, came easily because she'd played it for years. She let herself drift on its brawny flow.

"How do you know what you're doing?" Kamar asked.

"Rhythm," she answered over the shimmy of the high hat. "Everything is rhythm. Our bodies, time, the planet, man. It's all moving in beats you just have to catch."

Maggie struck a slow roll against the snare because she'd missed hearing the sound, her eyes closed so she could feel its hum deep in her fingers. She doubled her stroke, building to a buzz, then let the beads of the sticks roll against the toms before shifting to the pattern she'd dreamed up the night before and had been drumming into tabletops all day so she could get it into her hands. Within seconds, she found it and played the pattern until her muscles started to know the rhythm's shape.

But then something inside broke, and Maggie was slowing down, her body strangely out of rhythm. She tried to catch it again, but the clock inside sounded an extra beat or skipped, she wasn't sure which.

"Get me some water," she said, and Kamar went to the bar to get her a glass. Maggie wiped her damp brow and tried to even out her breaths. She went back to the beat. The rhythm returned, but she lost it again. Only when she stopped drumming did she sense the discordant pulse in her belly, thrumming stronger than the beat of the drums, deep down where she imagined the seed had planted itself.

"You okay?" Kamar asked.

Maggie backed away from the drums as if they'd spoken or cast a spell.

"Don't the drums sound right?"

"They sound fine." She handed him the glass, nodding for him to refill it. "I'm the one who doesn't sound right."

"I didn't notice. I never met a rock star before."

"I'm not the rock star, baby, Tip is."

"But that," he said, grin broad across his mouth, "that was something else."

Kamar went on about her playing as he walked Maggie back

to her room, miming her grip around the drumsticks and the way she hit. He told her about the clarinet lessons he'd had as a boy, but Maggie concentrated on steadying the rhythm in her body as she drew in and let out breaths, focusing on the one-two hoofing of her footsteps. The longer she walked, the steadier the march of her heartbeat until finally it calmed. When they reached the door, Kamar bowed and took his leave.

Inside, Tip Badgett was sitting in a chair across from the bed, slouched, his hands rolling in the pockets of a fitted wool coat buttoned up around his neck, a blue bowler with a feather in the band, tilted low so that only his jaw was exposed, a fine jaw, strong and proud. A delicate pang pulsed between Maggie's thighs when she saw him.

"You're giving me that hat later," she said, crossing the floor to him.

Tip looked up, his eyes bleary as if he'd been napping. "I've had this one for a long time. I did a lot of bad things in this hat."

"I like it."

"You like bad things." He took Maggie's hand, pressing his cheek against her open palm. "It's good to see you. There's no one I like seeing more than you."

Maggie cradled his chin, pleasured by the feel of his skin warm and earth colored. It was the precise architecture of his face that had always drawn Maggie to him. Everything about Tip was sharp—his keen-edged cheekbones and block chin, the pointed twists of his afro, his quick movements, his silver gaze that landed like an arrow.

"How'd you get up here without causing a scene?" she asked.

"All I do is get past people without causing a scene." He took Maggie's knuckle between his teeth. "Let's go to bed, sweetness. I know how much you like making love in hotels."

"Not today." Maggie slid her finger from his mouth. His gaze held hers, dry and hard but filled with need.

"Jack Knoxville gave me this hat." Tip took off the bowler and twirled it around his thumb. "He recorded his blues album wearing it, so I always thought it was lucky, considering that record made his name. I feel like I can hear that riff from 'Issaquena County' whenever I put it on. There was a period I wouldn't take it off. I was a young man then, and young men need to have something that defines them."

"A hat seems a little obvious for you."

Tip tossed the bowler so it landed on Maggie's head, and she turned to see herself in the mirror on the other side of the room. The vibrant blue collided with her dark skin, while the delicate plunge of its brim held soft against the angle of her jaw. The longer she looked, the more the colors and shape seemed to coalesce and fit.

Tip's eyes trailed the lines of her body. "Let's ditch this gig tonight and go find a preacher to marry us right now."

"Oh, Tip." She placed the bowler on his head. "You know we're not getting married."

"I'm only trusting what I feel. I've got love for you. I know you've got some for me."

Maggie toyed with the cashmere scarf around his neck. "Love is lonely, Tip. Just you and another person, and the rest of the world falls away."

"I want to grow with someone."

"People don't grow you," she said. "Keep playing music. Create things. Making grows you. Maybe what you need is something new to do that matters."

He shook his head. "You get to the point where you're not enough for yourself anymore. You need something lasting."

"If I wanted you in my life forever, Tip, the last thing I should do is marry you," she teased. "We won't love each other when we have to."

Maggie slid the end of Tip's scarf from his neck and draped it around her own, pulling at the hem to bring their faces closer. He smiled and opened his arms around her.

"Let me do something for you tonight," he said. "What makes you feel lucky? Is there something I can get you to make you feel lucky?"

"I have all the luck I need."

Tip held out his hand, trying to draw Maggie back, but she kept her distance. "What's going on tonight? Aren't you glad to see me? I don't feel you."

Maggie followed the furrows slinking from the corners of Tip's eyes and wondered what it was about her that became so impatient so quickly. Why generosity made her feel cornered. The longer Tip watched her and waited for kindness, the looser the pull toward him was.

She brushed her fingertips across his cheek, and he closed his eyes as if a wind had swept over them. As if suddenly taken by sleep, he rested against her open palm, which meant she could watch him without being watched. Tip's extraordinary face and body had always held Maggie in such a way that she never realized what she was finally coming to understand now that his proposal seemed real. She loved him like family, deep and eternal but in a way that didn't need her presence or promises to keep going. Then Circus's face flashed in her mind, the drop of his cheeks as he'd hovered over her body the first night in Miami and whispered "I love you" because the darkness seemed to give him courage. Maggie hadn't said it back. What she felt for him, she wasn't quite sure, but whatever it was, she missed as she stroked Tip's face. Something in the rumble of Circus's laugh, in his fragile moans against her neck, the way he could be consumed by her, then become so easily distracted, which put Maggie at ease because she didn't like being the focus of anyone's attention for too long. And while she sensed the ancestral link to Tip, for the first time she also sensed the mysterious link to Circus, seemingly more vital now that it was unraveling.

"Come rub my back." Maggie made her way to the bed. Tip followed, then slid his hands beneath her jacket, pressing his thumbs on either side of her spine.

"In 1967, my father drove my mother all the way to Las Vegas from Boston to get married," she said. "He couldn't wait to make love to her. The wedding was a secret, they had the real one months later as planned. You ever want to make love to someone that bad?"

"Those were different days," he said. "What made you think of that?"

"Hotels make me think of all kinds of things."

A chill passed through her, so Maggie inched across the mattress to press her back against Tip's chest. He pulled the covers around them. Across the room, the window snapped as if tiny drops of winter cold were rupturing the glass. They both looked up at the same moment the moon seemed to swell as if taking in breath.

Tip took her hand. "Life's been good to you, Maggie. I know you don't want for anything. But I don't think you want to stay in Boston forever. Come let me make you happier."

Maggie smiled when Tip started to hum the tune he'd sung on the diving board in Malibu, Smokey Robinson singing about butterflies caught in hurricanes.

"I'll think about it," she said.

Tip brushed his lips against her cheek, and she rested her forehead against his.

"Tip, can I tell you something?"

"Anything, darlin'."

When Maggie opened her eyes, he was looking down at her with such hope, she couldn't bring herself to tell him about Circus and what she was carrying. Instead, she kissed him. "I need a little sleep."

"Let's sleep then."

Maggie crossed the room to turn off the lights and leave the window ajar so she could taste the still winter. Her body seemed heavier as she climbed into bed beside him, positioning herself on the pillow so she could see the handprint at the top of the window, the beam of moonlight at its center no longer a blister but a powerful glow, the palm open, the fingers extended, reaching for something.

* * *

The leather pants Maggie brought to wear that night didn't quite fit over her hips, so she turned down the slice of buttercream cake the bride and groom sent to the band from the reception. Tip slid his finger through the cream and licked it off before heading to a lounge at the back of the stage where he'd been paid ten thousand dollars to meet the wedding party. As the door closed behind him, she caught a glimpse of the bride, the cascading fall of the girl's veil and the train of her gown reminding her of frothing waterfalls. Behind the velvet curtain separating the stage from the banquet hall, a Tony Bennett record played "Keep Smiling at Trouble," and Maggie whistled along. The band members got ready behind their instruments, while Kamar, who had volunteered to work the evening shift so he could listen to the band, swayed at a side bar and poured a ginger ale for Maggie's unsettled stomach.

"Believe this?" A tattooed blonde with a gap between her front teeth leaned on the wall beside Maggie, who needed a second to recognize her as the girlfriend of Tip's bassist.

"I heard the wedding cake cost five thousand dollars." The woman tittered. "I've been fantasizing all night what I'd do with that kind of money."

"That's a lot of trips around the world," Maggie said, then noticed the woman rubbing her stomach, firm and round as a basketball.

"I like his music so much I wanted it inside me." A shy grin spread across the woman's lips. "That's the joke I tell."

"How far along are you?"

"Seven and a half months."

"And when did you start feeling it in there, you know? The heartbeat?"

"You have to go to a doctor to hear the heartbeat," the blonde said.

"But you know what I mean. You feel it, right? At some point you know it's in there."

"She started kicking around five months. Is that what you mean?"

Before Maggie could answer, Kamar came back from the bar with her soda. "Mr. Badgett says you're on."

Tip stepped up behind him. "You ready, darlin'?"

When Tip reached out, she wound her fingers through his and followed him to the stage, taking one last glance at the blonde, who crossed her arms over her belly like a child with a toy she didn't want to share. Maggie took her seat behind the drums, while Tip placed the bowler on his head, giving Maggie a wink when she ticked her tongue at him. A voice from the other side of the curtain commanded the crowd to put their hands together for Tip Badgett, and the curtain parted, bathing the stage in the indigo light pouring in from the banquet hall. Maggie started a gallop on the drum as Tip slunk up to the microphone, the bridal party collecting at his feet.

All at once, the high she could reach only on her drums came full and rich, a lush tingle winnowing through her veins. The heat rose to her cheeks, to the flat of her chest and between her knees. She gasped quietly, then let out a laugh that made Tip turn his head. He bounced his chin to her beat, and they moved together against the drum and the run of the bass. The lead guitar came with them, blazing across Maggie's rhythm.

Tip started in on the next song, a tune so deep in Maggie's muscles, she no longer had to think about what she played and could drift. The high was there on the next song, and the next, each move to the next pattern smoother than a dance.

Then somewhere within a solo the lead guitarist took, the rhythm slipped from Maggie's fingers. Quickly, she retrieved it, but her balance was thrown. She was slower than she should have been, and there were those beats inside again, messing with her body's sense of time.

"Water," she mouthed to Kamar, then drank the entire glass while Tip made a toast to the bride and groom. When he turned back to the band to count off the next song, Maggie dragged the beat. Tip caught it and gave her a concerned twitch of his brow. She could feel her heart pulsing in her wrists, in her temples, in her throat, but now she was certain—no matter how impossible it seemed, no matter what the tattooed girlfriend had said—that another rhythm was coming down deep from her belly. Maggie laid into her snare drum to push against it, but the beat pushed back.

"You okay?" the bass player shouted over the music.

"I'm cool," she answered.

Maggie stopped pushing and closed her eyes to listen to the second rhythm, to hear its strange shape, whether it was truly there or only in her imagination. Breathing into it, around it, with it, she sensed its dull patter gain strength, and the sickness that had coaxed her to bed earlier that evening came up for one last spin before settling. Slowly the two beats seemed to find each other, growing so bold inside her gut, she thought she might pass out. She opened her eyes to steady herself. When she did, there was one rhythm clocking inside at the right time.

Maggie eased into it, the sweat rising in her pores. She let out another gasp, then another laugh, and Tip turned again, watching as the groove came back into her hands. The crowd watched Tip like a god freed from Heaven, but the rest of the players watched Maggie as she pulled them together like rings on a thick, healthy spine. She drummed harder than she had in years, sweeping the entire room up in the flow. The moment was strange and brief and resembled a dream, and she knew what it all meant only after Tip went to her at the end of the song to ask what had come over her. Maggie clicked her drumsticks above her head and told him, "Sugar, I'm having a baby."

The
Shape of
a Circle

*

Odessa

On a wall of the subway platform, someone had painted a mural of a figure walking a tightrope, the body in pale blue against a barren gray scrim, faceless. Odessa stood in front of the open doors of the train car as fellow passengers knocked into her on their way on and off, while she stared at the mural, her eyes following the lines of the wire and the walker's balancing pole. She remembered hearing somewhere that asserting the body against the constant spin of the wire was the only way to keep from falling, and she wondered what that kind of resistance felt like in the muscles.

"Are you in or out?" the conductor asked behind her. "Make up your mind, dear. We gotta keep moving."

Odessa stepped back from the yellow line and sat down.

"Let's go then," she said.

She'd meant to get off. She couldn't. All morning she'd been riding the train back and forth between the Oak Grove and Forest Hills stations, rising to exit when the train stopped at Green Street, which was the stop before Forest Hills, three blocks from the house where Ross Griffin had lived before his wife stabbed him in the throat. In the forty-six minutes it took the train to go from Forest Hills to Oak Grove, Odessa tried to work up the courage to step off the train and go to Ross's house, where she could finally put an end to the discomfort she'd felt since reading the news in the paper two weeks before. But every time the train screeched into the Green Street station, something brought her back to her seat.

The conductor eyed her in his rearview mirror as he closed the doors and put the train in motion. In her Calvin Klein wrap coat and high leather boots, she knew he wasn't imagining her a kook or a threat, though he must have wondered why a normal-looking woman was riding the train alone for hours on a Tuesday morning.

At the Forest Hills station, Odessa followed the boarding passengers to the back of the train so she would be out of the conductor's line of sight. The train lurched backward as it shifted tracks, knocking to the floor the sketchpad she'd taken from her purse to distract herself. She stretched out her foot to capture it under her heel, but another passenger had gotten to it first.

"Can I peek?" the man asked, sliding his thumb between the sketchpad's cover and first page. Odessa would have been put off by the intrusiveness, but he was handsome, and his smile, which seemed to lift every line on his face, was already flirting with her.

"I'd have to charge a fee."

The man reached into his pocket, fished around, then brought out a mint candy wrapped in pink foil, which he dropped into her hand.

"You have fifteen seconds." Odessa unwrapped the candy, watching as he paged through the book of her sketches, narrowing his eyes, nodding his head, grinning. She appreciated the diversion, the man standing above her, unaware of the strange business of her day thus far. He was big, lion big, with sturdy shoulders and thick muscle under his clothes. Beneath the flat cap he wore, he had a mane of tumbling curls and the face of a lion, too, with a slightly lazy, slightly lustful gaze and a slender snout sloping down to his mouth. His heavy lips curled, which made him seem vulgar and a tad belligerent. He had dark eyes, one of them a bit lazy, but there was that smile, and his gaze breached something inside her and left behind a weight.

"Oh, I like this," he said, showing her the page where she'd drawn a pair of eyes, lashes full, in the bottom corner. "Makes me feel seen. Can I have it?"

"They're just sketches."

Carefully, he ripped the corner from the rest of the pad. "Sign it for me, will you? Might make me a millionaire one day."

Odessa couldn't help but grin as she wrote her name on the back of the paper. He took it, nodded gratefully, and slipped it into his jacket pocket.

"If only I had more candies." He handed back the pad. "Pay you what this fine work deserves."

"You always walk around with sweets in your pockets to give to pretty ladies?"

"Just today, lovely, just today. I'm treating myself. I play music, y'see, and there's a producer in New York wants to hear what I can do. Big label, too. Best day I've had in a long while."

"Congratulations. I wish I had candies to give you."

"Thank you kindly. Glad I get to share my treats with you."

The train slid into the Green Street station, and Odessa lowered her eyes to her hands, picking at a chip in her nail polish as she waited for the shame—that she couldn't step down, that she couldn't yet find the guts to make her way to Ross's house—to pass.

"You hear about what went down here couple weeks back?" the man asked.

Odessa stiffened, preparing to feign ignorance when he mentioned the Griffins.

"Train derailed." He pulled a toothpick from the pack of cigarettes in his jacket pocket, sliding it between his teeth. "Buddy of mine was riding and got a mighty bump on the ol' dome. Oldest subway system in the nation, and they haven't updated it since they laid the first brick."

Chewing the pick, he glanced at the empty seat beside her. Odessa tried to come up with a reason not to let him take it, but figured a few easy moments with a good-looking stranger might calm her nerves.

"Sit down," she said. "This conductor drives like a maniac."

"Circus Palmer." When he offered his hand, she knocked her knuckles against his like they were clinking champagne glasses. He took up space when he sat, but she liked his manly scent of spiced aftershave. He started to say something else, but the chime of his phone interrupted him. Lifting it from his pants pocket, he scowled at the name on the screen and turned off the ringer, glancing at Odessa with an uneasy smile that still tried to flirt. But his mood had darkened. The two of them shared the seat in silence until Circus said, "You ever wish one of these trains you're on would slide into a tunnel and not come out the other side?"

The sound of his voice was cavernous, laden with something, though when she looked at him, she could see he was trying to seem mysterious, not gloomy.

"Where would it take you instead?" she asked.

"Now there's a good question." He rubbed his hands together as if a feast had been placed before him. Odessa wondered how he could move so easily from whatever grief the missed phone call left him with. She wished she could move as easily.

"All right, the train comes out into a kind of paradise, right," he started. "We're talking sunshine, all the trees and flowers in bloom. And it smells good, too. But what's it smell like?"

"The air just before it rains."

"I was gonna say bread baking, but I like yours better." With his finger, Circus drew a line across the back of the seat in front of him as if he were drafting a map. "Here, everyone's laughing, drinking wine, running around naked like animals. And maybe the real animals make music or something. They play instruments, that's what they do. Yeah, you got an elephant on oboe. A monkey on a trombone." He snickered. "Come to think of it, me and my daughter wrote a song about an orchestra in the jungle when she was just a tot. I imagine she was the one who came up with the monkey on trombone. Funny image, ain't it? Haven't thought about that in years."

Circus laughed, and the warm sound seemed to bundle Odessa into an embrace.

"You have quite an imagination," she said.

He gave a gentle nudge to her knee. "What's on the other end of your tunnel?"

Briefly, a flicker in her mind brought Ross Griffin back to her as if he were on the train suddenly, as if somehow the pull she felt toward this stranger were a betrayal so soon after Ross had been put in the ground. But as Circus watched her with an amused curiosity—unlike the prying, meddlesome curiosity she'd seen in Ross—Odessa wanted that pull.

"I'd just stay on the train," she said. "There is no other side. I like the dark and the quiet."

"Oh yeah?" His gaze lingered. "What's it like in there?"

"Peaceful."

He didn't say anything as his stare seemed to sharpen against her.

"There are better ways to disappear anyway," Odessa said. "Just go."

He chuckled, maybe because he thought he should, not because he thought the idea funny. It was a clipped laugh, lost in his throat before it met a natural end.

"Just go," he repeated. "All right. When do we leave?"

"We?"

Circus watched her as if she were a puzzle to figure out, his eyes narrowing as he slowly ground the pick between the teeth at the back of his mouth.

Odessa returned her gaze to the dark innards of the tunnel passing outside her window. "What makes you think I want to go?"

* * *

With Ross, she had come back into the world, lured from the seclusion she'd entered into in order to regroup after Ross's predecessor went back to his wife, an exile Odessa always imposed upon herself at the end of romances, but that she never stayed in long. Something about her had always put the chase in men, particularly men whose wives or jobs or geographical distances interfered with their coming fully together, a circumstance Odessa never wanted but couldn't help finding. That Ross was married, that he was her boss, made it easier to feel the tension she liked and deepened the strife and excess of feeling she needed to feel love.

The first night she'd slept with him, Ross asked, "What happens when you trail off like that—where do you go?"

They'd shared a shower after fucking in a hotel room twenty miles outside the city. Odessa was drying her hair and telling him about the fight her brother had gotten into with a stranger on a cruise. After Ross asked, she wondered what it was about him that sometimes made her forget she was speaking.

"Being around you gets me jumbled," she said.

"You know all the right things to say."

They'd met up at a colleague's wedding earlier that afternoon. Odessa had bought a copper fondue pot for the couple, and when she placed the wrapped pot on the gift table in the garden, Ross moved in behind her, close enough to feel his heat on her back. They walked together to one of the two tables where they and their colleagues were meant to sit, and Ross, unaccompanied by his wife who was home with a migraine, placed his seating card beside Odessa's. He invited her to study their names next to each other and to hear how the sounds seemed to sing together— Odessa and Ross, Ross and Odessa—just like the strings of the quartet playing on the lawn. Odessa told him she didn't hear it the way he did. She heard only the sibilant hiss.

She was forty-five when she met Ross. Twenty years earlier,

she'd buried a man she adored and spent the intervening years tying one strand of her life to another until the knots were snug. When asked, she'd say she'd known love and yearned for it again but recognized it now only when it came with desperation and fear. After six months of sleeping with Ross, she saw how he liked to wind his fingers in her untamed black curls, to sink as far into her as he could, to get lost. She would come to like the feel of him wandering around inside her, how he burned in there, how everything she sensed in him was need. She said "I love you" without meaning it because she wanted to say it to someone, which she understood now only because Ross was gone.

The cellist in the string quartet had nodded across the yard at her, and the day seemed to go gray around him while he filled with color. Then Ross was speaking to her. Odessa was listening, not hearing. She was saying things, not thinking about them.

Am I trailing off? she thought. *What happens? Where do I go?*

* * *

Circus Palmer didn't ask where she was headed, and Odessa was glad because she didn't know what to tell him. She didn't ask him either, and somehow their avoidance of this most basic of questions yoked them in secrecy as she imagined them headed away from or toward two separate but frightful things. Circus still appeared riled, perhaps by the phone call, as the grind of his jaw on the toothpick quickened.

"What do you wish you had in your mouth right now instead of that piece of wood?" she asked.

Circus looked over at her, confused.

She nodded toward the toothpick. "A cigarette or a drink?"

"I'd take either." He grinned and slid it back into the cigarette pack. "Although what have I got to complain about with a lady as lovely as you sitting beside me? How 'bout it? You up for a cigarette or a drink?"

"I don't smoke."

"A drink then."

"It's barely noon."

Circus's phone chimed again, and when he pulled it from his pocket, she saw the name *Josephine* flash on the screen and watched a different kind of scowl reshape his mouth. A harder scowl, less patient.

"You sing?" he asked, shifting in the seat to face her squarely. "You look like you sing."

"I don't see why."

"You got a face people wanna look at and a voice like honey."

"Are you trying to charm me?"

"Are you feeling charmed?"

"I think you're talking to me like you talk to everyone else. That's not how I like to be talked to."

Circus's smile withered. "How should I be talking to you?"

"Like I'm someone different."

He took the toothpick from the pack, gnawed at it. In his silence, Odessa heard the tiny crack of the wood.

"You are someone different," he said. "Why dull the moment with serious talk?"

"You feed people the same lines, you end up with the same conversations."

Odessa could sense his confusion as she drew a face in the condensation on the window, bucking against the walls inside that had risen against him. She could be kinder. Lighter. She wanted to be.

"All right then, I got something to tell you." An impish spark lit his eyes. "All this." He twirled his finger. "Life? It's not a line, it's a circle. It just keeps coming back around. Says so in a book I'm reading. Everything's already happened, and it's all gonna happen again. Over and over. On and on and on."

"Interesting theory."

"Ain't it, though? Except I don't know whether to feel comforted or bored."

"So it'd mean you and I've been here together before."

"I reckon," he said.

"So whatever happens has already happened."

He beamed and stirred her heart.

"Do you remember any of it?" she asked, easing into the tease. "Because I don't."

"Me either. But I have a feeling it was good."

A slinky feeling uncoiled in her belly as their eyes met. Odessa turned away, though she could see Circus was pleased to have charmed her. But the train rolled toward Downtown Crossing and he stood up to collect the bag at his feet. As he did, she sensed a mild panic in her belly, one she knew would rise once the train shifted at the end of the track and made its way back to the Green Street station, where eventually she would have to step off the train and do what she'd come to do. Somehow this man's presence had eased her nerves.

So when Circus said, "This is where I get off, Miss Odessa," she told him, "Stay." The look he gave her made her realize she'd come across too eagerly. With a tilt of her head and a sly curl of her lip, she said, "Ride another stop with me."

"Why would I do that?"

"We're having a nice conversation."

"So get off here and go my way."

Odessa watched the throng of passengers on the platform pull like a magnet toward the oncoming train as it rolled into the station.

"One break in a circle," she started, "and the whole thing disappears. I wouldn't want to be responsible for that happening. Would you?"

Circus looked at his watch, then at the door, then at his watch again. "I'm supposed to be in Watertown for a meeting. An important one."

"You don't seem in a rush." She stroked her collarbone, purposefully, slowly, the panic rising, rising.

"When you getting off?"

Odessa patted the seat beside her. "Soon."

* * *

Once, Ross told her about the time he'd capsized on a raft outside his family's cabin on Lake Winnipesaukee. He was six and daydreaming about the magic show he'd seen at a birthday party—he claimed to remember specifically—when a current hit and turned him, sending him into a greenish deep. He never knew who pulled him from the water, though he could still hear a gurgle that he thought came from the lake, which he soon realized lived in his own clogged throat. When Odessa asked what he remembered most about the day, he talked briefly about the pull of a tree limb or suck of mud at his ankle, he'd never known which it was. But he said it was the violent scowl on his mother's face that had truly gotten to him, the ferocity he saw when he opened his eyes as she, a giant in this fleeting moment, hovered over his limp body to breathe the life back into him.

And so as Odessa and her colleagues pieced together what they knew of what had happened between the Griffins that fateful evening, it was this image she kept returning to. The mother on her knees, clinging desperately to the last thing in the world she wanted to lose.

Odessa was tempted to confide in Circus in order to feel some kind of release—to expel from her body the worst secret of her life and watch it vanish within the blank space of their encounter as strangers. No one but her brother knew she'd been sleeping with Ross. Certainly, there was no reason to make herself known to Ross's jailed wife or their colleagues or anyone else, yet it didn't seem fair that she got off without making amends. But maybe it was too much to tell Circus, and where to begin anyway? All she really wanted was the courage to go to the Griffins' house and leave what wasn't hers before Ross's mother arrived. His assistant said the woman was coming within days to pack up her son's life.

They talked about music and work—Circus playing trumpet in bars around town, and Odessa's illustrations for ad campaigns at the firm. He told her about the bookcase he was making in his buddy's woodworking studio, the worst gig he ever played at an apple harvest festival in Vermont, the demo he was composing for the producer in New York. She told him about the time a woman she swore was Nina Simone crossed her path during a study abroad trip in France, the sketches she drew of people on the subway and tossed into the trash. He told her about his daughter Koko, a shy fourteen-year-old he said he wished he saw more often.

"Fourteen's the age when you worry," Odessa said. "So my brother tells me."

"Guess so." Fiddling with the zipper of his backpack, he asked, "You like kids?"

"More than grown-ups."

He kicked his bag under his seat, then glanced at the subway map above the door when the train pulled out of yet another station without Odessa making a move to disembark.

"Why do they call you Circus?" she asked.

Grinning, he flipped a quarter from his pocket in the air. "My sister, she had, what do they call it, a speech impediment. When she said my name, Cyrus, it sounded like Circus. So that's what they called me when I was a little man. Once I started playing music for real, my sister comes to one of my shows, calls me Circus in front of everybody. My man on bass says, 'Brother, I can't think of a better name for a jazzman than Circus.' Rest is history."

"Can I call you Cyrus?"

He let out a chuckle and pinched her chin. "Only my mama gets to do that."

They held each other's gaze for a sumptuous second.

"Last stop, Oak Grove," the conductor announced.

The heat rose to Odessa's chest as Circus glanced up again at the subway map. When he lowered his eyes, he took a quick skim of her face, peering as if she were a blurred photograph he was trying to decipher.

"Seems to me you're riding this train from one end to the other," he said. "Now why would that be, darlin'?"

There were moments when she'd believed the entry of Ross into her world was a sort of restitution for the great loss of her younger life. Tori Griffin had taken this from her the moment she drew that knife, and while Odessa couldn't blame the woman for her anger, she resented having become part of something she hadn't chosen, and the only way to regain her footing was to right it, then remove herself again.

"Maybe we should get that drink," she said.

The train came to a full stop at Oak Grove, and Circus watched as the car emptied out and a new batch of riders stepped inside. "I got somewhere to be."

"You must not want to be there badly enough if you're still here with me."

"That sounds like some shit I'd say."

Odessa batted him playfully. "You can tell me more about your music."

"I can't just follow some pretty stranger all over town."

He sank against his seat as if the duties he'd been avoiding had finally saddled him with their heft. He asked, "Why do you want me to stay?"

For this, she had no answer except that, of all she had to do in the world, it was this hardest of tasks she couldn't bear to carry out alone.

"I'd like a different kind of day," she answered as the train rolled into the next station on its way back to Forest Hills. "Where are you supposed to be?"

"If I say, you're gonna tell me to get off this train and go. If you're a good person, that is. Are you a good person?"

Their gazes locked again and seemed to fasten them together as Odessa understood that he truly needed to be where he was going but also wanted to stay with her.

"I don't want to say where I'm headed either," she said. "But I could use the company."

"What happens when we get where you're going?"

"I don't know."

The next three stops passed in silence, Odessa's nerves clicking as they came closer to Green Street. Circus must have sensed this and stretched his arm across the back of the seat behind her. She let herself fall gently against it. She tried to remind herself that nothing could really go wrong. No one knew about her and Ross. The rumor at the office said Tori Griffin believed her husband had slept with nameless women he met on business trips and at conferences. Even if someone spotted Odessa at the Griffins' house today, there were reasons she could offer for being there: she was an old friend who wanted to leave a note for the family. She was a buyer interested in the house. She was just passing by.

As the train pulled into the Mass. Avenue station, Circus nodded toward the exit. "Used to be a place at this stop called Gumshoe's. Played my first gig in Boston there. Nineteen years old, still at Boston Conservatory. I think about it whenever I pass through."

"I know Gumshoe's," Odessa said. "My cousin, Jermaine, was the owner. I was there all the time. I probably heard you play."

He eyed her as if she'd performed a magic trick he couldn't crack.

"When he closed," she said, "Jermaine gave me that picture of the lady in the chinchilla coat he used to keep taped to the side of his cash register. I still have it."

A grin spread over Circus's lips. "The love of his life."

"That's the story he told." Odessa shook her head. "Jermaine's parents took the family to Los Angeles, and one night they come across this woman who'd misplaced the coat and was running around Hollywood showing people that very photograph of her wearing it, thinking people might recognize it and help her find it. Jermaine's father thought it amusing and asked the woman if he could keep the picture. For some reason, she let him. But Jermaine found the whole thing a fright. He told me he'd never seen someone so sad. He was all of seventeen, and he'd known hard times. But he said seeing that woman that day made him wonder how anyone could bear loving something that much."

Odessa's imagination lingered on her cousin. The club's dank odor he tried to cover with sandalwood incense, the velvet hats he wore, a different color every night of the week, the stories he used to tell about the night he said Sonny Rollins stopped there to play. The photo of the woman in the chinchilla coat seemed as native to the place as the checked tablecloths and antique popcorn cart at the door, but only today did Odessa find herself wondering why her cousin kept the photograph on the register for decades until the club shut down. What did it oblige him to remember? What would Ross's mother keep for herself as she sorted through the belongings her son left behind? And why hadn't Odessa kept anything from the lover she laid to rest twenty years before? She wondered whether it was a sign of courage or cowardice.

Odessa brought the brooch from her purse, cradling it in her palm for Circus to see. Together they admired the gold plating wrought in the shape of a flower bursting with petals, the tips touched with olive and black stones, a sapphire at its heart.

"Whoa," Circus said. "Where'd that come from?"

"It's an heirloom that belongs to the family of a man I used to know. His mother gave it to him, he gave it to his wife, then he stole it back from her and . . ."

"He gave it to you," Circus finished her sentence. "I'm guessing he shouldn't have."

"I want to give it back." She zipped the brooch back into a pocket in her purse. "Is it all right if that's all I say about it?"

He nodded. "Is this a man you still . . . know?"

She shook her head.

"Okay, then." Circus settled into the seat. "Let's make a delivery."

* * *

A kid in a down parka played drums on the bottom of two overturned buckets on the platform of the Green Street Station. Both Odessa and Circus tossed him five-dollar bills as they passed the mural of the tightrope walker the kid played under and made their way through the turnstiles into the street.

"I dig that," Circus said. Odessa didn't ask whether he meant the drummer or the painting.

Never had she been to Ross's house out of respect for his wife. But she'd seen the Griffins' battleship-gray Colonial in a photograph on his phone when he was boasting about laying the granite for the retaining wall between his sidewalk and front lawn. She remembered Northwood, the name of the street, because she'd once had a friend who lived there, and she remembered the number on the transom—1030—because it was her birthday. She knew there were boxes in storage in the garage and a key hidden under a planter in the back garden. She'd planned to somehow make her way to the garden unseen and head into the garage to plop the brooch into one of the boxes for the mother to find later. But as she and Circus rounded the corner at Northwood Drive, Odessa understood the risk she was taking in the middle of the bright morning. The crime itself had taken place at the Griffins' vacation home on the Cape, but she imagined the neighbors kept a curious eye cast in the house's direction.

The Colonial stood at the end of the block in a way that was eerily familiar yet seemingly fake, as if it were part of the set of a film she'd seen. Odessa recognized the granite retaining wall and remnants of the snow-blanketed flower garden Ross used to say Tori tended the way she once cared for him.

"Who's this?" Circus asked.

Her gaze dropped from the front porch to the garage, where a white-haired woman lifted the door, bunched the collar of her jacket tightly around her neck, then went inside. Odessa took

Circus by the wrist and led him across the street to a playground where they hid behind a wooden tree house as Odessa eyed the woman through a window.

"His mother, I think," she said. "She must have come early."

Circus leaned down to peer through the tree house window at the woman as she took a broom from a corner of the garage and began to sweep.

"Well, let's go give her the thing," he said.

Odessa shook her head. "I don't want her wondering who I am."

"Maybe come back another day?"

"I can't go through this again. I want her to find it as if it were lost."

"Where is this guy?" he asked. "Why's his mother at his house and he's not?"

Odessa looked past him at a boy shaping snowballs and piling them on a bench. She tried to think of what to say, but the truth seemed too much to tell a stranger.

"Can I see the brooch?" Circus asked, and she handed it to him, watching as he delicately turned it over in his hands. She understood from his silence that he'd grasped something serious had happened to the man who lived in the gray house across the street.

Circus stuffed the brooch into his pocket, and before Odessa could stop him, he made his way across the street. At first she stayed behind, but as the woman turned to greet him, Odessa followed after.

"Sorry to bother." He offered the woman his hand. "Cyrus. I live in the neighborhood."

The woman pulled off her woolen glove to shake his hand, the good manners that seemed innate in her compelling her to smile though sadness dragged heavily at the corners of her mouth. In the woman's face, Odessa could see Ross's short nose and sharply angled jaw, though her eyes were silvery rather than night blue, their lids swollen and pink, tears glistening in them.

"One of the neighbors had a get-together a while back," Circus went on. "Your boy and his lady came by."

The woman flinched when Circus said "your boy," her lashes beating and wet.

He brought the brooch from his pocket. "This must've fallen off her dress. We wanted to get it back to you."

The woman peeled the brooch from his palm, glaring at it with mouth pinched, as she teetered slightly, causing Circus to hold out his hand to offer balance if she needed it. The day seemed to close up around them and lose sound, to ache, as Odessa and Circus, still strangers despite the grave intimacy of the last hour, glanced at each other across what seemed like centuries. She wanted to be somewhere quiet with him, somewhere warm, to either tell him all that happened or forget everything. But there was this woman, pretty and small and bearing so much resemblance to the dead man Odessa had slept beside only weeks before.

"I'm sorry," Odessa blurted. "Please."

And with this, the woman turned her gaze, seeing Odessa for what seemed the first time.

"Please?" the woman repeated.

Odessa's nerves rose as she imagined cold must have risen from the toes to the head when the body froze over.

The woman said it again. "Please?"

A gust of icy wind blew down the street, and the three of them looked toward it, watching a dusting of snow spill from the roof of a house nearby.

"This isn't mine," the woman said.

Odessa offered a polite smile. "Aren't you Ross Griffin's mother?"

The woman took one last glance at the brooch and handed it to her. "I don't want this."

Tightening the scarf around her neck, she went back into the garage, pulling the door closed behind her. Odessa stared into the space where the woman had stood, the brooch cold in her hand. As she slid it into her coat pocket, the tip of the pin pricked her thumb, but she didn't allow herself to acknowledge the pain. She deserved so much more of it.

"We shouldn't stay out here." Circus lit a cigarette and through a shroud of smoke said, "Come on, lovely."

He offered his elbow, and Odessa took it. There was an immediate ease as they strolled together, as if they'd already met and fallen in love some other day and had reunited, their bodies in a kind of slow dance down the sidewalk crisp with the last traces of the week's snowfall. She wondered if he doubted her or pitied her, whether he was bewildered or amused, whether he cared at all. Still, she felt glad to have him with her as they walked in silence to the end of the block.

"Why'd you come with me today?" she asked.

A gentle chuckle sounded in his throat. "Why do any of us do anything?"

Odessa looked up. Circus was staring back, the moment uncomfortable and intoxicating. She could have told him she loved him then and there if she believed in such things.

"Where were you supposed to be this morning?" she asked.

Circus hit his cigarette. "My kid's in trouble at school, wrote something strange in English class. The ex-wife and I are supposed to meet with her counselor."

"Oh, you should be there. Is it too late for you to go?"

"Maybe."

"Don't you want to be there?"

He glanced at her like a child afraid to ask permission for what he wanted. "Something happened here with us today."

"You were a kind person who did a stranger a favor."

"You know what I mean," he said, and Odessa could see he wanted to tell her more, but instead he seemed to sink into a submerged place inside himself where something else was happening that wasn't about his daughter or the trouble she'd gotten into at school. Whatever it was seemed to stop him from pressing on, and as he took another drag, Odessa saw dismay, then sadness, and even longing recast his handsome features. Then he shook himself from it.

"I got a gig just up the street tonight at O'Toole's," he said. "How 'bout coming by?"

A curl of smoke flowed from his lips, his gaze growing distant as he stared down the street as if, at the end of it, he could see where he needed to go but didn't want to be. Odessa liked looking at him. He was stylish, Circus. Hip. She liked the cashmere scarf draped freely around his neck, the flat cap and shined shoes. There was a sense of knowing him even though a world existed around him she hadn't begun to see. A feeling she thought it unlucky to walk away from.

"You should go," she said, already regretting whatever it was inside her that suddenly needed to get away from him. A yellow taxi turned the corner in front of them, and Odessa hailed it, telling the driver to take Circus wherever he wanted to go.

With a grimace, Circus tossed the cigarette into a snowbank and watched it smother. He nodded and slid into the back seat of the taxi.

"Circus," she said. "Thank you."

Sidewinder

*

Circus

The students were already practicing when Circus arrived at the Hemenway Street rehearsal room ten minutes late. They were several bars into the Lee Morgan tune, so he sat down, pressing his hand against the air to tell the drums to ease up. At the head of the ensemble, Panos Antonopoulos took a solo on his trumpet, climbing over the melody, his breath reaching for the higher intervals of the chords, fiddling with them until he fell into a movement the other students struggled to follow.

Circus couldn't stop himself from letting out a howl. "Find him," he shouted above the music. "Don't let him leave you behind."

Panos kicked the ground as he reached even higher while Circus watched. He admired the kid's confidence—the way he never glanced at Circus for approval during class—and he admired the sounds he found in the brass. Listening to him left Circus awestruck and proud, feelings he understood some men came to feel for their sons.

"You got the gift," he told Panos after class. "I feel blessed to play a part in shaping it."

Panos gave an odd smile and continued packing his bag.

"First year and already killing it. You're gonna be a solid jazzman."

"I'm not sure jazz is going to be my thing though," Panos said.

"Don't say that, man. You hurt my soul."

"It's the truth. I don't like how it makes me feel scattered."

"Music complicates you. Allow her the complications. Let everything else in the world be easy. You hear what I'm saying to you?"

Panos nodded. "I'll try to do that."

"Like Mingus, man, you never knew what mood you were getting him. He and his band would be playing, and if Mingus didn't like what he heard, he'd just cold stop and say, 'You already played that way. Do somethin' different.'"

Panos tugged at the ring on his thumb. "I think I've heard that before."

"That's what makes a man great. That's what makes a man Mingus. Trust me, I know the gift when I see it 'cause someone saw it in me when I was a young cat like you. You need a little vanity to you, son. Throw some gasoline onto that wild streak."

"*Wild?*" Panos shook his head. "That's not a word anyone ever used to describe me."

"They should," Circus said. "Make 'em."

"Are you saying I have to be crazy to be good?"

"I'm saying you got to be selfish."

Panos took a long sip of his coffee, unsure, it seemed, of what to say. Circus liked the silence, liked the weight of it, how it seemed to cast him in hallowed light. Giving the kid a gentle punch to the arm, he said, "Let's stay in touch when the semester ends. Jam together."

Panos ran his fingers through his wavy black hair and it flopped back into place. "Yeah, maybe. That could be cool."

"You know I got a gig Sundays at B.B. Kingfish. You oughta come by."

The odd smile returned to Panos's lips. "That sushi place in Cambridge?"

"Well, it's not just . . ." Circus watched him place his trumpet into its case and wipe a smudge from the bell, an unfamiliar desperation suddenly stirring in his gut. "There's a jazz brunch. Real elegant. You can't get a roll of sushi for under twenty dollars. It's a classy joint."

Panos snapped the case shut and slipped into his coat. "Maybe I'll come one afternoon."

"I'm holding you to it, brother."

Circus slapped him on the back, sensing the years between them though there was something pleasing about occupying that expanse, as if it kept him connected to a lineage and all that was vibrant and young in his own soul. Decades before, he'd walked through the classrooms and corridors of the Conservatory, and now he wondered which of his elders had watched him with pride.

"In fact, hit me up end of next week," he said. "I'm recording a demo for a meeting I got in New York in seven weeks and counting. Maybe I'll let you play on a track."

"Nice," Panos said. "Who you meeting with?"

"Graham something or other. I can't remember if that's his first or last name. A label called Fandangle or some such. A buddy of mine is making it happen."

The kid shoved his hands into his pockets, nodding. "Fandangle, huh?"

"Heard of 'em?"

Panos swirled the coffee in his cup. "They follow me online. They're a cool little label."

Shame hit like the swing of a fist, and he stood reeling from it, as if the expanse they'd reached each other across had closed up and Circus had fallen off the edge. As he watched Panos place his cup on the counter to zip his coat, he felt an urgent need to go back and rearrange the moment that had just passed, to reshape the way he imagined the kid was seeing him. Instead, he slid a cigarette from the pack in his jacket pocket and placed it unlit on his lip because it was a familiar act, a comfortable one.

"I should go to English," Panos said.

Circus held out his hand, and the kid shook it mightily, thanked him for class, and left the room. Circus watched after him, withered somehow by the distance growing between them.

* * *

His buddies called it an itch he could never fully scratch, while the ex-wife called it a weakness, but it was neither of those things, this constant reaching out. What need was there to name it anyway, though if he had to call it something, he'd have called it a moving into idyllic spaces, brief stretches of quiet time, loving time, between the accelerated hustle of living, like the quiet roads he'd traveled that connect Miami to Charleston to Baltimore to Boston. But loving wasn't what Circus was feeling tonight as he sat at one of his regular bars scrolling through the numbers in his phone. The conversation with Panos nagged him. When a message came from Josephine in Providence, the third she'd sent today, he deleted it without reading it. He liked the pulp of Josephine's body that moved marvelously under his hands, but it was too much out of bed, too overwhelming, when it wasn't secured beneath his hips. He liked the chocolates she brought him from her candy shop and the sweetness of her fingers in his mouth as she fed them to him. He liked how she was always grateful to see him no matter how much time had passed, how she welcomed him at any hour and held him snug against her in the dead of night. It was nice to feel love from someone who asked so little in return. But he grumbled to himself now about the number of years he'd been visiting her—five? six?—yet she still hadn't learned to leave him be when he wanted to do other things with his time.

The redheaded bartender came to refill his glass. "Two nights in a row at the Blind Fox?"

"You gettin' tired of seeing me?" Circus asked.

"Not even a little." She handed him a box of toothpicks, and he slid one between his teeth. She liked him, he knew, because she blushed whenever she poured his drink. He tried to remember her name as she gazed back at him through strange blue eyes, a gold blotch in the iris of one of them. The name was a word for fruit, Apple or Clementine. Beautiful girl. The body.

"I had a hankering for shepherd's pie," he told her. "And some company."

"Well, I've got plenty of both. It's too cold for anyone to come out tonight."

"And too cold to stay in. Alone, that is."

Like ribbon, her kittenish laughter unfurled around him. Her cheeks filled pink as she reached for a bottle of tequila, poured herself a shot, and clinked her glass against his.

"Winter's over soon." She downed the shot. "But we gotta stay warm until then, right?"

"Absolutely, Peach," he answered, glad to have remembered her name. "Absolutely."

Taking a handful of quarters from the register, she went to the back of the room, asking if there was anything he wanted to hear. He shook his head and glanced at the younger guy sipping beer at the end of the bar. Circus realized he'd been listening to their conversation. Frowning, the guy tossed ten bucks onto the bar, then went out the door after having one last look at the bartender wagging her hips at the jukebox.

"Which Tip Badgett album did you say your drummer friend played on?" she asked.

The thought of Maggie shrank something in him. The stampede of nerves he'd felt in Miami when she told him her news came back to his belly, so he took a hefty swig of his drink.

"How 'bout no Tip Badgett tonight, doll?"

She played something young with loud guitars, but it was too late, Maggie was with him. In his imagination, she was lying on the sofa in his living room, her bare feet dangling over the edge. He had an urge to squeeze her toes in the way that made her squeal and made him laugh. Maggie, the only woman with whom he slept through the morning. He wanted to go to her on this chilly night, to lie beside her in bed and watch the snow fall outside the window. He wanted to talk to her. To tell her about how good the kids at school sounded, something he liked to imagine he had something to do with, though now he was thinking of Panos Antonopoulos, and a different kind of burden rushed through him. He had slept so little in the three weeks since Miami, his nights haunted when he was alone, restless when he wasn't. And as the loneliness started to seep into him, he remembered Odessa, the subway car, the brooch. She hadn't come to mind since he'd met her two days before. He lingered briefly on her, and something in him warmed, but he wanted to think of Maggie, the closest he could come now to being with her. He imagined her peering through her bedroom window at the same cold moon and knew if he were lying next to her, if things were different between them, he might finally sleep peacefully.

"Hope you're hungry." The bartender slid a plate of shepherd's pie onto the placemat before him. "Manny gave you two servings."

Circus stared down, the gluey potatoes and scent of onions suddenly making his stomach turn. He took another sip of his drink. On the other side of the bar, the redhead glanced at her phone next to the register, got hooked by something on the screen, and started to scroll.

"Can I ask you something?" Circus pushed away the plate.

"Hmm?" she answered without looking up.

"How many people you follow online?"

She shrugged. "Couple thousand."

"You follow me?"

She glanced up. Grinned, tilted her head. "Not yet. Do you want me to?"

"You'd have to really dig someone to follow him, right? If you didn't know him. If he's just some cat playing music. He'd have to be special."

She looked at her phone, looked back at Circus, looked at her phone again.

"Never mind." He took a bite of the pie, washing it down with his last sip of bourbon.

The bartender poured him another glass, eyeing him with a smirk on her face.

"Don't laugh at the old man," he said.

"That's not why I'm smiling. And you're not old."

"You don't know what old is."

She poured herself another shot, downed it.

"I mean," he started, bashful, "how old do you think is, y'know, old?"

She ran her tongue across her teeth, considered. "Isn't age just a state of mind?"

"That's what they say, don't they?" He sipped the bourbon, letting it warm him. "'Older the fiddle, sweeter the tune.'"

"Oh, I like that," she said. "Age ain't nothin' but a number."

"Ain't that the truth. Hell, Monk put out *Brilliant Corners* when he was forty."

"That's good for . . . him."

Circus laughed, knocking his knuckles against the bar. "Aren't you just lifting my mood through the goddamn roof?"

"You didn't have a good day?"

He swiped the air. "Just a misunderstanding between me and one of my kids at school. We got a mutual admiration thing happening, right. I dig his playing, and he admires the hell outta me. We just got our wires crossed. But I feel good now here with you."

"I'm glad." She shimmied her hips to the growl of guitars behind them and lifted her glass.

"All right then." He clinked his glass against hers, the high hitting him now. "Seems we're gonna have us an interesting night."

What the Body Says

*

Peach

Peach woke to what sounded like thunder in her dreams but what she soon discovered was a ceramic plate crashing against a wall. Sprawled naked across the foot of an unfamiliar mattress, her limp arms and legs slung over the edges and still buzzing with sleep, she listened to the murmur of voices outside the room and tried to remember where she was. Her eyes adjusted to the morning's stale light and skimmed along the bed's surface, where she saw the cashmere scarf he'd tied around her wrists and remembered. Circus Palmer.

"How do you always end up at the Blind Fox?" she'd asked after serving him his first glass of Wild Turkey the night before.

"Who knows, doll," Circus had answered. "But something pushes me."

The bedroom had an unlived-in look. Peach assumed it was reserved for guests, though she imagined not many came, from the looks of its empty bookshelf and bare walls. Circus had told her the duplex belonged to a friend as they drove the two miles from the Blind Fox where her Chevy now sat in the lot, but the argument happening in the other room made clear he hadn't told the whole truth.

"Tell her to get out of my house," the woman in the other room said under her breath.

Mouth sticky and joints sore, Peach hauled herself to the ground and crawled across the carpet to the bedroom door, peeking through a crack into the living room at the other end of a hallway. She saw Circus briefly walk past in the slacks he'd worn the night before, his hands on his hips and a cigarette smoldering between his lips. She caught a glimpse of the girl standing beside him, who kicked at the shattered plate on the floor and the woman who spoke through a strangle of tears.

"Why did you bring her here?" the woman asked.

"You were supposed to be on the Cape," Circus said. "It's my house, too, you know."

"Not anymore, it isn't."

"Wherever my kid is, I call home."

"Now you're staking a claim."

Peach dragged her clothes from beneath the bed, then searched the room for her jacket until she remembered it crumpled in the passenger seat of Circus's Buick. Pulling her panties over her knees, she became aware of how rickety the hinges of her body were after a long night of drinking and dry fucking. Circus hadn't gone inside her because he said he needed to know a woman before he took her bleeding, though he asked for other things. The scarf around her wrists was his idea, as was the roughness, which she came to like because the slight sting of his hands pulled her deeper into her own flesh. A digital clock on the floor next to the bed blinked ten-thirty, reminding Peach she had a shift at the bar at eleven. She dressed quickly, smiling to herself as she imagined telling her friends how she'd finally gone to bed with Circus Palmer, telling them about the drama that came after. For a year, she'd been set on him, wondering whether his body moved with the same fierceness as the sounds he made on his trumpet on the nights he played the Blind Fox.

"I had one cocktail too many, all right," she heard Circus

say. "Your place was closer than mine. You want me to have an accident?"

"Should I answer?" the woman whimpered.

"I don't like ladies at my place."

The woman gasped. "I'm not your friend. Don't say things like that and expect me to understand."

As Peach tied her hair into a ponytail, Circus's phone vibrated in a pile of clothes on the floor. The name Josephine flashed on the display, and Peach shoved the phone under a pillow so as not to draw anyone into the room. As she reached for her earrings on the bedside table, she heard Circus lower his voice.

"Listen," he said. "The chick's only tits and a nice pair of legs. She's just a body. She's not about anything, Pia. There's no reason to blow a gasket."

Peach froze, her open hand suspended in midair. A note of relief sounded in the woman's voice when she said, "If only my life was as easy as yours."

Peach drifted back to the bed as the walls of the room seemed to narrow around her. Every pain the night had given to her body ached separately but deeply—hipbones in their sockets stressed by Circus's weight, nipples swollen from the tug of his mouth, thigh muscles raw. She had been through mornings like this one, mornings when the man who had eagerly mounted her the night before resented her the next day for enjoying his hands and looking the way she did. The difference now was she had to listen to it instead of reading it in his eyes.

There were two ways out. The window leading to the backyard, or the door leading farther into the house. Through the window, Peach saw a lime-colored ten-speed leaning against the garage. Leaving behind the earrings as evidence that she'd been there and it mattered, she opened the window, feeling the air in the room warm behind her as the late-morning chill flowed in, the hollow room like a hole in the earth she was suddenly afraid to fall back into. She crawled through. The sun came at her, flirting as it ran its hands over her skin and breathed out a slow, cool wind that glided up the hem of her skirt. She crossed the yard and climbed onto the bicycle, slightly too small for the long stretch of her legs. She apologized silently to the girl in the duplex and, bracing herself against the cold, turned the corner out of the drive. The sigh of the bicycle's tires against pavement and the shifting gears were the only sounds she heard as the world blurred past. But Circus's words echoed in her mind. He'd robbed her of a good morning—even the beaming sun distilled into mere yellowness and heat.

Peach stopped at a tiny supermarket en route, rolling the bicycle inside with her. She took a stick of deodorant, a tube of toothpaste and brush, and a package of cheap panties from the shelves and brought them to the counter, where a clerk with grease under his fingernails picked his teeth with a credit card. He smiled at her, leering the way men did. In the security mirror above them, Peach saw her mascara-stained eyes and wan cheeks, her unclean skin and unwashed hair, her sore body in yesterday's clothes. She took a pair of sunglasses from her purse to hide the tears brimming in her eyes.

"Everything okay?" the clerk asked.

No, she wanted to say. *Everything is wrong.*

Peach watched the clerk wipe his hands on his pant legs before handling the money. She wanted to catch his gaze, wanted him to ask her again so she could say something that could correct the morning. He only handed over her change.

* * *

She pedaled into the lot of the Blind Fox and through the opened back door, where she found her boss, Jason, unpacking crates of bottled wine. When she hopped off the bicycle, he took a hard look at her, spinning the ring attached to his pocket knife around his thumb as his tongue prodded the inside of his cheek, his eyes like hands prying apart her knees.

"Looks like someone didn't make it home last night," he said with a twisted grin. "If only my parents made me play trumpet instead of golf. I could be home sleeping off a night with you instead of working the lunch shift."

"In your dreams." Peach sashayed past him into the bathroom with the frank swish of her hips that she knew both intrigued him and kept him away. After twenty-eight years, she'd learned the right balance to strike with men she needed something from, and she liked her job at the Blind Fox. The tips were good, the regulars friendly, the hours hers to decide.

Her smile faded as soon as she met her eyes in the bathroom mirror. Peach scanned her face, her skin dried out from tequila shots and her blue eyes rimmed pink. The freckles on her cheeks, which her grandmother had once told her looked like sprinkles of nutmeg in milk, now made her pale skin look sickly. Whether it was the aching morning or Circus's words, Peach felt empty. Deboned. What was she anyway? Fingernails and teeth. Knees, belly, eyebrows, mouth. Breasts and neck. Legs. Pussy.

After moistening a paper towel, she washed between her legs and the inside of her armpits. She cleaned her face and brushed her teeth, pinned her hair and put in a tampon before sliding into a fresh pair of panties. Glancing at her phone in hopes of finding a call from Circus that would work loose the knot he'd left in her stomach, she found a text from a friend that asked, *How was last night?*

Peach typed the word *yay* and sent it with an image of a plump red heart.

*   *   *

As on most Monday mornings, Harvey Merrill occupied the center stool at the bar as he nursed a Guinness. When Peach stepped out of the bathroom onto the main floor, he folded his eyeglasses into his coat pocket and ran his fingers through his gray hair as if readying himself for a date.

"I was afraid you weren't working," he said.

Peach clocked in and started counting the money in the register, nodding toward the television humming above her head. "Who's racing this morning? Bowlby?"

"Bowlby's out," Harvey said. "He crashed last week. But no races for me today. We've got the news on here. You hear about that hole in Florida?"

"Is that code for something?" She winked. "Another round?"

Harvey drank the last sip of his beer. "Jason says you've got a new import from Belgium. Why not let me give that a whirl?"

"It's tasty." Peach placed her phone beside the register, checking one last time for a message. "My cousin just went to Germany. Maybe I should tell her to bring back a case for you."

Harvey's eyes narrowed. "You know where Belgium is, don't you, honey?" He smiled as if she were a child who'd just recited the alphabet incorrectly. "What a charmer you are."

Peach winked again for want of anything else to do, then made her way to the fridge for a bottle, casting her eyes around the room to get a sense of the afternoon ahead. Harvey was the only person in the place so far, though the ten tables in the room were clean, their silver in place. At the back, the spot that was emptied of chairs and tables on nights Circus and his band played was filled with seats, the dartboard replaced on the wall. Peach poured Harvey's beer into a chilled mug, yawning into her free hand.

"You're looking a little worse for wear." Harvey wiped a layer of foam from his upper lip. "What'd you get up to last night?"

"Yes, Peachie." Jason stepped behind the bar and started toweling a tray of glasses. "Give us something to think about later when we're in bed next to our wives."

Harvey blushed and turned his gaze to a blister in the meat of his hand, picking at it with his thumbnail. Peach gave Jason the finger. Jason licked the air.

"Don't listen to him, Harvey." Peach wrinkled her nose. "How about a Reuben for lunch? I'll sneak you an extra bag of chips."

Harvey nodded. "Yeah, a Reuben sounds good. Don't tell the wife, though. She's on me about the heart."

Peach keyed in the order, then poured herself a glass of water, eyeing the corner of the room where she'd watched Circus play. A lump rose in her throat just as her phone chimed with another message from her friend that said, *Tell me everything.*

Peach started to type a reply but instead found Circus's number.

Where'd I disappear to? Peach typed to him, adding a smiling face and pressing send before she had a chance to change her mind. She went to take drink orders from a group of men in suits who'd come into the bar. Circus would reply, she imagined. He would take back what he'd said, confess something private about his ex-wife, how he was still decent enough to care for her even if there was no love left. Peach would make him suffer a bit, though she'd forgive him in the end. The thought made her body lighter as she made her way back to the register, just as the door swung open and Stockwell, one of the Monday-morning regulars, bounded in with a younger man he worked out with at the gym across the street.

"Every day, dog, a gallon of water before I even get out of bed." Stockwell's voice rumbled through the room as the men made their way to their preferred table a step away from the bar. "Flushes out everything."

Stockwell tilted an invisible bottle into his mouth, so Peach popped the caps off two Heinekens, dropping them off as the cook came from the kitchen with the Reuben. Harvey slid his empty mug across the bar. "Hit me. The good stuff."

Peach poured him another Guinness, glancing at her phone again as she rang the beer onto his tab. No reply from Circus.

"Let me get a set of those darts." Stockwell stood at the bar, his pink skin blotchy from the workout, his body engorged with muscle and a slight stink. He was the kind of guy who carried a cup to spit tobacco juice into and called other men by their last names. His friend, Trujillo, was smaller but hard as rock, with a fine face and sensuous mouth. He never said much, and his eyes were serious, which made Peach wonder why he'd chosen Stockwell as a friend.

"You should check out my new rims." Stockwell placed his hand over hers when Peach handed him the darts. "I got them imported from Japan."

"I'm sure they're pretty."

"Sunsets are pretty." Stockwell smirked at Trujillo as if she were a joke between them. "A set of MT3s with snake-tongue spokes and alligator leather are ferocious."

"I don't think animals should be used to decorate cars."

Stockwell smirked again, but Trujillo didn't meet his eyes. Instead, he went back to the table with his beer, glancing at Peach as if he had something to apologize for. Beside her, Harvey sipped his drink and eyed their clasped hands.

"Be careful, friend, our girl's spoken for now." Jason came behind the bar to fill a rocks glass with ice and a shot of Jim Beam. He turned to Peach. "Do you even like jazz?"

"I like when he plays."

Stockwell clenched her fingers tighter. "You got a man?"

Peach could feel their eyes. Harvey. Stockwell and Trujillo. Jason. On her mouth, her breasts, her belly bare beneath the cropped top of her shirt. Like they were reclaiming her.

"Jason's being silly," she said. "There's no one."

Stockwell let go of her hand. "Well, you let me know when you want a ride."

Peach gave Jason a look as he disappeared down the hall toward his office. Stockwell and Trujillo started a game of darts, while Harvey stared up at the television and Peach wished she could tell one of them about Circus, wished she could find out whether they thought what he'd said about her was true. Maybe she wasn't about anything. She was twenty-eight, unmarried, a bartender and occasional student. Her ties—regulars at the Blind Fox, girlfriends she could party with, men she slept with—were light and simple. She didn't read books or know about current events, though she was drawn to people who did, like Circus, who once sat at her bar talking for hours about some policy the president was pushing. Peach had listened, rapt.

She had always been embarrassed by how lost she became in certain conversations, though she was kind and always thought that should count for something. But there were things she knew. As a girl, she'd memorized the pictures in medical books at her school library and learned the infections that could corrupt the body, the diseases it could carry. Now she was learning how the parts worked together—blood, vein, bone, muscle, organs, limbs—how to serve and save them. She didn't consider herself smart enough to impress most people, but what she knew was what she had always believed mattered most. The body and what it needed.

The suits ordered another round of gin and tonics, so Peach brought them over, glancing at the door when it opened. A wine rep stepped into the bar, asked for Jason, then made her way back to his office.

"Is this the sinkhole?" Stockwell asked, staring up at the television.

Harvey nodded. "They're still looking for her."

"Looking for who?" Peach asked.

"The woman who got swallowed up by the hole." Harvey shook his head. "Ask me, they're not going to find her."

"Was there an earthquake or something?"

"It's a sinkhole, honey." Harvey grumbled when Peach told him she didn't understand. "There's rock beneath the surface of the land, right? Well, when that rock dissolves, it can't hold up the surface anymore, so it collapses. This poor lady was just sitting in bed watching the tube when the ground below gives and the entire side of her house gets sucked into the hole."

Peach looked from Harvey to Stockwell, waiting for one of them to tell her they were teasing. "That doesn't happen."

Stockwell let out a snort and strolled to the back of the room where Trujillo was throwing darts. Peach looked up at the small blue house on television, the roof split in two, the fallen side suspended in a spill of rock, soil, drywall, and wood, the hole gaping in the earth beneath, black and seemingly without end. And there were colors and fabrics. Blue. Pink. Violet. Perhaps the woman's bed sheets or clothes.

"She's in there?" Peach asked.

"That's right," Harvey answered.

"She just fell in?"

"The ground took her."

"Could she live through something like that?"

"If there's an air pocket and they get to her in time."

"You think they're going to?"

Harvey offered an uneven smile. "Maybe. Probably."

"Hey, Peach Schnapps," Stockwell called from the back of the room. "Bring us some oranges, will you?"

Peach plucked a handful of fruit from a ramekin on the bar, breathing into the weight in her chest. She tried to focus on the chime of the cash register as she keyed in orders, but all she could think of was a dark cavity under the earth and a woman clawing rock.

"Maybe we shouldn't watch the news," Harvey said.

"I'm fine." Peach grinned through the quake at the corners of her mouth, making her way to Stockwell with the oranges. Trujillo sat slouched at their table but straightened his back when Peach placed the dish in front of him.

"You look pretty today," he said quietly, as if he didn't want Stockwell to hear. It was the first time he'd spoken to Peach in the weeks since he'd started coming to the bar. He looked away after he said it, his cheek dimpling. Trujillo smelled good. Fresh.

"Dog," Stockwell shouted, "I'm totally destroying you in this game."

He slapped Trujillo on the back, then grabbed three tennis balls from his gym bag and started to juggle. "Peach, guess which one of us benched the most today."

"C'mon, man." Trujillo shifted in his seat.

"I got ten years on this kid." Stockwell punched Trujillo's shoulder. "But I'm still ox strong. There are no limits. No one messes with me, dog, I can take anything down."

Peach collected the empty bottles from the table. "Another round, boys?"

"I don't see any boys here," Stockwell said.

Trujillo brushed past him, yanking the darts from the board as Peach stood in the trail of his cologne. Stockwell circled his shoulders and swiveled his neck as Trujillo tossed a dart, missed the bull's-eye, cursed. He threw again and came closer, glancing back to check that she'd seen.

"Your phone's doing its thing," Harvey called from the front of the room.

Peach ran behind the bar to answer.

You got my kid's bike? Circus had texted.

The hollow in the center of her chest seemed to fill with light.

I'm holding it ransom, she typed, then uncapped two Heinekens, leaving them on the bar for Stockwell and Trujillo. Harvey tapped the side of his empty glass, his eyes fixed to the television. She poured him another Guinness, waiting for the phone's buzz.

You at the Blind Fox? Circus replied.

Off at five, she typed.

Be there in a few.

Peach slid the phone beside the register. When she spun around, Harvey was watching her with a grin. "Good news?"

"Harvey," Peach began, tongue rolling against the inside of her mouth. "What would you say if you were telling somebody about me?"

"Oh, is this one of those games ladies like to play? If you were an animal, which would you be?" He tapped his chin. "A deer, maybe. One of those young ones with big, pretty eyes."

"Not a wolf or a tiger?"

"Why would you want to be dangerous?"

Peach feigned a smile. "You set for now, Harv?"

He gave her a thumbs-up, and she scanned the room to make sure no one else needed her. Slipping her makeup bag from her purse, Peach went down the hall to the bathroom where she dabbed her mouth with lipstick and refreshed her mascara even though she knew it wasn't her mouth and eyes that would lure Circus's gaze. But if he could only see her face, she wondered, what different things might he learn about her? Peach went to the dry goods room where the staff changed clothes before their shifts and found a hooded gray sweatshirt. There was a sense of disappearing as she slipped into it, of hiding. She preferred the denim skirt and black corset top she'd been wearing because she liked the heavier touch of the fabric and threaded seams, liked the exposure of skin, liked the heat and cold and wind that felt like hands caressing her.

A woman was pointing her finger into Harvey's face and whispering through screwed lips when Peach stepped back into the main room. The woman turned when she saw Peach, the pattern of wrinkles around her eyes burrowing deep. Harvey followed her gaze, reddening when his eyes landed on Peach. As she crossed the room to greet the new guests who had seated themselves, Peach heard the woman—dark-haired with gray roots growing in, heavy-featured, mouth bloated—groan under the weight of her hefty body and tell Harvey to order her a drink.

"The wife'll have a margarita," he said when Peach went back behind the bar.

"Mrs. Merrill?" Peach extended her hand, and the woman took it loosely, her fingers soggy and limp. "Nice to finally meet you."

"Don't bother saying Harvey's told you so much about me." Mrs. Merrill's voice made Peach think of sandpaper.

She tried to remember something lovely Harvey had told her about his wife, but she was right. He hadn't said much. She reached for the tequila, and Mrs. Merrill watched over the rim of her eyeglasses as Peach's fingers worked the lime around the lip of the glass, then rolled it in a plate of salt. Peach sensed the woman watching the bob of her ponytail, her breasts pushing against the zipper of the sweatshirt, and her long bare legs beneath the skirt. She asked Peach's name after she served the drink, wrinkling her brow when she answered.

"My mother was from Georgia," Peach explained as she made a round of mai tais for the new table.

Mrs. Merrill took a sip of the margarita, licking the salt from her lips. Even though she was from Charlestown, like Harvey, Mrs. Merrill had a way about her that reminded Peach of the southern women she used to meet during rare trips to visit her mother's family—drawling, oddly flirtatious, and always patting their collarbones as if the weather overwhelmed. Peach knew it wasn't polite to think such things, but she couldn't help but notice a pretty girl in the folds of the older woman's face. Not younger, necessarily, but buried.

"I wanted to see what's so special about this place to drag Harvey in every morning he doesn't have to be at the office." Mrs. Merrill dabbed her mouth with a cocktail napkin, and her rose-colored lipstick left a trace. "Must be the stiff drinks."

Harvey kept his gaze on the television. "They're getting ready to interview the brother of the lady in the hole."

"I don't care about any goddamn hole." Mrs. Merrill poked her thumb at Harvey. "This one loves destruction. Our neighbors at the end of the block dug up their backyard to build an addition, a deck or some such monstrosity. Everything was in a state, fencing rolled up like bales of hay, entire slabs of concrete piled over one another. Harvey reroutes his walk home from the train every afternoon just to have a look. I should have brought him his slippers and a tub of popcorn."

"How's it any different from the makeovers you always show me in your lady magazines?" Harvey asked.

"He likes what's new and clean," Mrs. Merrill went on. "And you sure are new and clean, aren't you, dear? But Harvey doesn't know it's your job to be nice. I know. First job I had was waiting tables at the Pufferbelly Inn on Mayfair Street in Medford. I used to wear shorter skirts than what you've got on. I had the kind of legs they wrote headlines about. I did what you're doing, batting my lashes and speaking like my vocal cords were made of baby powder."

"Mrs. Merrill writes romances." Harvey picked a chip from his plate. "Explains the colorful language."

Peach speared two cherries and placed them on the lips of the mai tai glasses. "What kind of romances do you write?"

"Books, dear."

"Oh, that's super."

"Is it?" Mrs. Merrill folded her hands on the bar. "And what's on your bedside table at the moment?"

Peach struggled to come up with a title she imagined Mrs. Merrill might admire.

"Leave her be," Harvey said with a groan. "Why don't you eat, Linda? Clearly, you're hungry for something."

"What's that supposed to mean?"

Peach placed a pitcher of Budweiser and the mai tais on a tray, delivering them to the tables before Harvey had a chance to answer. A rush of cold air made her teeth chatter when the bar door opened, but it was a friend of the guests drinking mai tais who came inside, not Circus.

"I heard her." Peach turned toward the amplified voice filling the room. Harvey, remote control in hand, had turned up the television's volume. On the screen, a man with tears in his eyes rubbed his hands over his balding head. The chyron beneath the image read BROTHER OF THE VICTIM.

"She was calling my name," the man said. *"I dug and dug, tryin' to get her. I said 'hold on,' and dug my fingers bloody. I can't feel 'em no more. But I couldn't . . . she just . . ."*

The brother's voice broke as someone out of frame reached her arms out to him. Mrs. Merrill snatched the remote, scolding her husband for not listening to what she was saying. The couple continued arguing under their voices while Stockwell challenged Trujillo to an arm wrestle. The house was on the screen again, pouring into the hole, but Peach kept thinking of the brother somewhere in Florida—in the same moment when she held a dish rag and stood in the center of a Boston bar—caught in the arms of whoever held him.

"Well, that's a load of bull." Mrs. Merrill threw down her napkin and climbed off the seat, ambling down the hall toward the bathroom.

"My apologies for the wife," Harvey said when Peach stepped back behind the bar. "Our oldest is headed off to college in the fall, and Linda's affected. I don't know why exactly, I mean, sure, it's change. But there's got to be something else."

Behind them, Stockwell pushed away from the table after Trujillo bested him in the arm-wrestling match. Trujillo grinned from behind his Heineken.

"I understand, you know," Harvey went on. "Linda used to turn heads, but not so much anymore. Four kids does that. What am I supposed to do?"

The door to the bar opened, but it was only the wine rep on her way out.

"Poor fella." Harvey grimaced at the television, but Peach wouldn't look. She turned off the sound, offering Harvey a slice of chocolate cake. By the time she keyed in the order and delivered another pitcher of beer, Mrs. Merrill had come back from the bathroom and sat sipping her margarita, her gaze fixed on Peach.

"Pretty sad about that lady in the sinkhole, right?" Peach slid a lime onto her glass.

Mrs. Merrill stirred the drink. "Don't let it get to you."

"You know," Peach said, "I don't only work in a bar. I'm in school, and I'm probably going to work in a doctor's office, like, as a medical lab technician or something. Maybe that sounds a little boring to a writer."

"A little."

"Well, but it's not." Peach moved to let Jason deliver the cake to Harvey. "I'm taking an anatomy class, and we're learning about the heart right now. Most people don't know how amazing the heart is. A pump, that's what it is really, a pump that just keeps filling up with blood. Isn't that romantic? Knowing the heart can fill up again after it gets empty?"

Mrs. Merrill nibbled at the lime.

"And you know the heart makes sounds?" Peach went on. "There's the lub and the dub. But for some people there are more sounds, and they call that a gallop. You have to get it checked if that happens. One night at the bar, I listened to Circus's heart. He's a guy who plays music here sometimes. I had my medical bag here with me one night after class, and he let me listen. And I heard extra lubs. Circus's heart doesn't beat. It gallops."

The thrill mingled awkwardly with sadness in her chest, and she glanced at the door.

"Lab technician," Mrs. Merrill said. "Lots of filing, I imagine."

"Oh, it's more than that."

"I've seen ads for such certificates late at night on television." She circled her finger around the mouth of the glass, licked off a spot of salt. "Is it a certificate you're getting, dear?"

"Linda," Harvey said, "give it a rest."

"Harvey, I'm getting to know your friend."

"No, you're being a shrew."

Mrs. Merrill leveled her shoulders. "Excuse me?"

Harvey's lips shriveled as if he'd bitten into an onion. "I hear you when you're not around. 'Is Linda going to think this shirt's the right fit?' 'Is Linda going to smell the one puff of a cigarette I allowed myself to take?'"

"You'd better not be smoking."

Harvey pounded his fist on the bar. "Let me have something for myself."

"How about another round?" Jason cleared their empty glasses, refilling the Merrills' drinks and nodding toward Peach to play a song on the jukebox. She started toward the back of the room, but the older woman grabbed her by the wrist.

Mrs. Merrill pointed her chin at her husband. "You think he's a nice old man. You have no idea what he's doing to you in his mind while you're prancing around back there."

"Get out of your head, Linda," Harvey said.

The guests at the other tables had stopped their conversations to listen, glancing at one another as if they were unsure whether to be worried or amused. Stockwell and Trujillo had stopped their game and were watching like spectators at a play. The Merrills didn't seem to notice.

"You can't take care of yourself when you've got a husband and children. You take care of everyone else," Mrs. Merrill said. "What you had before never comes back. Remember me, girly, when it happens to you."

Mrs. Merrill flung away Peach's wrist, then moved over a stool to leave a space between herself and her husband. Jason placed their drinks on the bar and picked up the remote, scrolling through the guide at the bottom of the screen.

"There's got to be a game on somewhere this afternoon, right, folks?" He landed on a listing for a hockey match, but before he could change the station, Stockwell asked, "Is that her?"

They all looked up at the television where a photograph of a woman was on display above a caption that read DOTTIE BED-GOOD, VICTIM. Her face was bulging, weighed by rolls of fat beneath her chin, her gaunt lips smiling around small teeth over-run by gums.

"Whoa," Stockwell croaked. "They'll need a crane to get her out."

"What do they use to push beached whales back into the ocean?" Jason asked.

Stockwell stepped up to the bar with his palm raised, and Jason slapped it as Harvey fidgeted on his stool, sensing his wife's ire.

Mrs. Merrill sat apart, her stare glued to Dottie Bedgood's image and moments later the sinkhole that had taken her.

"Leave her down there." Stockwell lifted his beer bottle into the air as if making a toast.

Jason snickered. "They may not have a choice."

Peach shoved him from her path as she slipped from behind the bar and went outside, shivering in the wind without her coat. A silver Buick drove past, and for a moment Peach thought she saw Circus at the wheel. She wondered if he was still at the duplex, if his ex-wife had forgiven him, if either of them had gone into the guest room and discovered her earrings and whatever else she'd left behind that was no longer worth going back for.

The door opened behind her, and Trujillo stepped outside. He offered a cigarette, then lit one for himself after Peach declined.

"It's cold out here," he said.

"Better than being inside." She picked up a stick and wrote her name into a snowdrift. "I should find another job. These people sometimes."

"The world's full of places to drink." Trujillo pulled off his coat and handed it to her. "Any of them would be lucky to have you."

Peach fit the coat over her shoulders, warmed at once by the musky scent of Trujillo's cologne steeping the fleece inside.

"I see all kinds of people coming in here," she said. "People you don't usually see in the same place together, like, old men and college girls and ladies who own companies and guys who play guitar and everyone else. What's weird is they're not doing anything when you think about it, y'know? All these places to drink all over the world. Everyone just sits there and talks and drinks and looks around. But sometimes I wonder if they're here doing nothing because they have so much to worry about when they're not here. And I wonder what they say to each other and how come I can't say stuff that makes people nod and agree and ask me things."

Trujillo was smiling, his dark eyes agleam as he rubbed his chin and listened. Peach noticed his lashes were long.

"Why do you hang out with Stockwell?" she asked.

He tilted his head to one side. "Everyone needs friends."

"You can find better ones than him."

"I'm not worried about myself."

Peach looked past him down the street, where an alley cat dragged something from an overturned trash bin. "I keep thinking about the woman in that hole. How you and I are standing here, and they're all in there drinking, and more people will be drinking here tonight. Someone's out shopping for groceries while someone else is making lunch and people are fucking, and she's in that hole."

Trujillo watched her through a haze of cigarette smoke.

"Do you think our minds really go into shock when stuff gets too scary?"

He took a pause, his gaze floating from her face to the street. "I think it's your body saving itself."

"What's she thinking about down there?"

Trujillo brushed his hand across her back. "She'll be all right. They'll get her out."

Peach skimmed the length of Trujillo's arms drawn over with tattoos—a mermaid straddling an anchor, snakes winding around the stem of a rose, a spider's web. Three dog tags on a ball chain were needled into his left forearm, and she gently held his wrist to read them.

"Who benched the most today?" she asked. "You or Stockwell?"

Trujillo grinned, sliding his wrist from her grasp. "I let him win."

"What makes you so nice?"

He flicked the cigarette into the street and slid his hands into his pockets. "I don't know. Time, I guess."

A man came around the corner thumbing a message into his phone, then stepped into the Blind Fox without acknowledging them or holding the door behind him. Peach gave back Trujillo's coat and followed, seating the man at a table by the window and asking what he wanted to drink. As he skimmed the menu, she watched Trujillo go back to the table where Stockwell had already ordered another round of beers. Trujillo took off the coat and draped it across the back of his chair. Peach imagined sliding back into it.

"She's dead," Mrs. Merrill announced from the bar, her hands slapping the wood. Harvey turned up the volume on the television.

"And we believe the hole's about twenty feet wide," said a man on the screen. *"The victim, Ms. Bedgood, is presumed deceased. At this time, we've determined the hole is too deep to recover the body without putting the safety of our team at risk. It has also been determined that in the interest of the community, measures should be taken to fill and seal the hole as quickly as possible."*

"What does that mean?" Peach turned to Trujillo, who lowered his head.

"They've called off the search," said Harvey.

"They're leaving her there? They can't leave her down there."

Harvey seemed not to have heard. He reached for Mrs. Merrill, and she scooted back to the seat beside him.

"Turn it off," Jason said, and Harvey clicked the remote, filling the room with a pained silence. A moment passed, frigid and bleak, then the room began to move again—Jason at the register, Harvey and Mrs. Merrill discussing whether to share a dessert, Stockwell plucking the darts from the board.

"Hey, old man." He tapped Harvey's shoulder. "You any good?"

"Used to be," he answered.

"Let's go a round? Trujillo takes winner."

Peach stood in the cold center of the room. "What about Dottie Bedgood?"

"Fuck her." Stockwell took a step forward and loomed.

He turned and tossed a dart that landed near the bull's-eye. Mrs. Merrill clumsily cheered, nudging Harvey off his stool. One of the men at the other tables called for Peach, but she'd already started down the hall toward the bathroom. Inside, she waited in the dark for tears to come, breathing into her chest where they pooled like sickness, but none came, so she sat down to relieve her muscles clenched with the strain of her cycle. Snapping on the light, she lifted the toilet lid and pulled her tampon, watching the plump drops of blood bead in the water below, the deep red and scent like sea giving her an odd comfort. Even the pain she liked in a way—its jabbing at the barrel of her belly and its grip on the base of her spine—because she'd always imagined the monthly event as her body asserting itself. But thoughts of Dottie Bedgood moved back through her mind, the woman wedged between rocks, choking in soil, weeds and tree roots winding around her limbs.

She heard a knock at the door and found Trujillo in the hallway when she opened it.

"You got a message." He handed her the phone.

Leave the bike in the back office, Circus had typed. *I'll get it next time I'm there.*

Peach placed the phone on the sink's edge. "You're here to tell me I have a text?"

Trujillo paused. Then he nodded, swallowing the way men did when they weren't telling the whole truth. Briefly, she imagined him in the faraway place where he'd fought alongside the three men whose names hung from the dog tags etched into his skin. There was rain, echoes of gunfire, the crack of buildings crumbling into rubble, scenes she figured she'd strewn together from movies. She imagined Trujillo shouting orders or knocking in doors, and quaked tenderly, eagerly, the way she knew certain women did when they imagined men and violence, though what excited Peach wasn't the danger but the fear behind it. She saw fear in the way the points of Trujillo's brow had drawn back as he watched her and waited for what to do next.

"I'm bleeding," she told him.

Trujillo took a cautious step forward and gently ran his fingers down the slope of her nose, brushing against her lips. He gazed at her mouth as if it cast a spell, but Peach realized a kiss wasn't going to be enough. Closing and locking the door behind him, she hiked up her skirt, then grabbed his hand, placing it between her thighs.

It was a slow, wandering pleasure, and Peach let herself fall, dropping deeper and deeper and nearer to the ground as Trujillo followed. She was vulgar on her haunches like the birthing woman she'd seen once in a picture from one of her schoolbooks, her legs wide, knees bent and pointing in opposite directions, but what she was working toward was the release, the break, then the lift upward. Whether Trujillo was glad or confused or thrilled or repulsed, Peach didn't know, because she wouldn't open her eyes to look at him and only helped his hand with the push and pull of her hips.

Loving You
Isn't the Right
Thing to Do

*

Pia

The dress was probably too much for a funeral. The champagne-colored silk, threaded with gold-tinted beads, shimmered over her body, Pia imagined, like the scales of a mermaid. The delicate V of the neckline lifted her small breasts like a polite offering, and the waistline—her mother called it Victorian—was proper, classy. Maybe there was too much dazzle, too much skin, but Pia decided not to concern herself about it as she combed a part into her blonde hair, tied it into a sleek knot, then carefully chose the strands she'd let fall to grace the back of her neck. She perfumed all her sweet spots with vanilla oil—behind her knees and the bends of her wrists—and fastened an orchid to the knot in her hair. She took off her wedding band, discolored on the inside, leaving a tan line she hoped no one would notice. In the mirror, she practiced her smile, fingers flitting over her collarbone as she parted her lips. She had learned to smile now in ways that hid the creases around her mouth, proof of how often she'd frowned over her thirty-six years. Pia took one last glance in the mirror. The dress was better suited for a cocktail party, as if she ever went to those, and the flower was too much. But she wanted to stand out. Patrick Hurley's wake was this afternoon, and Johnny O'Brien might be there.

* * *

Pia walked into the living room and placed a hand on her hip. "How do I look?"

Her daughter lifted the headphones from her ears. "Like you want a date."

Sitting on the floor, Koko extended her legs, which were losing their plump girlish swell and lengthening to womanly slender, and used her phone to snap a photo of her toenails painted green. The quick turn of her daughter's gaze made Pia shiver. There was a time the girl, whose moods and looks were dark like her father's, would have fussed over her mother's golden loveliness. But lately the fourteen-year-old had become more fascinated with herself, leaving Pia to bear an indefinable dread and to wonder what the point of having daughters was if they were meant to fall out of love.

She knelt down to peer at Koko's toenails. "The colors you girls wear these days are so unusual," she said. "I admire how little you care about being pretty."

Koko looked at her feet, frowned. "Should I wear a different color?"

Pia's dread lifted slightly as she watched Koko's bare face, her thick, unplucked eyebrows, the fuzz on her upper lip, and the tangled knots of her hair—still girl, still plain. Pia pinched her daughter's cheek. "How would I know? What you should do is get ready. Your father's on his way."

"Why can't I stay home?"

"You should take advantage of any chance you get to see that fool."

"He's just doing this to make up for fucking that girl in the house last week."

Pia stomped her foot. "My mother used to wash my mouth out with soap when I cursed."

"Explains a lot."

Pia went to the kitchen, where she filled a thermos with Grey Goose and tonic, slipping it into her purse. Back in the living room, the front door opened, and she heard Circus's throaty "What's up" and Koko's bored "Hey."

When she stepped into the living room, Circus was standing in the frame of the front door. His gaze slinked up her body in the silk dress and lingered at the orchid in her hair.

"Lucky corpse," he said.

* * *

Driving down the expressway past the harbor toward Quincy, Pia played the Cranberries' album she'd listened to back in college when she waited tables in Patrick's restaurant and Johnny O'Brien made drinks, flirting from the other side of the bar.

"'You know I'm such a fool for you,'" she sang quietly so as not to hear her own voice. She'd come across Patrick's obituary the day after discovering Circus in her living room and a pair of earrings in the guest bedroom. The woman, whoever she was, had left through a window. Patrick's eyes had gazed up at Pia from the dulled newsprint with the bleak, hollowed-out stare of the newly dead. The morning was darkened by the sudden resurfacing of her old friend, brought back to her by his passing, but it was Johnny she found herself thinking about the rest of the day. Johnny had a wicked temper and rumored connections to the Winter Hill Gang in Somerville, but he was blue-eyed and handsome. He'd always joked that Pia was out of his league. After two years working together, he'd finally taken her to dinner, then shyly made love to her that night. But a week later, Circus Palmer had played his trumpet on the restaurant's tiny stage, and Johnny had faded.

After reading Patrick's obituary, Pia had taken a bath with a vodka tonic on the rim of the tub and fantasized herself at the service, Johnny standing in a corner. He'd touch her shoulder and tell her how glad he was to see her again.

* * *

Pia took two generous sips from her thermos before walking into the funeral home, avoiding the open casket at the front of the room. She searched for Johnny in a corridor leading into the chapel, where a silver-haired woman wept as a man with tears in his eyes rubbed her back. Pia nodded her condolences to the woman, then went back through the hall into a visitation room, where she took a cracker and square of cheddar cheese from a plate on a table. Nibbling at the edge, she looked out a window into the parking lot. She saw a man she thought was Johnny but wasn't. Back in the room, a woman walked past, glaring at the orchid in Pia's hair.

"I think the guy you're lookin' for is up front in the box." A man stepped up beside her. Short with bulldog shoulders and a bloated face the color of bread dough, he sipped a small carton of milk through a straw.

"I'm looking for a friend," she told him.

The man nodded and took a sip. "Sad about ol' Pat, huh?"

"Of course."

"It's always the best ones that go too soon." A coy smile dimpled the man's round cheeks. "You don't remember me, do you?"

"I'm sorry. Should I?"

"Tom Fitzgerald. Everyone calls me Fitz. And now I gotta apologize. I know your face, but I don't remember your name."

"It's Pia."

"Right, I remember it was somethin' pretty." The man's teeth were yellowed when he smiled, but it was a friendly smile, and his accent told her he was a Southie boy, the kind her parents used to tell her to be wary of whenever she took the subway from Cambridge. "I'm a couple sizes bigger than I used to be, so you might not recognize me. I managed Sweet Charlie's, the bar next to Pat's place. Patty used to bring you guys over after closing time, used to tip the bejesus out of us, my God. Generous fella."

Pia twisted the fake diamond in her earlobe, nodded courteously, then scanned the room.

"So, how you been?" Fitz asked.

"Fine," she answered without looking at him so as not to deter Johnny from talking to her if he came into the room. "And you?"

"Guess I don't have a story you haven't heard before." He chuckled. "Marriage, kids, divorce. That's the order, isn't it? I got a house in Milton ain't bad. Well, until my wife swiped it in the divorce, but them's the breaks, right? Could be worse. This could be my funeral." He gestured toward the flower. "Interesting choice."

Pia looked past him down to the chapel. "Orchids are my favorite."

Fitz jiggled the carton, and Pia heard the splash of milk. "Those were good times, huh. Patty and the gang comin' out after the shows. What gets me, though, when these things happen, is how you never know how things are gonna end up. I think of sittin' at Patty's favorite table at Sweet Charlie's. And goddamn I can still see him, y'know? See him like he was then, drinking his Bud. And we're talking about who knows what and not one of us knows twenty years later I'd be at his funeral."

Fitz rubbed at his eyes, and briefly Pia's shame was stronger than her need to see Johnny. "What's nice is we get the chance to go back to those days," she said.

Fitz nodded, took a deep breath. "At least we had 'em. I met the wife at Sweet Charlie's, well, ex-wife. Kelly Martin, you remember her?"

"I don't think so."

"You wouldn't forget. She's got hair the color of fire." Fitz sucked in his cheeks as if to quell uncomfortable feelings. "You never noticed me back then, but I was there."

"I remember," Pia fibbed.

"Nah, you don't." Fitz's laugh was kindly. "Sweet of you, hon. I understand, I mean, you were the one with all the fellas around.

Mack and John O'Brien were always hittin' on you. I didn't stand a chance with those clowns around."

Pia pretended to be occupied by the loose clasp of her bracelet. "Johnny was the bartender, right?"

"He was."

"You knew him?"

"John and me are business partners, *were* business partners. We opened a couple boxing gyms together." Fitz straightened his tie, staring off into the distance. "Yeah, I know John. I know John real good."

"Does he know about Patrick?"

"I believe he does."

"Is he coming today?"

Fitz's eyes narrowed.

"Only because I remember how close they were." Pia folded her hands behind her back and watched a man dab a handkerchief against his eyes as he stood before the casket. "I'm sure Johnny would want to pay his respects, don't you think?"

"Nice of you to consider him."

"I'm thinking of Patrick." Pia pulled coyly at the fake diamond. "He used to say everyone at Sweet Charlie's was family. He would want everyone here."

Fitz took one last sip from the straw, then tossed the empty carton into a trash bin. He shoved his hands into his pockets, studying her. "Actually, John isn't comin' today. He asked me to pass his condolences to the family. But we're supposed to be meetin' after I get done here. It's just a mile up the road. If you want, come with and say hello."

Pia's pulse quickened. "Why on earth would I do that?"

"I imagine Johnny would be glad to see you."

"I'm sure he doesn't remember me."

"How could he forget you?"

Pia glanced at a clock on the wall as if she had elsewhere to be. Behind her back, she fiddled with the clasp of her bracelet.

"It's no problem," he said. "I'll take you over and give you a lift back, that is, unless John wants to bring you back hisself."

"I guess that's okay," she said, not sure if she was pleased. "Let me pay my respects."

Fitz stepped off her path, and Pia made her way to the casket, drawing in a breath before peering in. Patrick had aged significantly in the sixteen years since she'd seen him. For a brief moment that terrified her, she imagined her own body growing old beneath her dress. She stared down at the face, unrecognizable beneath caked makeup, to reassure herself that this man was someone she had once known. Maybe the soul didn't leave the body in the instant of death, she thought, but was always leaving every day, and maybe death was simply the soul's final withdrawal, like the way a tree could be dead inside for years before its limbs began to decay.

* * *

"You're meeting Johnny here?"

Fitz had driven down a mile of service roads into a gravel lot where an old warehouse had been converted into a boxing gym. The building was red, with poorly painted likenesses of Muhammad Ali and other fighters Pia didn't recognize on the facade. Fitz walked from the driver's side of his SUV to open Pia's door, then took a cluster of keys from his pocket and led her through a back entrance to the club. Inside, she heard the thump of gloves against leather bags, the skid of shoes on canvas floors, and the brutal grunts of men. The air smelled like raw meat. There was a handful of guys in the place but only one woman, a reedy girl wrapping her knuckles beneath a speed bag. Pia sensed all eyes on her as she followed Fitz into an office with pennants on the walls, photos of Fitz holding championship belts and trophies, a calendar of women dressed in skintight referee costumes. His desk held only a computer, a cup of sharpened pencils, and a Bible with Post-it Notes stuck to the edges of the pages.

"You seem nervous." Fitz took a bottle of milk and packet of honey from a minifridge, a straw from the cup of pencils. "Everyone's lookin' 'cause you're pretty. We don't get a lot of pretty ladies around here." He ripped the honey packet between his teeth and squeezed it into the bottle, watching the gluey threads layer, then disappear into the cream. "Somethin' to drink?"

Pia scanned the gym for Johnny as she took a seat across from his desk. "Nothing."

Fitz rubbed his hands over his balding scalp, swiveling in the chair to stare out the window as if he were suddenly alone in the room. Pia wondered whether Johnny was really on his way, realizing she had no way of knowing whether Fitz would lie about it or why. She tried to place him, the doughy cheeks, the soft bend in his nose. He might have been handsome back in the days of Sweet Charlie's, but he seemed too mild for Pia to have noticed him then.

"What time is Johnny supposed to get here?" she asked.

Fitz glanced at his watch. "Soon, hon."

"If I had his number, I would probably call him. But that's me."

He swiveled back to face her, stirring his milk with the straw and grinning as if he were interviewing her for a job. "What line of work you in these days?"

Pia stared into the gym as the girl knocked her knuckles against the speed bag. "Fund-raising. It's for a kid's music school. I assist someone, so my position isn't . . . essential."

He nodded toward her hands folded on her knee. "And how long since you took off your wedding ring?"

Pia hid her left hand beneath her thigh.

"C'mon," he teased. "I already know one of your secrets."

"What secrets would I have?"

"How 'bout the one where you went to a funeral to hook up with an old boyfriend?"

Pia bit her tongue to keep her eyes from watering, while the pale line on her finger ached tenderly. For fourteen years, she'd worn the ring—Circus had taken his off after the first six months—and continued even now, five years after the divorce. She'd been faithful, too, though she'd had little reason to be.

"Circus and I haven't been together for years."

"Circus?" Fitz sat upright in his chair. "Circus Palmer, that jazz guy?"

"You remember him?"

"He *married* you?"

Pia's throat tightened. "We have a daughter."

Fitz's lips twitched as if a thought had passed through his mind that he decided not to share. He settled into his chair again, nodded blankly. "Wearin' the ring won't bring him back, trust me on that one."

"You don't know anything about it."

"Maybe not."

Pia grabbed the thermos from her purse, took a gulp. "When's Johnny coming?"

Fitz watched her wipe a drop of vodka from her chin. "Any minute."

"I can't tell if you're honest or not."

"I'm always honest."

Pia scanned the photographs pinned to the wall. Fitz at the top of the John Hancock Tower. Fitz standing among a group of little boys wearing boxing gloves. Fitz in fighting stance. Then her gaze shifted to the brunette on the calendar's pages. She was the kind of woman Circus liked. Dark hair. Dark skin. Curves. Pia chewed the inside of her cheek, wondering why she still did this to herself.

"There was a party at Sweet Charlie's when I left," she said. "Johnny brought in a cake with a plastic violin on top because I told him I played as a girl. He used to say I should study drama instead of psychology because he thought I could be the next Grace Kelly."

Fitz slurped at the last drops of milk in the bottle. "I think I got that cake for you." His cheeks reddened as he pulled at the straw even though the bottle was empty. "I thought you should be celebrated."

He glanced at her with a look that said he'd suffered a little in telling her this. Pia wanted to thank him but realized how silly it sounded so many years later. He must have sensed her embarrassment because he blushed, then pulled two sticks of gum from his pocket and tossed one across the desk. "Tell me how close you came to being Grace Kelly."

"Oh, I never even tried," she said, politely sliding the gum back across the desk. "Circus was the star. He needed a home, so I made it. That's what you do when you're in love. No one likes to admit it, but that's what we do. Clear the ground so the person we want plants himself there, so we always have whatever it is we love about him. So it stays with us. My mother said something like that to me when I was young. She never understood what it was about Circus."

"I find myself wondering the same thing."

"I just couldn't imagine living without his voice and his laugh, the way he looked at me like he didn't deserve me. I could never do anything as well as he could. But he was mine. And then Koko came along, and children, well, they take everything. I was only twenty-two when she came, but God what she did to us. But I'm a mom, and that's the way I like it."

Pia sipped the Grey Goose and tonic, watered down now but still necessary. She realized how many times she'd said those words—*I'm a mom, and that's the way I like it*—and became bored with the clunk of the words, the singsong sound of her own voice as she said them.

"All of a sudden," she went on, tipsy now, "Koko was crawling, Koko was walking, she's talking. All my creativity went into raising her. When she was four, she wanted to be a chicken coming out of an egg for Halloween. So I spent a month making the best chicken coming out of an egg costume anyone had ever seen. And birthday cakes, my goodness. Koko loves M&M's but to this day she won't eat the red ones. For her fifth birthday, she wanted M&M's on her cake, and she wanted layers, so I made five layers and spent hours separating bags of M&M's by color, removing all the red and spreading the icing into perfect swirls. At three in the morning, Circus came down saying, 'Come to bed, buttercup.' And I said, 'Oh, just one more swirl.'"

Pia smiled, remembering when she served Koko the M&M's cake, a moment captured in a photograph framed above the fireplace at home. What Pia had loved most about those early years was how anything could surprise her daughter. The girl had been in a constant state of awe. Sitting across from Fitz, Pia thought about how she loved that little girl but feared it was the wrong feeling. She should have missed her.

"Once I had a dream my breasts were nozzles," she told him, "like at a gas station. Gas station nozzles, the part you shove in the tank. And there were all these cats suckling them, just hanging off my body."

Fitz didn't say anything. He was looking at her funny.

"I want to smoke," she said. "Can I smoke in here?"

"You don't seem like a smoker."

"Only sometimes. Keeps you skinny."

Fitz drew the blinds and closed the door as Pia reached into her bag for the pack of Virginia Slims she'd been carrying around for months. He brought a book of matches from his desk, lit the cigarette when she held it to her lips, and watched her take a slow drag.

"In a way, don't you think Patrick's lucky?" she asked.

Fitz raised an eyebrow.

"He's done. There's nothing more to worry about. Or want." Pia glanced down at her hands, cringing as she saw once again how much older they looked. "What I used to think was miraculous is really just common."

Fitz thumbed the pages of the Bible on his desk. Pia listened to the snap of the paper. His eyes moistened as he rubbed his hands together, lost momentarily in his own thoughts.

"Maybe you should call Johnny," she said quickly, "to make sure he's still coming."

Fitz rolled his tongue in his mouth, sneering like the gangsters she saw in old movies and scaring her a little. He reached into a drawer and pulled out a bottle of Jameson and two glasses. Filled them and handed one to Pia. She took a tiny sip. Fitz downed the shot, then pounded his fist against his chest. He slid the cigarette from her fingers, dropped it into her thermos, then guided her from the chair out of the office into the gym, where the noise and smell hit like a smack in the face.

"Take off your shoes," he said.

Clumsily, she slipped out of her heels. He placed them on a bench and handed her a pair of sparring gloves.

"What are we doing?" she asked.

"We're goin' a round."

"You're crazy." Pia held the gloves against her chest. They smelled like leather and sweat. "I don't know how to box."

"You know how to hit."

"I just want to see Johnny."

Fitz led Pia into one of the boxing rings, then helped her into the gloves. As he tied the laces tight against her wrist, she looked around the gym. The place seemed smaller than she'd remembered coming in, cramped, like a cavern hidden far away from the rest of life.

"All right." Fitz clapped his palms around the gloves snug on her hands, took a step away, then folded his fingers behind his back. "Now hit me."

"Excuse me?"

"Hard as you can."

Pia searched his eyes again. "I don't like this game."

"I'm not playing a game." Fitz slapped his stomach. "Hit me."

"We both know I'm not as strong as you, okay, you win."

"Give it your best shot. In the gut, hard as you can."

Pia lifted her arms, her wrists made limp by the swollen weight of the gloves. She knocked her fists against his stomach.

"You're not trying."

She knocked harder.

Fitz grabbed her gloved hand and shoved it against his hard belly. "You wanna hit something, I wanna get hit. So gimme everything you got."

Without thinking, Pia pounded her fist against Fitz's hard belly, but he barely moved. She took a step back to catch her breath. A man in a corner of the gym pretended to tie his shoes, but she could tell he was eyeing them. Two other men had stopped sparring in an adjacent ring to watch, while the reedy girl held the chain of the speed bag and stared. Fitz slipped his hands into a pair of focus mitts. "Circus Palmer, yeah, I remember that fella. He used to love the ladies."

"He never stopped."

Fitz raised the mitts in the air, nodded for her to punch them. "That was it then? A woman? Women?"

She thought of Circus shirtless in her living room a week ago and wondered whether he'd met up with the girl from the guest bedroom after he left the house that morning. Pia hadn't considered the possibility until now. In her belly, she sensed the heaviness she used to feel watching women ogle him from the edges of the stages where he played his horn, the queasiness that came on nights she spent alone in their bed not knowing where he was, smelling woman on him when he finally came home.

Pia found herself inside another memory, a more distant one. A snowstorm three nights after Christmas, when Koko was a five-year-old in footed pajamas, the cotton on their bottoms scuffed. A gust of wind blew outside, and the electricity spat, then clicked off in the devices around the house. Darkness filled every room. Before Koko could cry out, Circus scooped her into his arms and brought her to the kitchen, where they stirred a box of sugar cookie mix into dough and heated a pitcher of milk on the gas stove. He built a fire and pulled a blanket around their three shivering bodies. He sang to them. Louis Armstrong. Otis Redding.

Pia thought of the three of them under that blanket and wondered how Circus could have chosen to go. She thought of him taking his phone into other rooms in the house to answer calls, of his finally leaving in the middle of the night so she would have to be the one to tell Koko her father had gone for good. Pia thought about Circus so long, she forgot she was standing in the boxing ring, the gloves like weights in her hands.

"I don't like jazz," she said. "I never liked jazz."

Fitz snickered.

"I didn't want to be Grace Kelly either."

"Who'd you want to be?"

Pia thought about it. "Stevie Nicks."

Fitz lowered his hands, leaning against the ropes. "None of the fellas liked Circus Palmer. Too sure of himself. The kind of guy doesn't realize how lucky he is."

Fitz gently brushed her chin, then raised both mitted hands into the air. "You hit me, I call John. One-two punch, right then left."

Pia drew in a breath and punched, barely grazing the focus mitt on both swings. Embarrassed, she looked around the gym, but the men had lost interest. Only the woman was still watching.

Fitz took off the mitts and tossed them to the floor, spreading his arms in the air. "One-two punch. In the stomach this time."

"I feel ugly," Pia said.

"You're gorgeous."

"Fighting isn't pretty for girls."

"I don't see any girls in here."

She took a swipe and missed, then another that landed. Fitz let out a grunt. Pia's body was suddenly tingling, weightless, and so she didn't see what was coming next as Fitz leaned down to kiss her. The stale taste of milk in his mouth turned her stomach, and she pulled away.

He straightened his back, a wrecked look in his eyes. He unlaced the gloves, yanking them from her wrists. "John's not coming."

"Why not?"

"Because he's fucking my wife," Fitz answered calmly, as if he'd said Johnny was at the movies or baking a pie. "Some people get what they want. Most people don't. You know that by now, don't you?"

Pia climbed out of the ring, stumbling as she slipped through the ropes. Dropping to the floor, she walked quickly until she was outside the stinking, stifling gym. The door slammed behind her, surrounding her in a silence that was broken only by the cruel cackle of a bird cawing in the distance and the cold blue spill of the sky that deadened the day.

Fitz stepped through the door, head hung. He was carrying her shoes and knelt down to place them at her feet. Pia held his shoulder for balance as she stepped into them. When he stood up, he gently opened his hand. In it was the orchid, trampled and drained of color.

"It must have fallen in the ring," he said.

Pia took the flower as if it were an injured baby bird.

"Look," Fitz said, "the older I get, the less I understand about anything. All I know is I saw you and wondered what it'd be like to know you again. I mean, we don't have to get romantic or nothin', though you wouldn't hear me complain if we did. What I'd really like is to have someone to lie next to at night. That's what I want more than anything. Y'know?"

Fitz glanced up at her, and in his round face, she observed the features of the younger, handsomer man he'd once been. She wished she'd seen him then.

"I think if you saw yourself the way other people do," he said, "you'd be impressed."

Pia looked past him down the unfamiliar road headed to the funeral home, where her car was still parked in the drive. For an instant she knew was both silly and sad, she hoped to see Johnny driving toward them, or maybe Circus coming to bring her home, something sweet and unexpected. Nothing came but a quiet gust of wind. Pia slid the crushed flower behind her ear and started walking.

Opus

*

Circus

The first flickers of the oncoming spring couldn't burn away the chill lingering in the depths of the morning. Circus turned up the heat in the Buick as Koko slept in the passenger seat beside him, goose-bumped in a worn T-shirt. As a baby, she had smiled when she slept, which his grandmother back home used to say meant the angels were talking to her. He kept glancing over at the girl, charmed by the faint snore and her quaking eyelids, maybe in dream, maybe with the angels. He wondered if she'd let herself fall asleep so as not to have to speak to him, though he didn't mind. He had no idea what to say either.

"Hey." He nudged her after he pulled into the drive. "We're here."

Koko lagged behind as she followed him into his apartment, waiting at the door as he tossed his keys into a fishbowl full of matches, then cleared a space for her on the sofa.

"Your place is messy," she said.

He looked around at the clutter of instruments in the corner of the room, the unemptied ashtrays and half-full beer bottles, a bass guitar with broken strings on the coffee table and a wine stain on the wooden floor.

"You're welcome to clean if you're uncomfortable," he said.

Koko walked through the living room, sweeping her fingers over the keys of the piano before dropping like a sack of apples onto the sofa. "Last week I spilled candle wax on Mom's bedroom carpet. She freaked and started scraping it off with her fingernail, sobbing like a baby. Everything at home has to be spotless, so I guess it's cool to feel like I can just come here and toss whatever on the floor."

"Not exactly the vibe I was going for." He watched her pick at a scab on her arm. "You're gonna leave a scar."

"So? You have scars. Like the ones on your back you never told me about."

"I'm grown, I'm supposed to have scars." Circus collected the beer bottles on his way to the kitchen. "You hungry?"

"I could eat."

"What do you like?"

"Food."

He lit a cigarette on the burner of the stove and counted the number of hours he had to fill before he could take the girl back to her mother. The deal he'd made with Pia five years ago was that she could have full custody and he would visit whenever the mood or need struck. A child, especially a girl, needed her mother, was his thinking, and he'd convinced himself Koko would be satisfied with visits that were prompted by will rather than obligation. In truth, he'd already lost too much of himself by the time he decided to go. The time he'd made for his world outside wife and child had been too much for them and too little for him, even though he'd kept up with the gigging, the trips to play in nearby cities, the teaching, the women. Pia seemed able to tell herself stories about the women that made it all right until the day she and Koko ran into him with a woman in Somerville when he was supposed to be in the Berkshires.

Circus tossed two slices of bread into the oven and brought Koko jars of peanut butter and orange marmalade.

"Make yourself a snack," he said. "And see if you can find that cot in case you need someplace to sleep."

Koko winced at the jam jar. "I don't like fruit chunks."

"Spoon 'em out."

"What are you gonna do?"

"I got work to do. These are prime music-making hours."

"Whatever." Koko closed her headphones over her ears and stretched across the sofa.

"Yeah, whatever," he muttered on his way to the bathroom, where he took one last drag of his cigarette, tossed it into the toilet, then washed his hands before making his way into his studio down the hall. He clicked on the metronome to ease himself into a groove, a calming effect he'd needed more often lately. He listened to the tick-tock until a melody came into his head. He licked his lips, and brought his trumpet to them. The slinky melody had come to him in a dream and stayed with him for weeks. He blew it into his horn and listened to a piano play along in his mind. He played and thought of Maggie because the sound was like her. Fierce but major-keyed. Smiling briefly against the mouthpiece of the horn, he let himself imagine her in the room, curled in a chair and drumming a rhythm against her thighs. But before he could decide how to fit her snug into a daydream, his phone chimed with a message from the studio owner in Waltham where he was scheduled to start recording his demo.

We got paying customers those nights, the text told him. *Need to reschedule.*

"Fuck me." Circus placed his horn into its case and dialed. When no one answered, he tried again. The smell of smoke filtered into the room, but he ignored it and dialed a second time.

"Don't do this to me," he said after the voice on the other end of the line told him to leave a message. "You know how hard it was to get these guys together to play the same nights? I got a month to finish this record, or it's over with this producer. The bus leaves the station, man."

The smell of smoke tingled in his nostrils, so he brought the phone with him to the kitchen, imploring his friend to return the call. He found the bread in the oven had burned black, so he opened the windows just as Koko stepped out of the bathroom.

"Didn't you smell something?" he asked when she appeared in the doorway.

"I had my headphones on."

"And that affects your sense of smell?"

"Whatever." Koko snapped her gum.

"What's with you saying 'whatever' all the time? What exactly is 'whatever' supposed to express?"

"Whatever means whatever." She blew a bubble, popped it, sucked it back into her mouth. "Do you know who died?"

"Huh?"

"The funeral mom went to today."

"I don't know anything about your mother's life."

"God, do you even like her?"

"What kind of question you asking me?" He noticed an expression on Koko's face that he'd seen on his students' faces, an attempt to look indifferent when something really mattered. "'Course I like Pia. We bicker. That's what people who like each other do."

Seemingly satisfied, Koko blew another bubble. "What are you working on?"

The burnt bread singed his fingertips when he pulled it from the oven. "Don't worry about it."

Koko chewed with her mouth open, the gum crackling between her teeth. "Isn't forty kinda old to still be trying to have a career?"

"I have a career."

"Is that why you're interviewing at a car dealership?"

"Your mother tell you that?" He swiped the air. "Berklee's giving me less classes to teach, but that doesn't mean anything."

Koko watched him scrape the black from the toast with a knife. "Mom says you're bitter because you never got famous. She says it's because you never finish anything."

The bread split, then fell to the floor. Circus glared at it instead of looking at the girl. "Pia doesn't know jack about music, all right? I'm meeting with a record label. So maybe you can understand why I gotta think about that instead of keeping you entertained. Bet your mother didn't tell you that now, did she?"

"Well, did you tell her?"

Circus kicked at the blackened bread as Koko went to the cabinet for the broom and dustpan, then swept the toast and crumbs into a pile. "Whatever you were just playing was kinda cool. What's it called?"

"'Magdalena.'" He scooped the pile into a dustpan. "I don't know. Maybe."

"Where's Magdalena?"

"Magdalena's a person I know."

"The girl you had sex with in the house?" Koko pulled the gum into a long pink strand and coiled it around her thumb. She didn't blink or do anything that suggested she thought she was wrong in asking.

"Is Magdalena pretty?" she went on. "Why'd you write a song about her?"

"Darlin', most of my songs are about women."

She groaned and shoved the wad of bubblegum back into her mouth. "That's probably not something you needed to tell me."

The tick of the metronome still sounded in the other room, and Circus let himself be lulled. The melody was in his head again, louder and louder, until the room went away and there was only Maggie and sound.

"B-flat isn't right," he mumbled.

"Huh?" Koko was drawing a pair of lips into a napkin on the counter.

He nodded toward the second piece of toast. "You gonna eat this?"

Koko wrinkled her nose and went back to the drawing, coloring in the curved lines. "If you like Magdalena so much, why don't you see her instead of writing songs about her?"

"Writing songs is easier."

"Do you have a song about Mom?"

He tossed the bread into the trash. "You like pretzels? I think I got some pretzels in here."

"Do you?"

He slid a bag of chips from the cupboard across the table. "I wrote a tune or two about Pia back in the day."

"What kind of tunes?"

"Sad ones."

A sly grin turned the corners of Koko's mouth, and Circus could see where her habit of chewing her bottom lip had torn a hole in the skin. The smile made him notice that she'd started wearing lipstick and shadowing her eyes with blue powder. Her lashes were clumped with too much mascara, while her eyebrows looked as if she'd taken a tiny scissors to them but trimmed without following their shape.

"See what's on the television," he said. "There's something I gotta deal with."

She held the napkin over her mouth, the drawn lips in place of her own. "Why do you have different music playing in different rooms?"

"Koko, I need to work."

"I'm just asking."

"You ask every time you're here."

"Okay, so I ask once a year," she said. "Jazz is playing in the living room. The Roots are playing in the second bedroom, something I don't even know is coming out of your room."

"Play whatever you want." He started down the hall toward his studio. "Mi casa is your fucking casa."

"Why do you even play jazz? I mean, who listens to jazz?"

"I could give two shits who listens," he shouted. "I play to feel joy. Maybe you can't dig that because you're little, but I play, and the world gets easier. You should be so lucky to find something like that in your life. Now leave me be, Koko, for fuck's sake, will you?"

Koko watched him, chewing at the hole in her lip. A spot of blood rose at her teeth, and she dabbed it with the napkin.

"Sorry," she said, her voice shaky.

He knew he was meant to say something meaningful to her, something fatherly that was high-reaching and insulating, and as he struggled to find it, he also resented her for needing it and resented Pia for requiring this of him in the first place. He'd liked the horsing around when he lived with them, liked the funny expressions and observations Koko made as a girl, liked helping her tool around with arts and crafts kits, putty and tubs of clay, the violin she plucked at for a year, but this duty made him feel cramped.

"I imagine what I play's not your thing," he said, heading back into the kitchen. "What are you into? What do you like?"

Koko shrugged. "Do you know Lung Water? They're kinda rock, but also, like, sometimes they rap and it gets, like, you can dance to it. Oh, and I like Flower Girl. She's electropop, my friend Bree calls it, but also you know, indie. I guess Flower Girl's more indie. Bree says we should get into punk, though."

"Why's that?"

"She thinks we need to be more interesting."

"You're plenty interesting." He tossed out the stained napkin and handed her a fresh one. "I should introduce you to my friend Raquel in New York. She'll teach you a thing or two."

"You know people who do punk?"

"Raquel hung with all those cats back in the day. Had her own little band, too, what were they called? Ugly Mother, was it? I could only take so much, but man, she could screech the paint off the walls."

The grin on Koko's face reminded Circus of a time when she was smaller and he could impress her by staying inside the lines in one of her coloring books or shaping a lump of clay.

"Come on," he said and led her to the living room, where he took a seat at the piano.

The tune was called "Catalina" because of the T-shirt Pia had been wearing the first time he saw her at the end of her shift at Sweet Charlie's, where he used to play after college. CATA-LINA ISLAND was written in sensuous script on the pink cotton stretched across Pia's slight chest, which made him fantasize about the island, the water lapping the shore and the pretty blonde girl wading in the surf. The melody he made for Pia was delicate, chaste, and when he played it for her after their first date at a pizza shop, he saw love in her eyes, love he still saw all these years later, after his had long faded. He'd fallen for Pia as soon as he saw her tawny skin and blue eyes. She reminded him of the airily pretty blonde girls in his high school who were too idolized to notice a monstrous, awkward boy and his tiny horn. His love was rooted in reverence for her beauty and gratitude that he could be near it, but he was too young then to know this was the kind of love that moved quickly through him.

Playing the tune for Koko now, Circus could sense Pia in the sounds he once made for her. He might have missed her if their time didn't feel so far away.

"That's about your mother," he said when he finished playing.

"It's a happier song than I thought it'd be."

"She was happier then."

He winked and she lowered her eyes. On his way back to the studio where the metronome had stopped ticking, Circus pinched Koko's nose, then gave a kiss to her forehead. She rolled the napkin into a ball, picking at its edges.

"I guess maybe jazz isn't so bad," she said. "I like those songs you put on my iPod. Who was the guy you put on there?"

"Koko, please, I gotta get back to work," Circus groaned. "Dexter Gordon."

She flicked the napkin across the room. "What's the rush?"

"Every man has one perfect creation in him. This record is mine."

The girl snickered like her mother did when she was offended but too proud to admit it. He hadn't noticed Koko had picked up the trait.

"Listen," he said, "if you let me work for a bit, I'll take you out for ice cream."

"Ice cream?" She tsked. "I'm not five, you know. I'm almost fifteen."

"So you don't like ice cream anymore?"

Koko rolled her eyes and started sketching another pair of lips into a napkin. "Fine."

* * *

"Catalina" was a cut off the first demo he'd recorded after college, and he hadn't listened to it since. He slipped it into his player. There had been a rawness to his sound then, an eagerness he could no longer hear when he listened to his work now. He let "Catalina" fade into the next song, a ballad he'd written about his first shot of whiskey, and the next about his father sending him to the garden for a switch, and the next about the slink in the hips of a woman he'd watched walk across a moonlit street.

Circus lit a cigarette. He was forty. It hit him now. He turned off the stereo and flipped on the metronome, taking drags from the cigarette and concentrating on the tick, thinking of easier days and time running out. He needed to keep working, to make something happen. He rubbed his hands with sanitizer, grabbed his trumpet, and started pacing the room, prancing up and down the scales until the veins in his neck ached.

"Son of a bitch." He tossed the trumpet into the cushion of a chair, wiped his moist brow into the hem of his shirt, then took a bottle of Wild Turkey from a shelf and poured himself a glass. The drinking distracted him but wasn't easing his nerves. He needed to move, to let unravel whatever was knotted in his gut. He thought of sliding between a pair of open thighs and the release, imagining how sweet his sound would be in the aftermath.

What's up, beautiful? he texted Peach. *You crossed my mind.*

He felt thrilled by the nearness of pleasure, the woman reading the message and inviting him over. He could get through the writing and the afternoon with Koko if he knew a woman was waiting for him in the end. Lifting his feet onto his desk, he watched a bird glide across the sky outside his window.

"What do you think happens after we die?" Koko's voice startled him.

"What the fuck, man?"

She was standing at the door, anxiously twisting the knob back and forth. "It's just that I don't know what religion you are."

"Christ, are you trying to get on my nerves?"

"Sorry," she whimpered as if holding back tears. Then the words poured out. "It's just that I got an A on an essay I wrote about God, and I was just thinking how we've never talked about what you believe, and there are so many things happening, like, Mr. O'Rourke got fired, and he was the only person at that stupid school who thought anything I do is cool—"

"Mr. O'Rourke?"

"—plus I'm in drama club now, and he won't get to see me perform, and you don't care even though I have a singing part in *Bye Bye Birdie,* and I wanted to tell you how the performing thing, like, I probably got from you."

The girl stood in the frame of the door, her hands pressed against the wooden panels as if held in place by them, and Circus knew there was more in her to be set free, though he was unsure whether he knew what to do with it.

"I'll come see your show." He pinched her chin. "But right now, I need to work."

The outpouring seemed to calm Koko. She sat down on the floor. "Who's Odessa?"

She tossed a tiny piece of paper to his feet. On it, two eyes with thick lashes peered at him, and the name Odessa was written on the back. Seeing it brought him back to the subway car, and he wondered what had happened to that woman after they'd delivered the brooch, why she hadn't gone to his show after he'd invited her, what might have been different today if she had.

"Where'd you get this?" he asked.

"In your jacket."

"Why you going through my closet?"

"I'm bored."

Circus rubbed at his temples. "This is my house, Koko, my time, I decide how I'm going to spend this day, you hear me? I didn't ask to see you today. I'm sorry if the time you get isn't good enough, but I gotta do for me. You have no idea the weight I got on my shoulders, man, so I don't have time to sit around shootin' the shit 'cause your momma's too much of a basket case to talk to you about Heaven."

Koko ran down the hall into the bathroom, tears welling in her eyes. Circus groaned when he heard the turn of the lock and followed after her. From the other side of the door, he could hear the steady stream of the shower, which meant Koko had turned it on to muffle the sound of her crying, just like her mother used to do.

"Listen," he said through the door, "one day you'll understand. You'll want to be something someday."

"I already am something."

"I won't stand out here and beg."

Koko didn't answer, so Circus went back to his studio for another bourbon. On his phone, he found a text message from Peach.

Lose my number, she'd typed.

Sucking at the inside of his cheek, he considered napping to get to the end of the day faster until he saw the single mother who lived in the house next door outside filling her bird feeders, her nine-year-old racing toy cars on the sidewalk. He dialed her number and watched her take her phone from her jacket pocket, perking up when she noticed his name on the display.

"You finally calling to ask me to dinner?" Donna answered.

"What's shakin', Mama?"

"Everything. When are you going to fix my piano?"

"Is that still broke?" Circus chuckled, then lowered his voice. "Listen, gorgeous, what you got going on today?"

"I'm around, why?"

"You want some company?"

"Always."

Circus took another sip of his drink, watching as Donna combed her fingers through her hair and checked her makeup in a window. He would have liked her more if she tried less.

"My kid's here, and I got work to do," he said. "I'll give you thirty bucks to take her and your boy out for some pizza."

"You're going to break that girl's heart passing her off on me all the time."

"She'll get over it," he said. "Her mother's taking her to Sanibel Island next week."

"I'll do it only if you promise to take me out one of these days."

"You got it, doll."

Circus finished his drink, then went back down the hall toward the bathroom, knocking on the door. Koko opened it. She was sitting on the edge of the tub, tear stains beneath her eyes, the worn spot on her bottom lip colored with a tiny patch of blood.

"I got a surprise for you," he said.

"Oh no."

"You like Donna next door." Circus pulled his wallet from his back pocket and handed her three ten-dollar bills. "She invited you out for pizza with her boy. Nice, right?"

Koko scowled at the bills before snatching them from his fingers. She slipped past him down the hall into the living room and slid the money into the pocket of her backpack. She yawned and stretched, then dropped onto the sofa, balancing her bare feet on a pillow. As she fit the headphones over her ears, Circus started to speak, but Koko raised a finger in the air.

"Go do your work," she said.

He tried to say something, but Koko fired a glare across the room that stiffened his back. His daughter smiled, an odd womanly smile that made him feel like a ruse was up, a smile that might have inspired him to invite her into conversation, but Koko had already closed her eyes and chosen sleep.

Boy

*

Koko

Koko spent the morning waiting for him to come outside.

"Come out of your house, boy," she whispered. "Come out here and see me."

The boy had appeared in town the evening after Koko arrived with her mother. For a week, she'd watched him sip lemonade on the porch of a beach house two doors down from her grandmother's place and stare into a distance that seemed to reach across the ocean. He read books in a hammock hung between two trees. He sat on the beach smoking cigarettes. But he never noticed her. The boy was a mystery, a secret, a dream. He was a fist in the center of her chest that clamped whenever he walked past her across the sand, his swim trunks wet against his thighs. The muscles in his legs, in his shoulders and arms, were smooth as the marble museum statues she was made to stare at during class trips, and the sun colored his pale skin like honey.

This morning Koko sat at the feet of her mother, grandmother, and aunt, who were perched on lounge chairs under separate beach umbrellas. The blonde women kept complaining about the Florida heat that day, but Koko loved the way the sun burned the sand and deepened her brown skin to copper. On the blanket beside her, Cressida, Koko's sixteen-year-old cousin, lay on her stomach timing her soak beneath the bright sky, which she said she wanted to turn her skin pink like a rose. A long time had passed without anyone saying a word, so Koko could concentrate on the boy's house as if her stare might open the front door.

"My goodness"—her grandmother's voice broke Koko's concentration—"how is it I always look forward to coming down here yet become so quickly bored?"

"Maybe because we're here in March," Koko's aunt answered. "It's not the time."

"Oh, I get so tired of Boston right about now," the old woman answered. "At least we have a hint at summer today."

It was the last morning of the eight-day trip in a rented condo on Sanibel Island paid for by Koko's grandmother, and the women had lost interest, which made them turn on each other. The good manners their shared vacations always began with had, as usual, crumbled by the second day. Koko prickled in their silences and the sneaky ways they could be mean, like pointing out fat on each other's bodies that Koko couldn't see. Only during these reunions did she feel lucky to have a body thick and dark, because she went unnoticed by these willowy females combing their fingers through their yellow hair and hissing at each other like snakes.

"Cressida, dear," Koko's grandmother said, "sing 'Greensleeves' for us. You know, Koko, your cousin trained with a singer from the Royal Academy when she was in London this winter. She has the voice of an angel. Sing for us, darling."

Cressida opened one of her green eyes. "Now?"

"Please." Their grandmother removed her sunglasses.

Cressida rose to her knees, and Koko watched as she sat on her folded legs and laced her fingers as if she were kneeling on a church pew. A gentle wind lifted the edges of her blonde hair as she parted her lips and let free the same sound the pretty girls made in choir. Koko looked at her mother, whose head was turned away, and at her aunt, watching with a pained grin, and at her grandmother, whose chin swayed back and forth as if keeping time with an orchestra.

"Wonderful." Her grandmother swooned when Cressida hit the final note. "When I was a girl, I was a soprano, too. Aren't we a couple of larks?"

Cressida smiled plainly and lay back on her blanket.

"You know, Pia"—her grandmother turned to Koko's mother— "Pauline and Cressida were in London for a wedding."

"She knows, Mother," Koko's aunt said, swirling the ice in her glass.

"Who got married again, dear?"

Aunt Pauline slipped a cube between her lips, chomped into it. "Art's nephew."

"Yes, the composer," her grandmother said. "Art's family is so cultured. If my ailments weren't what they were, I would have gone with you. I feel so at ease with those people."

Koko watched her mother dig a hole in the sand with her foot.

"Maybe next time you go to London, Koko can tag along." Her grandmother slid a cigarette from the chrome case she always carried with her. "She needs her horizons broadened."

Koko reached up to squeeze her mother's hand. "I'm going for a swim."

"The water's too cold," her mother said.

"Not for me."

"Don't go out too far. Stay where I can see you."

"For heaven's sake, Pia." A line of smoke trailed elegantly from her grandmother's lips. "She'll only go out farther if you insist she stay close."

Koko walked to the water and dove in, cracking the sea's sleek skin and falling among broad-shouldered waves. Salt water fizzed in her ears and bubbled in the kinks of her hair as she let herself fall. She opened her eyes. The sun was spilling down from the sky into the water and streaming in zigzag patterns. She dove deeper, pretending to be a mermaid beating its fins in the ocean, where she imagined kingdoms made of sea gods and starfish and coral reefs sprouted up like tiny clay castles. Koko found a spot below the water, her spot on the planet, and listened to the water clog her eardrums. She opened and closed her legs so the small tide would roll between her thighs, up where she stroked herself sometimes when she found courage. She pulled down the straps of her bathing suit to free her breasts and let the cool water touch them. Deep down in the water's shadows, she let herself drift until it was time to come up for air.

Koko swam back to shore and lingered in the surf. Up the beach, the women sat in their chairs—mother, grandmother, aunt—slender and shining, their pale skin protected under wide-brimmed hats and sunblock. They held lit cigarettes in one hand, thermoses of vodka tonics in the other, and stared out from their own private worlds. Cressida, just as lovely and pale, lay at their feet, the small hump of her bum bridging her slender legs and the soft plane of her back. The sun seemed to shine directly on the four of them. Koko, dark like her father, imagined herself a swollen blot on the family portrait and imagined the ocean carrying her away.

She had started to swim back to her space in the sea when she noticed the boy smoking a cigarette and strumming a guitar in a beached kayak on the shore. Koko floated on her back until she was in the stretch of water in front of him. When she saw him looking in her direction, she left the water the way she'd seen Cressida do. Thumb and forefinger plugging her nose, she dropped her head back to let the water slick her hair, even though her curls only coiled tighter. She stepped out of the water and imagined the drops streaming over her as she walked over to him.

The boy's legs hung over the edges of the kayak as he rested his head against the back, eyes closed now and cigarette dangling from his lips. Koko could see he was older than she was, probably a senior in high school. She liked his bony wrists and fleshy mouth, the way the light shined in his messy butter-colored hair.

"My dad plays music," she said.

The boy opened his eyes. His gaze rolled against her body—hips, tummy, breasts—and something swirled warm inside her, up where the waves had just rolled in.

"Yeah?" he asked. "What kind?"

"Trumpet."

"Trumpet's badass."

The warmth swirled up again, giving Koko the guts to say more. "You're not afraid to get in trouble?"

"In trouble for what?"

"They probably don't want you playing guitar on the beach."

"Who's they?" He took a dramatic pluck of a string.

"Are you writing a song?"

"Maybe."

"It's the first day of spring. You should write about that."

"Why?"

"The day and night are exactly the same length."

The boy shrugged. Koko ran her hands over her hair and was ashamed it hadn't fallen slick like Cressida's. She took a hair tie from her wrist and twisted her curls into a knot on top of her head. "You'd think my dad was badass if you met him."

"Where is he?"

Koko tried to think of an answer to impress the boy until she heard her mother's call. She turned and saw the women staring over at her, Cressida at the edge of the blanket, mouth gaping. The four of them reminded Koko of swans, their eyes wide and long necks curved.

When she turned back to the boy, he was grinning. "Look who's in trouble now."

She crossed the beach back to the umbrellas, where her mother yanked her by the arm. "What's wrong with you?"

Koko prayed the boy wasn't watching.

"You can't just go around talking to random boys on the beach." Her mother pulled down the skirted hem of the one-piece she'd insisted Koko wear. "They'll get the wrong impression."

"So?"

Her mother took an oversize T-shirt from a bag at her feet and shoved it against Koko's chest. "Put this on."

"Koko"—her grandmother's voice stiffened like a teacher's— "you already have a wild look about you. Don't make it worse."

"I can handle this." Her mother's grip tightened.

"I'm simply commenting. This doesn't come from our side of the family. Her father's blood runs thick." Her grandmother shook her head and took a long pull from her cigarette. "What girls learn these days. And for God's sake, Pia, take some wax to the poor girl's upper lip. You're not doing her any favors."

"Mother, give it a rest."

Koko's grandmother shook her head. "At least your father had the decency to keep his girlfriends out of my house. Pauline, did your sister tell you what her jewel of a husband did?"

"Not interested," muttered Aunt Pauline.

"Ex-husband," Koko's mother said. "And he thought we were out of town."

"Well, pardon me." Her grandmother tittered. "That makes all the difference in the world. You see, Koko, this is the nature you've inherited. You'll be battling it all your life."

"Jesus," Aunt Pauline said. "She's fourteen. Let her talk to a guy."

Koko looked back at the boy, but he wasn't looking at her. A trio of other boys stood around him, slapping one another's palms and backs. She tossed the shirt to the ground. "Why don't you cover up Cressida?"

"Cressida's not my daughter. And she hasn't been cursed with curves."

Koko looked down at her cousin's body in a sailor-striped bikini. With her blonde hair and lean frame, her cousin looked more like her mother than Koko did.

"Anyway," her mother said, "you don't see me flaunting myself."

"I'm not like you." Koko watched the boy lead his friends from the kayak up the beach away from her. "I don't want to be like you."

Her mother's grip loosened and slid from Koko's wrist. When she looked down, her mother's lips were quaking.

"You hurt my feelings," she whimpered, nudging Koko with her toe. "Say you're sorry."

Koko glanced at her grandmother and Aunt Pauline, who sipped their drinks as if they hadn't heard a thing. Cressida shifted her body on the blanket to watch from the corner of her eye.

"Sorry," Koko mumbled.

"Give me a hug so I know you mean it."

Koko knelt on the ground so her mother could take a hug. The scent of tanning lotion and liquor filled Koko's nostrils as her mother held her. Satisfied, her mother flattened the chair and lay prone, covering her face with her hat. Her grandmother and Aunt Pauline smiled briefly at Koko, then turned their gazes back to the sea. Up the beach, the boy was leading his friends toward the clam shack by the pier.

"How was the water?" Cressida asked when Koko sat beside her on the blanket.

"Good. I saw a stingray."

"No, you didn't."

Her cousin tied the straps of her bikini top and rolled onto her back, slathering her legs with sunscreen. Koko took a dollop and mimicked her, even though her mother said she was dark and didn't need protection. As Cressida sat up, her hair fell softly across her shoulders, one of her ears peeking through the blonde. Koko understood there was something flirty about it and wished her hair did the same. Her cousin swung her hair across her back, and Koko touched the coarse knot on top of her head, thankful the boy couldn't see her failing to be pretty.

"It's always fun to see you," Cressida whispered. "But I'm telling my mom I want to stay in D.C. next year. My boyfriend misses me when I'm gone too long."

Koko pulled a rock from the sand, stroked it between her fingertips. "You must really like having a boyfriend."

"It's exhausting." Cressida pushed her sunglasses up the bridge of her nose. "Boys always want to do it, if you know what I mean."

"Yeah, totally, I know," she said, hoping she sounded convincing. "So have you?"

Cressida shook her head. "Justin's going to Duke next year, and I figure he won't forget me if I let him do it the night before he leaves. I let him do other things, though. You've got to pretend you like it."

The gentle swirl came again between Koko's legs. "What if you really like it?"

"My God." Cressida patted her knee. "You're so young."

* * *

Boys. In blue jeans hanging below their waists, in boxer shorts with pin stripes, football team logos, smiley faces. Boys in baseball caps turned backward, their concave chests starting to fill in, shoulders bony and struggling to take shape, jawbones starting to square. Boys made Koko excited and messy inside. She wondered what it would be like to be a girl they wanted. Like Cressida. Like Natalie De Luca, like Millicent and Kima, and all the girls at school who didn't seem to have to do anything to get noticed but wear short skirts and twirl their hair. Only old men seemed to notice Koko. She caught them eyeing her swelling breasts and moon-shaped ass that the boys at school made fun of.

But this boy. He'd noticed. This boy made her want to cry.

"Mom?" Koko slipped into the oversize T-shirt. "Can we go get some clams?"

"Clams make us fat."

"Please?"

"Oh, for God's sake." Her grandmother reached into her purse and handed Koko a ten-dollar bill. "Darling, treat your cousin to some clams."

Cressida slipped into a beach dress and tied her hair into a loose knot, which made her look even more grown-up and more like Koko's mother. Koko was about to change her mind, fearing the boy would like Cressida and not her, but her cousin had already started up the beach. Cressida went on about the wedding in London, though Koko barely listened, skittish against the nerves in her belly as she walked toward the clam shack far out of her mother's sight.

The boys were gathered around a picnic table, their fingers greasy in baskets of fried clams and potatoes. Along with Koko's boy were a skinny redhead with acne scars and a pair of blond twins, handsome and square-shouldered, their matching polo shirts with collars lifted. One of the twins stood on the table as if he'd just been crowned prom king, then balanced a tennis ball on his nose like a trained seal, the redhead counting the seconds. He clicked his fingers when he saw Koko and Cressida coming. Just as Koko had feared, all eyes turned to her cousin.

"Well, this day just got good." The boy jumped off the table and tossed aside the ball, sizing up Cressida like someone used to getting things he wanted. "Are you two girlfriends?"

Cressida blocked the sun with her hand to peer up at him. "She's my cousin."

His gaze flicked over at Koko, lost interest, and went back to Cressida. "I've never seen you around."

"We come every year, usually in the summer though," Cressida said. "Our grandmother brings us."

"How long you here for?"

"We leave tomorrow."

Koko looked at the other boys, who now seemed bored. The redhead scooped a handful of glass pebbles from a flowerpot near the clam shack's door and hurled them one by one against the ground. The prom king's twin chewed his fingernails and paced a trail in the sand. Koko's boy seemed the least interested as he sat quietly smoking on the bench, his back turned.

"You can't leave yet. We just met." The prom king ran his

thumb across his bottom lip, his eyes on Cressida's mouth. "We were about to take a walk, weren't we, guys?"

"Nah," the redhead said. "We were about to hit Chaffee's barbecue."

The prom king's gaze dropped to Cressida's chest, which was reddening like it did when she was embarrassed. "You should come with us."

Cressida tugged at the belt loops of her dress. "Where are you going?"

"Not far. Just over the dunes. The guys want to see my motorboat. You want to see?"

"Our moms are waiting for us," Cressida answered.

"We won't be long." He winked. "You can bring your little cousin."

Cressida glanced over at Koko.

"We'll go," Koko said.

"I'm Tyler." The prom king slipped his arm around Cressida's shoulder and led her down the beach. The twin trailed them, yelling at the redhead, who threw pebbles at his feet as he walked. Koko's boy stayed several paces behind, hands in his pockets. She walked beside him, too nervous to speak. In a tiny patch of grass, she saw a dandelion springing up and picked it, closing her eyes and holding it between her fingertips. The dandelion blossoms left grains of wishes on her lips as she blew the cotton from the stem without quite knowing what to ask for.

* * *

The overturned boat was past a run of dunes and hidden within a sea of grass. The redhead sprinted ahead of them into a blue shed beside the boat and brought out a case of beer, handing a bottle to each of them as they formed a loose circle. Koko looked over at her cousin for guidance, but Cressida only worried at the label with her thumbnail. Koko's boy broke away from the circle to sprawl across the sand, an open bottle balanced on his bare chest.

"One beer, then we're out, right, bro?" The redhead shot Tyler a look.

"I'm fine here, Tyler." The second twin's voice, tight and cracking, reminded Koko of the boy who lived on the other side of her duplex back home, the boy who needed pills to stay calm.

"Why go when there's fun to be had here?" Tyler sat on the boat's edge, patting the space beside him. Cressida sat down, holding the bottle between her knobby knees and shrinking as he roped her into his arms. She no longer looked like a grown-up.

"How do you guys know each other?" she asked.

"Most of us live around here." Tyler pointed his thumb at his twin. "You can guess how I know this asshole."

His brother flipped him the bird.

"This asshole I know from school." Tyler pointed to the redhead who was sneaking toward a seagull, stirring the pebbles in his pocket. "And Ian? Let's see, Ian's family has been coming here forever. I knew this kid since he was in diapers. Isn't that right, bro?"

The boy lifted his beer in the air. "Whatever you say."

Ian. Koko said the name again silently, imagined it with her own. Ian and Koko. Koko and Ian. *Hey, Koko,* she imagined him calling in the middle of the night. *It's me. Ian.*

"Ian doesn't like talking much," Tyler went on. "At least he doesn't like talking to me."

Tyler grimaced, staring at Ian as if he wanted the boy to tell him he was wrong.

Ian lifted himself onto his elbows. Took a long sip of beer. "It's all good," he said.

"What's Ian got to say anyway?" the second twin muttered.

"Tyler." The redhead chucked a pebble at the bird, then watched it fly away. "What are we doing back here? I thought we were going to Chaffee's."

"Relax." Tyler took strands of Cressida's hair in his hand, smelled them.

"There's gonna be a girl for everybody there." The redhead kicked a spray of sand at his feet. "Girl by the name of Molly, if you know what I mean, brother."

"I'm not doing any of that shit," said Ian.

"Chaffee's barbecue isn't going anywhere." Tyler pulled Cressida closer. "And I want to learn about my new girlfriend."

Cressida's chest blazed in shades of pink. She didn't see the smirk Tyler gave the redhead, and Koko couldn't tell whether her cousin liked the boy or feared him. Tyler certainly liked Cressida, but so did his brother and the redhead, who both stole glances. But Koko didn't care about them. She cared about Ian, who was sitting up now, his eyes drifting along the slope of Cressida's legs.

"Cressida has a boyfriend," Koko blurted out.

Her cousin stared back at her, lips parted, confused.

"She won't do anything with her boyfriend"—Koko couldn't stop—"so she won't do anything with you."

Tyler chuckled and took a sip of his beer.

"Koko's hungry," Cressida said. "She gets grumpy when she's hungry."

Ian was still watching her cousin, his eyes lingering on her knees.

"Cressida gets rashes on her stomach," Koko said, and Ian blinked. Now he was watching her. "Sometimes they spread all the way to her back."

Her cousin looked at Koko as if she were a stranger.

"Well," Cressida started uneasily, "she . . . she has blueberries on her underpants."

"Cressida still wears a training bra."

"Koko," she cried and covered her chest with her arms. "No one likes mean girls."

"Cressida's part blind in her left eye."

"Koko's part black."

They were all looking. Tyler and his twin. The redhead and

Ian. Staring. Cressida covered her mouth as if she wanted to stop anything else from coming out of it.

Ian stood up and twisted the cap off Koko's beer. "Cool."

Koko took a short sip of beer so she wouldn't cry, cringing at the bitter taste.

"Tyler?" The second twin was pacing again. "What are we doing? Let's do something."

Tyler clapped his hands together. "Have no fear, brother."

He pulled a joint from his shirt pocket and twirled it between his fingers. The redhead snatched the joint and quickly lit it, watching as the smoke billowed from his mouth. As the high hit, his face melted into a devilish grin. He passed the joint to Tyler who drew in two staggered breaths, then howled. He handed it to his brother, who dropped slowly to the ground as he took a long drag. The twin held out the joint to Cressida, but she shook her head.

"C'mon." The redhead rubbed his running nose into his collar. "You'll like it."

Cressida shook her head again.

"Let me." Koko took a step forward, and the twin handed her the joint. Cressida got up from the boat and stood beside her, glaring. From the corner of her eye, Koko watched Ian take a bottle of water from the shed and sip, his expression blank. Koko held the joint to her lips, inhaled, listened to the burn. The smoke seemed to grip the back of her throat and blister in her chest. She doubled over and hacked up a line of bile, spitting it to the ground. She thought she might die there, and her father flashed into her mind. She suddenly missed him terribly.

Tyler and the other boys laughed as Cressida patted her back.

Then Ian was at her side. "Drink." He placed the bottle of water in her hands and guided it to her mouth. Koko took sips between coughs until she could breathe again.

Ian took a quick hit of the joint, then passed it to the redhead. "What a waste of a day." He circled the boat, drumming his knuckles against the hull. "Is this the best we can do?"

Tyler's smile faded. "What would you rather be doing?"

"Well, there's the problem. I don't know. But I'm tired of feeling like it's all the same fucking day."

Tyler's eyes darted around the circle, desperate, it seemed, to come up with a way to please Ian. His gaze landed on Cressida, who seemed on the verge of tears. Tyler edged up beside her as if she were part of his new plan.

"Did you go swimming?" he asked.

Cressida kept her gaze on the ground. Nodded.

"Was the water cold?"

"A little."

"What happens when the water gets cold?"

Cressida peered up at him.

He looked over at Ian and winked, nodding toward Cressida's blushing chest. "Beneath your top."

Ian tsked and turned away, but the redhead and second twin were focused now on Cressida, quiet, waiting.

Tyler said, "Show us what happens under your top when you get cold."

Cressida reached for Koko's arm. Koko stiffened, rooting in the sand. Her spine seemed thicker, and she lifted her chest as she thought of coming home three weeks before with her mother to find her father stepping out of their guest bedroom where a woman waited for him. Koko had stood beside her mother as she cried, beside her father as he made excuses, all the while trying to see through the slight crack in the door and understand why her father had ruined so much to have whatever was in that room.

"I'll show you," she said.

"Koko." Cressida elbowed her.

Koko shook her head, her gaze fixed on Ian's back.

"We have to go," Cressida said. "I'm leaving, and Koko, you have to come."

Koko took off the T-shirt and tossed it to the ground. The boys circled, scorching the air around her with their big impatient bodies. The redhead glared at Koko's chest as he toyed with the pebbles in his pocket, tongue rolling against the inside of his mouth.

Beside her, Cressida's breath sounded in tiny, frightened gasps. "I'm counting to three, then I'm going," she warned.

Ian turned, his gaze landing on the ground at Koko's feet, then slowly rising to her eyes.

"Don't bother counting," Koko said.

Cressida slowly backed out of the circle, running as soon as she hit the dunes. But the boys were no longer paying attention to Cressida.

"Do it," the second twin said, his hands nervously squirming in the pockets of his shorts. The redhead took a step closer, biting at his dry, pink lips. Koko cringed at the smell of his body, like seawater and dirty clothes. He hurled his pebbles at the wall of the shed behind her and smirked when the clack made Koko jump.

"Do it," the second twin demanded, thumping his palm against his forehead as if something hurt inside.

"My brother gets angry easily, little girl," Tyler said. "So don't tease us."

The boys' slow movements toward Koko had backed her against the shed, close enough to grab her if they wanted. The second twin kept looking at the shed's open door as if he were thinking of dragging her inside. Though the sun continued to beam down on them, Koko sensed a chill beneath her skin as if the sky had suddenly fallen dark. Her armpits were moist. She needed to go to the bathroom. To throw up. To cry.

"Don't be a punk, Tyler," Ian said from somewhere behind them. "Leave her alone."

The other boys didn't seem to hear him. The twin reached out to touch the hem of Koko's swimsuit. She braced herself when his fingertips grazed her skin and was about to let out a cry when Ian came up behind him and smacked the back of the twin's head.

"What's your problem?" the boy shouted.

The wall the boys' bodies had raised around her fell as they all turned to Ian. Koko slipped into the T-shirt and took a deep breath to stifle the tears.

"Chill, bro," the redhead said. "She wanted to show us."

Tyler slapped Ian's back. "You said you wanted something different."

"You're a shithead, Tyler."

The handsome boy reeled as if Ian had taken a swipe at him.

"Bro," the redhead offered, "let's go to Chaffee's. That's where we need to be."

Tyler straightened his collar, then nodded toward his brother, who trailed him back over the dunes. The redhead punched the air and followed.

Ian was about to join them when Koko touched his back. When he stopped and looked down at her, she didn't know what to tell him.

Ian gave a thumbs-up to the redhead. "I'll catch up in a minute."

"Suit yourself," the ugly boy snickered and was gone.

Ian went back to sit on the hull of the boat, glancing at his wrist, then tsking as if he were used to wearing a watch and was disappointed not to find it there. He kicked at one of the red-head's pebbles left behind in the sand.

"I don't want to go back yet," Koko said. "I like it here."

Ian tugged at the drawstrings of his swimsuit.

"Do you want more beer?" she asked. "I can get you some. I have ten dollars."

"What'd you say your name was?"

"Koko," she answered. "There's a song called 'Koko,' and I'm named after it. My dad said he wanted a girl so he could name her that. He was waiting for me."

"You sure talk about your dad a lot." He took a lighter from his pocket, tossed it from one hand to the other. "So what do you want to do?"

Koko had fantasized about this moment but didn't know what to do now that it was happening. Ian kept playing with the lighter, his patience waning, it seemed, with each toss. Koko grabbed it from the air.

"Whoever can hold their hand over the flame longest," she said, "gets to make the other one do whatever they want."

Ian's eyebrows lifted when she lit the wick, then held her open palm over the flame. The lick of heat quickly burned, and Koko let out a yelp. She pressed her mouth against her hand and passed the lighter to Ian.

"Man," he said, striking the thumbwheel, "you're crazy."

"You like it, right?"

Ian grinned, then lit the wick. The flame bobbed beneath the cave of his hand, but he held it there, kicking his heel against the ground. Within seconds, he snapped off the lighter and pressed his mouth against his palm.

"You win," she said. "What do you want me to do?"

Ian blew into his palm. "You like to hurt yourself?"

Koko tried to guess how he wanted her to answer. "Maybe."

"I know girls like you." He went to the shed and brought back two unopened bottles of beer, holding one against his fresh wound and handing the other to Koko. "Kinda weird, but I guess it keeps things interesting."

Ian watched her as if he was noticing her for the first time, as if he liked what he saw, so Koko feigned interest in a dragonfly buzzing in the dunes.

"You like Sanibel Island?" he asked.

"I don't know." She held the cold bottle against the sore. "Do you?"

"It's cool when you're a kid. But every year? Everyone who comes is the same, you know what I mean, like, all the ladies wear the same outfits and smell the same. All the dads look bored and fat. The conversations are the same, everyone's talking about the same movie. Nothing happens that's new."

Koko twisted the cap off the beer and took a small sip, hoping he would say something she had an answer to.

"I don't want to be like everyone else," he said.

"Me either."

"But maybe I am."

"No, you're not." Koko sat beside him on the boat. "You're not like those other boys. I don't know if they're the everyone else you mean. But you're not like them."

He nodded, cracked open the bottle. "You really have blueberries on your underpants?"

"I don't know."

Ian took a sip as if to hide his smile. Koko kicked sand at his feet. He kicked sand back. She pushed him, he pushed harder. She poked him in the ribs, and he tossed his beer in the sand to grab her hands. She pretended to struggle as he pinned her arms behind her back.

"Don't," she whispered. "I'm a girl."

The skirt of her bathing suit had ridden up, and Ian noticed.

"You still have to tell me to do something," she said softly. "What should I do?"

Ian blushed and let go, tugging at the crotch of his swimsuit.

"Did I say something wrong?" she asked.

He swallowed, as if something painful stuck in his throat. "I don't think so."

Koko picked up his bottle, wiping the sand from the glass with the hem of her T-shirt.

"Do you want to know about me?" She handed him the bottle. "Ask me a question."

"What kind of question?"

"Anything."

The boy sipped the beer. "I can't think of a question."

"Do you want to know if I have a boyfriend?" Koko's armpits began to sweat again. "Because I want to know if you have a girlfriend."

"Of course I do." Ian snickered and tugged his crotch again. "Lots of girlfriends. More than I can count sometimes."

"Oh, I do, too." The lie spilled out. "I mean, I have a boyfriend.

His name's Eric. We went to the movies, and the next day, like, he told everyone he was my boyfriend even though we never really did anything. Except at this party in January, it was my friend Emma's birthday and we kissed in her closet. But I mean, he kissed Emma, too, because we were playing Truth or Dare. She didn't really like it, I guess, you know, because she likes this other guy David Johnson. David's little brother is deaf and he's afraid of dogs."

When Ian turned his back, Koko lifted her arms to let the warm breeze dry her armpits. He lay on the ground beside the shed, dug a hole for his beer in the sand, then sighed and stared up at the sky.

"Am I boring?" she asked.

"I guess not."

"Can I lie next to you?"

"I guess so."

Koko sat beside him, imagining resting her head on the hill of his chest. "If you're not going to tell me to do something, can I tell you to do something?"

"You can ask."

She scooted closer to him. "Will you touch my hair?"

The boy paused before reaching up to tap the coiled ball on top of Koko's head. She took out the band, combing her hair into shape with her fingers, and lay beside him. Ian swallowed loudly, nervously, then burrowed his fingers in her hair. The scratchy sound of the curls against her scalp and Ian's fingers made Koko sleepy, and she closed her eyes, letting her hand drop against the boy's knee. He stroked harder than she wanted, but soft enough to feel good. Everywhere was warm.

"Why do you want me to do this?" Ian asked.

Koko opened her eyes. "Nobody touches me."

Soon Ian's fingers were gliding up the length of her arm. Koko held her breath and shut her eyes. When she opened them again, he was hovering above her, his thing against her leg, hard like the handle of a baseball bat. He looked down and licked his lips. The boy, his body strong. His mouth the color of strawberry taffy. Slowly, he placed his trembling hand against her chest where the two sides of her ribcage met. Between Koko's thighs, there was rolling, rolling.

And then he moved his hand. Over the collarbone, inside her T-shirt, and down the top of her bathing suit. With clipped breath, he closed his eyes and cupped her breast. He squeezed, he patted, he pinched, and Koko sensed a tingle in her knees, across her thighs, across her tummy, and up again to her neck, where her tongue seemed to thicken. And up between her legs, where Koko touched herself, was a tingle so deep it started to burn. The boy pressed gently as Koko lifted her back, as if she were floating from the ground. But when she reached out to bring his other hand to her chest, Ian jerked away.

The boy stood up, his brow sweating, his thing like a tree branch high in his swim trunks.

"I should go." His voice cracked.

"What's the matter?"

"I should go home now."

"What'd I do wrong?"

"I thought you haven't done this before."

"I haven't."

"You don't act like it." Ian coughed, and his thing bobbed in his pants. He tried to push it down, but it sprang back up. "Look, my mom will kill me if I'm late for dinner. She gets really mad when, you know, I don't come home after she takes all this time to cook dinner for me and my stepdad. I think she's making pot roast, and um, it takes a while because she has to peel carrots and onions. And potatoes. That takes a long time. Potatoes do."

Ian waved a quick goodbye, then started across the sand, tripping on a rope that hung from the boat's hull. Regaining his balance, he turned and had a last look at Koko before he went away.

Koko watched him lope down the dunes until he was almost

out of sight. In the opposite direction, she saw her mother and Cressida coming toward her up the beach. Soon her mother would be standing before her in her sunglasses and wide-brimmed hat, hands on her hips, mouth pursed, and Koko would have to make excuses. Until then, she wanted only to think about the boy's warm hand and feel her skin perk up again. Koko lay on her back. She listened to the waves rush against a distant shore, then peeked up at the sky, grinning like an angel in the sand.

Pretty Children

*

Angela

In the small of his bare back, sprouting up from the base of his spine and in the shape of a *V*, were scratches. Angela saw them after Circus pulled off his shirt, then slid belly first into her bed, his arms hanging over the edge of the mattress as he waited for her hands. As he lay there, she saw the two welts between his shoulder blades he said were left from a bicycle wreck he'd had as a boy, scars she'd noticed the first time they were in bed together. What was new were the scratches—long, slender slits, like the veins of a leaf, a flower even, with beaded blood drops tiny and hard. She imagined the scrape of a woman's fingernails, could only imagine a woman, her legs open around his hips and her hands clasping his shoulders, hands that slid down as the pleasure he gave her swelled.

"Have you been seeing someone?" she asked.

At first, he didn't answer. "Nope."

Angela swallowed the lump rising against the back of her throat, then softened her voice for the lie. "I wouldn't mind if you have."

He dragged a pillow across the bed, thumped it, and placed it beneath his chin. "Then why you asking?"

Angela grabbed the glass of water from the floor, rubbed the cold drops from its surface, and pressed her hands against her suddenly flushed face. Their romance, affair, she wasn't sure what to call it, had lasted three weeks, then stalled without Angela knowing why. More than two months had passed since she'd seen him, and though she'd mostly forgotten Circus Palmer, she now knew he'd been with someone else—somewhere in that time was another person. Then came an urge to punish, a need that intensified the longer she contemplated the scratches and imagined the other woman's hands.

"Turn over," she said, and he did, his smile cocky as he waited, she imagined, to be impressed. From the table beside the bed, Angela took a cloth napkin she kept nearby for spills and unfolded the four corners between Circus's thighs. Tying her hair into a knot at the nape of her neck, she unzipped his pants and, sucking in a breath, opened her mouth around him. The stale scent of sweat between his thighs disappointed, but she breathed through it as he dug his fingers into her hair. She counted off the list of ingredients to her favorite bread pudding recipe—pumpkin, anise, brown sugar—to occupy her mind. Circus moaned, Circus begged her not to stop, Circus praised God. He reached for her, she pushed his hands away. He called her name, she kept silent, amused by how easy it was to weaken him. And when he finally came, she pinched a nub of flesh on his stomach to leave her mark. Circus let out a howl.

"You're a champion," he said as he slid across the mattress. "Golden."

Angela delicately folded the four corners of the napkin, then stood over Circus's body that seemed smaller now, helpless.

"You should go," she said.

"Come again?"

"I'm done. It's time to go."

He nestled into the blankets. "Ah, c'mon, princess. Just a while longer."

He tried to pull her to him, but she stepped out of reach. Curling up against him would only dull the need she'd stirred, and Circus seemed the type to want what wasn't easy. Slipping into her robe, Angela focused on binding the ties around her waist instead of his warm, sturdy body, instead of the bed where she was about to lie alone.

"You should go."

* * *

He wasn't her type. Bulky. Dark. His body beastly and thick, his features heavy, his voice a lazy growl. There was something unmannerly about him, too, vulgar. When Angela saw him for the first time at a café—elbows on the counter, toothpick between his teeth, thumb stroking his bottom lip—he was sipping a shot of Wild Turkey, even though it was light outside, and telling the waitress brewing coffee how pretty her hair was. Angela had noticed only because his approach seemed so silly, so obvious. The cashmere scarf draped round his neck, she found elegant, and the flat cap barely containing his mane-ish fall of dark curls was stylish, but in her thirty-eight years, Angela had preferred men who wore pressed shirts with buttoned collars and fitted suit jackets. Men with clean shaves and neat haircuts. Polite and cultured men who built distinguished careers and worked during daylight hours. Her ex-husband was that kind of man.

After the waitress served him a slice of lemon meringue, Circus invited her to a gig he had playing trumpet that night. He brushed his thick knuckles across the freckles on the girl's cheek, and she blushed, tugging at the strings of her apron, which gave Angela an unexpected shiver. She wondered what those knuckles felt like.

Maybe it was the way he finally turned and noticed her in the back of the café, then took the toothpick from between his teeth, slowly, his smile slowly widening. Maybe it was the way she imagined an animal stalking as he walked across the floor to get to her, the way he told her she was going to dinner with him that night instead of asking, or the way he noticed little things about her during the three weeks they spent together, like the birthmark behind her left ear and the flecks of silver in the irises of her eyes. Maybe she wanted him because he was the only man who touched her so indelicately that something animal in her seemed to emerge, loosening her like fossils from a rock.

* * *

The morning after she told him to go, Angela sensed the scratches again beneath her fingertips, rubbing them together as if rolling the tiny blood beads like crumbs. The longer she lay awake, the more vividly she imagined the other woman's legs open around Circus's back, his hips rising and falling, the woman's nails notching his skin. She wondered what the woman looked like and whether she—with her blue eyes brazen against ivory skin and long hair like a stream of black ink—was enough to hold him in place. Once he told her he liked that she taught theater at Brandeis, that she corrected his grammar and told him stories she'd heard about important people he didn't know, Stanislavski and Strindberg. The teaching, Circus said, was noble. Angela wondered whether the other woman had a life he admired.

Slipping out of bed, she went to the kitchen to eat two boiled eggs for breakfast and compose the day's list of things to do, writing and rewriting the list a second and third time until she was pleased with the way her handwriting landed on the page. On her predawn walk, she found herself imagining a girl in her twenties, moody and cigarette smoking, who got Circus to notice her by opening her knees at the foot of the stage where he played his horn. She thought of him hovering over the girl's body on a thin mattress in some ramshackle apartment. She stayed with the image, certain that only a foolish and young woman could fall for such a ridiculous man. It embarrassed her to have become that kind of woman and in such a short time.

Breath puddling in the chilled air of the spring's first days, Angela closed her eyes, counting up to ten and back and making herself think of good things: the view from the top of Mount Washington in summer and the sound the leaves made when the air ran through them. When her phone chimed in her pocket, she reached tentatively for it, but the message wasn't from Circus. It was from her twin sister.

I miss you, Amy had typed. *It's time. Come meet your niece.*

Angela's skin grew hot, even though the morning breeze was frigid. She deleted the message and made her way home, though now she sensed her sister with her, behind her it seemed, and following. On the train to school, during her lectures, and in the middle of meetings with students, she sensed Amy lingering like shadow.

The next morning a second message came from Amy asking Angela to visit, Ryan would soon be out of town for business. She'd sent two pictures: one of herself holding the baby, and a second of the baby in a yellow dress with ladybugs woven into the pockets. The little girl wore a lace bonnet on her head, her grin pink and toothless. But Angela didn't look long enough to come to know her niece's face because she was too distracted by Ryan's hands holding her, his fingers with knobbed knuckles and tidily clipped fingernails, the mole on his right ring finger and the gold band on his left. A year had passed since Angela toasted Ryan on the day he married Amy—an exemplary tribute, said their father, who'd told Angela she was obliged to rise above the fact that her husband had left her for her own sister. Angela had risen. But she wasn't ready to see the baby.

* * *

Two nights later Circus was back. He brought a baked chicken and pecan pie in a grocery bag, presenting them as gifts, though he ate most of both. Angela sat with him in the kitchen as he described an antique trumpet he'd seen in a shop window. He told her about starting his first lesson as a boy and practicing in his mother's closet because the clothes muffled the noise, but his stories made her testy, eager to turn the conversation to herself and the things she'd done. Angela forced a smile and went to the drawer for a spoon, which she dug into the center of the pecan pie and scooped out a bite.

"Why jazz?" she asked, knowing the question would poke at him. "No one listens to jazz anymore."

He tore a hunk from a chicken leg with his teeth. "Why do you teach?"

"It's not the same. I'm always necessary."

He bit off another hunk of chicken. He smacked his lips as he chewed, fat glistening at the edges of his mouth. Somehow the great mess of him gave her a thrill.

"I got a gig at a sushi joint in Cambridge," he said. "Sundays, if you're ever hungry and wanna groove."

Angela quietly ached to feel him watch her as if she held some kind of marvel, but he continued to sloppily chew, finally wiping his mouth and tossing the napkin to the side of his plate.

"It's new every time," he said. "You got the notes and arrangements, yeah, but once you start playing, something different happens. You don't know what's gonna come. That's what it is about jazz. Everything else about living stops surprising you at some point, right?"

"I suppose."

He took a can of beer from the paper bag, popped the tab. "Everyone wants to sound the death knell on this music, and yeah, you got a lot of lean times and young cats coming up with fresh sounds no one's heard before. But I can't worry about what it is or isn't, or where it's going. I just gotta do what I do."

Staring into the empty air, Circus took a sip so wistful, Angela thought she saw tears in his eyes. Wherever his imagination went was taking him out of the room, away from her.

He reached for the pack of cigarettes in his pocket and slid one into his mouth without lighting it. "You sure I can't smoke in here?"

Angela snatched the cigarette from his lips, tossed it into the sink, and dropped into the chair, convinced momentarily that she'd had her fill, that the absurdity of their pairing had struck firmly enough for her to finally want him gone.

"Why do you come here?"

The awkward pulling he did at his beard told Angela he wanted to come up with a response she liked. "Well, what can I say? You're not exactly the kind of woman I'm used to, all right, you're in a whole other league. You're special."

"Special?" She swiped the air. "How can I be special when I have, quite literally, spent my entire life seeing myself in another woman's face? No, special I am not."

"She looks just like you, huh?"

Angela pointed her finger at him. "Don't you dare tell me your schoolboy fantasy about twin girls. I've heard it a million times. I don't have the stomach."

"I wasn't."

She calmed and had another bite of the pie. "No one could tell the difference between us. In eighth grade, she and I switched places, and her little boyfriend had already run his hand up my skirt before he knew it was me. She told me to do it. She said she wanted to see if he could tell. We said nothing would ever come between us. Nothing should come between women. We have enough to deal with, for God's sake. I believe this, you know. Especially sisters. Though I suppose now she's gotten back at me since she's taken my husband. Oh, don't look at me like that. I didn't want him anyway. He's dull. She's dull, all right, they're both endlessly dull."

Angela pulled the catering menu from the grocery bag, pretending her attention had been captured by the list of desserts. *Help*, she heard the voice in her mind cry. *Everything hurts.*

"Ask me, it's his loss." Circus leaned in to kiss her neck, but she pulled away even though she wanted to capsize against him, against anyone, against anything.

* * *

The new mark was on his belly beside the one she'd left. Purplish in the light of the candles she'd placed around the bedroom, the mark was a small eruption on his skin, puckered as if the woman had drawn his flesh between her lips. Lifting herself onto her knees to let her hair drape over his body, she pressed her thumb into the mark, circling it with her fingertips, circling and circling before slowly digging in her nails.

Circus was gone before sunrise. Sleeping in someone else's bed, he told her, was something he couldn't do.

* * *

Angela woke up on the bedroom floor with no memory of how she got there. A light from the hall shone into her room, so she could see the wine bottle, empty beside her. She reached for her phone to look for Circus online, hoping that whatever it was about him that made her curious might draw her in further. She found a black-and-white photo on his website, Circus standing beneath a spotlight, only the brass of his trumpet in color. His hair was shorter and face thinner, an older picture, Angela assumed. She found an album cover, Circus staring back at her, his younger face swathed in ocean colors, his hair catching blue light. A calendar on the final page announced the recurring Sunday brunch at the sushi restaurant in Cambridge and another gig Thursday nights at a club called the Lighthouse.

There was Circus in a skullcap on the deck of a ferryboat. Circus chalking a cue in front of a black velvet pool table. And finally, Circus standing with a famous musician Angela tried to place. Between them stood a black woman with a lush afro. Her face, a beautiful collection of angles and curves, stared out from between the men with a boldness that thrilled and embarrassed Angela cowering in the dark. The caption listed the trio as Tip Badgett, drummer Maggie Swan, and local musician Circus Palmer. Angela studied the picture, measuring the distance between Tip Badgett's body and Maggie Swan's, between Maggie's body and Circus's. She tried to decide whether Circus's arm around Maggie's shoulder or Tip's arm around her waist reflected the greater intimacy. She thought of Maggie Swan stretched across a mattress, Circus lowering himself between her thighs, her fingernails carving into his back. The woman's brown skin and daring eyes made Angela feel flat and dull. Fading.

He called two nights later, at midnight.

"You're on my mind." His voice was bluesy on the phone in the dark. Angela imagined grain and honey, black coffee and cigarette smoke.

"It's late," she said, rising out of sleep. "You should have phoned first."

"What do you think I'm doing?"

Mouth parched, she went to the kitchen for a glass of water but found a bottle of vodka. She opened the bottle, sniffed, poured a glass. "You couldn't wait until morning?"

"Why wait?" he asked. "A song in your head means you want to listen to it. I'm thinking about you, princess. And I'm digging the little shiver I get doing it."

The sound of his voice rustling within the black night gave her a charge as she stepped through the halls back to her bedroom. He could be there within minutes, pressing his chest against her naked back and taking up the space on the other side of the bed. Angela wanted him there, but this wasn't something to tell a man, especially a man as slippery as Circus Palmer.

"Why should I let you come?" she asked.

"Because I miss you." He took a sip of something, wherever he was.

Angela sat at the edge of her mattress, sheets twining ankles and pillow between her knees. She sipped the vodka, which she drank now from a coffee mug because she didn't want to see through a crystal glass and admit she was drinking alone. Shoulders pressed against the headboard, she let the edge of the wood prod the spokes of her spine.

"Come," she said.

Angela had a steam in the shower, sprayed perfume between her breasts and behind her knees, then applied enough makeup to make her skin appear smooth and her blue eyes shimmer in the pale but not enough to make him believe she had spent much time. In the mirror, she smiled at herself, pouted, smiled again, regretting how grueling it had become, this performance of being female and coaxing out love.

Twenty minutes later he was at her door whispering against her neck, "I been thinking about those lips since I left."

Gently, she pushed him away, and his crooked smile told her he appreciated the move. She slinked down the hallway, thrilling at the heat of him following behind. In the living room, she poured him a glass of vodka as she waited for him to notice the Tip Badgett song playing, the sound turned low so it might sneak up on him.

He glanced at the speakers, seemed to recognize the song, then started whistling the melody, his tongue at the roof of his mouth. "I got a friend played drums on this record."

"Is that right?"

"She's from around here."

"How does she know you?"

"It's a small town. You meet people."

"She must like working with Tip Badgett. He's sexy."

"He's lucky to have her," Circus insisted, his words weighted in a way that filled Angela with resentment. But before she could think of what to say to push deeper, he took her hands and led her to the loveseat. "What are you doin' way over there? You're not acting glad to see me."

Angela didn't move. "Can't you at least ask about my day?"

He kissed her fingertips. "I want to know about all your days. But everything will come out over time."

"Are we going to have that? Time?" It was a slipup, she knew right away.

Circus settled into the sofa, pulled a lighter from his pocket, and without looking at her, flipped the metal cap. "We got time now."

He lit the lighter's flint and stared into the flame. "What do you want to tell me about your day?"

His smile was wide, kindly, and she realized it was possible he was truly interested. She went over the events of the day in her mind, but there was nothing to impress a man who knew rock stars, drank bourbon in the middle of the day, and slept with women who left marks on his body. And so she made it up.

"I stole something."

For an instant, the lie seemed real, and Angela felt relief having told it. She was even more relieved when Circus glanced up from the lighter, grinned. "What'd you steal?"

"Lipstick," an answer came quickly. "Red lipstick. Does that excite you?"

He spread his arms over the sofa's back, waiting, it seemed, for her to go on.

"I was at the drugstore." Angela was surprised how easily the story slipped off her tongue. "I had mostly odds and ends in my basket, you know, paper towels, toothpaste, and the like. Then I walked down the cosmetics aisle like I always do and I sampled a red I hadn't tried before. I liked it and was about to drop into my basket. But then, I don't know, I just wanted to take it. So I did."

There was a giddy feeling, like what she imagined naughty children felt sneaking behind their parents' backs. It was new. She liked it.

"Sounds like an eventful day." He sat up to take her face in his hands, and she allowed herself to be looked at, allowed him to look, staring into the empty space behind him and softening her eyes so he could be left with the bare fact of her beauty. His gaze crossed her forehead, drifted down the crisp line of her nose and the squares of her cheeks.

"Damn, you're pretty as a doll." Lifting her blouse to kiss her stomach, he asked, "Is tonight the night?"

Angela stopped his traveling hands. "I said I don't want to. Not yet."

"But we did before."

"Then you left, and I never heard from you. You don't deserve a reward."

He eyed the buttons of her blouse, his fingers drifting up the length of her arm. Angela liquefied under the solid weight of his hands as he pulled her to the floor. She was glad he'd come. But she was also looking for a mark. She found one—a thin scratch in the meat of his thigh—moments later when Circus took off his pants.

"Hey." He seemed to notice her change in mood. "Why so sad?"

"I don't get sad."

"Every woman gets sad."

"Not me." Angela smiled, but the corners of her mouth creaked. She kissed him so he couldn't look into her eyes. When he moved his hands up her blouse, Angela arched her back. When he lay on top of her, she ran her lips across his shoulder. And when he parted her knees to lie clothed against her, Angela sank in her teeth.

* * *

Twice more Circus came to see her, and Angela found marks—a scrape beneath the hairline of his neck, a pinch in the flesh behind his knee. And she left them—a bite between his thumb and fore-finger, a bruise her mouth made on his chest. As the days went by, she knew it could go on like this. Circus would come as long as she offered herself. And so she let it continue without asking the woman's name or what she was to him because she thought it might be a pleasing thing to make choices without knowing good things would come from them. She let it continue because she understood it wasn't the prize she wanted, but the winning. A night would come, and there would be no marks. Sometimes she decided it was Maggie Swan who marked him because she needed to perceive an actual woman on the other side of his skin, to dig into the space a real woman had made in him and wrest her out.

Until a week passed without word from him. Until she sent messages Circus didn't answer.

It was Thursday. Thursdays, she remembered, he played the Lighthouse, and she went. Inside the club, she ordered a red wine, keeping an eye on him onstage in front of a four-piece band. She walked the perimeter of the club toward a seat in a dark corner behind the stage where she figured she wouldn't be noticed. Circus seemed more massive than usual, and more striking, his suit tailored but loose around his body, the pin stripes glimmering against the lights. The cry of his horn swirled through the air like something thicker and heavier than mere sound, and the crowd drew toward him, stilling their glasses to listen and watch as the trumpet squealed, then hopped. Circus took rutted breaths, evened out when he relaxed his shoulders.

She didn't like the music, not the muddled sounds or the melody, too hard to follow. But she finally understood what it was about Circus Palmer. He made the horn sound like it was laughing, like it was sobbing, like it was fucking. As he played, he seemed to promise something potent, something that made a woman wonder what she could access through loving him. Angela imagined what it might feel like if he would have touched her then, if he would leave a mark. And for a moment that was gorgeous and brief, she saw herself as the woman who had finally gotten to this man and imagined all the other women in the place watching her with longing because he'd let himself belong to someone now. She shifted her eyes to the crowd and saw them. Beautiful, enraptured women in love. After his solo, Circus took the horn from his lips, rubbing his thumb against the brass pipe like the inside of a lover's wrist and the women applauded madly, all of them, swooning and making love to him with their eyes. He could have had any one of them, so how could he turn away? Why would he? Angela tried to resent him but couldn't. Instead, she wanted what he had.

One of the women in the audience was looking back at her. She looked at Angela, looked at Circus, looked at Angela again. Angela glanced up at the stage. Circus had spotted her, his eyes cast in shadows, glaring.

* * *

She found him leaning against a brick wall in an alleyway behind the club, having slipped out through a back door. In sunglasses, he smoked a cigarette and scrolled through his phone, not acknowledging her when she stepped onto the street. A pipe dripped into a drain somewhere, amplifying the silence between them.

"I shouldn't have come," she said. "I know that now."

"Free country," he mumbled without looking up from his phone.

"You're good. I imagined you would be."

Circus kept scrolling.

"Next weekend my play opens." She unpinned her hair so it would fall across her shoulders in a way she hoped he'd notice. He didn't. "You'd think I'd be used to the nerves by now but . . . I wish I could just sit in the audience and watch what I created without thinking about anyone else. Do you ever feel that way?"

He flicked an ash to the ground, his eyes still on the screen.

"I'm sure you can understand," she tried to put a lilt in her voice. "I wanted to see what you looked like outside a bedroom."

Finally, he lifted his head. "This is my space."

"And what should I take that to mean?"

"You weren't invited tonight."

"My God, you say the most laughable things."

Gaze locked on her, body menacing, he said, "I fucked you one time. All right? So I'm not interested in hearing what love story you got cooked up in your head and how much you care about me. I've been getting off on this little tease you got going, fooling around like we're teenagers afraid to get caught behind the bleachers, but there's nothing else to it."

Circus crushed the cigarette beneath his boot and moved past her toward the club door.

"Care about you? You don't think anyone cares about you, do you?" she snickered, not recognizing the force with which she came at him, the desire to claw and be clawed. "Oh, you poor man. You're a cigarette, sir. A shot of cheap liquor. You're maddening, that's all you are."

Moving closer to him, Angela snaked against the thistly heat of his anger. "Those women fawning over you? They don't see you like I do. You don't fool me. I know what dreams look like, and I know what a life looks like when they die. You're just a beautiful, beautiful failure."

Circus drew back, and for a second she thought he might hit her. "I go anywhere in this town, and I can play, all right," he said. "I got friends everywhere. And you are far, far from being the only chick I can call on a Saturday night."

He should've turned around, she thought, and headed back into the bar. Instead, he lit another cigarette and stood there like he wanted a response, like this exchange of venom had seized him in a way their lovemaking hadn't.

"Do you know how lucky you are to stand here with me? I'm a goddamned gift," Angela said. "How did things go so wrong that you seemed like an interesting thing to do?"

"Listen, it's not my fault you're no movie star and your sister stole your boyfriend. Don't drag me into your shit."

Sweat was forming at the small of Angela's back. She thought she could feel the hair on her arms rising. "Oh, my shit, yes. You know, sometimes I imagine the babies. They've got one now, they'll have more. I imagine something happening to their babies, some disease maybe. They can't walk and have to wear braces on their legs. I'm ashamed by how glad it makes me. I want to imagine that the two of them aren't happy. But they are. I don't want them to be. For God's sake, why would I?"

Angela let out a long, delicious breath. She wanted to lie down and sleep for days. She closed her eyes.

"The scratches on your body," she said. "Who's doing it?"

"Scratches?"

Angela let her silence compel him.

He groaned and hit the cigarette. "Maybe I've been going harder at the gym. That's all I know about any scratches."

"I wish I could see your eyes."

"They're not doin' anything special."

Angela listened to the soft pop of his lips on the cigarette's tip. He was lying. He lied, which meant he needed this moment as much as he needed whatever he was keeping from her.

"Let's go back inside, princess," he said.

Circus reached out his hand, but Angela didn't take it and moved past him into the bar as he said things to her. That he had to play the last set. That he'd get her home afterward. That she was going to be all right. That he'd lie next to her and stay through the night if she needed. He seated her on a stool at the bar and placed his cap in her hands, kissing the top of her head before heading back to the stage.

"Another drink?" the bartender asked.

The trumpet wailed. Circus swayed his hips as if nothing had happened between them. His world had fallen into place again. Angela held the hat, the wool scratching her skin.

"You'll be okay." The bartender uncorked a bottle of red wine. "I tell you, the number of women I've found crying over Circus Palmer . . . there's no loving worth that kind of pain."

"I'm not crying." She slipped off the stool and tossed the cap onto the bar. "And I won't be needing this."

* * *

The house where she'd once lived stood at the end of a cul-de-sac, nestled within trees coming to bloom. Daisies were painted on a new tin mailbox at the end of the drive, and bird feeders hung on the front porch, the ground beneath pebbled with seeds. The gold knob on the front door gleamed under the porch light, and Angela wondered whether Ryan had installed it himself, gratefully locking himself into this new life.

Amy opened the door and Angela let herself be held.

"You're here," her sister said.

Amy's belly and breasts slumped against Angela's body though her grip was strong. When she pulled away, Angela could see the lines around her mouth had started to deepen, her always-unkempt hair beginning to gray.

"Thank God you called." Amy beamed. "You look perfect as usual."

The furniture in the house was still efficient and plain, just as Ryan had wanted, though Amy had certainly chosen the new carpets in orange and yellow patterns. Open magazines were splayed on the coffee table beside crumpled candy wrappers, and Christmas tree lights hung from a windowsill even though the holiday had long passed.

"When Ryan's away, the clutter comes out to play." Amy scooped the wrappers into her hand and straightened the sofa pillows on her way to the kitchen. "What are you drinking?"

"Whatever you are."

The house smelled of baby. Fresh linens, warm milk, soiled diapers, talc. Pink pajamas and bibs were folded in a laundry basket in a corner, and toys were strewn across the floor. On the wall behind the sofa hung framed photographs of the family. Faded black and whites of her father as a young doctor and her mother in her Wellesley graduation robes. There were photos of Amy and Ryan looking out from the back of a limousine after they'd been married and standing in front of a sunset in Maui during their honeymoon. There were photos of Angela and Amy as girls in matching dresses at a cousin's wedding and braiding their hair into a single knot. There were communions and birthday parties and family vacations. And there were photographs of the baby in her lace bonnet and toothless smile.

Amy came back from the kitchen with two glasses of apple juice, which she placed on the coffee table, then flopped onto the sofa the way she used to as a girl, her bare feet shoved underneath the cushions.

"I was watching a documentary about frogs." Amy stuffed a pillow between her knees. "They have teeth. And there's this frog, it's got a chemical or something in its skin, and just one ounce of it could kill, like, a million people."

Angela sipped the apple juice, grinned. "You sound bored."

"I'm happy." Amy shrugged. "Maybe happy is bored. Or bored is happy? But really, I just don't know what to say." She looked over at Angela. "Should we . . . talk?"

"Not yet."

"But tell me you feel better about things."

"I'm here." Angela glanced at a photo on the wall of the sisters riding the same pony at a zoo. "Do you ever wonder who you would be if I weren't here as a constant reflection?"

Several seconds passed before Amy answered, "I love that you're here. Do you wonder that about me?"

"Yes."

The two of them drank their juice, glancing at one another, smiling and turning away.

"Where were you tonight?" Amy asked. "Mom said you're doing another play?"

"I was at a show," she answered. "A jazz thing."

"I didn't know you like jazz."

"I don't think I do."

Amy giggled, then raised a finger when a sniffle came through the baby monitor. She listened for several seconds before returning to her drink. "I feel like we should remember something together. Like, we could talk about trips to Grandpa's lake house. We should laugh together, don't you think? We have to get back to the way things were."

"That's not going to happen."

"Why not?"

"Because it's now," Angela answered. "But I do want to feel . . . better."

Tears brimmed in Amy's eyes as she held out her hand.

Angela took it and let her gaze drift to the peaceful sprinkling of rain falling in the moonlight outside the window.

The baby's cry sounded again in the monitor. Amy took one last squeeze of Angela's hand, then disappeared down the hall. Once she was gone, Angela went to the window, where she became lulled by the misty silence outside.

"Say hi to Ellie," Amy said on her way back into the room.

Angela didn't notice anything that made the girl different from other babies. Ellie was small, round-cheeked, pink, her eyes clear. She was bundled in a cotton-candy-colored blanket, her tiny head poking from the top. But as Amy brought her closer, the girl seemed to recognize Angela and let out a coo. The love was instant, crushing, and hurt Angela's heart.

"She's so beautiful," she said. "Just perfect."

Amy held out the baby, and Angela enfolded the girl into her arms. Ellie cooed again, sucking at her fingers.

"I'll make a bottle." Amy kissed the baby's forehead and disappeared into the kitchen. As Ellie blinked up at her, Angela remembered a lullaby her mother used to sing and hummed it while pacing the room.

"I'm Auntie Angela," she whispered. "We're going to do lots of things together."

She held the girl close, imagining the books she'd read to her one day, the pastries they'd bake together. She imagined taking an older Ellie on her first hike up Mount Washington and a teenage Ellie calling Auntie Angela for advice she wouldn't ask for from her mother.

The baby shifted in her blanket and croaked unhappily.

"Are you itchy?" Angela lowered Ellie into the playpen in the center of the room. Rolling the baby onto her back, Angela pulled the blanket from her body.

The mark was at the top of her thigh. Like a red brushstroke of paint on a pink canvas. Angela saw it and bit her tongue. The baby yelped and kicked, her mouth twisted as if ready to release a loud cry as Angela drew in a heavy breath and, with an eagerness that was both thrilling and ripe with shame, slid her fingers through the playpen's metal bars.

The Time You
Fell in Love

*

Circus

Carmen Julia swept out of the café with her silk wrap billowing behind her and the hem of her skirt rippling as it caught the rise and fall of the breeze. Nearly twenty years had gone by since Circus had last seen her, but he recognized at once the severe part of her black hair spooled at the nape of her neck, which was lean as a flower's stem, the round face with the forehead he used to say was mango soft as he bent to kiss it. He recognized the swift, theatrical pace with which Carmen imposed herself upon the world and remembered how she could enter and exit a room with the drama of a flock of doves taking flight. He watched her step to the curb as her eyes passed over the road that lay before her as if deciding where to take her day. She stood proudly, monarchical, with hips squared as if she could bend the sky, the day, and everything in it to her whim. She cast off into the street, scarves trailing.

Circus followed after her. He needed to be seen by her. He needed her to remember him. The man he had been way back when Carmen knew him had never seemed so far in the distance, and he recognized it now only because this lovely presence from the past was being offered up to him. Already he was imagining Carmen looking up at him and seeing in his ripening features the young man she had once loved. He wasn't usually in this part of town, so he wondered if fate had delivered him to this spot half a mile from where his interview at the Cadillac dealership was scheduled, knowing he wouldn't make it an hour without feeling throttled by the necktie he wore, knowing he'd stop for a shot of bourbon at the first bar he saw once he hit Norwood Center, knowing Carmen Julia was going to step out of the café next door in a flowing skirt and backless blouse and that Circus would leave a ten on the bar and follow.

The warm tar of the newly paved roads relented beneath his scuffed leather shoes as Carmen made her way toward the town square, the muscular thew of her back reminding him, as it used to, of outstretched wings. He sensed both a compression and a stretching of time—the faint memory of their final morning together looming near enough to make him feel as if it had happened only seconds before, yet far enough away to make him doubt the moment had ever happened at all.

Carmen strolled up the pathway toward the old white gazebo in the center of the square, lingering at the bottom of a row of stairs, while Circus waited yards away to see if she was expecting someone. She paced back and forth, taking an elegant spin at each turn. He remembered then how she could never stand still, how she danced even when she wasn't on a stage. She swung her arm through the air as if she were rehearsing one of her routines, her limbs rippling as if her body couldn't contain its own rhythm, without caring, it seemed, whether anyone noticed.

Circus pulled off his tie and shoved it into his back pocket, untucked his pressed shirt, and made a mess of his hair. He sprinted across the grass, then walked up slowly beside Carmen, who had begun to make her way back toward the street. A sly grin spread across his mouth, and his heart filled as he waited for her to sense him. When she finally looked over, it took a beat longer than made him comfortable for her to recognize his face.

"Good morning, beautiful." Circus bowed, shoulders drawn

forward and ready to fit the bulk of his body into her slight embrace.

But Carmen didn't open her arms to take him in. Instead, she took a step away, tapping her finger against her lips. "How strange."

"A blast from the past."

She stared as if she imagined herself in a dream.

"Carmen, it's me. Circus Palmer."

"You're still here," she said quietly, a downward tilt to her mouth. "You never left."

"Well, that's not exactly true." His fingers found a coin in his pocket and rubbed at it. "I've been places over the years. New York awhile. But yeah, Boston is home. I got lots going on here."

Her gaze drifted down his body to examine his suit, which had been one of his favorites until now, as Carmen turned up her nose.

"I was on my way to buy a new car." The lie made him blush lightly, something he hadn't done since he was a younger man and more comfortable with making up stories. "Cadillac. You know how I do."

She smiled plainly, then started away. "Lovely to run into you."

"Tell me how you've been." Circus interrupted her path, his armpits beginning to sweat. "It's been a minute."

Carmen laced her arms across her chest, and he watched her decide to indulge him. "I moved to Manhattan briefly to dance with Francesca DeMille."

"I remember."

"Then I was in Paris." She took a casual glance at the manicured fingernails of her left hand as if to let him see the gold band tight on her ring finger. "And now I have my own dance company in London, where I live. With my husband."

She'd said the word deliberately—*husband*—and Circus gritted his teeth. "So what are you doing in town?"

"My father's remarrying and moving back to Puerto Rico," she said. "I've been here with him and my brothers to help him prepare."

Carmen turned her face as if to brave an unanticipated swell of emotion privately, and Circus could faintly see the twenty-year-old girl he'd first passed in the halls of the Conservatory in his last year. During the ten months of their romance, he had been transfixed by her smooth skin, her black hair coarse and wild, her mouth fat as a bruise. The way Carmen moved mesmerized him, her body alert and always sensing music. Some nights she would turn off the lights and ask him to play his horn, then sway to his sounds in the dark. He used to thrill at the wide breadth of her movements and her lush depressive moods, the delight of never knowing whether he'd come home to find her sobbing or dancing in the living room. She had the same sweeping moods of his mother, let out the same wolflike howls of grief, except that Carmen would let him comfort her. When they made love, she would whisper things—how beautiful he was, how ample he felt inside her, how close she felt to God—that filled his eyes with tears. Carmen stood before him, a woman now, and Circus was just as painfully drawn, even more so, maybe because she was the first woman, the only woman, to whom he'd said "I love you" and allowed the feeling with all its terror to live deeply in him.

"Your husband," he said. "I'd like to meet him. Tell him he's a lucky man."

A fire flashed in her eyes. "I suppose you still play your trumpet?"

"Always have, always will."

"And have you won your Grammy?" she asked without looking at him. "I don't remember you talking about much else."

He didn't like her question, didn't like her tone. Glancing over her shoulder, he saw a vintage car at the curb, so he pretended to find it more interesting than what she'd asked. He circled the car like a potential buyer, and Carmen seemed amused by the boyish glee he took, pointing out its shiny grille and hubcaps, so he kept on.

"My old man had one of these," he said. "Nineteen seventy Pontiac GTO. Only drove it on special occasions. Usually when he visited his girlfriends. He'd leave me in it while he was up with his woman, and I'd sit behind the wheel pretending the car was mine. There was a nick in the foam wheel, and I swear to you, I can still feel it in my hands." He stretched his fingers like he was trying on gloves, glad to see Carmen still intrigued. "One day I'm twelve, thirteen. I beg him to leave the keys 'cause one of my favorite tunes is playing on the radio. The song ends, I'm waiting, waiting. I decide to drive the car around the block—bam—hit a goddamn telephone pole. Old man whipped my ass, boy. I never got behind the wheel of that sweet ride again."

Sweat pooled in his armpits and in the small of his back, though the air was cool. Carmen was watching him, interpreting. Circus could feel the dissection.

"What would I do with a Grammy anyway?" he asked. "I'm a superstar at Berklee. Got gigs all over town and make good cash selling my CDs after shows. Tomorrow I'm in New York for the weekend, playing a fancy hotel and meeting with a label. They've been wanting to see me for a while." A panic set over him, but he didn't want Carmen to see. He gave her his easiest smile. "Yeah, I got music. I don't need any award."

Circus felt a need to even things out between them so let his gaze move from Carmen's eyes to her mouth to her collarbone and hips. She'd never liked how his eyes climbed all over her body, that was what she called it. She used to say it emptied her out. He saw a flash in her eye. The stormy spirit had been nudged.

"Good to see you." Jaw set, Carmen spun on her heels.

"Hey." Circus took her by the elbow, deciding in that moment to miss the interview. "I'm sorry. Just have a coffee with me."

"I'm meeting someone."

"I want to talk. We started a conversation twenty years ago we never got to finish."

"That's not what I remember." Carmen slid out of his grip and straightened the cuff of her sweater. "I'm walking. What you do is your decision."

She crossed the square without waiting for him. Circus followed as she strode down the main street gazing through boutique windows, then stepped into an antique shop. He walked beside her, still nervous, still rubbing the coin in his pocket. Within the musty smell of the shop, he could smell her perfume, and though he couldn't identify the scent, he imagined that if gold were liquefied, it would smell like Carmen.

"You are from a very long time ago," she said.

"Not so long."

"It was a lifetime ago." Carmen took an old biscuit jar from a shelf, lifted the silver lid, and smelled inside. "A time I barely remember."

He started to feel angry, erased. "You aren't looking at me like I'm someone who didn't matter."

Carmen peered up at him and smiled genuinely for the first time. She replaced the jar on the shelf and continued down the aisle. "You are handsome as ever. But a little fat."

"Not you. You're still perfect. Forgot how tiny you are, though."

"I'm not tiny. You're just large. I can be large."

Her smile deepened, and Circus felt emboldened. "How long you in town? I'm back Monday for the marathon. What say you and I hit that dessert spot at Park Plaza you used to like? See if your name's still carved under our table in the corner."

"I don't think my husband would be happy."

"Tell me about him. Could I take him?"

Carmen shook her head, tsked. "You're still ten years old."

"Ten wasn't a bad year."

She stopped in front of a shelf full of antique toys, pensive as her gaze moved from one to the other. "Simon is a conductor with the London Symphony Orchestra."

"Cool." Circus steadied his voice, though he felt dumb having boasted about his little gigs at bars. "Why didn't he come with you to Boston?"

Carmen ran her fingers along the tin casing of an antique Pinocchio on strings. "He's staying with the children. Our youngest is very good at cricket. He has a tournament this week. Simon wanted to be with him."

"Lucky kid," he said. "All I ever got from my old man were promises to play catch."

Carmen eyed him in a way that suggested a mystery had resolved itself. Gently, she took Pinocchio from the shelf, coiled his strings around her slender fingers, and made him dance. "And you? There must be a woman in your life. Or women, if memory serves."

"Not fair."

Carmen kept her eyes on the toy. "You haven't grown sentimental, have you?"

"I'm sensitive," he said. "You never knew that about me."

"I knew."

Circus skimmed the record of his life. There was Pia, the wife he had been loosely married to. There was a handful of women with whom he'd spent time in the decades since Carmen knew him, but none who had dug deep enough to mention. And there was the ever-changing inventory of females with whom he'd relieve the tensions music couldn't get rid of. But it was Maggie who came into his mind when Carmen asked. What surprised him even more than the thought of her was the yearning, the sorrow in not having seen her for so long. It was supposed to be easy to go on without Maggie, but somehow she'd managed to lodge herself in him no matter how hard he was trying to bleed her out.

"There's nobody," he said. "Maybe nobody's been able to take your place."

Carmen smirked and took a toy acrobat on a wooden trapeze from the shelf, squeezing the handle and watching the acrobat flip over the bar. "I very much liked you. You made me infatuated. A little crazy."

Her gaze suddenly dreamy, Carmen coiled a strand of hair at the back of her neck around her finger, her tongue ticking against her teeth.

"You know how many times I've thought about you over the years?" He took a step closer, leaned in. "I've written songs about you."

"Don't be silly."

"You broke my heart." An immense sadness swept over him, as if he could have dissolved onto the ground. "You're the reason I can't stick around for anybody. I haven't been the same since you left."

"After I left?"

"You graduated and went to New York. We were gonna go together."

"Is that so? Why would we?"

"We were in love."

"No, we were sleeping together." Carmen looked up at him as if he were telling a joke. "Are you sure you're thinking of the right girl?"

Circus slid the cigarette from behind his ear and slipped it between his lips, nibbling at the stub. He didn't like what was happening inside him, his stomach churning, his mouth growing dry. Carmen tittered—about the flipping acrobat, about him, Circus wasn't sure. She grabbed a basket from the ground and tossed the acrobat in, perusing the shelf for other toys. He felt destabilized, like waking up in an unfamiliar room. Carmen glanced over at him, and her lips perked like a mother soothing a child.

"You would like me to say I missed you, too," she said. "You would like me to say I haven't stopped thinking of you. I want to be with you and leave my husband, pick up where we left off. What would you do if I said this? Truly?"

All at once the gloom that had overtaken him deepened into something angry and hard. Carmen turned back to the toys.

"What I remember most is the way you used to cling to me when you slept," she said. "Always I would wake in the middle of the night because you were holding me too tightly. If I turned my back, you'd hold tighter. If you turned, you would still reach back to put your hand on my leg. You needed to be touching me. You needed to hold on. I thought of it once when my son crawled into bed with me after a nightmare. He attached to me the same way, and it brought back the memory. I always wondered how you could speak so much of freedom when you were awake, yet hold on like the devil was after you in your sleep."

Carmen began dropping toys in her basket—a cymbal-clapping monkey, a bear on a bicycle, a spinning top—saying the names of her children with each toy. Teresa. Aidan. Michael. Circus was impatient, suddenly hostile. The last thing he expected her to be was content, so he prodded at it, unsatisfied.

"You sure aren't the woman I expected to meet all these years later," he said. "This sure isn't the life I saw for you either. Kinda simple, ain't it?"

Unruffled, she said, "Perhaps."

"That's not how I'm doing things, man. Not me."

Carmen took the acrobat from her basket, squeezed the handle, and watched him flip over the trapeze. "I had one of these as a girl but I never liked it. Rise and fall, rise and fall, but he never gets off the stick."

Carmen tossed the acrobat back onto the shelf and chose a tin airplane instead. Perfecting the lay of scarves around her neck, she strolled up to the counter to pay, as Circus glared at the acrobat, the tin body contorted beneath the trapeze after she had put it back so carelessly.

He didn't remember feeling much when she left all those years ago. He'd simply walked back into his own life—it had seemed fertile and full of promise then—so that he wouldn't have time to regret. Now it came, twining in his gut. Worse than the regret was sensing all the holes he'd left untended, which he saw when Carmen crossed his path to remind him of what he used to want. She'd left, and her life had begun. Circus was still waiting for his beginning. Standing in the shop, he wanted whatever had begun to calcify in him all those years ago to break apart and recover its flow. He wanted to slide a needle through the last moment he'd seen Carmen and this current one, when he'd watched her step out of the café, wanted to pull the thread and close the gap. He waited for Carmen to glance over her shoulder at him as she made her way out of the shop door—he knew when parting lovers looked back it meant something. But Carmen never looked.

Salvage

*

Koko

The Blind Fox stood between a bank and the shop where Koko and her neighborhood friends used to buy comic books before the girls in the group decided they were too old for little-kid things. Koko had always been curious about the bar, with its black facade and red-rimmed windows lined year-round with green tinsel, the orange fox painted on the door sipping wine. Before the trip to Sanibel Island with her mother, her father had promised to stop there and pick up her bicycle though he made no mention of the woman who had stolen it. When Koko came back from Florida eight days later, her bike still wasn't in the garage.

Standing in the parking lot behind the bar, bookbag heavy on her shoulder, Koko waited for a cook or manager to step outside to empty the trash or receive a delivery, knowing she wasn't allowed inside. She would ask for the bike and offer her school ID, which she held ready in her hand to show.

She heard the slam of a car door and the click of heels on pavement. She recognized the woman right away as she slipped through the pub's back door. The tall body, the red hair, the big eyes and pointy chin Koko thought made the woman look like a baby deer. Neither of her parents had noticed that morning, when

Koko backed away from their argument after seeing movement through a crack in the door of the guest bedroom. She'd watched the woman escape through a window, then take the ten-speed from against the garage and ride away.

Koko circled the block to settle her nerves and walked as calmly as she could to the entrance of the bar, wavering for a moment before pulling open the door and stepping inside. The darkness seemed to close around her as if she'd been sucked out of the bright afternoon into a dank cellar. The place smelled like stale food. The wooden floors looked sticky. The red walls held crooked pictures in old-fashioned frames. Koko wondered why her father liked the place and figured it might have something to do with the dartboards at the back of the room, the huge bowl of chili she saw a couple sharing at one of the tables, and the redhead behind the bar, tying her hair into a ponytail. Her eyes seemed to blink even bigger when she noticed Koko and stared back at her as if she weren't sure whether to seat her or tell her to go.

"Are you lost?" The woman's voice was high, girly with a slight rasp to it, like a sprinkle of salt. Koko wished her own voice sounded as cute. She shook her head.

"Is it Girl Scout cookie time?"

"I wish."

Her gaze flicked down to Koko's toes and up again, and Koko regretted wearing her jacket with a rip in the fabric.

The woman tilted her head and her ponytail bobbed. "Did you come to eat?"

"Can I?"

Koko looked around the room. Two men at the bar sat with three seats between them as they nursed their beers and watched a baseball game on the television above their heads. An old man read the newspaper at one of the tables near the couple finishing the last bites of their chili.

"It's probably not allowed for you to sit at the bar," the woman said. "Is a table okay?"

Koko nodded and followed her to a booth at the side of the room. The woman went back to the bar and grabbed a plastic menu, wiping it as she brought it to the table.

"Something to drink?" she asked.

Koko ordered an iced tea mixed with lemonade, thinking it sounded fancy. She kept her eyes on the menu, unable to concentrate on the food listed on it. The day had become much too exciting.

The bartender came back with her drink, placing it atop a cocktail napkin that Koko promised herself to take home as a souvenir. "What can I get you?"

Koko knew she had seven dollars in her bag, left over from her allowance, so she could only afford a cup of clam chowder. "Do crackers come with it?"

"They sure do." The woman smiled. "What's your name, sweetie?"

Koko's stomach clenched. "Jenny."

"I'm Peach. Tell me if you need anything, okey doke?"

"Okey doke," Koko answered and watched her walk away. She had hips like the women Koko saw in magazines—narrowing at the waist, then rounding out into soft points. Her Spandex skirt clung to them, the hem high above her knees showing off her long legs.

From the other side of the room, the old man peered at Koko over his newspaper, giving her the once-over, as if to tell her she wasn't supposed to be there. She sipped her drink to hide her smile, relishing the satisfaction of getting away with something. Still, she didn't know what to do as she waited for her soup. Doing homework would make her look like a kid, looking at her phone even more so.

And she didn't know what to do about Peach. An odd sensation had passed through Koko the morning her parents fought as this unknown woman moved behind their guest room door. It was the same sensation she'd once had staying at a house her friends said was haunted, and she learned frightening things could come into her world without being seen on the way in or out. Koko had never expected to be sitting yards away from the woman. But now that it was happening, what was she supposed to do?

Peach stood at the end of the bar chatting with one of the guys watching baseball, glancing over every so often and wriggling her fingers as if she and Koko were friends. Koko found herself wishing they were. Whenever Peach turned her attention back to the guy, Koko studied her body, the way she held herself and moved. How every part of her looked skinny and long yet still curved. How her breasts bounced when she laughed and the silver pendant at the end of her necklace seemed so perfectly placed between them. How when she listened to the guy talk, her mouth perked like a red bow, and when she giggled, she pressed her fingers against the bridge of her nose or let her mouth fall open and her shoulders bounce.

One of the cooks called out from the kitchen, and Peach walked back through the hallway, her hips swaying and reminding Koko of a bell. She looked down at her own thighs heavy in her blue jeans, spread like globs on the puffy seat of the booth. After envying the fanlike spread of her cousin's blonde hair across the sand on Sanibel Island, Koko had woken up an hour earlier every morning to flat-iron her hair, but she knew it still had no spring, not like Peach's.

Peach came from the kitchen with the chowder and cracker packets heaped in her hand.

"I got you extra," she said, scooting into the booth across from Koko.

"Are you allowed to sit here?"

Peach shrugged and lifted her legs onto the seat. "I did everything I need to do before the dinner rush, which isn't happening for, like, two hours. And as you can see, nobody's here." She rolled her eyes. "This isn't the hardest job in the world."

Koko stirred a fistful of crackers into her soup and sensed the blood rush to her cheeks.

"So, Jenny." Peach leaned against the wall and laced her hands behind her head. "Do you go to school around here?"

"I go to Roosevelt."

"What year?"

"Freshman."

"Yikes." Peach wrinkled her nose. "That was the hardest year for me. You're probably doing all right, though. You seem pretty cool."

The blood rushed quicker to Koko's cheeks. "Where did you go?"

"Not anywhere you know. I'm not from around here. San Diego, that's where I grew up. I followed my ex-boyfriend out here." Peach tapped her hand against the table as if it were a judge's gavel. "Piece of advice? Don't follow a boyfriend, like, anywhere."

Koko giggled into the napkin. "Why not?"

"They ask you, but as soon as they see you're coming, they don't think you're so cute anymore." She ran the pendant of her necklace up and down the chain. "It's okay here, though. Cold as heck in winter, but it's been good to me."

"I'm leaving one day."

"Oh yeah? Where to?"

Koko took in the spicy scent of Peach's perfume, which briefly wafted across the table. Her own body had started to produce strong odors, and the powder-scented deodorant and coconut shampoo her mother bought her had made her smell sweet, but not, she now realized, womanly and grown. Peppery fragrances made girls into women, as did high cheekbones and dangly earrings and the right color of red lipstick, which Peach made her understand.

"I don't know," she answered. "Maybe someplace they speak another language. Like, Spain. We learned about flamenco in my music class."

"I took French in high school," Peach said, just as the door opened and two groups walked in. "Guess what my French name was."

"Monique?"

She stood up and with her hands lifted dramatically in the air, said, "La Pêche."

Peach pursed her lips, then sashayed to the door, grinning at Koko as she led the diners to separate tables. On her way back behind the bar, she reached into the pocket of her apron and dropped a handful of quarters onto Koko's table.

"Play something fun," she said, nodding toward the jukebox.

Koko slid the four quarters into her palm, making her way to the jukebox while attempting the same soft swish she saw in Peach's hips. None of the songs in the box she liked, so she chose an Aretha Franklin song, her father had once told her everyone loved Aretha. When she turned back to the bar, Peach gave her a thumbs-up and mouthed along to the words "What you want, baby I got it."

Quietly, Koko strolled through the room, staying close to the walls, where she pretended to be interested in the framed pictures but was secretly practicing her new walk. On the other side of the bar, the door opened, and Peach squealed, running into the arms of the man who walked through. He was smaller than Peach but had a face Koko liked, and his small but muscular body and the tattoos on his arms made Koko blush. Peach draped herself around his neck and kissed him, so Koko turned back to the wall. She was reaching out to straighten a crooked frame when she realized her father was staring out from the picture. Circus wore a woolen coat Koko remembered him wearing when she was still in grade school. He was lifting the collar as if the person who snapped the picture had just caught him getting into it. A strand of beads hung from his neck and drifted into his pin-striped shirt, unbuttoned low enough to show the hair on his chest. His beard was thick, his hair tied into the knot he used to wear, his eyes boring into the camera lens.

Koko took a step back as if he'd walked into the bar and caught her there. But then she moved closer, first reading the bold type at the bottom of the picture—THE CIRCUS PALMER TRIO,

SUNDAYS—because it was easier than looking into his eyes. But then she looked. The face, she knew. The hair. The left eye a little lazy. The hands. But he didn't look like her father. Something Koko recognized in him wasn't there, or maybe something she didn't recognize was, she wasn't sure which, though she saw that he was handsome, and it filled her with a sense of pride. Staring into her father's eyes, Koko knew what she needed. She wanted Peach to tell her who this man was.

Peach made a cooing sound at the bar, and the boyfriend nuzzled her neck, his arms around her waist. She stroked his back, her body suddenly airy as they gazed into each other's eyes. Until then, Koko hadn't understood that men could make women happy, and she thought of her mother on that morning over a month ago, throwing a plate against the floor and crying in her bedroom. Koko thought of all the times her mother had cried. Thought of all the broken plates.

Peach pranced across the room toward her. "Want to meet my boyfriend?"

"You guys have music here?" she asked before Peach could lead her away.

"Some nights. Also trivia on Mondays. I keep saying we should do a comedy night, but Jason never listens."

"What kind of music do they play?" Koko pointed to the men in the photograph next to her father's.

Peach leaned in closer. "The one guy looks kinda rockabilly. Maybe rockabilly?"

"What about him?" Koko pointed to her father.

Peach wrinkled her nose. "Don't ask."

"Why? What's wrong with him?"

Peach grimaced. "Remember what I said about not following a boyfriend anywhere?"

Koko nodded.

"It goes double for musicians." Peach waved her hand toward the bar. "Come over and let me introduce you to a real man."

The boyfriend was called Trujillo, Peach said, but she called him by his first name, Danny, and since Koko was her friend, she could call him Danny, too. He seemed shy but friendly, as if he wanted to say the right things to Koko so that Peach would be pleased. He asked her about school and complimented her sneakers even though she knew they were worn. He asked if he could treat her to another iced tea and lemonade, but Koko said she'd probably had too much sugar. Peach and Trujillo cozying against each other made her feel like she'd stayed at a party too long, so she asked for the bathroom. Peach pointed her down the hall.

Koko went in and closed the door behind her. She washed her hands, then sat on the toilet lid, glancing around the room. On a small wooden cabinet, she noticed a bottle of hairspray and a makeup bag, which she unzipped and sorted through. Inside she found mascara, blue and black eyeliner pens, blush, and a tube of lipstick. She took the lipstick and spun the cap until the gunk pushed through, the thick red paste the color of apples. Koko went to the mirror and slathered it onto her lips, pushing harder than she knew she had to but suddenly needing the pressure. Koko slid the lipstick into her back pocket and stared at herself in the mirror, admiring the fullness of her lips with this new shock of color. Already she thought she looked older. Her face could change. Her face was changing.

Koko rubbed away the lipstick before she went back into the main room. When Peach saw her, she smirked, then took a napkin from the bar and wiped off the lipstick's last traces.

"Sorry," Koko said.

"No worries." Peach wiped a smudge from Koko's chin. "But you shouldn't wear other people's makeup. You'll get cooties."

Peach smiled, then brought a grocery bag, folded neatly at the top, from under the bar. She passed it to Koko.

"I have to leave?" she asked.

"Well, the other girls came in for the dinner shift, and you're sitting in one of their sections. And it's about to get busy."

"Don't I have to pay for the chowder?"

"It's on me, pretty lady."

In the bag, Koko found a lidded cardboard bowl she assumed was another serving of chowder, two pieces of chocolate cake in a clear plastic box, and a sandwich wrapped in paper.

"You know, my family didn't have any money either," Peach said quietly. "It was just my mom and me, but yeah, there were days when all we ate was tuna out of the can. There's nothing bad about asking for help." She patted Koko's shoulder. "Take it."

The shame blazed in Koko's cheeks, and she had an urge to throw the bag to the floor and run out of the place, but she didn't want to humiliate herself even more. She thought about telling Peach she wasn't homeless or starved or whatever Peach had imagined, but the embarrassment tied her tongue.

"Thanks," she croaked and went back to the table for her jacket and backpack, slinging it over her shoulder. She decided to confess to her mother that her bicycle had been stolen but that someone from the Blind Fox called to say they'd found it. Her mother would come back to get it. She shoved the grocery bag under her arm and started toward the door. But as she passed the bar, the sound of Peach's happy squeal made her spin back around.

"My name's not Jenny," she said. "It's Koko. Circus is my dad. And you stole my bike."

* * *

Peach paced the floor of the storage room at the back of the bar as Koko sat on a beer keg and waited for her to speak. Her ten-speed had been tucked into a corner, raggedy towels hanging from the handlebars. Peach seemed worried, her forehead crinkled and big eyes bright as though fear had lit a lightbulb behind them. She rubbed her bare arms even though Koko thought the room too warm.

"You don't look anything like him," Peach finally said. "Well, I don't know." She skinnied her eyes. "Maybe I see it. He always made it sound like you were older. In college or something. Far away. I didn't know you were here."

Biting at her fingernails, Peach sat on a second beer keg as the night with Koko's father seemed to replay in her mind. "We had so much to drink. I mean, like, I was blotto. He didn't tell me where we were going. I thought we were going to his place or a friend's house, I mean, God, what guy brings a girl to his ex-wife's house? And I didn't mean to steal your bike. I didn't know what else to do. Circus said he was coming to get it."

"I didn't think you did it on purpose."

Peach's mouth quaked as if she were holding back tears. "Why did you come here?"

"I don't know, my bike, but . . ." Koko dragged the towels from her bicycle and tossed them into a nearby bucket. "I guess I also wanted to see you myself."

"Do you want to yell at me?"

"I don't think so."

"What then?"

Koko ran her fingers over the handlebars, picking at a spot of rust. There were flutters in her belly and a clogged feeling in her chest, as if her own tears were in there but she couldn't get at them.

"He doesn't like me," Koko said. "Not as much as he likes you."

"Oh, he doesn't like me." Peach gripped the handles of the keg as if she were afraid to slip off. "And of course he likes you. He's your daddy. He loves you."

The word sounded strange on someone else's lips. *Daddy*. Years had passed since Koko had called him by the name, she didn't even remember the last time. And though she knew most little girls called their fathers Daddy, she didn't like anyone else using the term to refer to hers.

"Why do you think he's not a real man?" Koko asked. "What's wrong with him?"

"Oh, sweetie." Peach placed her hands on Koko's shoulders.

"Nothing's wrong with him. I shouldn't have said that. It's just . . . sometimes, okay, sometimes things don't go the way a girl wants, and she feels, I don't know, mad about it. Maybe I wished I meant more to him."

"Obviously you mean something."

Peach tsked and flicked her hands into the air. "I mean nothing to him. Trust me."

"But he brought you to our house," Koko said. "My mom's house. My house. Why would he do that if you weren't important?"

A tear rose in Peach's eye, and she sucked in a breath. Outside the door, Koko heard the floorboards creak as someone walked past. She looked at Peach, whose face had crumpled again with worry as she chewed at her thumbnail and stared at the floor. Koko wondered if Peach made him laugh. If she knew how to get him to talk about the things she liked. If she'd ever cried with him, if he'd ever comforted her, and if he did, what he said.

"Is there something you do that I could learn to do?" Koko asked.

Peach's mouth twisted, and she collapsed into tears, sobbing into her pretty, pretty hands. She folded Koko into her arms and held her head against her chest.

"I'm sorry," Peach wept. "I'm so, so sorry."

Koko let the woman cry, just as she always had with her mother, and as Peach's sobs grew thicker and heavier and more desperate, Koko felt her own sadness seep away, even though she'd wanted to feel it, knowing it had to get out somehow.

Some Kind
of Love

*

Circus

A man in a tailored suit, dirtied at the bottom hems, leather shoes scuffed. He was mumbling to himself, not like a madman, Circus thought, but like someone so lost in himself he'd forgotten where he was. Moments earlier the man had asked him for a cigarette. Now he stood in a corner peeling away the paper and mumbling. This was a subway platform in New York City, and Circus knew to expect strange moments. Still, he watched the man out of the corner of his eye.

This was the day, his day. Circus had woken up before dawn, swum ten laps in the hotel pool, spritzed himself with cologne after his shower, and eaten a nourishing breakfast of grapefruit and a spinach omelet. He wore his favorite suit, his demo snug in the chest pocket. Everyone he passed in the street, he smiled to, and he whistled as he walked, taking a nod at the sunshine. And then this. Something about the way the other man's nerves seemed to shudder through his limbs and deform the features of his face made Circus feel those nerves in his own body. But as he tried to walk farther down the platform, the man's pacing only brought him near again. Circus seemed to be the only one who noticed the man, noticed the pacing and the speed with which he went from jumpy to frenetic as he inched closer to the edge of the platform toward the tracks. Closer, closer. A train was coming, barreling across the rails.

"Hey, man," Circus whispered from too many yards away, extending his hand, afraid to get too close because now the man seemed to be leaning over the tracks. For a moment, Circus wondered if they were in a dream.

"Hey, man," he whispered again as his soul seemed to leap up, even though his body took a giant step back and away. The man was falling over the edge as if in slow motion. There was noise and there was chaos and there was a scream, but then someone reached out and stopped the man's fall. Bodies huddled around, then guided him to a wooden bench. Someone draped a coat over the man's shoulders.

The train screeched into the station. Circus stepped on and took a seat. As the doors closed, a terror grew in him as he tried to avoid but couldn't help looking into the eyes of the man still sitting outside on the platform. Not because a man could arrive at a moment like this. But because when he did, maybe no one would reach out for him.

* * *

The kid wore thick-rimmed eyeglasses, a mustache curled at the tips, and scuffed Vans beneath jeans gently folded to expose pale, scrawny ankles. He didn't look like a jazz fan, but he spoke like one, the way he talked about the squawks of a Coltrane solo and identified the kinds of mutes he heard on Circus's record as he listened through gold-plated headphones and paced the studio floor. The inside of Circus's hands were sweating. He waited in a butterfly chair too small for his massive frame and watched Peacock Evans, whose rickety body lay on a hammock strung from hooks in a corner, puff at a freshly rolled cigar.

"What's the third track called?" The kid lifted the headphones from his ears.

"'Magdalena the Swan,'" Circus answered.

"This one's tight. You're alive on it."

"I'm not alive on the others?" Circus tried to joke.

The kid replaced the headphones over his ears. "The piano on this track is sick."

"Graham likes the keys," Peacock croaked from the corner. He nodded lazily, then went back to his cigar as Graham paced the floor, poking the air with his fingers in time.

The stuffed head of a black bear that was mounted over the console stared down at Circus, its cold yellowed eyes like a threat. Maybe it was those eyes or Graham's relentless walking back and forth, or thoughts of the man on the subway, or the awful bellow the man had let out as he fell toward the rails before someone pulled him away. Whatever it was had scared Circus in a way he was having trouble braving through. Biting his thumbnail to the quick on one hand, he rubbed his knee with the other, counting the tick of the metronome in his mind. He wanted a drink desperately.

"You all right, brother?" asked Peacock.

"I had a morning."

Peacock nodded toward Graham as if to tell Circus to direct his attention to what was important, so he tried to focus on the quirks of the Williamsburg studio and the kid listening to his record, perhaps on the verge of changing his life. But he kept seeing the other man's fall toward the tracks.

Graham pulled off the headphones by the cord, then tossed them into a director's chair.

"What is this record?"

Circus glanced at Peacock, who shrugged.

"A biography," Circus answered. "That's how I think of it. About the people I've known. About the man I am."

"There are only five tracks."

"It's not finished."

"You said it was a masterwork." Graham snickered, sounding like a kid again. "You brought me an unfinished masterwork?"

"I had trouble making it all come together, but I made a good go of what I had."

"You ever made a record before?" Graham asked.

"Depends on what you call a record."

"Sounds like you mean no."

Circus eyed Peacock's cigar, regretting he'd turned the old man down when he offered one. "I've recorded a trunkful of CDs over the years. They sell well when I gig."

"A trunkful?"

Circus looked to Peacock, but Peacock wasn't looking back. "I don't seem to be saying what I mean to be."

The kid pressed his hands together, skinnying his eyes as he took Circus in. "What is it you'd like me to do for you?"

Graham loomed higher than his height should have allowed, likely because the black bear was watching over his shoulder.

"If you don't mind," Circus said, "I'd love if you'd just let me know what you think."

Graham paced the floor, hands on his hips and eyes darting behind the thin lenses of his eyeglasses. Circus wondered whether they were real.

"No one's rushing to record jazz anymore, you know it, I know it," Graham said. "I lucked out when I found Hot Swallow. You know that band?"

"Hot Swallow . . ."

"They're like an updated King Oliver's Creole," the kid went on. "They're tight, you should check them out. You want to know where things are going, you check out Hot Swallow."

"Listen, friend." Circus had the urge to throttle the kid's throat but chewed at the inside of his mouth instead. "Peacock here thought you might be able to help me out. I'm looking to take things to the next level."

"Always happy to do my man Peacock a solid." Graham crossed the room to slap hands with the old man. "But I've got to really love what I hear, and I've got to think lots of other people are going to love it, too."

Circus wiped his moist palms into his pants. "And do you think people are going to love what you heard?"

Graham sat across from him in the director's chair, carefully lacing his fingers between his open knees. "Things are going in a direction you don't sound like you're headed. You're good, though. You know the language. But you're not . . ." He sighed as if it pained him to go on. "You're not interesting."

Circus's hand dropped against his chest, a move that surprised and embarrassed him.

"Sorry, bro," Graham said.

Across the room, Peacock stood up from the hammock and rubbed the watch chained to the inside of his pocket, his mouth suddenly drawn and severe. Circus tried not to look at him as his cheeks blazed with shame.

"You know, I just thought of the meter where I parked my car," Circus's voice cracked lightly. "I should put more quarters in it. Or move the car maybe. Do they check the meters here? Back in Boston, boy, those bastards show no mercy."

"Why don't I walk you out?" Peacock tossed him his jacket.

By the time they reached the elevator, Circus had already forgotten how he'd thanked and said goodbye to Graham but hoped he'd done both gracefully. Peacock had been kind enough to stay silent on their way out of the studio, but once they hit the street, the old man reached into his pocket for a pack of cigarettes, offered one to Circus, and took another for himself.

"What just happened?" Circus asked.

"Business," Peacock muttered.

"I wish you weren't there to see it."

Peacock grinned, revealing the tooth that had always been missing, now replaced with silver. "Don't worry about me."

A breeze from the East River rolled up between the warehouses lining the street and gave Circus a chill. The sky, puffed with swollen gray clouds, made him feel like the entire planet had grown cold save for one streak of sunshine that poured onto a spot on the Manhattan skyline and filled him with a regret he couldn't place.

"This day, man," he said. "April isn't supposed to be this somber."

"What's going on?" Peacock asked.

Circus thought his knees might fail, shaky as they'd become. He had an urge to call Maggie—she'd understand and soothe him—but he couldn't bear her knowing what was happening. Then the man came to mind again, his buckled body sitting on the wooden bench as he looked back at Circus with the hollowed-out stare of a person who wanted to die.

"I'd rather not say," Circus answered. "It's embarrassing. My life's embarrassing."

Peacock blew a ring of smoke and swirled his wrinkled finger through the center. "We don't always have good days."

"That kid doesn't know what he's saying. You heard the record. It's interesting, right?"

"How do I know from interesting nowadays? What matters is what you believe."

Circus pinched the bridge of his nose to stop the water filling his eyes. "I believe I've been looking for a feeling I can't find anymore. I keep looking in the notes and scales and everything else, but it never comes. Where is it, man?"

"You wanna know what I think?"

"'Course I do."

Peacock ashed his cigarette, gaze set on that distant point of sunlight. "You always been afraid, and nothing kills good sound more than fear. The notes are waiting for you to take 'em and let 'em do what they wanna do to you. But you gotta be wide open, brother. Stand naked. Don't stop when you get to the brink. You control that horn like a woman you don't trust."

Circus rubbed at his eyes as if he were tired when really he was blinking away tears. "No use now. That kid was my last shot."

"Don't let that boy stop you."

"I'm forty, man. When am I gonna get things off the ground?"

Peacock shook his head. "Life is long. You got plenty of time to do." He slapped Circus on the back and watched him with the kind of look Circus knew he would remember once the old man was gone, an eerie moment that made him fear that day was coming soon.

"Life is long." Peacock tapped the rim of his hat and smiled that silver grin one last time before starting down the street in the direction of the sunlight, leaving Circus standing under a dark patch of sky.

* * *

He woke up sprawled across the tiles of his hotel bathroom, a splash of vomit in the tub and two bottles of cheap bourbon empty on the counter. He had no idea of the time but noticed the room outside was dark, the hotel around him quiet. On his phone, he noticed he'd sent a message to Josephine at some point in the night, asking why she loved him, and she'd responded twice. *Just come see me,* she'd written. *Just come.* He regretted reaching out and deleted the messages. As he pulled himself from the ground, the pressure held hard behind his eyes. The hotel phone rang in the main room, and when he went to it, he saw the mattress upturned on the floor and had a brief memory of capsizing the bed in his anger before opting to lose himself in the bottles of bourbon instead.

The man who had booked him at the hotel that weekend was calling, Circus assumed, to reprimand him for missing the gig. He ignored the call and lit a cigarette even though it was a non-smoking room. The clock on the nightstand said it was four in the morning, while the city outside his window was quiet but still buzzed the way he remembered from when he lived there as a younger man. Back then, he had imagined the city would one day open its arms to him as it had for so many others. How tragic, he thought, to find himself looking at it through a window like an outsider.

A copy of the CD he'd given to Graham sat on the bedside table next to his player. He slid the disk inside, playing it low. He listened to the piano introduction, then the drum kick in, and then heard himself on trumpet, the soft murmur in the brass flirting with the piano. He tried to find what he'd heard the many times he'd listened to the disk, but the kid's voice was in his head. His sound was unoriginal. Rote. Circus pulled the CD from the player and cracked it in two.

* * *

A woman would sit in the audience or walk by the stage. Maybe it was her smile or her scent when she passed, the way she sipped her drink or shimmied her shoulders when she danced that would bring Circus to the right notes when he played that night. Once a woman's girlish giggle bubbled up from the back of a club and made Circus's horn coo. Another night, Peach tending bar at the Blind Fox wrapped her lips around a cherry in a way that made him reach the highest note he'd ever played and hold it until he thought his lungs might burst.

But the woman eyeing him from the bar as he played that night at the hotel made his sound messy, as if he were hurting instead of loving the brass. She was lanky with a blonde pixie haircut and wide, silly eyes blinking blue. Pretty, but another man's kind of pretty. He hadn't noticed her come in but had scanned the room after a solo and caught her staring back at him, already in some kind of love.

"Are you here with someone?" she asked when he stepped up to the bar at the end of the set and ordered a shot.

"I'm here with everyone."

"Be here now with me," she slurred, slapping the stool next to her, blue eyes glistening. "I just ditched my date in the restaurant across the street. He's probably still sitting staring at his phone not noticing I left. Funny, right? I just up and left, just . . ." She slurped the last of her cocktail, snickering into her straw. "He bored me, and I don't like to be bored. I told him I needed to powder my nose."

Circus knocked back the shot, then ordered two more, pretending the second was for the woman. He drank both when the bartender turned his back.

"Why don't you buy me a shot?" Her eyes narrowed as if she needed glasses but had forgotten to wear them.

Circus ordered another round. The woman clicked her glass against his and downed her drink before Circus had a chance to bring his to his lips.

"You're good." She pounded the empty glass on the bar. "I mean, the trumpet playing."

"Maybe."

"I wish I was good at something."

Circus knew this was the moment he was supposed to ask what it was she did or wanted to do, but he didn't have the energy. The room had cleared except for the pianist and bass player from the quartet and a couple kissing in the corner—a desolate scene, but less desolate than crossing Manhattan to his run-down hotel and heading up to his room alone.

He took a handful of peanuts from a bowl on the bar, tossed them into his mouth, then pushed the bowl toward the woman as an offering. When she took a nut between her manicured fingers, he noticed the charm bracelet around her wrist, a leaf, a heart, and a star dangling from the chain along with a thin plate with the name *Patsy* etched in script on its surface.

"You live around here?" he asked.

She shook her head. "Jersey City."

"You don't sound like you're from Jersey."

"I grew up in Mississippi. You probably can't hear my accent because school took it out of me. They don't like how the South sounds up here."

Circus detected the drawl, though he acted as if he hadn't, figuring she'd want it that way. "You're not still in school, are you?"

"It's been three years. Almost. Being out's a lot less exciting than I thought it'd be." She let out an exaggerated groan and crossed her eyes, a batty look he imagined she thought charming but that only made him regret sitting next to her.

"Get us more to drink," she said, clapping her hands against the bar. Circus ordered another round, reassuring the bartender he'd take care of the girl, who was growing drunker, though he was starting to have his own trouble sitting squarely on the stool as the buzz took hold.

"You don't look like you're from around here either," Patsy said. "Are you, like, Spanish or something? Or Dominican? Oh, that would be cool."

"You got it, doll." Circus took a toothpick from the bar and chomped it firmly between his teeth. "Dominican Republic's where I'm from."

A dazzle of light flashed in her eyes as she ogled him with a new fascination. "Santo Domingo must be amazing."

"It's something all right." Circus felt a little bored, though she had become prettier to him under the dull light. He watched her take a sloppy sip of her martini.

"You think he's still sitting over there?" she asked.

"Your fella? Damned if I know."

"You ever do that to a girl?"

"Probably."

An exaggerated pout twisted her mouth as she chased the olive around the bottom of her empty glass with a sword-shaped pick.

"Come on now," he said. "You women act like we're the only ones who ever did anything bad to anybody."

"I'm a little trickster then, aren't I?" she asked with another cross of her eyes. "What am I going to say to someone talking about molecular whatever it is he was talking about? Who knows what that even is? I bet he doesn't even like jazz. I haven't really heard much, but I liked what you were playing." She moved to the edge of her stool. "It sounded like you were making love to me."

The words were meant to move him, he knew, but they landed like a note played off-key.

"We should go somewhere," she whispered.

"It's late, doll. Not much open but hospitals and knees."

"This is New York, everything's open. And I have lots to drink back at my place."

"You wanna go all the way to Jersey?"

"Well, what do you want? I'm feeling wild tonight. Don't you want to start a riot?"

Circus looked into the woman's dewy eyes and wished she knew him in a way that would make it all right to answer truthfully. Maggie. He wanted to see Maggie. To call her. To tell her a joke over the phone and listen to her laugh. To feel the lush thrill as he made his way to her in the night. It was always best with Maggie, the fucking and the cozy aftermath in a sweltering room, the reaching out for her in the morning across a wide mattress. She was the only woman he spent the night with, and after all these years, she still made love to him in ways that made his body quake days later in the remembering. But more than lying in her bed, Circus wanted to tell her about his days, to be held and to nuzzle her neck.

Missing Maggie bothered him more than the kid in the studio, so he took Patsy's hand, guided her from the chair, and led her into a corridor where they wouldn't be seen. Her mouth tasted like the olives in her drink when he kissed her, but Circus kept on. When he opened his eyes, Patsy was unbuttoning her top to show herself to him.

"Let's make a memory." She nudged him toward the women's bathroom, and Circus let himself be pushed, pulling her into a stall and locking the door behind them. He slid his hand up her skirt, and Patsy gasped, her blue eyes reeling beneath her lashes. As he looked down at the woman delirious with pleasure and gin, as he heard their noise echo against the laminate panels of the stall, a cold sadness streamed through him. He pushed through it, gripping Patsy's ass so he could feel her breasts bounce against his chest. Eagerly, she squealed beneath him. The nothingness of it all was what he needed then to make everything right. The stinky fuck and hard, empty come.

Before he could unzip his pants, the girl bucked in his arms. She wheezed, went limp, then dropped onto the seat of the toilet, her head drooping against her chest as she fell quickly to sleep. Circus tapped her shoulder, shook her, called her name. Nothing. But before the panic could set in, Patsy woke up and blinked her eyes.

"Sorry," she said. "That happens sometimes."

"What wrong with you?"

"Sometimes when I get excited—"

Outside, the bathroom door creaked opened, and he covered Patsy's mouth, cursing himself for being in the room. He heard a woman's heels click across the floor, then heard the woman at the sink. He heard the rush of water, the wet rubbing together of her hands, the splash as she rinsed. He turned back to Patsy to signal for her to stay quiet, but she'd already fallen back to sleep. He listened to the woman at the sink drag a brush through her hair as a light hum sounded in her throat. He listened to her uncap a lipstick and remembered how he loved watching Maggie color her lips. The woman's phone rang.

"Is he still up?" her voice rasped. Circus closed his eyes to listen. "Put him on."

Patsy wriggled on the seat. Circus held her against him to keep her quiet.

"Why can't you sleep, baby boy?" The woman sweetened her voice as she spoke into the phone. "Yes, Mama's far. I'm so far away, it's another time where I am . . . look at your clock and tell me what time it is . . . that's right. Now guess what time it is here."

The trill of the woman's laugh put Circus at ease, and he imagined himself on the other end of the line.

"It's twelve-thirty here," she said. "Isn't that funny? We're in different times and different places, but here we are saying 'I love you.' Baby boy, will you go to sleep for Tía? Mama will be there when you get home from school tomorrow. . . . Do you want to say your prayers? Let's do it together."

Circus closed his eyes to listen, but the woman walked out of the room, the rasp of her voice trailing off. He peered down at Patsy, hoping she'd awakened so they could share whatever it was the woman had left behind, but she was asleep. He tried to pull himself from the corner of the stall where he'd hidden, but something weighed him down as if his will had left him, or something greater, like his spirit, like his very soul had ticked out gradually over the years so that now barely a trickle remained. His limbs quaked.

Gently, he positioned Patsy on the seat, then went back to the lounge for his horn. He asked the bartender to reserve a room and went back for Patsy, gathering enough strength to pick her up and carry her through the corridor into the lobby, where he told the night clerk to slip the room key into his back pocket. Cradling the woman in his arms brought back the nights he'd carried a sleeping Koko from her car seat to her bedroom, and a longing passed through him.

Patsy mumbled as Circus laid her in the hotel bed, tucking the blankets around her. He filled a glass with water from the minibar and placed it on the bedside table just as she reached out to him from under the sheets.

"You don't have to leave," she said. "It's warm here."

She looked up at him with her blue eyes, but there was no longer anything silly about them. He sensed the heat in the bed layered with blankets and pillows, and missed the feeling of sleeping next to someone, their bodies and breath in tune. But even though he could reach out to touch her, even though he only had to slide in bed beside her, he felt like he was looking into a warm room from the cold outside.

"What do you wish you were good at?" he asked.

"Hmm?"

"Earlier, you said you wished you were good at something," he said. "So what would it be?"

Her eyes blinked heavily. She was already fading. "I haven't figured that out yet."

Patsy snuggled into the blankets, and the delicate whimper that fell from her lips pulled him toward her but in a way that was too strong, too insistent, and Circus had a queasy feeling as if he were tumbling in a dream. He kissed Patsy's forehead, held the trumpet case against his chest, and made his way out of the room.

"Let me know when you do," he said, closing the door.

Places Where People Are Happy

*

Raquel

"Our old place," she said. "Twenty minutes."

Raquel hung up just as he whispered thank you on the other end of the line. She turned up the Buzzcocks vinyl playing on her stereo and finished her cigarette in the dark. She took her time with each drag. Let him wait. The hour she wasn't certain of, nor the day of the week, though the slim light coming through the slats in the blinds suggested morning was long over. A matchbox from one of last night's bars lay at the edge of the kitchen door she'd pulled from the hinges years ago to use as a coffee table, a name and address she didn't recognize scribbled on the back.

"Come by anytime," whoever it was had written.

Raquel pulled out a match, dragged it across the strip of sand on the box's side, savoring the tang of wood and fire that burrowed so deep inside her nostrils, her eyes watered. She brought the flame to the paper, then dropped it into an empty cup, watching the name burn to ash. Her head hurt. Her tongue tasted of bile. From the windowsill, she took a tin of aspirin, popped two into her mouth, and swallowed them with a lukewarm sip of coffee. Crossing the room to the antique trunk she'd kept since girlhood, she fished through the heap of clothes and pulled out an old muscle shirt and leather biker shorts she liked because of the way they held tight to her body. She dressed in front of the bathroom mirror, staring back at her eyes smudged with mascara and her skin thirsty after too many shots of cheap whiskey.

A glass of wine she'd poured at some point after coming home stood on the floor beside the tub, and she thought to drain it until her eyes found Zuzu's earrings stuck between the basin and the wall. She reached for the two tiny playing cards—the ace of diamonds and the queen of hearts—dangling from silver hooks as the memory of Zuzu picked at the calm Raquel had settled into that morning. Behind the flat of her sternum, plump beneath the bone, sat an ache she'd needed to dull or release since Zuzu left the month before, a soreness that she imagined like the tears her friends on Prozac always said they could never fully shed. The nights out were supposed to get rid of the ache, but every morning Raquel woke up to its swell.

She downed the wine and started out of the apartment but had only walked a few steps toward the door when she saw Zuzu's faux fur in the hallway, the butterscotch pelt in a heap on the floor like an animal curled up to sleep. She hadn't seen the coat since Zuzu left and couldn't remember why it lay there now. An ache in her belly grew so full it might have pitched her against the wall if not for her lingering buzz. Raquel slid into the coat and a pair of snakeskin boots and made her way out the door.

* * *

Circus Palmer sat on the back patio of the East Village diner chewing at the end of a toothpick, a glass of bourbon at his fingertips. He hadn't changed much in the two years since she'd last seen him, though age had started to line his face and stroke his hair with gray. He seemed on edge, his knee bouncing beneath the table and jaw tense around his powerful bite.

"It's been more than twenty minutes," he said when she took the seat across from him.

"But you're still here."

Circus folded his arms, his shoulders hunched as if his body were caving in on itself.

"Gimme one of those." She nodded toward the cigarette pack on the table.

He lit one for her and handed it over as his eyes scanned her body. "Looks like you haven't slowed down."

"I'm out Friday night, I'm in Sunday morning." She took a sip of his drink, watching as he cracked the toothpick between his teeth. "So what's wrong with you?"

Before he could answer, a waiter approached the table, awkwardly yanking at the hem of his apron. "Ma'am, you can't smoke out here."

"I come here all the time. Benny lets me." Raquel kept her gaze fixed on Circus, who had retreated into his thoughts. She ran her foot up the length of his calf to bring him back, and he flinched as if wrenched from a dream.

"Bring me something with whiskey in it." Raquel tugged the waiter's necktie. "And a plate of fried eggs. Lots of salt."

The waiter glanced at her cigarette, and she figured the regret in his eyes came from a wish to either challenge her or take a drag. Cheeks reddening, he went back inside the restaurant.

Circus slipped the toothpick from his mouth, pointing it at her. "You haven't changed."

"Why would I?"

He crushed the empty cigarette pack in his hand. "How do you live here, man? It's bananas, this town. Madness."

"Come on, you're a big boy. And this town's a pussycat. Nothing's gone on in years."

He eyed the cigarette as she took a drag. "Today I saw a dude try to jump in front of a train at the Canal Street station. Someone grabbed him before he . . . fell."

"Is that all? Be glad for him, honey. He gets another swing at the ball."

The corner of his mouth lifted as if he thought he should smile but couldn't.

"So," he asked, "whose bed did I get you out of this afternoon?"

"Don't flatter yourself. You're not worth getting out of someone else's bed." Raquel blew a line of smoke across the table. "You wouldn't have liked her. It was quick, just how I like it."

"You're worse than me."

"I had to send her away, be by myself for a while." Her voice quaked though she'd meant to seem unmoved. She stamped out the cigarette, then immediately craved another as a breeze wafted a hint of Zuzu's amber perfume from the fibers of the faux fur. Raquel took off the coat and slung it across the back of her chair. "I only like about eight people anyway."

Circus chuckled and reached for her hand. "I missed you."

"Well, that's a crock. You only remember me when you're here."

"And how often do I cross your mind?"

"Don't make me hurt your feelings."

Circus Palmer. Uneasy as he seemed, she still wanted to take him to bed just as she had the first night she saw him plugging his ears at a punk show in Brooklyn fifteen years before. She'd noticed him because he seemed out of place in his loose jacket and Blue Note T-shirt, but Raquel soon discovered he liked being where no one expected him to be, liked the way it rattled him. Sitting with him now, she understood she'd come to meet him out of a reflex that reached back to when they used to phone each other and meet after the bars closed. Back then, Raquel was a session singer staggering toward the end of a coke habit that Circus picked up before he crashed and went back to Boston. She used to let him into her bed because he had a strong body and a thick cock, because he gave her the roughness she liked without needing it to mean anything, because he knew music and made her laugh on occasion. But she didn't like him. He was vain without deserving it, frightened by living though he tried to be hard. Their encounters during his occasional visits to New York in the years that followed were tied to that distant time, and Raquel groped for whatever was back there that might fuel him now because she was sitting there needing to get rough.

"How's your kid?" she asked.

"Fine, I guess. How am I supposed to tell? She's a teenager now. That's when you people start becoming women, right?"

"And what are you going to do about it?"

"Fail. Fail probably." He spun his spoon against the edge of the table. "I told her about you. She's been into punk lately. Wants to meet interesting people."

"Aren't you interesting enough?"

The waiter brought a plate of eggs and an old-fashioned. Raquel slid a bite into her mouth, studying Circus as he combed his fingers through his beard.

"I can't get this picture out of my head of that back room at the Dirty Kiss," he said. "Peacock Evans was onstage going to town on his horn. There was this cat in the audience not paying attention, right, he's just yammering on about Lord knows what to his woman. Peacock stops playing. Just cold stops. The crowd gets quiet, man, you could hear a pin drop. Peacock hangs back like he knew this was some high drama he was fixin' to stage, then he walks right up to the table. 'You got two options: leave of your own accord or let me show you the door. Either way, the pretty girl stays with me.'"

Raquel sensed the old charge she used to feel when Circus told his stories, the heat that seemed to rise in his body and the spark in his eyes.

"The other cat tries to start something," he went on. "Now Peacock, so the legend goes, he could throw down in his day. But when I met him, he wasn't no spring chicken. So here comes me, right, I've been in New York all of two weeks, a young lion not long out of Conservatory. The cat comes at him with a right hook, but I block it, take a swing, and clock that motherfucker square in the jaw. That big dude who used to work the door tries to throw me out with the other cat, but Peacock says, 'You ain't taking him.' Next thing I know, I'm on stage playing trumpet next to Peacock goddamn Evans."

Circus sat back in his seat, stretching his fingers as if he'd just thrown the punch.

Raquel lit another cigarette, drew from it, and passed it to him. "You tell that story every time you come to New York."

"It's a great story. Maybe the last great story I've been able to tell."

He took a slow drag. The smoke trailed from his lips, and with it, Raquel imagined, went the heat.

"I can't figure out what it was we saw in this place." He scanned the patio. "A little square for you, ain't it?"

"I used to live around the corner," she said. "Me and this diner have lots of history. Back when I was a kid and couldn't get any work, I used to steal food whenever the cook went back to the kitchen. Cream pies and pudding cups from the glass case. They used to have one of those old lady cake stands with banana bread and iced cookies under the lid. I took those."

"I remember that apartment. Wasn't much but a room with a mattress on the floor."

"It was simple and right. I miss those mornings. Waking up all alone, just before the sun comes up. Listening to the wild parrots gossip in the trees outside my window."

He watched her take a drag, leaning in close. He looked old and beat-up, his skin grayed and dry, yet he still looked at her like he had the right to have her if he wanted, which made her dislike him as powerfully as she wanted him.

"I think about seeing you the first time at that club in Queens," he said. "You walking across the floor, looking like trouble. You told me to come home with you, said you were good luck."

Raquel ashed the cigarette, smiling in spite of herself. "I am good luck."

Circus laughed easily then, his body softening as he sank back in the chair. Then the edge seemed to hit again, and he folded his hands behind his head, letting out a dull sigh. "I turned forty back in February."

"And?" she asked. "I'll be fifty in November."

"You ain't bothered?"

"Why would I be? It's only time."

He picked up the lighter from the table, fondling the spark wheel with his thumb. "Things can still happen, right?"

"Things are always happening."

"But is it good? You all right with how everything played out?"

"That's not what I care about," Raquel said, impatient. "I live how I want, I do things I like to do. I don't worry about the world or Armageddon or what I thought was meant to happen. I just rock, man. Sometimes when the monsters need to come out and play, I go onstage and let them free. People listen sometimes. I just play, that's what I do. Just rock, man. Just go, go, go."

Circus's eyes were trained on her, and the way he was watching made her feel caught in a lie, as if he could sense the pounding beneath her breastbone. She tossed the balled cigarette pack into a bin in a corner to distract them both but missed, and the pack rolled back to them.

"It's just that things are starting to weigh on me in a way they didn't used to," he said.

"Don't bother me with your troubles," she said and pushed her toes into his crotch. He caressed instead of grabbed them, so she pulled her foot away.

Circus retreated into himself again, his gaze on the ground. Raquel left him to it. She spotted a bruise blossoming purple on her thigh and traced it with her finger, trying to recall what had happened the night before to cause it and pushing her thumb into its violet center so the pain would come again and remind her.

Circus pulled his phone from his pocket, scrolled through a series of pictures, lingered on one, then handed it to her. She recognized Maggie Swan in the photo, smiling from the other side of a table lit by candlelight.

"That's still going on?"

Circus nodded as a vein at his temple quaked.

"Lucky son of a bitch," she said. "I heard she's touring again with Tip Badgett."

"Apparently."

Maggie Swan had a way about her. Raquel had seen it in person at a party in Brooklyn years before, a vibrant light everyone around her seemed to chase. Even on the small screen of Circus's phone, Raquel had an impulse to go after it in the same way she'd wanted what shone inside Zuzu. But in Zuzu, there was fluorescence rather than fire, a light that came not from heat but from cold, like a constant run of electricity. She had been humming with it when she arrived at Raquel's door, backpack slung over her shoulder, freshly arrived from Beijing. A photographer friend had hired Zuzu for a shoot after seeing her bee-stung lips in a perfume ad and paid Raquel to let her sleep on her sofa. Zuzu, deafened by disease as a girl, never spoke during the three weeks she stayed in the apartment, so Raquel came to know her through the charge she gave off as she walked through the halls. Though Zuzu was peculiar—she wore a different wig each day, collected books in languages she didn't know, bathed in cold water—she wasn't peculiar in a way that normally intrigued Raquel, who liked unruliness and danger over quirk. It was the silence that bothered Raquel, the incessant hush thickening the air as Zuzu passed her notes instead of speaking, the soft patter of Zuzu's bare feet on floors and the sighs she made alone in her room. Silence enclosed the young woman, barely thirty, yet she seemed so content inside the quiet that Raquel began to fantasize what was in there and what would happen if she was let in.

Raquel slid the phone back across the table. "Why are we talking about Maggie Swan?"

Circus stared at the screen. "I knocked her up."

He glanced over as if he expected surprise, but Raquel only ashed her cigarette into his empty glass. "I always figured there were children all over the world you don't know about."

Circus ticked his tongue. "I'm careful. Maggie's the only one I let things slip with."

"So what are you doing about it?"

"I don't know. We haven't been talking."

"Since when?"

"More than two months by now. I left her in Miami after she told me."

Raquel fought the urge to toss her drink into his face, to spill her eggs into his lap as he sat there like a dejected boy. "You're a class act, bub."

"Sometimes I think she's too good for me," he said.

"She is. She's a rock star and you play in shithole bars in a tiny shithole town. She's massive, you're a tiny boy. You're lucky you ever got to touch her."

The corner of Circus's mouth pinched, and Raquel was pleased to see him hurt. "Show me the other pictures," she said.

"Other pictures?"

"Your other women. I want to look at sexy girls."

"There aren't any," he said. "Not of faces anyway."

"Only Maggie."

"I like to look at the picture sometimes."

"And why?"

"I like looking at pretty things," he said.

"Then why don't you have a picture of a sunset or a starfish?"

"Because it's Maggie."

Raquel watched him take a bite from the plate, watched a dab of oil drip down his chin.

"You're a fool," she said.

* * *

On the train back to Brooklyn, Raquel sucked a raspberry lollipop and sipped coffee from a paper cup as the car bucked against the tracks. There was a time she used to look forward to rides on the subway because of the overheard conversations and missed stops that delivered her to new places, the brief threats of violence, of seduction, of connection that provoked and reshaped her. But over the years she came to find comfort standing alone in the car during those isolated stretches of time when all the city's disparate souls were thrown together, locked beneath the earth's surface and away from their lives, sequestered momentarily as if in a respite from the task of living.

There had been times, too, when Circus Palmer accompanied her during late-night trips home, their arms and fingers and tongues entwined, embarrassing other passengers. But now they sat on opposite sides of the aisle, every so often nodding like strangers noticing each other with only the faintest interest. Next to Circus, a man let his eyes ride Raquel's shinbone up between her legs, then turned away when she parted her knees to tease him. Circus noticed, gave her a dutiful tsk, then went back to reading the dated sign above her head celebrating the New Year. Raquel found the bruise on her thigh again, pushing into the violet. All she felt was numb.

* * *

What was left of a brief spring rain steamed the windows of her apartment, and Raquel watched the drops shimmy down the glass. On her back, knees lifted, she pressed down on Circus's head so he would bury his tongue deeper inside her and find the right spot. When she opened her eyes and saw him, whatever sweetness she'd found went away. There was no reason for what they were doing. The pleasure would rise and fall, but her world before and after would remain unchanged. Raquel kept her eyes shut, concentrating on the feel of Circus's skilled tongue until she sensed the rise of heat, widening her legs to tighten the muscles at her hips so she could reach for the come, but she couldn't find it.

He hadn't kissed her. She hadn't wanted him to. They'd walked arm in arm from the subway station to her apartment, but the link was loose, routine. She'd poured them each a drink, then slipped out of the leather shorts before Circus could say anything else about the man on the subway, about turning forty, about Maggie Swan. She'd placed the glass of wine on the floor beside the sofa, then slid out of Zuzu's coat, dropping it to her feet, as Circus dropped to his knees in front of her.

Now he backed away and told her to take off her boots. Raquel slipped them off and slipped off the shirt, eager for the calloused touch of his fingers, though when he pinched her nipple, she felt only the dull snap of skin. Circus gazed at the span of her collarbone like a pillow where he wanted to rest his head. Before she could turn away, he looked into her eyes as if he needed to say something but didn't know how. Then he climbed into her lap like a dog unaware of its size.

"What are you doing?" she asked.

"Just put your arms around me."

"I don't want to." Raquel pushed him. "Do something to me. Something I can feel."

Circus lay back on the opposite end of the sofa, cradling the mound of his belly. He reminded her of a spoiled child, pouting and twiddling his thumbs. She thought of telling him to leave until he leaned forward and said, "Get on the floor."

Raquel lowered herself to the floor.

Circus took a magazine that lay beside him on the sofa and rolled it tight. "Come here."

She crept toward him, tingling at the thought of what he might do next.

"Not so fast," he said. "I'm watching."

She slowed her pace, thrilling against the scruff of the carpet on her knees.

Circus took a cigarette from a pack on the coffee table and slid it between his lips. "The girl you sent away. What's her name?"

Raquel stopped. A vein beneath Circus's eye twitched, and he smirked when he realized he'd struck something. A light chuckle sounded in his throat as he nodded to himself, pleased, and lit the cigarette. He spooled the magazine again and slapped it against his palm. Sliding it beneath her chin, he lifted her face to meet his.

"Where did she touch you?" he asked. "Show me."

He stared at her mouth as if it were a fruit he wanted to sink his teeth into.

"I said, show me." He nudged her, and Raquel toppled onto the faux fur. Her fall awakened the grains of Zuzu's amber perfume that clung to the weave of the coat's shell, reminding her how it had landed in the hallway floor. The night before she'd pulled it from the closet to bury her face in the pelt.

"You're not fooling me, I can see it in your eyes." Circus hovered over her, teeth bared like a canine cornering its prey. "You didn't tell her to go. She left. She didn't want you."

Raquel looked up without knowing what she needed from him. She'd needed to tell someone about Zuzu. How she'd whispered "I love you" to the girl's back as she stirred a pan of spaghetti in the kitchen or disappeared down the hall to her bedroom at day's end. How she'd screamed "I love you" from her bed at night and listened to her voice echo against the walls. How much it hurt not to touch or be touched as the girl lay beside her on the sofa, giggling at the television, cradled by her world without sound. But Circus wasn't the person to tell.

"What do you know?" She kicked him in the shin. "You're a frightened dog who can't go a night without some woman petting him behind the ears."

Circus yanked the scarf from around his neck, glaring as he held her wrists behind her back, then bound them.

"And now?" she asked, calmed by the quiet thrum of her own voice. "Do you feel like a strong boy?" Raquel rose to her feet. "Untie me."

Circus poured himself more wine from the bottle on the coffee table, his fingers nervously drumming out a rhythm on the side of his glass. Finally, he stepped behind her to loosen the knot of the scarf. Raquel sensed the delicate slide of the fabric from her wrists.

"Hand me my boots," she said.

Circus pushed them toward her with his foot.

"Pick them up."

He gave her a look, took them from the floor, then slid them onto her feet.

"Take off your clothes," she said.

Circus shook his head.

"Take off your clothes."

He crossed his arms over his chest.

"Take them off. Or go."

* * *

Circus sat naked in the chair Raquel made him drag from the kitchen into the living room, his wrists tied to the back with a pair of her stockings. She'd switched off all the lights except for one slender beam from a floor lamp pointed at him.

"Open your legs," she said from the sofa.

"I don't like this anymore."

A clock on the bookshelf ticked as night loomed outside the window and began to swallow them in gray colors. Eyes closed, Circus gently parted his legs, limp but starting to rise. Raquel plucked a handful of grapes from a plate on the cushion beside her, eating them one by one as Circus groaned, his stomach busy with nerves.

"Tell me where Maggie touches you," she said. "Tell me what she does that you like."

"I'm not talking about Maggie."

"I want to imagine the two of you." Raquel went to him, walking her fingers up his thighs. "Tell me what she thinks is so special about you."

"Not a goddamn thing."

"Yet she let you give her a child."

"She won't keep it."

"Why not?"

"I told her not to." Circus's voice cracked, and he pitched forward like he'd been sucker-punched. The air went out of the room. Time seemed to lock around them. Raquel wondered if he might be sick.

"It's probably already gone," he whimpered. "She got rid of it. She got rid of me."

"Then you're glad."

Slowly, Circus lifted his head, nostrils flaring. The sight made Raquel's fingers tingle.

"Fuck you," he mumbled, and his eyes watered. Raquel watched as he shook his head back and forth, pulling at his tied wrists.

"I'm awful," he cried, his voice hoarse. "I'm fucking nothing. You're right, I'm shit."

His body lurched forward when she walked back to the sofa.

"Stay here," he begged. "Hurt me if you need to. Let me have it. Just get it out of me."

Raquel lay on the sofa and pulled Zuzu's coat over her body.

"Get it out," he pleaded.

Raquel turned off the floor lamp and nestled into the coat, immersing herself in the warm rinse of darkness.

"Fuck you, man," he whimpered, more to himself, it seemed, than to her. "Goddamn you."

Raquel listened to Circus's moan, the richness of it like sugar in cream. Under the blanket, eyes closed, she stroked her skin. Her body hummed as she pushed her finger into the bruise on her thigh and sensed the pain of the wound blossom. She was in her body, there she was again in her flesh and belly and blood. What had bulged beneath her ribcage, she let come now, let it crack the surface and pierce the bone.

"There it is," she said and opened her eyes.

Birthday
Girl

*

Koko

The day after Koko's fifteenth birthday, two bombs went off during the marathon in Boston, eight miles from where she lived with her mother. She was at the mall buying a bottle of perfume called Reckless when her mother phoned to see if Koko had heard from her father and to tell her to come home. Koko bicycled through the streets, her legs—made clumsy by their pubescent lengthening out—now worked effortlessly, spurred on by fear. The television was on when she got home, her mother chewing at the palm of her fist and watching the footage play on a loop. The crack of the blasts at the finish line made Koko jump, while the gush of smoke swelling in the air reminded her of a dream she had had once of ghosts. The shattered glass and wrecked sidewalks, the rupture of people and clamor of screams began to haunt her until she grabbed hold and pushed it all firmly away, like so many other awful things. Still, the chill of it all made her forget for the moment that her father had forgotten her special day.

Four days after the blasts, school was canceled, and no one was allowed to leave their houses as the police searched for the bombers. Koko watched news footage of the two suspects crossing the sidewalk near the marathon finish line, backpacks strapped to their shoulders. A photo of the second suspect flashed onto the screen as Koko nibbled at her thumbnail and a tickle rolled through her belly.

Have you seen him? Koko sent a text message to Bree. *The younger one. He's beautiful.*

Just thinking the same thing, Bree replied.

No one so beautiful would do this. He must be innocent.

He better hope so.

Koko's mother blustered into the room, a gust of breathy sobs and wet tissues tumbling from quaking hands. Her robe flapped behind her as she sipped an orange juice with a splash of vodka Koko could smell. She hadn't left the house or changed clothes since the bombings.

"I can't get hold of your father." Her mother's birdish trill always sounded more brittle when she was frightened or needed something, which was often. "You try him."

"He doesn't answer me either."

Her mother pulled the phone from the pocket of her robe and dialed. "Circus, we need you here. Goddamn it, look what's happened. Those guys are out there somewhere. What if they come here, what would we do? Your family needs you."

Through the sheer cloth of her mother's nightgown, Koko watched the footage of the blast play again on television, the crack of the bomb, the plume of smoke, the bodies rushing. Her mother tossed the phone onto the sofa, let out a raw cry, then slunk back through the hall toward her bedroom. Koko tried to take the scene in as something real, as an actual event that had occurred a mere bicycle ride away from where she watched on television. But a bombing couldn't happen. Not in real life.

Only the face of the younger boy seemed fathomable, the smooth milk and honey skin, the slinky mouth and tousle of dark hair, the shadowy eyes lit with danger. Koko imagined he was looking back at her through the TV screen, and she blushed as if she had a fever, though it felt good.

Impatient, she texted Bree. *I want to find him.*

Nuts.

I need to meet him.

As if.

We're smart, we know people. Someone we know must know him, she wrote. *Whoever finds him first, wins.*

* * *

Hours later the suspects were identified—two brothers, nineteen and twenty-six, the elder one killed by police. The nineteen-year-old had escaped to the town where Koko lived, so soldiers were searching her neighborhood door to door while she found him online—photos from the boy's prom and wrestling matches, a picture of his family cat. She found the high school he went to and sent messages to everyone she knew with connections there. No one knew anything. On the boy's Twitter feed, she found a quote he'd posted a month before the bombing that read, "If you have the knowledge and the inspiration all that's left is to take action." Koko wrote the words in permanent marker on her forearm, then quickly covered them with her sleeve when her mother called from her bedroom.

Koko grumbled and went to her. Lying on her side beneath a pile of blankets, her knees at her chest like a diseased child, her mother said, "What a disappointment everything has turned out to be, hasn't it?"

"I don't know."

"Sweetheart, will you bring me an aspirin?"

"They know their names," Koko called on her way to the bathroom.

"Monsters."

"I think he's beautiful," she said when she got back to the bedroom.

Her mother lifted her head from the pillow. "Who?"

"The younger one."

"You're out of your mind."

"We don't know if he did anything. And if he did, I'm sure there was a reason."

"What possible reason could there be?"

"I don't know. Someone must have hurt him."

Her mother downed the aspirin with a swig of the vodka orange juice, then drifted back onto the pillow. "I haven't slept. I'm starving. I haven't eaten since yesterday. Where's your father? Why isn't he thinking of us? I'm so, so hungry." She reached out, and Koko loosely took her hand. "We're so alone, you and me, aren't we? I'm sorry, sweet girl, I didn't want us to be so alone. This wasn't how anything was supposed to turn out."

Koko slid her hand from her mother's clammy fingers and folded her arms over her chest. Even sick and drunk she was still pretty, her mother, her blonde hair flowing over the silk pillow-case, gold-colored and shimmering like some holy light. "Do you want me to make you something to eat? Tomato soup from the other night?"

"Would you do that for me?" Her mother sniffled. "That would be so nice."

Koko went to the kitchen and took the pot of soup from the fridge as her mother's phone rang. Hoping it was her father, she ran to the living room to answer.

"Darling!" Her grandmother's voice boomed at her. "How are you?"

"Okay, I guess."

"How absolutely terrible." Koko could hear her grandmother exhale one of the cigarettes she kept in a chrome case, the ones that smelled like clove. "Darling, there are terrible, terrible people in the world, but we mustn't allow them to frighten us. That's what they want, and we mustn't give those brutes anything they want."

"I'm not scared," Koko said. "I know one of them."

"My God, Koko, call the police."

"Well, I don't really know him. I just feel like I do. And I don't think he's terrible."

Silence on the other end of the line, an exhalation of smoke. "Put your mother on."

Koko brought the phone to her mother and went back to the kitchen.

"I've already called and he's not answering," she heard her mother say. "Why do you ask when you know I have no idea where he is? You just want to torture me."

Koko slid on her headphones and listened to her favorite song of the week, the one about kids shooting kids, the one with the easy beat, the one her dad liked to whistle. As she stirred a dollop of cream into the tomato soup, she imagined the younger suspect at the front door, and a shiver passed through her. He would look down at her ready to defend himself and see she wasn't afraid. He would sense how she could see he was gentle deep down, that she understood him. She would sneak him into her room and make him something to eat, watch him take a bath, wash his back. If her mother came in, she would hide him under the bed. At night, she would crawl under to sleep beside him.

Did you see the latest photo? Bree texted. *Oh my god, wicked hot.*

Koko turned off the burner and ran back to the living room television. In the photo, the boy wore a black graduation gown with a red carnation in the lapel, handsome with a smirk on his pout of a mouth. She was slightly sick, slightly thrilled.

I love him, Koko typed.

Her mother blustered down the hallway to the front closet and put on a down winter coat.

"You're cold?" Koko asked.

"No." Her mother curled up on the sofa. "We should stop watching."

"Did you hear from Dad?"

"Guess." She groaned watching the footage of the suspects crossing the sidewalk with their bomb-packed backpacks and used the remote to turn down the volume.

"Mom?" Koko started nervously. "Can I tell you something? It's kinda private, but I want to tell someone."

"Of course, you can tell me anything."

"You won't be mad?"

"Tell me, sweet girl."

There was a lump in Koko's throat. "I know I don't know him, but I feel like I miss him. Is that weird? I just miss him."

"Miss who?"

Koko nodded toward the image of the boy on television.

Her mother tsked. "You don't know what you're talking about."

"Don't you feel bad for him? Just a little bit? I mean, he's only nineteen."

"He can go to hell for all I care," her mother said. "He's evil. You don't know evil yet, but I can tell you, that's the face of it."

Koko's throat thickened with tears, but she swallowed them. She'd learned early on, her mother was the crier in the family.

"Sweet girl," her mother said, "come sit with me. We can keep each other safe."

"You don't know how to protect anyone."

Tears bloomed in her mother's eyes. "Why won't any of you care for me? I try so hard."

"You don't understand anything." Koko was on her feet, yelling instead of crying. "He doesn't have anyone. He needs people behind him. He needs someone to stand up for him, to believe in him. To fucking love him. No one's got his back."

"Dear God, I hope they get that boy soon." Her mother pinched the bridge of her nose. "I don't know how much more of this I can take."

Koko's phone buzzed. She prayed it was her father. He would understand. He knew how complex life could be. But it wasn't a message from her father. It was Bree.

I found him.

* * *

Bree's message said Jenny Parker lived near the suspects' uncle over by the high school, and the rumor was the boy was hiding there. Bree sent the address.

I'm going. Koko texted back. *I want to be with him before they catch him. Maybe they won't catch him.*

They'll catch him.

I want to be with him.

That would be so rad. You'd be famous.

That's not why. Koko stared at the photo of the boy in his graduation grown. *I want to make a bed out of his hair and swim through his eyes. I want to hold him, to tell him everything will be okay.*

Well, it won't, Bree texted. *He'll be in jail soon. Or dead.*

Koko switched off her phone to ignore whatever else her friend had to say. She went to her room and slid into a leather miniskirt, cowboy boots, and a T-shirt with the word FREAK scrawled on the front, a touch she thought the boy would appreciate. Bree called it her Fuck Me Gear, which she'd put together after her adventure with Ian, the boy on Sanibel Island—a style worn in contrast to her saintly looking mother, who didn't seem the kind of woman to be since her father barely came around. Koko had spent the birthday money her aunt had given her to buy straightener for her hair, wax for her upper lip, and a kit to shape her eyebrows. Knowing the boy would soon see her, she was glad she had. She checked herself in the mirror and packed the boy a turkey sandwich along with a sweatshirt and a box of bandages in case he was hurt. She checked to make sure her mother was still transfixed by the television and went to her room to steal the bottle of vodka and a credit card from her wallet.

Just then her mother's phone rang. Koko stood motionless in the other room. If it was her father, she would consider it a sign and stay. If not, she would go.

"Hello?" her mother answered sleepily. "Yes, Mother, I've locked all the windows."

Koko slipped out the back door.

* * *

She pedaled her bicycle through the deserted streets, the brilliance of the spring day hollowed out by the stark absence of life.

Everyone was inside their homes. She could sense the jangling of nerves behind bolted doors and windows. The silence, punctured every few minutes with the scream of sirens in the distance, rattled her, so she focused on the smooth grip of her bicycle tires on the road. She stopped to sip the vodka, not enough to truly taste it but enough to imagine it kept her focused. The address was in the next town over. She continued on her bicycle, passing by a cemetery and through a playground where she was spooked by children's toys abandoned in midplay—a pair of badminton rackets, a tricycle, a basketball under a hoop. Farther on an old woman on a cell phone watched her, mouth hanging open, from the window of an apartment as Koko passed. Her palms were sweating on the handlebars, her pulse ticking mightily in her throat. But she kept on.

A fleet of police cars rushed toward her on the main road, sirens crying. Koko steered her bicycle into an empty lot behind a gas station to wait for them to pass, fearing the boy might have heard the sirens, too, and would move on. She imagined him trembling in an alleyway praying to God. Imagined him hidden in the toolshed of a stranger's house. Imagined him halfway to Canada. Koko climbed back onto her bicycle and raced to the address.

* * *

The house was unremarkable, with green awnings and decayed brick, a pale yellow door. The porch was teeming with potted trees and plants, strands of green leaves and tangled stems that crawled over the rails and banisters as if the earth had opened up and sprung through the slatted floor. On the front stoop, a dirty white cat twitched its tail, then slinked away. The windows of the house were dark except for a light in a tiny window on the attic floor. The boy must have been hiding there.

In a schoolyard across the street, Koko laid her bicycle in the shadows of a tree and picked at her lip, pulse drumming, as she waited for courage to walk to the door. She took a generous sip of the vodka, retched, then went up the steps and knocked. When no one answered, she knocked again, then backed up into the yard to see if there was movement in the attic window. Someone had switched off the light. She knocked one last time, then pulled a pen from her backpack and scribbled onto an envelope she found in the mailbox.

I'm here, she wrote. *I believe in you. Flash the light to give me a sign, and I'll come up. Love from Koko.*

She opened the screen door and dropped the note inside before heading back across the street to her bicycle to wait. The house remained still. Lying in the grass, Koko watched whipped-cream clouds slowly somersault over the roof of the house and imagined the boy lying beside her holding her hand. She thought of him in his graduation gown, thought of him pinning his red carnation to her prom dress in a few years, imagined dancing with her head against his shoulder, his arms strung around her waist. What was he thinking? she wondered.

Koko closed her eyes, giddy but slowed by the vodka. She peeked up at the house one last time before drifting, unwillingly, to sleep.

* * *

She wasn't sure how much time had passed when she woke up. The sky was starting to find its predusk blue, dreamy and cold above her. Everything everywhere was still silent. When she switched on her phone, it chimed with messages from her mother and a text sent ninety minutes before from Bree.

Where are you? the message read.

At the house, Koko texted back.

Bree replied, *What house?*

His uncle's house.

Shit, Ko, didn't you get my text? News says the kid isn't anywhere near there.

Then where is he?

Just go home and be safe.

Koko tossed the phone back into her backpack, her throat swelling with tears. She swallowed them with a sip of water and got back onto her bicycle, slowly making her way through the streets farther from home. Turning onto a main road, she looked through the windows of a Laundromat, an Italian restaurant, and a pet shop, all of them empty. Even the gas station at the corner was lifeless. The whole planet seemed to have gone and left her behind.

Up ahead, Koko saw a flickering light and pedaled toward it, arriving at a tattoo shop with curtains drawn, a neon sign out front sputtering. A man inside sat in front of a television. She could see him through the glass door, which she banged on, and the man jumped before clomping over to answer.

"What are you doing out here?" He sounded like a parent, even with his hulkish body covered in tattoos. He pulled her inside, locking the door behind her.

Koko tugged at her earring, glancing past him instead of into his eyes. "I want a tattoo."

"You shouldn't be out here. Do your folks know where you are?"

"Yeah." She caught sight of the television where footage of the bombings played. "So can I get a tattoo?"

"What the hell kinda tattoo do you want so bad to come out in this?"

Koko lifted her sleeve to show him the quotation. *All that's left is to take action.*

"How old are you?"

"I just turned eighteen."

"I'll ask you again."

Koko blushed when she saw the boy's photograph on the screen. "Fifteen."

"Well, I can't give you a tattoo without your parents' permission."

"They're okay with it. Please," her voice cracked. "I need to get it."

The man followed her stare toward the boy's photo on the screen, the graduation gown, the carnation. He looked back at Koko, a vein in his neck throbbing. "Tell you what. We don't need to tell your parents so long as you give me some basic info. Protects me, see. Just your name, birth date, an emergency number. That'll do. Cool?"

He handed her a slip of paper where she wrote down her birth date and home phone number. "I'm Koko."

"Lemme go get the equipment ready." On his way out of the room, the man took the television remote and flipped to a music station. "You don't need to see any of that."

On the waiting room sofa, Koko flipped through a magazine past photos of women with tigers inked down the length of their legs and tattooed college girls in fishnet stockings. She saw herself as one of them, traipsing down the hallway of her school past Natalie and Millicent and Kima, who would watch her and wonder what she knew now that they didn't. She imagined a thorny rose painted over the length of her thigh. The boy would like it.

"Just gotta give the equipment a chance to heat up," the man said when he came back several minutes later. With his elbows on his chubby knees, he looked like a bullfrog sitting in the folding chair. "This channel cool with you?"

She nodded and took the sweatshirt from her backpack, draping it across her knees. Absently, she watched the music on the screen, struggling again to keep her eyes open.

"How long will it take till you're ready?" she asked.

"Haven't used the machinery all day, could take an hour to be ready. But we'll get that tattoo on you."

The man didn't say much, only glanced every so often at text messages on his cell phone and checked a compass-shaped clock on the wall. Koko pulled up her sleeve and traced her fingers across the quote, picturing daisies laced through the words.

Twenty minutes later there was a knock at the door. The shape behind the glass in the window seemed to cast a beam of light into the room, and Koko saw the towering body. She saw the mess of dark hair and immense shoulders. She saw a warrior, a titan, saw him as she always had. A king.

The tattooed man unlocked the door, and her father stepped into the room.

* * *

The ride in the car started in silence, her father's jaw pulsing as he kept his gaze fixed firmly, angrily to the road. Koko toyed with the ties of her sweatshirt, wanting him to speak first.

"Are you mad?" she asked.

"We're not supposed to be on the roads. We're breaking the law being out here. You know that, don't you? You're lucky you weren't in Watertown where the feds are looking."

"What'd Mom tell you?"

"Who knows? I couldn't hear anything through the blubbering. Barely got the address to the tattoo parlor."

Koko gazed at the houses on the street as they passed, each of them lit with the glare of televisions beaming through windows. "You forgot my birthday."

"Huh?"

"My birthday was Sunday."

"Is that why you did this?" He cursed himself. "I'm sorry, baby. I'll make it up to you."

"Were you worried about me?"

"Shit, of course."

"Then why didn't you call? Mom tried to reach you."

He wrapped his knuckles against the steering wheel. Being around her always seemed to make him nervous, as if she had him on a leash he wanted to chew through. "I got a lot going on, Koko. I think about you all the time, baby, but there's, you know, so much going on." He glanced over at her. "You're shaken up, huh?"

"A little."

"This kinda thing messes with grown-ups, too." He put a hand on her knee, squeezed. "I just needed to be someplace I could wrap my mind around it, you know. Feel all right."

"How come that place isn't home with us?"

He took a toothpick from his pocket and started gnawing at it, letting several moments of silence pass again between them. "So what are you, fifteen now?"

"Yeah."

"How's it feel?"

"Okay, I guess."

He let out a low chuckle. "I remember fifteen. Wasn't one of my best years, but I can tell you, it gets easier. Don't get me wrong," he said, his voice melodious now, warm. "There's still lots that's hard, but you just start to realize you're getting closer to when you're in control of things. You know you're gonna be free one day."

They drove in silence a bit farther. Koko kept her gaze outside the window. "Where are we going?"

"I got a friend in Waltham. He's got a place we can rest till the streets open again. He's a good guy, you'll dig him. There's a pool, you can dip your feet."

"Cool," Koko mumbled, looking around inside the Buick. As always, the car was cluttered with her father's life—sheet music strewn on the floor, wires crammed into the deck beneath the rear window, suits in a garment bag hanging from a hook, boxes filled with copies of his CDs. Only the trumpet case was set apart from the rest of the clutter. Koko had always loved to watch her father play—liked the sight more than the sound, imagining the horn made from elephant tusk and her father a medieval hero blowing into it to announce the hunt. The case, strapped safely behind a seatbelt in the back seat, was a source of life. She could sense it like another body in the car.

"Does your mother know you were gonna get a tattoo?" he asked.

"Not really."

He shook his head back and forth, a slight smile on his lips. "What were you gonna get?"

Koko pulled up her sleeve.

He stopped at a red light and read the quote. "Where'd you hear that?"

"The second bomber." She was blushing again. "The younger one. He wrote it."

The smile on her father's face faded. He cracked the toothpick in half with his teeth and tossed it into the ashtray.

Koko got a strange pleasure having shocked him. "I love him," she pushed harder.

"The bomber?"

"The younger one," Koko said. "I love him."

Her father turned away so that she stared at his face in profile, at the crown of tousled hair, the majestic shoulders, and the mighty jaw. He was like a character in a comic book, a warrior draped in animal skins, wielding a sword. She imagined crawling over the seat into his lap.

"Well," her father said quietly, "I'm sure he'd love you, too."

Koko turned away to look through the window into the dark houses on the street, then settled back into her seat as the tears gently and finally came.

Blonde on Screen About to Be Kissed

*

Pia

He would say she looked nice. If he was trying to be friendly, to stave off conflict, "nice" was what he'd say. If he meant it, if he really noticed her, he would say she looked beautiful. Gorgeous, maybe. He might roll the tip of a cigarette across his lips and take her in, lighting up while his eyes stayed fixed on her. She wore a dress in springtime colors to stir him and tied her hair in a braid draped over her shoulder the way he used to like. She imagined he might tug at the knot to flirt.

A waitress stepped through the sliding-glass doors of the terrace where Pia sat at one of two tables, and poured her a second cup of coffee. The woman's smile said she hoped the person Pia was waiting for would come, as she left behind a plate of shortbread biscuits and mints in plastic wrappers. Pia dipped one of the biscuits into her coffee and bit off the edge, eyeing the door on the other side of the small dining room where Circus would come. Through the glass doors, she watched the waitress step back behind the bar and twist dirty water from a dishrag, then circle her wrists as if they ached.

The place was farther than she and Circus had been together in years. Pia had asked him to come because she wanted to know if she could still convince him to do things he didn't want to do, and she wanted to see if traveling to this town, thirty miles from the city where their lives played out, might release them from a shared past so they could meet each other anew. During their marriage, the farthest they had traveled together was to Salem, thirty minutes from Boston, when Koko was four and went through a phase of being fascinated by witches. Lately, Pia had been thinking a lot about those days and about Koko as a girl. Even the pub, which overlooked the Ipswich River, its watery trickle playful against the slick mud beds, jogged her memory. The terrace where she waited stood suspended above the stream, so she could take in the slightly salty, slightly sour odor of stagnant river water. The smell, like the slight drop in temperature, reminded her of the days Koko had dug rocks from the creek near her grandparents' cabin in Maine. Pia smiled, remembering the little girl's exhilaration over discovering a misshapen stone she imagined was a fossil.

Through the glass doors, Pia saw Circus step into the restaurant in his flat cap and scarf, a toothpick between his lips. She felt what she hadn't in years—a spinning in her belly and a lightness in her limbs as if her heels were caught in an undertow—the same feeling she'd had nearly seventeen years before, when he'd been only a boy she liked. Half a decade spent missing him after the divorce had blunted those tender feelings, and Pia wondered why they were coming back now.

"Looking good," Circus told her when he arrived at the table. He spun the chair around and sat with his heavy arms folded across the back. He'd always reminded Pia of a bear, with his hefty body and savage moods, especially today as he hulked over the tiny chair and nibbled the end of the toothpick like a grizzly chewing the stalk of a pine.

"We're far," he said. "Why are we so far?"

Her palms were sweating. "Don't you find it charming?"

"The drive was nice. I like driving. Clears the mind." He leaned back, scanning the place. "Romantic joint here. Candles on the table, a babbling creek. You trying to seduce me?"

Pia lowered her gaze into her coffee cup just as the waitress came back to the table, grinning as if relieved to find her date had come. Circus ordered a cup of coffee, then changed his mind and asked the woman to bring him a bourbon, neat. He followed her with his eyes when she walked back through the doors into the restaurant, though not with the desire Pia had become used to bracing herself against when he watched other women, but with a vagueness she didn't recognize.

"You and I've known each other a long time," he said, his eyes still locked on the waitress's back. "You ever think about that? How long we've known each other. How long you've known some people."

"It feels like you're the only person I've known a long time."

Circus turned to her, the vagueness still dulling his eyes.

"Does it make you happy?" she asked. "Knowing someone this long. Knowing me?"

"Guess so. People need grounding."

His gaze shifted to the river below, sharpening as he leaned forward to see the creature that had just dived into the water with a splash. Pia glanced but saw only the rings spread out, then ebb over the wet surface.

"Where were you after the marathon?" she asked him.

"I don't want to talk about that."

"With some woman?"

"I was by myself, if you must know. A hell of a time to be alone, but goddamn it, I was." Circus sighed as if something hurt deep inside. "Listen, I don't have a lot of time. Only reason I agreed to meet you out this far is I got a buddy in these parts I owe a visit to. You said something happened with Koko, so why don't we get to it."

"We see each other so rarely, and when we do, we yell. Can't we catch up a little?"

He turned the chair around and tapped his watch just as the waitress dropped off his bourbon, offering Pia a friendly nod. She recommended a basket of battered shrimp to split between them, or slices of fresh-baked pie if they were in the mood for something sweet, both of which Pia declined.

"Can't you guess what we have to talk about?" she asked after the woman walked away.

"Are we playing a game?"

Beneath the table, Pia pinched the stretch of skin between her thumb and forefinger, stifling a sudden urge to cry. She tried to remember the last time she was in the same room with Circus and sensed anything close to love in him. Nothing came to mind. The grace he had once seen in her body, her face, her voice had long ceased to touch him, so it was only his occasional interest in Koko that kept them linked.

"We need to talk about that attention-seeking adventure she took on her bike," Pia said.

"That's not why she did it."

"What other reason could there be?"

"She's a teenager, she saw a boy she liked."

"She could've gotten herself killed."

"But she didn't, did she? We protected her. This isn't why you brought me here, is it?"

Pia picked at a chip in her coffee mug, her body and voice hardening in a way she hadn't expected. "You know, she's dark, that girl. She's always been a dark child, but the things she's interested in lately are horrifying. The shows she watches."

"It's what kids are into. You're not supposed to get it."

"The music she likes."

"Some of it's kinda hip."

"And the clothes." Pia lowered her voice. "They're getting tawdry."

"Koko's got her own thing."

"You're a father. You're supposed to be protective."

After Circus groaned and covered his face with his hands, Pia waved the waitress onto the terrace and asked her to bring a shot of rum for her coffee. Circus slid his phone from his pocket and scrolled through his messages as he waited for the woman to go to the bar. Pia studied the gray flecks in his beard and the wrinkles that had come to his eyes. He was plumper than she'd ever seen him, worn. She couldn't understand why he still cast a spell.

"I found a shoebox under her bed." Pia stirred in the rum after the waitress poured it and went back inside. "Wrapped in gold paper. She'd written 'Joshua' in red marker and drawn little hearts on it. There were cutouts from magazines of women's eyes and lips. Mouths kissing."

"This doesn't warrant a meeting either."

"It wasn't the box that worried me," Pia said. "It's what was inside."

"Why were you in her shit?"

"She's my daughter."

"You look for reasons to punish her. Leave her be, it's been a rough time for all of us."

"Do you want to know what was in the box or not?" she asked.

"I don't think I have the right."

Pia turned her gaze out the window to a pair of doves circling the river before floating down to shore. One of them took a stone into its beak, and Pia watched, hoping to see what would happen if the bird swallowed.

"Christ," Circus mumbled. "I'm gonna think the worst if you don't tell me."

Pia kept her eyes on the doves as she quietly thrilled against the warmth of Circus watching her. There had been few men she'd invited into her life since he left, so any touch, even an unloving one coming from a distance, lit a wick.

"Joshua's a boy at Koko's school. Apparently, they call him the Tower, God only knows why."

"He's probably tall."

"The box was full of things she'd stolen from him," she went on. "There was one of those winter caps boys wear, the knit ones, with a Pistons logo on it. A wad of chewing gum, that was strange. A ballpoint pen with the cap chewed, crumpled math homework. He failed the assignment, by the way. There was a copy of *The Great Gatsby* he must have been reading for class. A baseball with grass stains."

Circus seemed confused when she turned back to him. Outside, the dove toyed with the stone, and she watched, relishing the great pull between her and Circus that came with the revelation of this secret that only they could share, a crisis that concerned only them.

"Why did she steal those things?" he asked.

"She likes him."

"Funny way of showing it."

"When he drops things or leaves things behind, she admitted she takes them. Sometimes she says she sneaks into his locker."

Eyes on the water below, Circus gnawed at the wooden pick. "I'm disappointed. He sounds like a boring kid."

"That's it?"

"What do you want me to say? The girl's flooded with impulses she doesn't get. So they're coming out kinda strange, what of it? She'll figure things out." Circus took a sugar cube from the edge of Pia's saucer and popped it into his mouth. "You never did like anyone having fun when you weren't."

"Stalking boys is fun?"

"Koko ain't stalking. She gets crushes. Leave her be."

Pia slid the cloth napkin from beneath her silverware and unfolded it onto the table to steady her hands. "I have fun, you know."

"Is that right?"

"I'm in a book club." She ironed out the edges of the napkin with the tips of her fingers. "We get into some rowdy conversations. And I have a swap group with some of the ladies in my neighborhood. We exchange clothes and shoes, purses we don't use anymore, knickknacks from around the house. I got a skirt from my friend Eileen. My friend Mary and I are taking a belly dancing class. Well, we're signing up for one."

Circus watched her knead the napkin's threaded edge.

"You only married me because of that girl," she said.

"That girl?"

Pia wound the tip of her thumb into a loose string hanging from the napkin's border, watching the rush of blood as she tightened it. "You know, men still like me. I get catcalls and whistles. There's a man right now who's over the moon about me. He's a boxer and so, so strong," she said, thinking of Fitz, whom she'd only seen once since Patrick Hurley's wake and whose numerous invitations to dinner she'd ignored.

"Good for you." Circus's eyes lazily skimmed the span of the river.

"You think I don't want things," Pia went on. "You think you're the only one who wants things. What I wouldn't give for a little more of your world and a little less of mine."

"My world ain't so rosy, buttercup."

The pet name hit unexpectedly, softening Pia like a warm body holding her on a chilly night. He used to call her buttercup when he thought she needed comfort, or wanted some of his own. She sighed gratefully as if he understood her now.

"All I do is spend time with a child who doesn't like me," she conceded.

Circus's gaze narrowed, a vein at his temple ticking. "Koko likes me, right?" he asked. "There's nothing about me a kid wouldn't dig."

"She likes you because she misses you."

Circus stared blankly at her, and Pia wished she could access him as she once had. He shook his head as if to knock unpleasant thoughts from his mind and reached for his wallet, tossing a twenty-dollar bill onto the table.

"You're leaving?" she asked.

"We're done, ain't we?"

"I haven't told you the worst part."

"There's no problem here—"

"There was a pair of boy's underwear in the box."

Circus flinched, so Pia pushed, desperate to keep him in the chair.

"I don't know how Koko got them," she said. "We can only assume."

He shifted in his seat.

"They looked as if they'd been used. I don't mean they were dirty or anything—"

"Christ, Pia," he said with a wince. "Spare me the details. I get it."

Circus pulled a second toothpick from the cigarette pack in his jacket pocket and slid it between his teeth. A calm came over her. Finally, he was inside the moment with her, he was inside the story and its strain. He motioned at the waitress to bring them another round, then sat scratching his beard, lost in thought.

"You should talk to her," he said after the waitress delivered their drinks.

"Of course I did, and I put her on punishment. She was already grounded for two weeks because of the marathon incident, and now it's a full month because of this crazy shoebox." Pia savored the smell of rum in her coffee. "I'm glad you finally see what we're dealing with and that we're still in this together."

"Here's what I want you to tell her—"

"I beg your pardon?"

"Tell her she's a good girl, but she's gotta keep her eyes open."

"What makes you think you can give me a script?"

He shook his head. "I feel like I asked you to keep watch over something, and you keep causing damage."

"She's not a sofa," Pia said. "And what about you? She sees you twice a year and sometimes on holidays, if she's lucky."

"This is about Koko, not us. You need to get her some pills or rubbers or whatever."

"Is this what you consider parenting? Are you proud of yourself?"

"You make it harder than it has to be."

"You wouldn't feel this way if you were doing it yourself." Pia tightened the thread around her thumb. "And the stealing? Breaking into someone's private property? What kind of girl does that?"

"I could care less. Just make sure she's safe."

"She's only fifteen. That's too young. She'll get a reputation or worse."

"Christ, you're more like your mother every time I see you."

"Take it back." Pia lobbed the balled napkin across the table at him. "You take it back."

Circus only glared.

"This is your fault, you know," she went on. "You can't come and go as you please. You know what that does to a woman?"

"I'm here, aren't I?"

They sat quietly nursing their drinks, bodies pressed against the backs of their chairs as if to widen the distance between them. Pia sensed a flattening in her gut as she realized how little she cared about the shoebox and its contents, even though she'd spent so much time crying after the discovery. The underwear, Koko had confessed, she'd stolen from the boy's gym bag left on the bleachers during basketball practice. Pia believed she understood her daughter well enough to know she wasn't sleeping with the boy. Koko didn't yet have that kind of courage. Pia glanced at Circus, studying his face and body and posture for something that might turn her off, and though he was older and heavier and slumped, she still wished he would look across the table and love her.

"What was it about me?" she asked. "In the beginning. What did you like?"

"I don't remember."

"Think about it."

He gave a casual shrug of his shoulders. "You were out of my league. It was cool knowing a woman like you dug me."

"That's how I made you feel. But what was it about *me*?"

He took the last sip of his bourbon, twirling the empty glass between his fingers. Then he smiled. "I never told you?"

Circus settled into the chair. "I came up with this kid, Mac, lived down the street from us. Not much interesting to say about the cat, but he had a mother who wanted to be an actress. She collected all kinds of antique books and magazines about Hollywood, you know, from Betty Grable days. Mac comes across this book of old film stills. Mostly pinup girls and whatnot. So we're sitting in his shed, that's where we used to get into shit, you know, cigarettes then booze and grass. We were young, too, no more than thirteen.

"Mac shows me this book of stills, and I'm getting off on those fat white asses. But then there's this one picture of an actress. She's got those sculpted waves in her blonde hair they used to have, you know, like butter frosting, and she's slender, not like those juicier girls. This girl, she seemed delicate. Like the crystal in the china cabinet my mother would never let me and my sisters touch. But it was the look on this girl's face that did me in. Her lips were parted just right, like some dude was fitting to plant one on her and she was excited about it but trying to stay classy. When I was a kid, I couldn't put words to it, but I get it as a grown man. She was a certain kind of woman, you know, where the more she reveals, the less you know. That's some bewitching shit. I told my boy Mac that's the kind of girl I'd marry."

Circus touched the back of Pia's hand. Timidly, she let him hold it.

"First time I saw you, I thought of that picture," he said. "Thought I'd found that girl. That was the first time I'd thought about it in years, probably the last time. Well, until today."

Pia watched his fingers stroke the inside of her wrist. "How did I lose you?"

"It's not about having and losing."

"You can't keep saying silly things like that."

"But it's real."

"Why would loving me be so bad? What does love take from you?"

Circus ran his lips across her fingers. "Other day, I see this old couple on the subway. They're not saying jack to each other for several stops, so I don't even realize they're together. Then the lady pipes up and says, 'That was a short distance between those two stations.' Her old man says, 'The next one's even shorter.'"

"So?"

"Who wants to have those goddamn conversations?" He shook his head. "You knew who I was from the beginning. I haven't changed."

"I never wanted you to change," she insisted. "How am I supposed to let go when you never leave completely? Your late-night visits—"

"Hasn't happened in years."

Tears rose in Pia's eyes. This time she didn't stop them. "I'm just trying to be happy. And I'm trying to make everyone else happy."

Circus lifted himself up, burdened, it seemed, by his own heavy body, then went to the terrace's edge and leaned against the railing to watch the trickling creek below. As she imagined running her fingers through his hair, she knew there was nothing she wanted to change about him, except whatever it was that kept him from loving her. But what she realized in a moment that struck painfully was that every event in his life, every memory and conversation, every cell in his body had coalesced to make Circus Palmer the man he was, and changing that one thing, whatever it was, whatever its size, would have made him a different person, perhaps a person she wouldn't love back.

"I never wanted to play violin," she said.

Circus looked over his shoulder, brow drawn.

"When we met, I told you I loved playing violin," she went on. "I only said it so you'd find me interesting. My parents made us choose an instrument, but I couldn't choose, maybe because I didn't want to play. My daddy bought me a violin, and he always looked so pleased when I played well. So I stuck with it. And I don't like powder blue, no, it's not my favorite color. Someone must have told me it looked pretty on me once and I believed them. I like purple. I like . . . orange."

Pia sensed a greater height in her body when she took a step toward him, aware now of why she'd come. "I never wanted to take anything from you. Just let me tell you things."

"You've told me plenty today. You feel better?"

So many times had she looked up at him, stared at him, observed him from the other side of a room or from the foot of a stage. This handsome face she had always imagined it impossible to live without. She had seen this face overjoyed, seen it raging, seen it gnarl in ecstasy, but she had rarely seen the eyes stay steadily on her, to learn her face as well as she'd learned his.

"You don't have to be with me," she said, throat tight. "But you need to be with Koko."

Circus gave the braid of her hair an easy tug. "Darlin', there's something you need to know. It's about a woman."

Pia tried to back away, but Circus held her.

"She's been in my life a spell. Her name's Maggie."

"Don't tell me her name."

"Truth is"—Circus paused, sucked in his lips—"we had a slipup."

Pia snatched her hand from his grip and shoved him. Circus fell softly against the railing, holding his fist over the spot on his chest where she'd pushed.

"I'm not trying to hurt you, buttercup," he said.

"Don't call me buttercup."

"I thought I should tell you."

"Do you love this person? You couldn't possibly. You're not capable."

Circus looked past her into the budding crown of a tree at the terrace's edge, the grimace on his lips turning into a slight smile.

"I got feelings," he answered. "We haven't seen each other since she told me, and truth be told, I miss her when she's not around, man. I'll be on my way to see her and can't get there fast enough. She's the only woman who still makes me nervous. Then this happens, and it's got me thinking about what her and I got, where I am now. Maybe she's a chance to finally feel like what I'm doing means something."

Pia cupped her hands over her ears and let out a scream, a deep, abrasive shriek that burned the back of her throat. The sound spewed out as tears soaked her lashes. Circus reached for her again to shush her, but Pia backed away, slamming into the table behind her.

"Ma'am?" The waitress had opened the glass doors and was standing behind them on the terrace. Through her tears, Pia saw the woman look over at Circus as if he were obliged to tell her what happened, but he only scowled and slipped past her out of the place.

"Tony, bring me that bottle of Bacardi, would you?" Pia heard the waitress call into the restaurant, then felt the woman's strong grip on her arm as she led her back to her chair. She watched the woman dip a cloth napkin into the water glass, listened to the crack of ice against the crystal edge, and quaked when the woman held the wet napkin against her forehead. Pia heard the glass doors ride their track as they opened and closed, heard the waitress thank Tony for bringing the bottle, and watched her pour a shot of rum into a coffee cup and place it in her hand.

"I don't know what that guy said to you, honey, but I'm not surprised he said it." The woman wiped her own forehead in the wet cloth and ticked her tongue against the back of her teeth. "I can spot men like him a mile away. Who knows what it is about them, huh? Boy, could I tell you stories."

The woman folded her arms and balanced her chin in the palm of her hand.

"My ex-husband had the same, what do you call it, vibe," she went on. "Went to work one morning and never came back. My sister ran into him six months later with his arm around some seventeen-year-old girl at a Bertucci's in Worcester. But wouldn't you know, I'd still answer the phone if the bastard called."

The woman soothed Pia's nerves, but she had stopped hearing the words. She was imagining the drive back to Boston, the whine of the garage door closing behind her after she pulled in, the familiar creak in the floorboards as she stepped from the front door to the living room where Koko would be sprawled across the sofa with her bare feet on the coffee table even though she knew Pia hated it. A calm ran through her as she imagined the girl slowly taking over the house, her discarded soda cans collecting in the pantry and her clothes on the floor without Pia to pick up after her. Finally, the girl could take down the lace kitchen curtains she despised and paint her room the garish mint color Pia forbade.

"I could see it as soon as he walked through the door," the waitress said, snapping Pia out of her daydream. She didn't know whether the woman was talking about Circus or her ex-husband, but when she looked into the woman's face, she envied the airiness with which the woman talked about a pain she was done with. And so she sat with the waitress, the two of them looking in the direction of the breeze coming in.

"Clean yourself up, honey." The waitress handed her a compact mirror from the pocket of her apron. The metal lid was scratched, its gold tone faded and scalloped edges dulled, though the red rose painted on its surface shone boldly.

"Nice, huh?" The woman winked. "I bought it from this old witchy woman at a flea market in Brimfield. She said her mother used to carry it. Who knows why she was selling it."

Pia opened the lid and noticed a crack down the center of the mirror.

"That's what makes it special." The waitress nudged her playfully. "The woman said the seven years of bad luck ended 'cause the mirror's already broken. It only brings blessings now. And

I'll tell you, I've had a great few years since I've been carrying it around."

Pia stared at her own reflection, and though the crack drew a line across her face, she recognized what Circus had seen that reminded him of the actress in the photograph—the calm yellow of her hair, the polite curve of her mouth, her readiness to be transported.

"It's yours, take it," the waitress said. "I like to pass good fortune along."

Pia parted her lips just right to see what Circus admired.

"You think you can get yourself home, honey?" the woman asked. "You live far?"

"I'm not going home," Pia answered and slipped the mirror into her bag.

Bullfight

*

Josephine

Tonight he was coming, and Josephine was restless. She could hear his cracked harness boots on the sidewalk outside her open window and feared when he stepped through the door that this night would be like all the others. Pacing in the dim light of her kitchen, she sipped a glass of cold lemon tea and listened to the rain fall in rhythm with his footsteps. She was wearing his favorite nightgown—a white linen sheath—something he said a nun might be made to sleep in. High collar, lace, ribbons. He said he liked its shock of white against the dark and how its dowdy lines were corrupted by the healthy curves of her body. Josephine listened to the scuff of his boots on the porch stairs. With one hand, she stirred honey into her tea, the drops clumping in the cold. With the other hand, she held the gun.

The front door of the triple-decker opened and closed, and she heard Circus tromp up the stairs to her apartment on the top floor. With each step he made toward her, Josephine's heart drummed more forcefully until she thought she might be sick. She could smell him now, the musk in his cologne barely concealing the meaty scent of his body. Circus stood at her doorstep, the notes of some jazz tune she couldn't identify sounding on his lips.

"Little woman," he called from the other side of her door, "let me in."

"One minute," she whispered.

"Josephine, doll." He knocked. "You in there?"

* * *

For eight years, Circus had come to see her in Providence when he was in town to play his horn, though he only came at night, like Eros slinking through the atmosphere toward Psyche sleeping deep as though a poison were running through her. The first night she heard him play, Circus was practicing in the second-floor apartment below her, owned by a friend of his who was out of town for the week. That night the trumpet's wail had woven through the threads of wood in Josephine's floorboards and welled in the air. She'd been sweeping and stopped to listen, lowering herself to her knees to get closer to the sound she imagined like grains of brown sugar knocking around the belly of the brass. It got so she planned for the private shows, dimming the lights and burning candles to listen. Something about his music made her want to take off her clothes, to be kissed, to dance, even if the heat it broke between her thighs made her shy.

At the end of the week, she introduced herself with a box of candies she brought from the shop she owned—almond clusters and butterscotch chews, chocolate fudge and mint patties. They ate them together that night in the backyard and made love in the grass. He told her his life was in Boston. She told him he could come when he wanted. She thought it loving and generous. Though she saw him only on occasion and briefly, she felt him a part of her, like her own heartbeat, blood and bone. There had been other lovers, men who noticed her because they sensed something deep and lonesome and vigorous sweltering inside her. But Circus Palmer was different. Maybe because he never made a fuss over what seemed wounded in her and only came to her to be loved. Maybe because she discovered that Circus was a blaze.

Every time he stepped into the room, it seemed to swelter. This must have been what love was, she figured, since, in her thirty-five years, nothing else had burrowed deep enough to make her feel so sick. The distress of loving him let her know he was calling before the telephone rang, let her know he was standing at her front door before his finger pressed the bell. Love gave her chills in the middle of summertime, made her sweat in her sheets on cold nights, watched her at the supper table thinking of him—soup spoon in midair and soup gone cold. The longer Circus stayed away, the deeper love dug in. When he did come, Josephine lay with him, feeling each second of time tick past and away, bringing her nearer to the final moment when he'd be gone, a moment worse than death inching closer.

She'd always known about the wife who kept Circus from her, but lately the fact was getting to her, and there was too much shame in her to tell anyone he was still in her life. Her girlfriends had started sneaking each other glances whenever she brought up Circus Palmer during their nights out at salsa clubs. The young clerks at her candy shop had long grown tired of hearing about him. Her mother wouldn't allow his name to be spoken in her house.

But when Josephine was alone, his prolonged absences left her crying for weeks, daily, seemingly without end. Deep, rich cries that made her hungry afterward. He'd go, and the sense of loss was immediate, hollow, like falling in a dream. In the mornings, she'd lie breathing Circus from the sheets, wondering where he'd been since she'd last seen him and how to ask why he'd gone. Her nights had become restless as she tossed in a bed too big in a room widening out around her. It was the emptiness in her apartment Josephine disliked most about the night, as if she would roll into it and disappear. What she missed most were touch and whispers in the dark. Without them, she'd become desperate. Clumsy.

And now, for the first time since he'd been coming around, Josephine hated him for not loving her back, for not sensing what he was doing to her. The gun, which she'd bought two weeks earlier after a string of thefts in her neighborhood, was a purchase she would never have imagined making, though she found herself glad to have it in the apartment. She didn't know whether she'd have the courage to use it once Circus arrived. She'd had fantasies of turning the gun on him or turning it on herself so she could be with him forever in the way the dead lodged themselves in memory. But all she really wanted was to keep him in the room.

She went to the bedroom to slide the gun between the mattress and box spring, then stopped in front of the mirror by the front door to accentuate what Circus liked in her, the red of her lips and the intense black of her hair, which she knotted into a loose bun. Anger had brought a flush to her cheeks and a pool of sweat to the small of her back, which he'd want to slide his tongue through. When she opened the door, Circus charged. She took a step away so he would have to reach for her, and he grinned, catching her waist in his hands. There was something worn about him tonight, his eyes dull and beard overgrown as if he hadn't slept for days. He placed his trumpet case on the sofa, pulled the toothpick from between his teeth, and spread his hands across her back. He looked down at her, gazing at the silver cross at her collarbone.

"I've got a song in my head," he said. "Guess what it's called."

"'Josephine,'" she said, knowing her lines.

"'Josephine,' that's right." He let out a crackling, cigarette-stained laugh. "And what do you do when you can't get a song out of your head?"

"Listen to it." Josephine whispered into his mouth, then took his hand, leading him down the hall toward the bedroom.

"Easy there." Circus stopped in the doorway of the kitchen. "You're not being a good hostess. Aren't you gonna let me take off my coat?"

Josephine quickly removed his jacket, sensing the vigor in his shoulders still humming with the music he'd played hours before.

Without looking at him, she folded the jacket, placed it beside the trumpet case on the living room sofa, then went back to him in the kitchen. When she tried to lead him away this time, Circus's body stiffened, his eyes narrowing as if he could sense something different in her.

"You got anything for me to drink?"

"I only have half a bottle of bourbon left," she told him. "I'm not buying any more."

"Why's that?"

"No need."

"I'll have a glass."

She felt him watching her legs beneath the swirling hem of her nightgown as she crossed the kitchen floor to the cupboard, where she poured him a glass of Wild Turkey. Josephine didn't like the taste of alcohol, didn't like what it did to a person either, but she'd bought it and served it to him, one of a long list of things she did in hopes he'd stay. She held the glass at arm's length as she crossed back to him, and Circus eyed her before taking a sip. He leaned back against the counter, his legs open and taking up space, as he held his glass in the lamplight and stared at the beams shining through the crystal.

"How was your night?" she asked.

Circus poured himself a fuller glass as Josephine sipped her tea. He told her about his gig that night and how hot his trumpet sounded as it flirted with the drum, told her about the fight he had seen in an alleyway after the show, throwing a right hook to mimic one of the fighters and watching his imaginary opponent fall to the floor. It was this that pulled her, the drama Circus made of his own life. He was loud, Circus, he bumped into furniture. His laugh always made the neighbors knock at the walls to quiet him down. He never quieted down.

"When you were in Miami," Josephine started, "what'd you miss most about me?"

Circus took a daisy from a tiny vase on the table, sliding it behind her ear. "I like these flowers. Only time my mama let me close was when she tended her garden. She let me put my hands on hers so I'd learn. I never understood why we had to weed out those pretty daisies."

"I asked you something."

Answers seemed to filter through his mind. "Your eyes. Lying in your arms while you tell me things."

"I make you feel good."

"That's right."

Josephine pulled the stem from behind her ear and spun it between her fingertips, staring into the yellow yolk of the flower. "You tell me things you don't tell anyone else."

"I reckon I do sometimes."

Josephine scratched her fingernail against the zipper of his pants. "You know they have a name for what I do for you. I let you come when you want. I listen to your secrets. I comfort you and let you leave when you're ready. Some women get paid good money for those services."

"Worth every penny." Circus took Josephine's teacup and placed it in the sink before pressing his mighty body against her. She wished she was a different kind of woman then, the kind of woman who could relax like he wanted her to, the kind of woman who didn't need so much, the kind of woman love didn't make smaller.

"You're strange tonight," he said. "Something wrong?"

An awkward silence passed between them with a strange surge of heat. "I keep having bad dreams. There are women with spiders in their hands, and they open their fingers and the spiders crawl out. They crawl all over me."

"It's only a dream."

"You're there. Laughing."

"Then you know it's a dream." He squeezed her knee. "You won't hear me laughing with any spiders around."

"You haven't answered my calls," she said. "I didn't know if you were coming back."

"Where else am I gonna go?" he asked in a way she imagined he thought sounded playful, though she heard only resignation.

"Are you here to tell me something?" Josephine shrank when he took a step away. "Is there something?"

Circus plucked a ribbon from her collar so her gown opened up more to him. He ran his thumb across her bare throat. "Now I feel like you're accusing me of something."

"Why? Do you feel guilty?"

"All I've thought about all day is seeing you, and I walk into this."

"I had another dream—"

"Why you always getting all worked up about a dream?"

"—you were with someone else."

Circus sat in one of the chairs at the table, staring up at her as if she were diseased and he didn't know how to tell her.

"The problem is I love you," she said. "And it's getting worse."

He took a pack of cigarettes from his pocket and lit one, all the while studying her and deciding what, she didn't want to imagine. Josephine wanted to see into his eyes, but his defiant gaze—she wondered what about her he needed to defy—wouldn't let her. He went to the bay windows at the end of the hall, shoved one open, and sat down, rubbing the chill from his arms. He took a drag and blew the smoke through the screen while Josephine stared at his face in profile, the slender muzzle sloping down to his woolly beard, his mouth vulgar, a tad belligerent, but handsome just the same. There was some perverse pleasure in imagining his massive body collapsing around the bullet of her gun, imagining the flow of blood over her hands. The thought sent a shiver through her.

"What were those candies you brought around that first night we met?" he asked. "The ones you made from sugar."

"Pastillage."

"Think you could make me some of those?" He tugged awkwardly at his beard. "My kid, man. I forgot her birthday, and I think she'd like those little candy sculptures. They look like the porcelain figurines she used to collect when she was younger. You know, those trinkets girls like? Unicorns and dolphins. Dragonflies. I thought of those just the other day. I kinda missed when she used to carry them around. Could you make something like that for me?"

He rested his forehead against his thumb and watched her with a look Josephine had never seen from him before. Solemn, wistful. He held out his hand, and she settled into his lap as his thick arms slid around her waist. They sat together in silence as Circus finished his cigarette and stroked her hair. He began to hum, and Josephine relaxed against the purr in his chest. Something seemed to have changed. Something promising.

"I'll make them for you," she said.

Circus coiled his fingers around hers, kissed them. "How did you learn to make something so delicate and pretty?"

"It's all about heat and air. Shaping what's there from what's not."

"I guess it's the same with music sometimes. The magic's in the silences."

Circus widened the window, and the hall filled with the smells of blooming trees and fresh soil, the scent of newly sprouted spring. He flicked the cigarette outside and watched it smother in the wet grass below. He scratched at his beard, his gaze still fixed to the ground outside. "I don't know what I'm doing, but I don't think I should be doing this anymore."

Her body started to tense, but she stopped it with a dig of her fingernails into her thigh. He brushed a loose hair from her forehead, his eyes taking her in as if he could read their entire history in her face and was pleased by what he saw.

Josephine edged away from him, the backs of her knees starting to sweat. "Then why did you come?"

"I don't know."

"See? You're not going anywhere." She lifted herself from his lap, emboldened when he kept hold of her wrist. "Clean yourself up and come to bed."

Josephine listened to his steps through the hall into her bedroom and the attached bathroom, listened to the zip of his pants and the soft drop of his clothes to the floor. She heard him whistle with his tongue at the roof of his mouth, heard the creak of the door to the shower, then the spray of water as his body splashed against the flow. The gun was still a presence, a spot of heat in a cold space. Josephine was drawn to it. She went to her bedroom and crept into the bed, sensing the gun beneath her back. Listening to Circus's breezy whistle, she realized she'd never be able to stop herself from opening the door to him and lifting her skirt. She used to like it. It was love, wasn't it? But love that felt like a sentence, like sin.

"Josie," he called from the shower, "come wash my back." He kept whistling. "'Summertime'"—she recognized the melody—"'and the livin' is easy.'"

"Come to bed," she said. "I want you here."

"And I want you to wash my back. Come take care of me."

Josephine crawled out of the bed and stood at the bathroom door, watching him reach an arm over the line of the shower curtain as he scrubbed at his pits. Carefully, she let her nightgown fall to the floor and stepped into the shower.

He smiled, his eyes on the cross at her throat. "God can't see you in here."

He handed her a block of soap and turned his back. Josephine lathered her hands and flattened them against his skin cratered by the two stretched scars between his shoulders he'd said he got during a fight as a teenager. She drew her thumb up the length of his spine, spreading her fingers across the fan of muscles at the small of his back, curled them around his shoulder blades, then stroked the bone bulging between them as he lowered his head. She sketched triangles into him with her fingernails, every so often digging, thrilling silently when he flinched.

"Easy," Circus warned.

Josephine lathered her hands again, letting the soap puddle in the arc of his back. As she slid her fingers down the tiers of his ribcage, she fantasized pushing a finger beneath and pulling at the bone, fantasized rubbing herself into his body, scouring the skin until it chafed and split open so she could slip inside. She grabbed a clump of his hair and yanked.

"Jesus," he said, nudging her. Josephine stumbled.

"Why aren't you being nice to me?" he asked.

"I'm always nice."

Circus thrust open the shower curtain, and the shriek of the metal hooks made Josephine jump. He stepped out of the bath and wrapped himself in a towel. She calmly retied her hair, slid into her gown, then went back to the bed, letting the hem twirl as she walked, letting him see. But he didn't touch her and instead slipped into bed beside her, rolling onto his back, the look in his eyes far off again. She held him, and before long, he nestled against her neck. She could feel his breath on her skin, could smell the stale scent of cigarette smoke and booze. Then his eyes were closed and he fell asleep. She prodded him awake.

"It's nighttime," he mumbled.

"But it's our time together."

He kissed her shoulder. "Let me rest my eyes a second."

A second turned into five minutes, turned into ten. She elbowed him, but Circus only rolled to the other side of the mattress and sank deeper into sleep. Josephine lay contemplating his back, lulled by the slow rhythm of his breath, then went through the apartment shutting the drapes and turning the locks on all the doors.

In the living room, a stroke of light sneaked through a slit in the curtain and caressed the trumpet case on the sofa. Josephine opened it and watched the light slink over the horn. When she picked up the trumpet, it was awkward in her hands, the brass slightly cold. When she tapped the buttons, the valves scratched as they popped down, then up again. She liked holding it, liked placing her finger where Circus placed his and laying her thumb in the rest where his had been. She took the mouthpiece from its velvet cradle, twisted it on, and blew. Her breath echoed through the horn like rushing water until she remembered the need to hum. Josephine licked her lips, buzzed, and the horn cawed out of tune.

She heard Circus jump up from the bed. He came running.

"Stop," he shouted. He took the trumpet, cradled it like a newborn, and gently placed it in its case before carrying it back to the bedroom, leaving Josephine alone in the dark. A chill passed through her. Everything seemed empty at this late hour, as if she and Circus were the only people on the planet awake, and anything could happen without the world listening.

Circus returned dressed, trumpet case in hand.

"You're leaving?"

He didn't answer and only crossed the room toward his jacket and shoes.

Josephine lunged for him, but he shook her off like a loose thread on his sleeve.

"It's that wife of yours, isn't it?" she asked. "You think she needs you. She doesn't. You've outgrown her, and that means she's probably outgrown you."

She watched him place the cap on his head and slip into his jacket, wanting to trap him in the room somehow.

"You always come back, Circus, you can't quit me." Josephine broke through the tremble in her throat. "Hell, you could marry somebody else, and you'd still want to come around. A wife hasn't stopped you before."

She knocked him against the door, and he bristled, nostrils flared. She ran to the bedroom for the gun and returned to the living room, holding it so he could see. Circus drew back, his eyes holding on her. Her nerves stilled. Now she had him, every part of him was hers. She sat on the sofa and placed the gun in the center of the coffee table.

"Me or you," she said, her backbone feeling thicker. She imagined she had the strength to lift the house from its foundation.

Circus picked up the gun, opened the chamber, and glanced over at her when he saw it was full. Gently, he put the gun back on the table and had another look at her before pulling off his jacket and tossing the cap to the floor. He went to the kitchen and came back carrying two orange juice glasses and the bottle of Wild Turkey. He placed the glasses on the table, then slid a chair from the desk on the other side of the room, positioning it across from her.

"All right," he said, folding up his sleeves. "Me or you."

Josephine had fantasized an apology, fear in his eyes, begging. She hadn't expected this. The inside of her palms itched. The hairs on the back of her neck pricked. But she stayed in the room, trying to calm herself by watching the bourbon dribble into the glass as Circus poured two shots and pushed one across the table.

"You know I don't drink," she told him.

"You're the one who brought the guns and the threats." He held the bourbon to his lips. "Only thing missing is liquor."

She was sweating in her nightgown, her gaze passing between the bourbon and the gun.

"You sure you wanna do this?" Circus was grinning behind his glass. "'Cause me? I can do this."

He raised his glass into the air. Josephine raised hers. They watched each other drink. She cringed as the liquor trickled down her throat, while on the other side of the table, Circus pounded his chest and let out a howl.

"My old man used to take me shooting," he said. "Only thing he liked doing with me. Every weekend he'd polish his guns with the same care he gave his Pontiac. There were guns all over the house, like trophies. You'd be surprised the terror that strikes in a kid's heart." He watched her like a boy making a dare. "You learned how to use that thing?"

"I've practiced," she answered.

"You a good shot?"

"I've hit the target."

He nodded, thumping his fingers against his chest, and Josephine listened to the hollowed-out sound. His gaze flicked down to the gun, then back across the table at her as he poured another shot and waited for her to drink. Josephine coughed after she took a sip, while Circus downed his in one swallow.

"Well," he said, "this is more fun than I expected to get into tonight."

"This isn't a joke," she said, trying to toughen her voice. "I'll use it."

"I believe you."

Outside the window, the moon was a slit in the sky, and Josephine imagined pushing her finger through it so she could peel back the heavens to climb into them and away.

"You didn't call after the marathon," she said. "You didn't check in to see if I was okay."

"That's not what we are, doll."

"Weren't you worried about me?"

Circus downed half a shot, then placed the glass on the table beside the gun. "I don't think we see this thing the same way."

Josephine rubbed at the center of her chest, aching as if her heart had risen there and clotted. "What do you think happens when you don't call or see me? You leave my house and everything stops, is this what you think? I'm not a figment of your imagination. You don't think I have my own life to figure out? Don't you know I'm sitting there thinking I'm boring or stupid or not pretty enough? Don't you see me?"

"Women," he said with a snicker. "You all think you're so damn special."

"I should shoot you right now."

A vein in Circus's temple pulsed, and a grin curled his lips—wicked, cruel—at the same time that a deep shame spread through Josephine's body. This was more than love she had for him, more than a need to have him lie beside her and say things that were true. This was madness, but madness that made her feel vital in a way nothing else did.

"I love you," Josephine said. "Don't you see where all this is coming from? Can't you feel it? I'm in love with you. Completely. I can't shake it, it won't let me loose. I need you, and you need me, Circus. You come here because you need me."

He twisted the tip of his beard. "Do you have any idea who I am?"

Josephine didn't know how to answer. His gaze was fixed on her.

"You're smart," she said. "And talented. You march to your own drum."

"You could be describing anyone." He watched the perk of her lips as she took another sip. "Describe me."

She ran her finger around the rim of her glass. "I like your passion. It makes me remember to be brave."

"That's about you, not me."

"But it comes from you," she insisted. "It's inside you."

"See?" Circus raised his glass as if toasting a win. "You don't know me well enough to love me."

"Don't smoke in here," she said when he lit another cigarette.

"Be fair, doll." He smirked. "This could be my last one."

She kicked the edge of the coffee table. "You don't take me seriously."

A strand of smoke curled from his mouth. "Make me take you seriously."

Josephine reached for the gun that seemed heavier now. Before she lost her nerve, she turned it on him.

Circus wouldn't look at the gun. Instead, he looked at Josephine, then closed his eyes, the vein in his temple ticking. She might have lowered the weapon, but there was something marvelous about pointing it at him, pinning him against the chair, compelling him not to move until she decided, as if everything she had been through with him fused into one ache she could be free of with a quick pull of the trigger. The days without contact and the cold absence left by him, which she suffered during trips to the grocer's, the bank, the Laundromat. She felt his absence behind every conversation, beneath the print of the newspapers she read in the morning, within the plots of movies she watched with friends. Nights came filled with dreams of Circus making love with other women, Circus always leaving, leaving, gone. But Josephine was at peace now. Her aim steady.

"My mama pulled a gun on my old man, one of his favorite pistols," Circus said. "You're sitting across from me, but I feel like it's her I'm seeing."

He made a noise like a whimper, and a tear rolled down his cheek, dissolving in the graying hairs of his beard. He wiped away its trail and shifted in his seat so the gun wasn't pointing directly at him. Josephine kept her grip on it, unsure of what was happening.

"You don't need me, man, I'm already dead." When he looked up, his eyes were wet. "What do you want me for? I was never gonna be great. You know what it is to realize something like that?"

This was what Josephine had wanted to see in him. Tears. Collapse. But instead of tasting vindication, she resented him for stealing the focus from her, from them. She watched as he spun the empty glass on the table.

"A selfish son of a bitch, that's what I am." His voice flattened. "I fail everybody, I fail myself."

Circus dropped his head in his hands, muttering like the drunk men Josephine avoided late nights on the subway.

"A woman is supposed to forgive everything," he sniveled. "They're supposed to be tender that way. What a man needs is someone who can tolerate that son of a bitch when he creeps up in you."

Josephine lowered the gun and placed it on the table. "I can."

Circus looked up as if he'd forgotten she was there. Josephine could see clarity sharpening in his eyes.

"You aren't listening," he said. "All you're thinking about is what you wanna get."

"You're destroying me."

"You can blame me," he said. "But you must like how it feels."

Circus winced as if maybe he knew what he'd said was too much, but instead of apologizing, he finished her shot of Wild Turkey and rose to his feet, sorting through his pockets as if he were preparing to go.

"You're not leaving your wife, right?" she asked. "That's what you came to tell me?"

Circus got back into his jacket and cap. He gave her shoulder a squeeze. Quietly, he said, "The wife and I haven't been together for years, doll. I reckon it's time you knew."

Josephine had the sense of falling again, the weakening of muscle.

"There's a woman though," he said. "Maggie and I've known each other a good while."

"And you're here to tell me you love her?"

He didn't answer.

"Are you going to be with her?"

"I don't know if she'll have me."

Josephine heard herself make a sound like a hiccup. Her body seemed to cave in on itself. She pressed the palms of her hands into the hollows of her eyes, and her mouth hung open, but the only words that came were "you" and "no" and "you" and "no." The tears rose in her eyes as the woman stepped out of her nightmares and into life, real and full. The fire Josephine had sensed in Circus's soul was gorgeous and essential, but Maggie was the spark. Josephine loved Circus, and Circus loved Maggie, and maybe Maggie wouldn't have him because she loved someone else. This seemed to be how love worked. This was Josephine's life, her friends' lives, the lives of almost everyone she knew, though she imagined someone, somewhere who received the accumulation of all that love. She wanted to know what it might feel like.

"You're a good woman, Josie. You made a silly man feel happy on many a night. I'll always be grateful to you." He leaned over to pinch her cheek. "If you feel I've done you wrong, well, I'm sorry about it. But I can say I've been lucky to know you."

The sweat rose again to the back of her neck. "This is the last night."

Circus kept looking at the door. She watched him check his pockets again, then go for the trumpet, but Josephine got to it first.

"Give it to me," he said.

"Play me a song."

"I'm not fucking around, Josephine, give me my horn."

"Just one song." She opened the case. The trumpet gleamed where the light stroked its bell. "I want to see you happy before you go."

Josephine placed the case on the coffee table beside the gun. The red velvet lining cradling the horn reminded her of the inside of a coffin.

"I can't play with dirty hands," Circus said.

Josephine listened to the run of water in the kitchen, closing her eyes against the fear that she would break as soon as he left the apartment. He came back to the room, took the horn, and brought it to his lips. The sound came through the brass, and Josephine sensed all over again the endless agony of wanting Circus Palmer to come up to her from the second floor as she knelt on the ground to listen to him. She sensed all over again how Circus had swallowed up everything in her life. But now there was nothing romantic or beautiful about it.

Circus finished the tune and put the trumpet in its case as the notes hung in the air. The night outside was still, the building silent. Josephine imagined there was no one around for miles. He lit another cigarette, breathing out a trail of smoke as he walked toward the window, picking at a hole in the pane. "What is it about those little porcelain trinkets girls like anyway?"

"They can break," she answered. "You feel responsible."

The horn was in its case, rock hard but lifeless, an anchor in the quiet chaos of the room. "I never asked why you chose the trumpet," Josephine said.

"You don't like the trumpet?" Circus chuckled, standing at the window, his gaze fixed on the sky growing melon-colored with morning. "The horn has been the only thing that doesn't change. The notes are always right where I expect them to be. The things I say to my trumpet, I can't say to anyone else, and it's always said things I can't say. I become part of it, you know, put my breath right into it. That's my soul. Maybe I needed a safe place to put that breath. And I tell you, I haven't found a safer place than the inside of a horn."

He was smiling when he looked back at her. "You knew who I was from the beginning, sweetheart. I never lied to you."

"You're right." Josephine smiled back before reaching for the trumpet, her fingers where Circus placed his, her thumb where his laid in the rest. The brass felt cold against her skin yet seemed to burn at the same time. The moment curled and held snug around them, neither could get away or prevent what was coming as she held the trumpet in the air, and Circus watched in terror as if the horn were a child being held by the throat. Josephine peered through the terror to contemplate the angles of his face, the unkempt shag of his handsome beard, the slightly lazy eye because this was the last time.

She slammed the horn against his mouth. There was a snap of bone, there was wailing and a chip from his tooth on the floor. Circus was on the ground holding his jaw, bloodied spittle seeping between his fingers. He grabbed the trumpet from her hand and scrambled out the door. She heard him clamber down the steps, heard the building's front door slam shut behind him.

The next morning Josephine couldn't recall exactly what had

happened. The liquor had made her woozy. The only evidence that anything had occurred at all was the spot of blood on the floor. After days passed and she no longer heard the sound of the trumpet coming from downstairs, or Circus's knock at her door, she knew he was really gone. There would be no more music. But the dreams stopped. And that was good.

What
Goes
Around

*

Circus

The girl. Presented to him in a tartan coat and stiff dress he imagined she wouldn't have chosen to wear—gray, the bottom flared. Her grandmother stood by her side, dusting something from the girl's shoulders as if Koko were a table hauled up from the basement to sell. A suitcase stood on the steps behind them, a pillow slipped into a Day of the Dead cover roped to the side handle, both dampening under a spring drizzle. Koko's face had thinned since Circus had last seen her, narrowed by hunger, he assumed, since her grandmother, Joan, had told him over the phone she hadn't been eating. He watched them through the window, knowing he had to let them in. When he finally opened the door after the second ring of the bell, Circus lied about an appointment he had to get to, but Joan snapped her fingers, grabbing at the air like she'd caught a dog by the collar before it could run.

"What happened to your face?" Koko asked.

"Slipped in the shower," he answered, sputtering between his still-swollen lips. "I'm getting it fixed next week."

"You look gross."

"Thanks, kid."

Joan's prim mouth tightened into the same phony smile she'd always worn with him. "Well, won't you invite us in anyway? I actually do have somewhere else to be today."

Circus opened the door so they could pass, dragging in Koko's suitcase after the older woman waggled her fingers in the air toward it. He rolled the heavy case inside, his ankle aching where he'd twisted it on the sidewalk on the way out of Josephine's building only a week before. Joan was peering around at the mess of his living room, her nose wrinkled as if she were repulsed by the room's smell of cigarettes and stale vegetable oil from the chicken he'd fried up the night before but couldn't eat because of his busted mouth. For a second, he thought she might change her mind about leaving Koko with him until Joan turned to her granddaughter, patting her gently on the head. "Uncle Ken will bring the rest of your things tomorrow."

Circus blocked Joan's path as she started toward the door. "How long do you think . . ."

Koko's lashes fluttered as if she were holding in tears, so he didn't finish the question. Joan politely folded her hands, head tilted as if she were addressing a child. "Pia hasn't been in contact except to send Koko a goodbye note, which I'm sure she'll be happy to share with you. And let me spare you the displeasure of trying to phone Pia. She doesn't answer."

The corner of Joan's mouth quaked, and she continued toward the door. "Now, I'll leave you to take care of your daughter while I go pray for mine."

When she made her exit, the air in the room seemed to leave with her. Koko circled the sofa and glanced around as if she were seeing the place for the first time, her teeth biting a hole into her bottom lip. Circus watched from the door, already sweating, the girl like a wrestler he feared finding himself pinned beneath.

"You got school tomorrow?" he asked.

Koko snapped the wad of gum in her mouth. "I guess."

"How are we supposed to get you over there?"

"I don't know." She blew a bubble, then sucked it back into her mouth. "Drive?"

The leather chair across from the sofa respired like an old man as she dropped into it. Her gaze flitted across the cluttered bookcase to the *Godfather* poster framed on the wall, her lips sounding out the title stenciled in Italian across Brando's face in profile.

"I watched it," she said. "Well, I started watching, me and my friend Bree. Her dad likes it, too. We couldn't stick with it, though. So boring."

"You'll appreciate it when you're older."

Koko shoved her finger beneath a rip in the seat of the chair. "The things your dad said you'd appreciate when you got older. Do you appreciate them?"

He rested his hand on the doorknob, fiddling with the lever of the lock. "I don't recall my old man saying much about appreciation."

Koko's thumb crawled deeper into the seat of the chair, jabbing at the underside of the leather. "Why's the poster in Italian?"

"Guess it's got a certain style."

"Have you ever been to Italy?"

"I haven't."

"Do you speak Italian?"

"You ever heard me speak Italian?"

"Who do you think the Italian will impress?"

He didn't know whether the girl intended to rile him, but he answered her the way he always answered females who tried to cut into him. With silence. Before Koko showed up that morning, he'd been contemplating his next move in the chess match he'd started with a friend the night before, glancing every so often at the television, where highlights from the Knicks game played in silence. He went back to the chessboard, held an ice pack against his mouth, and turned up the volume on the television.

Koko folded into the leather chair, her knees at her chest, her arms strung around them. "What do you usually do on Sundays?"

"You're looking at it."

She picked at the pink polish chipping on her thumbnail. "I usually see my friends."

"You wanna ask one of them to come over? I got classes to plan for anyway."

"I'm not in the mood." Koko let out a sigh. "Do we have to watch basketball?"

"This is my house."

"But I'm here now."

Circus grabbed the remote, chucking it to the floor at her feet. "Watch what you want."

"You don't have to get mad."

"What the fuck happened, Koko?" he asked, and the girl flinched either from the push in his voice or from the cursing.

"I don't like watching sports."

"That's not what I'm talking about. I saw Pia a week and a half ago. What'd I miss?"

Koko combed her fingers through her hair, pressed straight now, so it swept across her face and hid her eyes, lashes thick with mascara. The girl was pretty, graceful even, and the realization embarrassed him briefly.

"Mom went out one day, then she called and told me to go over to Grandma's." Koko picked more vigorously at the polish on her nails. "She didn't come back. That's the story."

"She sent you a letter?"

"I don't want to talk about it."

"Why don't you call her?"

"She doesn't answer."

"All right, but you must have a theory about what's going on here."

Koko huffed as her body folded deeper. "There was this guy, Fitz, who came around once, a boxer or something, kind of a meathead. He was sending her flowers, but she always said no when he asked her out."

"You think she went off with him?"

"No, she wasn't into Fitz, but he was the only unusual thing in her life lately. Maybe if she gave him a chance. He really seemed to like her. Why don't grown-ups like being happy?"

The room fell silent.

"I don't feel good." Koko crept out of the chair and stood, her knee bobbing back and forth so that her whole body shook. She pulled at her bottom lip, wincing when the sore left a spot of blood on the tip of her thumb. "Can I go lie down?"

"I haven't cleaned out the second bedroom," he said. "My equipment's all over the place, there's shit everywhere in there. I have no idea where that cot you used to sleep on is."

Koko's knee bobbed harder, faster. Circus saw the tremble in her hands. "Go lie down on my bed," he said.

Koko hurried down the hall and quietly shut the door, leaving Circus crowded by the walls of his own home. He pulled the metronome from his pocket and let it tick as he considered his options. He could come up with a reason Koko should stay with her grandmother, maybe he'd promised someone else the extra bedroom. He could persuade the parents of one of Koko's friends to take her in. He could hunt Pia down himself. He poured a shot of Wild Turkey, even though his dentist said not to, and dialed his neighbor, Donna, flirting until she was softened enough to coax into staying with Koko. He drank the last of the bourbon before heading back to the bedroom, where Koko lay on his mattress on her back. The late-morning sun was bold and clear since the rain had passed. Now it tried to stream through the windows, but Koko had drawn the curtains, the dulled light wrinkling within the folds of the blankets heaped at her feet.

"Your grandmother buy you those clothes?" he asked.

Koko nodded.

"Doesn't seem your style."

"What's my style?" she asked breathily, as if she'd just stopped crying.

"I don't know. Funkier."

"I kinda like the dress."

Circus spoke gently. "Hey, so I promised a buddy I'd meet him for a drink at a joint down the street."

"It's noon."

"We got business to discuss so, yeah, Donna's coming over to hang with you. You need something, you ask her."

"I don't need anyone to stay with me. People pay me to babysit their kids, you know."

Circus grinned, won over by the uneven sound of her voice pitching between the undisciplined squawk of a girl and a woman's mellow croon. "I bet those kids dig having you around."

She didn't move or say anything, so Circus started out of the room.

"Is this how things are going to be?"

"You like Donna," he offered.

Koko pulled the blanket up around her body and shifted on the mattress so Circus faced her back, a slight back but one he used to wash and wonder how those scrawny little girl muscles and thin bones, how those slight and yielding shoulders, could ever fill out into something strong enough to sustain itself, but there it was, a wider back with firm shoulders, tall and turned against him.

* * *

"Circus Palmer." The barman poured him a Wild Turkey. "What's going on, brother?"

"Nothing but the rent."

"Looks like your mouth had a meeting with somebody's fist?"

"Slipped in the shower." He glanced in the mirrored wall behind the bar, sliding his tongue over the bulbous swell of his bottom lip and sensing the sting where the wound hadn't yet healed. "Booze helps, right?"

The man slid a bowl of pretzels across the bar, took a handful for himself. "I wouldn't know. But sit here long as you like and find out."

The barman reached under the counter and flipped a switch. A new Tip Badgett ballad in midsong came over the speakers, one Circus knew Maggie had drummed on. Closing his eyes, he listened to her rhythm, sleek as her body lying next to him. When he opened his eyes, he saw his reflection in the mirror, saw the swollen lip, the cracked tooth and purplish welt on his cheek. The sight put him on edge. He was fed up, chafing as if stuck in a game he'd suddenly grown tired of playing. He took his phone from his pocket and placed it on the bar, drumming up the nerve to call. When he finally dialed, Maggie didn't answer.

I shouldn't be thinking of you, he typed into a text message. *Or I shouldn't be telling you. But I am.*

Circus took sips of his bourbon to keep calm until Maggie responded.

"Who's up?" he asked the barman, who watched a game on a television in the corner.

"Cubs versus Pirates. Who you rooting for?"

"Baseball ain't really my game, man. I'm more into boxing."

"You see the Panchak and Granados fight?"

"Had money on it."

"Those were some rock-solid punches Granados threw, right?"

The barman went on about the fight while Circus nodded without quite listening. He had his eye on his phone, sensing its imminent buzz.

Minutes later Maggie replied, *How'd I get lucky enough to sneak into your mind?*

It's been happening, Circus responded, eager to make peace. *Always happens. But I'm the one who's lucky.*

I believe you are.

I like being in your company. I miss it.

Circus swirled the last sip of bourbon in his glass and waited.

Then you should cherish it more when it happens.

The shame spread quickly through him, so he picked up the phone and dialed.

"I deserve that," he said when she answered.

"I'm glad you realize."

He weakened at the sound of her voice. "What are you doing?"

"Packing."

"Another trip?"

"You could say that. What's wrong with your voice?"

"Just a little accident." He dug his fingernail into a gap in the wood of the bar. "I did the wrong thing, all right, I shouldn't have left. I shouldn't have disappeared for so long. I wish I could take it all back."

Circus pressed the phone closer to his mouth so he could whisper to her, turning so the barman couldn't hear. "You know me, Maggie. You see everything."

"Do I?"

"You're the only one."

"This sounds like liquor talking, Cyrus," she said and sent a flutter through his chest. Maggie was the only person who called him by his real name. "Have you been drinking?"

"Little bit."

"How come you do this?"

"I like taking you drinking with me."

Maggie sounded as if she were settling into a sofa or bed. "Where are we then?"

"That hole in the wall down the street from my place. I'm here with the regulars. Maybe I'm a regular. It's one of those places holding on even though the neighborhood isn't what it was. They're not moving on. But I'm here so what does that tell you?"

Maggie chuckled, and he wished he were with her.

"This is the kind of place where a cat like me gets messed with if he says the wrong thing to the wrong person," he said. "What if it happened, Mags? Would you hold an ice pack on my broken nose? I want to put my arms around you while you hold an ice pack on my broken nose."

"How much have you had to drink, sugar?"

"Doesn't matter."

"Are you alone?"

"Always. I'm lonely all the time," he said. "Other night I went to a party. My buddy's wife comes up to me and says, 'We're worried about you.' Like I'm not happy or something."

Maggie's silence left space for him to go on.

"I don't like how bad I wanna see you," he said. "I never like how bad I wanna see you."

"It sounds like you're going through something. Why don't you go home and rest?"

"Don't go," Circus begged, louder than he'd wanted. "Stay on the phone with me."

"My god, Cy, what's wrong?"

He pulled a twenty from his wallet, left it on the bar, and hurried out into the street. "I don't know what to do, Maggie."

"About what?"

"Anything."

"Well"—Maggie let out a sweet sigh—"whatever you decide, I think you're all right."

Circus grinned broadly and dropped onto a bench at the end of the street as if his body had given way. "You know I think the same about you. More than all right. I get flushed when I think of you. It just happened. It's wild."

"How come you never want to come see me when you feel like this?"

"'Cause I'd never leave." He saw a flower stand on the opposite side of the street, scanning the bouquets for roses in hopes she'd ask him over, and he could bring her one. "Why you being nice to me? I've been such a shit."

"Because I'm leaving."

"When are you back?"

Maggie didn't say anything for several seconds, and he could sense her reluctance to answer. "I'm not coming back."

* * *

Circus peeled out of the parking lot, the Buick's bumper scraping against a dip in the road and knocking something loose, but he kept driving. He sat rigidly at the wheel as the slowed traffic seemed to press him against the seat, poking at an impulse to jump out of the car and run because he might get to her faster. Turning onto a side street, he slammed the gas, coasting down a hill toward the highway. Out of the corner of his eye, he saw a young woman walking up the street in the direction he'd come, her back to him, her long black hair catching sunbeams and shining. She had the same small frame and swift gait as the girl on the beach in Miami. Luz, he remembered the name, and with it everything else came back—the Miami sunset, the warm breeze coming off the water, Maggie beside him on a chaise longue stroking her neck and telling him their news—and for a strange, brief moment that he immediately understood to be absurd, he imagined this was a do-over, that time had brought him back to Luz so he could reset that first moment and make everything right. He let himself live in the fantasy a little longer until he recognized Koko's tartan coat.

Circus pulled to the curb and lowered his window. "What the hell, man?"

Koko frowned in a way he assumed she must have used to ward off strangers until she realized it was him. "I didn't want to stay with Donna."

"Get in the car."

Koko slid into the passenger seat without looking at him.

"Donna tell you where I was?"

"I know that's your bar. The place I got the high score in pinball," she said. "I cut out when Donna was in the bathroom. The one in your bedroom, by the way. You know she goes through your cabinets, right?"

Circus glanced at his phone and noticed three missed calls from his neighbor. He sent a text telling her to go home.

"I'm on my way across town," he told Koko.

"So take me."

"It's not that kind of situation."

"Well, I'm here." She slumped against the door. "Deal with it."

Jaw set, Circus put the car in gear. "You're not in charge, you know."

"I don't want to be."

"There's nothing I like less than kids barely out of diapers thinking they know more than everybody else."

"I bet there are worse things not to like, and I haven't been in diapers for thirteen years." She rolled down her window and drew in a strong breath. "Where are we going?"

"To see a friend."

"Guy or lady?"

"You're staying in the car."

"Is it a drug deal?"

Circus tsked when he looked over but saw from her timid smile that she was trying to make a joke. "It's my friend Maggie."

"The one you love so much you wrote a song about her?"

"It's impolite to pry."

"You don't have to get mad just because I know you love someone."

Circus relaxed his grip on the wheel, rolling his head from one side to the other to loosen the knotted muscles in his shoulders. "You know, I didn't ask for this."

"Me neither." Koko lowered the back of her seat, stretching out her legs. "Obviously."

The edge of a disc hung from the player on the dash, so Circus slipped it inside, rapping the steering wheel with his thumbs when the song streamed out from the speakers.

"Jelly Roll Morton." He nudged her. "'Wolverine Blues.' Remember, I used to play him for you? Listen to how he's riding those notes in time. Ba-da, ba-da, ba-da. Hear that swing? You remember this? He played life like an instrument. Used to say, you gotta play jazz—"

Koko watched him tap music into the air. "Yeah, I remember all that."

Circus nodded his head in time, tongue patting the roof of his mouth. "When I was your age, I practiced the fingering on these runs until my fingertips calloused up. I got it in the end, though."

"Can we listen to something else?" Koko asked. "Something quiet?"

"Of course." Grimacing, he ejected the disc. "Whatever you want."

* * *

The sun had bled white against the spring sky and cast the day in blanched light by the time Circus pulled onto Maggie's street in Brookline. The trees bordering the road had always reminded him of soldiers guarding the path to her house at the bend of a cul-de-sac, though this afternoon he imagined them as witnesses lowering their eyes as he made his way toward a sentencing. He parked in the drive, then slid a five-dollar bill from his pocket, handing it to Koko, who yanked off the headphones he was grateful she'd slipped on after they hit the highway.

"Go get a snack," he said. "There's a bakery up a block. They make good danishes."

"No one eats danishes." She passed the bill back to him. "I'm not hungry."

"Man, I wish you would've stayed at my place. I gotta have a serious conversation with this woman, a private conversation, all right, and it's gonna take time."

"I'll wait."

"I can't leave you here."

"I'm fine." She reclined her seat, folding her legs against her belly. "I'll read a book."

"You don't have a book."

Koko held her phone out for him to see, scrolling through the text on the screen before replacing the headphones over her ears, already gone before he had a chance to disapprove.

Circus stepped out of the car, combing his hair with his fingers as he walked to the front door. On the porch, he saw a down coat folded into a box marked "donations" and remembered the first time he'd seen it. Maggie had come back from a trip to Vancouver in the dead of winter, her flight landing just before sunrise when the cold was at its peak. Circus had offered to pick her up at the airport because he hadn't stopped thinking about her since they'd last met up. When she walked out of the terminal, her thin body, easily chilled, was covered in the floor-length down coat that made her look cocooned. Circus found it charming. During the drive, she talked about the music festival she'd gone to with a girlfriend and invited him in for coffee when they arrived at her house. Inside, she turned to him at the front door, a coy smirk on her lips.

"Want to see something?" she asked.

Circus had watched her undo the lengthy chain of the zipper, the teeth unlocking and spreading open to reveal the black blouse and skirt she wore underneath. But when the zipper's slide reached the bottom, it stuck. Slowly, Maggie stepped out of the parka one foot at a time, dropping it to her ankles.

"So," he said. "Getting out of your coat is like getting out of a dress."

They didn't make it to the kitchen for coffee but made love on the living room sofa until morning turned to afternoon turned to dusk, pausing only for meals and wine.

As he rang the doorbell now, Circus imagined Maggie retrieving the coat from the box so they could relive the day.

"It's open," she called from inside the house.

The place smelled like Maggie. The cottony scent of the laundry soap she used to wash her clothes and the lavender flowers of her perfume. He waited in the living room, where a painting of Nefertiti stared back at him and a crystal chandelier hanging from the ceiling softened the room with light. The quiet slap of her bare feet against the floor sounded in the hallway, and Maggie stepped into the room.

"There you are." Circus moved toward her, arms extended. "There you are."

"My God, Cyrus, what happened to your mouth?"

Circus hugged her body against his. "Don't ask yet."

She rubbed his back, and his heart purred. "What happened?"

"I had a fight with an angry woman and a trumpet."

She pulled away slightly, her eyebrows cocked.

"A woman hit me with my own goddamn horn," he said. "You believe that?"

Maggie shook her head. "What's the doctor say?"

"I haven't been to the doctor. I've been to the dentist, though."

"Should we ice it?"

"I don't know, my lips are starting to feel like mush."

"Don't mess around, Cy, you need to see a doctor."

"I don't want him telling me I won't play again." His eyes watered after he said it, and Maggie reached up to run her fingers across his bruised cheek. Circus dropped his chin against her open hand.

"You come to me smelling like a brewery?" she tsked.

"Stop," he said. "I need you to be nice. *We* need you to be nice."

Maggie slid out of his embrace, leaving one last stroke of her fingers against his cheek. She moved a pile of vinyl records from the sofa to the floor, offering him a seat he didn't take.

"I came by after those bombs at the marathon," he said. "I wanted to see you."

"My sister told me."

He took her hand. "Don't leave. What's still in New York for you?"

"Everything I'm about."

"What about me?"

Maggie squeezed his shoulder. "You want some tea? Let's have a cup of tea."

Circus followed her through the hallway toward the kitchen, stopping to look at a collection of family photos on the wall. There were portraits of her parents as Morehouse and Spelman students, portraits of Maggie and her sister from high school, a family dog, a cottage somewhere, Maggie and her sister as girls collecting seashells on a beach.

"You've seen those pictures a hundred times," she said.

"I like them just the same." He pulled one from the wall. "I like knowing who you were before I knew you. The you before we met."

"Laying it on thick, aren't you, sugar?"

"I mean what I say."

"I know." She handed him a cup of tea, blowing the heat from her own. "This is what you do. Bleed the passion out of something, then miss it."

"Is there someone else?"

Maggie shook her head, smiled. "Though Tip did ask me to marry him again."

"How am I supposed to compete with Tip Badgett?"

"You're not." She replaced the frame on the wall, letting her gaze linger in her own younger eyes. "I'm not marrying anyone. That's not how my love moves."

Circus took a sip of the tea, staring down at Maggie playing with the curls of her hair. Briefly, she lifted her head, but he couldn't translate her expression.

"You're the notes I know best, Maggie," he said. "You're in my fingers. Don't leave."

"You talk like I'm the one not handling things. Refresh my memory, Cy, which one of us left that hotel in Miami?" She waited, letting the silence humble him. "The difference between you and me is you never think yourself responsible for the feelings you stir in people."

"Listen, I know I did wrong. For a long time now, I haven't been feeling myself. I'm just roaming, man, roaming the same worn-out path." Circus fidgeted, needing her to touch him again. "All I'm feeling is how sensitive I am. I'm needy, baby. And, Maggie, I want to be with you more than I want to be with myself sometimes, and I don't like how it feels. I panicked, all right."

Circus's knees slightly buckled, and Maggie looped her arm through his, leading him back to the living room. She nodded toward the sofa, and he took a seat as she dropped the needle on a record player in the corner, moving her hips when the old Bill Evans tune they liked to listen to together began to play. When she settled between his legs, easing her back against his chest, Circus cloaked her body within his and rested his chin against her shoulder. The warm light in the room and the scent of chamomile in their cups gave him a sense of place, a sturdiness the past months had sapped from him. He traced the supple lines of Maggie's shoulders with his fingers, following the sweep of her ribcage and edging down to the small of her back.

"My people are in Brooklyn," she said. "I miss New York, Cy, I miss my brownstone and my neighbors. The music. The space I have to create. So I'm going to do what I always do." She sat up to face him. "And I'm going to do this."

She made a circle with her hand over her belly.

"You didn't . . ."

She shook her head.

"Why didn't you ask me?"

"Ask you?" Maggie laughed. "Asking permission isn't something I do a lot of."

"I wish you . . ."

Maggie clasped her hands in her lap, her lips pursed. "What? What do you wish, Cyrus? Think about it long and hard."

Not only was Maggie beautiful, but there was a kind of honesty about her he had never fully recognized until now as she sat with him, clothed, in the light of day and on her way out of his life. Until now, he'd thought they were living the same story, wandering separate paths yet moored by the places where they came together and secured to each other by what they weren't saying or allowing to take root, which still thrived beneath the surface like the braided roots of a tree. They loved each other in their own way, he'd thought, even if they were telling each other it didn't mean much. They could have gone on like this forever, but what he realized as Maggie gazed back at him, comfortable with the decision to take herself and what they'd made together away from him, was that he was the only one who'd been lying.

"I should check on Koko," he said, a sudden pang in his chest as he thought of the girl curled up on the passenger seat.

"She's at your place this weekend?"

"She's outside in the car."

Maggie leaped off his lap. "You left her?"

"I'll get her." He stood up to make his way outside, but Maggie had already passed through the hall out the front door. Circus went to the kitchen to dump the tea and search for something stronger but found nothing in the fridge or cupboards. A wooden crate on the floor held an unopened bottle of Rémy Martin, and he contemplated whether to open it, ultimately leaving it in the crate to keep his head clear.

The screen door squeaked on its hinges, then slammed shut at the front of the house. "Are you hungry?" he heard Maggie ask.

The two of them stepped into the kitchen, Maggie the only one acting like there wasn't anything strange about it. Koko seemed either timid or annoyed as she hid behind the sweep of her hair and kept her eyes off him.

"Let's see." Maggie stared into the fridge, pulling out a glass bowl of spinach salad and a hunk of Swiss cheese. She disappeared into the pantry and brought back a baguette in a wicker basket and a jar of raspberry jam.

"Belinda made this," she said, taking a seat at the table and waving Koko over. "Belinda's my sister. She's a sweet little homebody."

Koko glanced up at Circus as if awaiting permission to join Maggie at the table, then sat down when it didn't come.

"Bring us some plates, would you?" Maggie asked him.

He brought a stack of plates from the cupboard and a collection of silver from a drawer, placing them on the table without sitting down. Maggie opened the jam, eyeing him as she spread a dollop over a slice of bread.

"What do you like to eat?" she asked Koko.

The girl folded her arms and kept her eyes on the floor.

"Me, I like everything," Maggie went on. "Even had snails once. I didn't think I was going to like them, but you put enough butter on something, it'll go down."

Koko swung her feet beneath the chair, her mouth pouting rudely. Circus wanted to scold her but also thought it might convince Maggie to send her back to the car.

But Maggie seemed amused as she went back to the pantry and brought out a cake plate, lifting the lid to reveal an apple pie she set in the center of the table. She sat down, pretending to enjoy the taste of her raspberry jam while she watched Koko steal glances at the pie.

"You want a slice?" she asked.

Koko didn't answer but had another peek.

"I'll give you one if you say something."

Koko unfolded her arms. "Something."

Maggie winked and cut her a slice. "I knew it. You have that haven't-eaten-for-days kind of crankiness."

Koko took a bite of the pie and spoke with her mouth full. "My grandmother can't cook."

"What does she make that's so bad?"

"Roasts and stuff," she mumbled. "Everything she makes is dry. The other night she made a pot roast I could've used as a doorstop."

Maggie let out a raucous laugh that echoed in the room and made the corners of Koko's cheeks dimple as she smiled beneath her hair like she hadn't intended to be funny but was glad she was. Maggie told her about the lamb shank her grandmother used to roast on birthdays, and Koko watched her as if from a distance, quickly becoming mesmerized.

"Sit down, Cyrus." Maggie nodded toward an empty chair. "The apples in the pie are soft enough for you to eat."

"Cyrus?" Koko sneered at him. "Mom doesn't even call you Cyrus."

The room filled with silence as Koko looked back and forth between them, teetering, it seemed, on the edge of understanding something she wasn't sure she wanted to know.

"Tell me where he got the nickname," Maggie said, and Circus knew she was trying to set Koko at ease since he'd told her the story years before.

Koko stared at the inside of her hands. For a moment, he thought Maggie had lost her.

"Aunt Ruby, right?" Koko asked. "She had a lisp when she was a little girl and couldn't say 'Cyrus.' It came out sounding like 'Circus,' and the name stuck."

"A lisp like your daddy has now." Maggie grinned. "Say 'she sells seashells by the seashore,' Cy."

Maggie winked at Koko, who hid another smile, glancing up at him like she wanted to hear him try. He sat down, picking at a plate of spinach salad after Maggie passed it to him from across the table. A muddled panic set in as he listened to the voices he knew well but had never heard in the same room—Maggie's easy tenor and Koko's higher pitch. He didn't know yet how to feel about it. He tried to remember which of them he'd been hiding from the other and why, unsure of what was so alarming about the two of them in the same room, though now that he was seeing it, he couldn't help but feel there was something good about it. He'd always imagined his life had paged through many chapters with more yet to come, but now he feared he'd arrived at the close of something much larger, that he'd made a permanent turn, and nothing would best what had come before. It was all too much to take in.

"What grade are you?" Maggie scooped raspberry jam onto her plate.

"Ninth," Koko answered.

"Do you like it?"

"I have to say yes."

"You don't have to say anything." Maggie licked the jam from her spoon. "I didn't like school either. Not until I started a band."

"Do you sing?"

"Only in the shower, girl."

"What do you sing in the shower?"

"'Proud Mary,' Tina's version." Maggie snapped her fingers in the air.

Koko beamed. "You're lucky. My voice is bad."

"No, you have a nice, strong voice, I can hear it. It's clear, and that's good on a woman."

Koko scooted closer to the table. "What do you play?"

"I play drums with some bands."

"Cool." Koko reached for the jar, the two of them taking turns scooping out spoonfuls of jam. "I do plays sometimes."

"You're in theater?" Circus asked.

Koko rolled her eyes. "I played Helen in *To Kill a Mockingbird*. I invited you."

She went on to Maggie about the boy who played Tom, how a teardrop trickled down his cheek during one of the performances and made the rest of the cast believe he'd been moved. Later, the boy confessed to Koko that dust had fallen into his eye and caused it to tear. Maggie listened, her mouth and eyebrows showing her surprise and glee, which charmed Circus, just as Koko's enthusiasm suddenly charmed him because he'd rarely seen or heard it. He liked sitting with Maggie, both of them holding their attention on Koko. He liked seeing who the girl was when she wasn't looking at him.

"Next year, they're doing *Arsenic and Old Lace*," she said. "I don't know if I'll try out."

"You should." Maggie patted her arm. "I can tell you're good. Don't you think, Cy?"

Koko turned to him. All he could do was nod. Speaking might have ruined him.

Maggie held his gaze as if sensing the stir of emotion inside him. "I was in a play once in college. *A Midsummer Night's Dream*. They wanted me to play Titania, the fairy queen, but I insisted they let me play Puck, the sprite." Her fingers danced in the air as she lifted her shoulders and declared, "'Lord, what fools these mortals be.'"

Koko mimicked the rise of Maggie's shoulders, then dropped against the chair with the same shy grin she'd worn in the car, gazing at Maggie with love. But when she turned to Circus, her smile faded. "Dad, are you okay?"

He didn't realize his face was showing the turmoil he held inside. He tried to nod, but his lips quaked. He pressed them tight.

"Koko," Maggie said. "Have you ever seen a chicken coop?"

"I don't think so."

"My sister raises chickens in the backyard. Why don't you go outside and have a look? They might have laid some eggs."

Koko gave a nod of her head and excused herself. Moments passed, Maggie circling the rim of her teacup with her finger, Circus watching, swallowing the lump in his throat.

"Her mother left," he said. "We don't know where she is, but it doesn't seem like she's coming back anytime soon."

"Oh no." Maggie shook her head. "Poor child."

"She seems to like you." He cracked a smile. "Maybe you should stick around."

Maggie paused as she stroked her neck, her gaze following the path Koko had just taken outside. They sat together for several moments until Maggie stood up to refill their teacups. She moved onto his lap, and he held her.

"The other night I dreamed a melody," he said. "I woke up to hum it into the recorder I got next to the bed and listened the next morning. It was 'Moonlight in Vermont.'"

She chuckled. "I've done the same thing."

"Lately I've been wondering if my best memories were only dreams I had."

"Oh, Cy, don't be so dramatic. You're going to be all right." She kissed the top of his head, stroking his back.

"When are you leaving?" he asked.

"Next week."

"That's quick."

"It's been a long time coming."

"Is this the last time I'm going to see you?"

"I said 'Next week,' didn't I? And New York's only a car ride away."

He rested his head against her chest, listening for her voice's echo. "Tell me about the night we met."

"Why?"

"I want to live it again."

"You're not getting soft on me, are you?" She sank deeper into his lap. "Stevie Chan's garden party, was it? I was sitting by the pool, and you were about to jam with the guys."

"But then I saw you."

"Then you saw me, and you walked up looking like an Adonis, boy, like some warrior in ancient Greece."

"What'd I say?"

"You said, 'I was looking for you.' Then you corrected yourself and said, 'I was looking *at* you. I've seen you before. We've met.'"

"Did you think it was a line?"

"Well," she said. "I'd never met you before in my life."

He shook his head. "I wouldn't forget you."

"You got real close," she said. "I could smell your cologne, something stout and musky. You were so close, I could see the wad of gum in the corner of your mouth, this green pulp you chewed at like an addict getting over something. You pulled the cap off your head and shoved it into my hands. That's your move."

"That's my move."

"I asked if Circus was your real name, and you told me that's what everyone calls you. And I said, 'I don't want to call you what everyone else calls you.' And you said . . ."

"'I'm Cyrus.'"

"And I handed that hat right back to you and said, 'I'm Maggie,'" she said, tears filling her eyes.

Circus held her tightly as he finally realized what was coming for him once Maggie was gone. He placed his hand on her belly even though there was no bump there yet to hold on to. He wanted to explain, but he didn't know what needed explanation or how to give it words.

"You do what's been done to you," he said, voice cracking. "I got scared when Koko came along. You scared me all over again."

Quietly, Maggie nodded, resting her hand on his. She sat with him, tracing his fingers with her thumb. Circus chewed at the inside of his mouth to keep himself from crying. The light in the room seemed to shift as if the day had turned to night and back into day, though he understood only a few minutes had passed.

"All right, Cyrus Palmer, you be happy. You hear me? You find a way to be happy." She cupped his chin and kissed his forehead. "Go on now. Your daughter's waiting."

* * *

Circus started the car after Koko told him they'd been sitting at the curb outside Maggie's house too long. His silence was making her sad, Koko said, and she worried Maggie would look out her front window and see them. He pulled away from the curb and away from the house he'd left so many times, the streetlamp at the sidewalk's edge receding in his rearview mirror. But unlike before, he had a sick feeling, like a death had come, and the grief would always travel with him.

"I get why you like her." Koko carefully placed the basket of eggs, plucked from the chickens' nests, between her knees. "Are we going to see her again?"

"I don't have an answer for you."

Koko nodded, rolling an egg in her palm. "Are you going to tell me things?"

"What kind of things?"

"About you. About us."

"What's to tell?"

She swallowed nervously. "Like, the scars on your back."

A cold washed through him as if his body had filled with gray. "My father and a pair of matches."

The wound on his lip pulsed, sending a fleeting pain through his jaw as he swallowed the spit, tinged with stale blood, pooling on his tongue. He tried to concentrate on the rickety hum of the Buick's engine, but he couldn't get around the feeling of collapse beneath everything he'd laid his life upon. Only Koko distracted him. What made him smile was the care with which she was positioning herself around the basket of eggs.

"You wanna be an actress, huh?" he asked after giving her a playful nudge.

"Not really."

"You said you were in theater."

"Just something to do."

"So what are you into?" he asked.

"I don't know."

"There's gotta be something. I owe you a birthday gift, kid. Let's go get you one."

Koko leaned her head against the window but didn't answer. Circus tapped his hand against her knee. "Well, I didn't know what I wanted to be at first either."

"I thought you always wanted to play music."

"Not when I was real little. When I was real little, I wanted to be a cheetah. I used to practice in my backyard."

"Practice what?"

"Running," he said as if the answer were obvious.

Koko smiled and slipped off her shoes, opening the window a crack. Eyes closed, she took in a deep breath, then let it go. As she straightened the hem of her dress and licked her chapped lips, Circus noticed for the first time how many years had gone by, how old she looked now, how much she looked like him.

"What are we going to do?" she asked.

The warm air outside flowed in through Koko's window, and Circus relaxed into it. He imagined the second bedroom where she would sleep, the old instruments and speakers he'd have to find a new place for, the furniture he'd have to buy—a mattress, a dresser, and whatever girls liked—his routine, his habits, and everything else he'd have to rearrange. A fury rose in him, but at its end was something unexpected, a moment of clarity, accidental but stark, that told him he might not want to be a different person—he couldn't possibly be—but somehow the man he had already become was enough for this girl, and she could show him ways to be better. But this, Circus didn't think he should say aloud, not here, not yet, so he only took his daughter's hand, comforted by how baby soft her skin still was and by the part of him that wanted to tell her, *I will give you anything if you only love me. Forgive me. Listen.*

What Would You Do Today if You Knew Jesus Was Coming Tomorrow?

*

Pia

Just after dinnertime, a shuttle bus wheezed into the lot of the King of Prussia Holiday Inn that Pia had made home for the last week, blocking her view of the full moon. Earlier in the day, a woman netting dead leaves from the hotel swimming pool told Pia this was a Milk Moon because the cows and sheep were full with milk, and all the flowers wanted to bloom. Pia believed the woman because she wore beaded scarves around her waist like a gypsy, though she didn't think she was free to call anyone a gypsy anymore. Pia had been smoking a Pall Mall cigarette, which she could feel tarring her throat with each drag, and peeling an orange, so soot lay in the beds of her fingernails and juices stickied her hands. When the bus rolled in, she spat into her palms, rubbed them together, and wiped them against her unwashed skirt, feeling a need to prepare for whatever the bus was going to bring. The immense silence with which it had arrived and its timeworn metal frame seemed to open up a mystery.

The people filing out of the bus were nothing special, like people stepping off any bus anyplace in the world, she imagined. Pia watched anyway. Not much had crossed her path to look at in the ten days since she had left Boston, and she didn't want these tugs of boredom sending her home. A teenage boy stepped off the bus and shaded his squinting eyes with a magazine as if he'd been sleeping. After him came a father and son with Eagles duffel bags. A big woman in a too-tight dress. An afroed woman with an acoustic guitar.

He came backwards. Feet first. Ass. Back. He dragged his wheeled suitcase from the bus to the ground, then slowly turned with a look of awe as if he were arriving in Paris or London and not King of Prussia, Pennsylvania. From the slight distance and in the growing dark, she could see the slender mass of his body under his blue raincoat, could see the wheat-colored layers of his hair and the hewn angles of his face. The bus riders ambled into the hotel, and she followed several steps behind, sorting through a pile of gossip magazines on a coffee table once she got inside.

"We're the Mercersburg folks," said the old man at the head of the throng to the clerk at the front desk. "'Bout ten of us. You said you'd set us aside five or so rooms. Don't worry—boys and girls in separate quarters."

The corner of the clerk's mouth lifted in a practiced, dispassionate smile, which made the old man blush. He turned back to the rest of the group and instructed them to take out their licenses. The man in the blue raincoat dropped behind the rest of the group to unzip and search his suitcase, kneeling within arm's reach.

"Where's Mercersburg?" Pia asked him.

He glanced up, letting his gaze move up and down her body, but not with the lust she'd been seeking for so many years. He looked with pity, and Pia realized how long it had been since she'd given her hair a good combing and her face a good wash. She licked her lips to give them a momentary gloss.

"I'm new to the area," she said, knowing right away how silly it was to say at a hotel. "What's your name?"

"Gilbert."

"Seriously?"

He looked back at her, apparently not hearing anything to doubt or joke about.

"Gilbert's a nice name," she said. "Unique. I like it."

"I appreciate the kindness." He offered a wide, childlike grin, then returned to his bag, sliding his wallet from an inside pocket.

"I'm Pia. I'm passing through."

Gilbert nodded and brought his license to the front desk as Pia took a peek into his half-open suitcase but could see only what looked like stacks of sweaters, a flashlight, and the worn corner of a book. She opened to a random page in one of the magazines before he turned and saw her snooping, but she watched out of the corner of her eye as he closed the bag.

"How long will you be in town?" she asked.

"Around five days, I believe." He had a thin voice, weak almost, but it made her feel more confident, as did the lack of lines around his mouth, which told Pia she had a few years on him. "And you?"

"We'll see," she tried to sound mysterious. Gilbert only beamed again like a boy. She asked, "Did you have a good trip?"

"Any trip where I reach my destination is good in my eyes."

"Oh, I like the way you think." She toyed with a button on her jacket. "Although it's kind of nice not to have a destination. You just go and let your destination find you."

Pia clasped her hands behind her back, proud of herself for coming up with such a smart thing to say.

Gilbert nodded as if she'd told him a riddle he was slowly figuring out.

"What brings you here?" she asked.

The rest of Gilbert's group disbanded and headed to their rooms. He looked after them, seemingly concerned he should join. "We're on a retreat. There was no more room at the venue itself, so we're here. I'm not one for cabins, so I'm grateful for the warm bed."

"Cabins? What kind of retreat?"

"My apologies"—he folded his hands over the center of his chest—"but I've had a long day and need to get something in my belly. I hope you won't be offended if I excuse myself."

"The place across the street has a fun menu," she said. "I usually go around seven."

The old man brought Gilbert his room key, watching Pia with slightly skinnied eyes.

"We got a long day tomorrow, son." The man slapped his back. "You best rest up."

Gilbert bowed his head as the man walked off after shooting Pia another glance.

"Kind of you to make the recommendation." Gilbert reached for his bag, touching the center of his chest again. "How lucky we crossed paths."

* * *

Back in her room, Pia stepped into the shower for a thorough cleaning, digging the dirt from beneath her fingernails and scrubbing the grime from the bottoms of her feet. She washed her hair twice and sprayed perfume in it, rouged her cheeks and mouth. She slipped into the prettiest, cleanest dress she had—cotton with pink and blue stripes. In her bag, she placed a lipstick beside her wallet and keys, a handful of peanut butter candies so she could offer him one, and the Henry Miller novel she'd found at a rest stop near Hartford but hadn't started reading.

The waitress at the diner knew her now so brought a cup of creamed coffee with two sugar cubes. Pia had ordered Reuben sandwiches all week for dinner, but tonight she needed something lighter, something that would blend with the natural fragrances of her body so Gilbert would smell sweet things when he sat across from her.

"I'll have a fruit salad and strawberry shake."

The waitress grinned. "Don't you look pretty? Expecting company?"

"Maybe," she answered, and felt like a girl.

Pia checked the door before turning to the first page of the book, deciding she would flip to the middle when Gilbert came to make it appear she'd been engrossed. She read the opening line aloud to herself in a whisper—"Once you have given up the ghost, everything follows with dead certainty, even in the midst of chaos"—but whatever it meant didn't register so she read it again and again until she wasn't reading at all but only staring at the page. It was seven o'clock. A Tuesday. Koko had her piano lesson and Pia wondered if Circus had driven her. Neither Koko nor Circus had reached out during the last few days, though in the week following Pia's leaving, they'd bombarded her with phone calls, none of which she'd answered. She'd thought of turning off the phone or blocking their numbers but realized she would miss the prickle of delight that came to her belly with each chime of her phone, knowing how insistently she was occupying their minds. In fact, she longed to hear one of those chimes now and reached for her phone, reading Circus's last text from three days ago: *Come get your daughter.*

The waitress delivered the milkshake and five minutes later brought the fruit salad. Pia picked at the melon and pineapple. Took light sips of the drink. Through the window, she watched the hotel, thrilling whenever the lobby doors opened but suffering after they closed and Gilbert hadn't passed through. She waited an hour, paging through the book so no one in the diner would see her and feel pity.

"Exactly what I needed," she said when the waitress delivered her bill.

The first steps Pia took back across the street dragged, her body weighed by regret, a familiar burden she couldn't remember not feeling. And then the archive of things that hadn't worked out in the last two decades of her life passed through her mind—minor crushes stalled, friendships drifting apart, prospects to help her out of a dreary desk job fading, appeals to Circus to stop fucking other women during their marriage and to Koko to show some love. Pia's body settled into the strange comfort that came with relentless disappointment, until she arrived at the hotel doors and realized she'd made a choice in leaving Boston. A choice to separate herself from those moments and no longer slump her shoulders in the face of whatever life handed her.

Inside the hotel, Pia slapped her palms against the front desk and the clerk jumped, lost in his computer screen.

"I'd like you to tell me which room Gilbert is staying in," she said. "He's the gentleman I was speaking to earlier."

The clerk glanced around as if looking for someone to give permission. "I don't think I'm allowed to do that."

"I'm allowing you," she said, feigning a confidence she didn't know whether she deserved. "I'm the customer. I get what I ask for, yes? And I won't tell a soul."

"I don't know who Gilbert is, ma'am. People come in and out. Hard to remember a particular person."

Her knees quaked. Her voice threatened to crack. But she kept her gaze fixed on him.

"And, y'know, what about"—he absently tapped the computer keys—"privacy?"

Pia fought the urge to cry, though she knew the tears wanted to come only because she didn't like how vulnerable she felt making demands.

"I need to get in touch with Gilbert," she pushed on. "Are you going to help or not?"

"What's his last name? I could call him."

"Can't you just search for the name Gilbert? It's unusual enough."

"Our computer doesn't work that way." He reached beneath the desk and brought out a pad of paper and envelope. "How 'bout leaving him a note? I can try and make sure he sees it in the morning."

"I want to see him tonight." The urgent need started to hurt her stomach.

"I'm sorry, ma'am"—the clerk lowered his voice—"I can't lose this job."

Pia slid the pad of paper to the edge of the desk so the clerk couldn't see. Quickly, she wrote, "Can you come see me? It won't take long. Pia. Room 212."

"I'll do my best to make sure he gets it," said the clerk.

"Please do better than that."

Pia made her way through the hotel, checking the halls for him. Doors opened and closed, coins clanked in the vending machines, and she turned to see whether Gilbert was the one making the sounds. Sliding beneath the covers of her bed, the cotton dress snug against her body, she stared through the dark and imagined Gilbert heading to her room having retrieved the note. She would open the door to him, she might welcome him inside, but the vision stopped there because she didn't know what she needed to happen next. The thought of him walking through the corridor searching for her room was enough tonight. She wanted someone to come after her, to come get her. To find her.

* * *

The knock on her door the next morning was tentative.

"A minute," she called, then ran to the bathroom to quickly wash her face and run a comb through her hair. She brushed her teeth and changed out of the cotton dress into a romper she knew showed off her legs.

When she opened the door, Gilbert glanced up from her note, which he held in his hands, and looked at her as if he wasn't sure he had the right room. He handed her the note like a passenger on a train handing over a ticket. Pia followed the lines of her own handwriting—the swirl at the top of her *o*'s, the circle over the *i* in Pia—to stall for time as she realized she hadn't come up with a reason to ask for Gilbert's help.

"Did you rest well?" she asked.

"Sure. Thank you for asking."

"It's been restless. My sleep."

Finally, she looked up from the note and caught his gaze fixed on her bare ankles, bare shins, knees. She could see now he wasn't much younger than her, perhaps in his early thirties, but there seemed to be a lack of having experienced the world or having been damaged by it, which explained the innocence she read in his blue eyes.

"Are you wearing socks?" he asked. "Whenever we couldn't sleep, my grandmother told us to put on our socks. She wouldn't let us go to bed without them when we slept at her house." He scratched at his forehead, the apple of his throat jumping. "Is that why you asked me to see you?"

Pia liked how his nervousness felt on her skin. She didn't say anything for several moments so she could feel its light prickle. Gilbert slid his hands into his pockets.

"Do you want to come in?" she asked.

"I don't believe that would be right." He cleared his throat again. "Why don't we take a walk?"

"There's nothing around here to see."

"Actually, I was thinking we could walk to the pop machines," he said. "They've got a cherry cola in there, and I haven't had one of those since I was knee-high. I'm happy to treat you if you're thirsty."

Pia joined him. Gilbert walked beside her, his hands in his pockets, his gait slow.

"Maybe we should eat something?" She tried to put a lift to her step to show him what a fun girl she was. "I could eat a horse."

"Have you tried the breakfast downstairs?"

"Not this morning."

"They have tasty waffles. You can make them yourself."

Pia found their walk romantic, with Gilbert's leisurely stroll and awkward smiles. The way he looked around as if they were outside surrounded by pretty trees and passing butterflies. He went on about the hotel breakfast, describing what the other members of his group had chosen to eat that morning and glancing bashfully at her.

At the vending machine, Gilbert bought a cherry cola, popped the tab, and took a generous sip. He held out a fistful of coins. Pia thanked him and shook her head.

"Okay then." He picked at the tab of the can. "What did you need to talk about?"

Pia hadn't come up with an answer and sensed the tears welling in her throat. Every day since she'd left Boston, something had made her cry so hard she thought her soul had emptied, yet there was always more sadness.

"Maybe I will have a soda," she said.

Gilbert began dropping coins into the slot. Pia pressed the keys and watched the can of iced peach tea fall.

"Actually," he said, popping the tab and handing the can to her, "I think I know what you want to talk about."

"You do?"

"I could sense it in you immediately. The longing. I know how it feels. That's what it is, right? Longing?"

She smiled at a family who passed in their bathing suits apparently on the way to the hotel's indoor pool. She let her gaze linger after them so that Gilbert wouldn't see how rattled she was, but when she turned back to him, his eyes were still fixed on her.

"I guess," she answered. "I guess that's what it is."

He glanced at his watch, sucking at his bottom lip as he seemed to make calculations in his head. "How long would it take you to get ready to start your day?"

"I'm ready now, I thought."

"Where we're going you should dress," he paused, glancing down at her bare legs and blushing. "Warmer."

* * *

Three cars waited in the hotel lot for Gilbert and the rest of his group, their drivers eagerly greeting them as they stepped out of the hotel. In blue jeans and a loose sweater, Pia stood at a distance until she was welcomed into the back seat of one of the cars, an old Chevy with a cross hanging from the rearview mirror. The woman driving introduced herself too quickly for Pia to get a name. Sliding back behind the wheel, the woman turned up the volume on a baseball game and nudged the man in the passenger seat, who offered Pia a tip of his soiled Sunoco cap. Gilbert climbed into the seat beside Pia, thanking the drivers for their kindness.

Pia gently tapped his knee. "You haven't told me where I'm going."

"The retreat, of course."

"What kind of retreat, though?"

Gilbert pulled a manila folder from the backpack between his knees, reading from a pamphlet inside. "Today we're talking about acceptance. Pastor Williams says nothing enslaves us more or brings us farther from the Lord than searching for acceptance."

"Oh," she said. "This is a . . . this is religious?"

He smiled like a father hiding a gift from a child. "This is what you need. Trust."

Pia kept her gaze on the landscape passing outside the car window. The town looked like so many others she'd passed since she'd stepped out of the café in Massachusetts and hit the highway, stopping only to buy a suitcase full of clothes and cosmetics at a department store in Worcester, and a steak dinner outside Darien, Connecticut. She'd ended up in King of Prussia because she saw a sign for Valley Forge from the highway and decided her unplanned adventure needed markers to give it significance. The tour of the park offered her spirit a sense of rebellion and pride that faded by the evening when she arrived exhausted at the hotel.

Most of the week that followed she'd spent in bed crying, snacking, watching television, sleeping. Once she'd ventured out to a farmers market to buy fruits that now sat rotting on the bathroom counter. Another day she went to a zoo and wept in front of a field of prairie dogs burrowing into their dens. The landscape through the window didn't offer much, mostly shopping malls and stretches of budding trees, but the sights were recognizable, unlike whatever she was riding toward.

* * *

The grounds reminded Pia of the camp her parents used to send her to during summers, with its cluster of cabins circling a main house, where she now stood at the back of the room with Gilbert. The rows of wooden folding chairs and the aisles in front of them were filled with people—young, old, hopeful, stricken—as children ran through the empty spaces in the room, their mothers hushing or chasing after them. Beside her, Gilbert pressed his palms together and closed his eyes in prayer, so she had a chance to stare at his handsome jaw and the lush waves of his hair. He seemed unaware of how beautiful a man he was, and Pia wondered how it was possible. Not once had he looked at her with smug desire, not once had he spoken to another person as if his interest had to be earned, not once had he walked into a room like he was the person who most deserved to be there. Things Pia knew beautiful men did. Things she'd watched Circus do again and again. It had broken her every time.

Silence passed through the crowd when a man stepped through the entrance at the back of the meeting house and moved with determination up the center aisle to an elevated stage, where a crimson rug had been unrolled, it seemed, to receive him. The beam of light that shone down on him from a lamp above seeped into the angles of his face so that he looked like he'd been carved from pale wood. He stroked the cross pinned to his bright yellow necktie, a gesture that seemed to deepen the silence. Pia shifted in her seat, desperate for him to speak and bring the air back into the room. A baby croaked from somewhere within the stillness.

"God's telling me there are a lot of seekers in here this morning," the man said, eyes closed. "Do you feel the grasping of the souls around you? Do you know what they're grasping for?"

He opened his eyes. They were hard, Pia thought. Demanding.

"Do you feel the souls around you waiting?" He moved to the edge of the stage. "They're waiting for someone to tell them they're okay. You. You are waiting for someone to tell you you're okay. Is that what brought you here today?"

He paused, glancing around the room. No one moved or answered.

"Would you like me to tell you that I approve of the way you're living your life?" Pastor Williams asked. "Okay then. I'll tell you. You're okay. I approve."

Nodding, he waited, his gaze moving over the crowd. "You don't feel better, do you?"

The tension eased slightly as a hum of laughter filtered through the room.

"Why don't you feel better?" Pastor Williams smoothed the bottom of his necktie like an executive running a meeting. "Because I'm just a man. The people sitting around you? Just men. What we think of how you're living makes not a whit. What God thinks? Now there's something."

Gilbert's gaze stayed fixed on the pastor. Beside him, the man in the Sunoco hat called out, "Praise Him."

"I understand," the pastor said. "You're only trying to figure out why you're in this life. And I'm here to tell you. God is the reason."

Murmurs of "yes" and "speak" and "praise the Lord" filtered through the room.

Pastor Williams crouched down to sit on his heels. "Turn to the person next to you and tell him he's smart."

Gilbert turned, a tear wet in his eye, and quietly told Pia, "You're smart."

"Tell him he's doing a good job at work."

"You're doing a good job at work," Gilbert said.

Pastor Williams said more, but Pia wasn't hearing his commands. She only heard Gilbert who, on the pastor's order, told her, "You're beautiful. You're a good person. I appreciate you."

He turned back to face the stage, rapt by Pastor Williams, but Pia wanted him to look at her again, to say more, to unclasp his hands and put them on her.

"Maybe you feel good to hear such kind words from another person," the pastor's voice broke through her daze. "We like being paid attention to, don't we? But if you're ready, I'd like to show you today what it feels like when the Lord pays you attention."

Gilbert patted Pia's back as if together they'd won a prize.

"Let us pray," said Pastor Williams.

The people in the room bowed their heads. Except Pia, who quietly backed away from Gilbert deep in prayer and slipped out of the house, across the lawn, and into the sparse wood behind the row of cabins. Reaching into her pocketbook for the Pall Malls, she snickered, thinking of the pastor's melodrama, though she noticed how heavily her hands shook. Boston felt so far away. Pia missed the plump cushions of her living room sofa. Missed the smell of the apple trees that budded in spring outside her kitchen window. She missed Koko when she allowed herself to think about it. The loneliness she'd known back home felt far away, too, and she still hadn't settled into the utter freedom that replaced it. She should have been doing more with all that space and time, she knew, but couldn't imagine what. Gilbert was an answer. The two of them could curl up together on her hard hotel mattress, speaking softly and stroking one another's hair as she told him about the wrong turn she took near Worcester, almost ending up in New Hampshire, and the five-car pile-up outside Newark that had given her nightmares for days. She fantasized his lips brushing across her stomach and his hands spread across her back. She thought of the last time she'd touched herself—hidden in her bedroom closet months before—and had a good shiver.

* * *

Pia sat at a picnic table nibbling at the hot dog on stale bread that someone had smothered in mustard and placed on her plate. Across the lawn, Gilbert listened intently to Pastor Williams, whom he'd sought out before lunch began. After the meal, the woman pastor who had blessed their food separated the women from the men and guided them toward the cabins to study their Bibles. When one man dropped back from the throng and made his way toward the parking lot, Pia went after him. He was headed back to the hotel, he said. A spot of pain in his belly. She told him she had a headache and rode with him. At the hotel she drank peach iced teas, watched cop show reruns, and bought jade rings from shopping channels, her eyes drifting every so often to the window where she hoped to see the cars come back from the retreat. She watched until she fell asleep, only to be awakened what seemed like seconds later by the chime of her phone.

I needed that dress I asked you to hem for Nicolette's wedding this weekend, Koko had texted. *Thanks a lot for not doing it.*

Pia tossed the phone to the foot of the mattress, expecting the usual shame to hit. Instead what she felt had the same dull texture of what she used to feel fighting with her younger sister or taking her turn getting slighted by the popular girls in high school. Testy. Worn. Lighting a cigarette, she pulled out an atlas someone had left in a drawer by the bed. Dropping it between her open legs, Pia closed her eyes, opened to a random page, and pointed her finger. Billings, Montana. She did it again. Mound City, Kansas. Troutville, Virginia. Silver Springs, Colorado.

At seven, she went to the diner across the street and ordered a basket of onion rings and a root beer float. The Henry Miller novel sat in her purse, but she couldn't bring herself to read it.

Instead, she paged through a John Deere catalog someone had left in the booth.

"Want some company?"

Pia looked up. Gilbert stood with his hands in his jacket pockets.

"Please," she said, brushing her fingers through her hair. "Are you hungry?"

Nodding, he sat down. "Order me something? I can't figure out my appetite."

Pia ordered him a ham sandwich and bowl of chicken soup, sliding her root beer float across the table when the waitress brought it. Gilbert hesitated before sliding over the straw and taking a sip from the edge of the glass.

"My mother always said we should only allow ourselves one special thing a day." He wiped a dab of ice cream from his lip. "That was my special thing."

"Only one sip?"

"I'd say there's enough sugar in there to last me a week."

The waitress delivered the basket of onion rings, and Gilbert took one without asking, which Pia hoped meant an intimacy had come into bud between them. He pulled the crisp bread-crumb shell off the onion like paper from a straw, then placed both pieces onto his saucer.

"You left the retreat early," he said.

"You come to scold me?" she flirted.

"Today's study was about finding grace in the middle of suffer-ing. Seems a discussion any woman could use."

"Do I not seem graceful to you?" She twirled the braid in her hair around her fingers. "Some people used to say I look like Grace Kelly. Do you know who she is? Do you think they're right?"

He looked at her with narrowed eyes, assessing her but seem-ingly not getting a read. "Why are you here? Do you live in that hotel?"

"Heavens, no. I'm just passing through town."

"You said that before." He rubbed his greasy fingertips together. "What's it mean? You don't seem to be in a hurry to get wherever you're going."

Pia uncapped a bottle of ketchup and poured a pool onto her plate. "Why be in a rush?"

"Depends on where you're headed. Where *are* you headed?"

"I have no idea actually." She reached across the table and tugged the sleeve of his jacket. "Want to come with me?"

Gilbert quickly slid the sleeve from her fingers as if an insect had landed there. Pia withdrew her hand, slipping it beneath her thighs. "I guess I'm having a journey. Trying to discover something new."

"The Lord is discovery enough for me."

The waitress placed the soup and sandwich in front of Gilbert, who reached for his knife and neatly cut away the sandwich's edges. Pia watched the care with which he handled the bread, his strong, unscarred hands gently maneuvering the knife and pulling at the crusts.

"Do you want to hear my story?" she asked, suddenly fearful of his answer.

"I know your story, Pia. You're seeking, like Pastor Williams said."

"There's more to it, though. Isn't there always more to it?"

He took a careful bite of the sandwich, his teeth leaving a perfect semicircle in the bread. "Everyone thinks there's something more to life. But life is God, and He's enough. Your journey's already decided."

Gilbert took another bite of his sandwich, ignoring the dollop of mayonnaise left on his bottom lip. Pia had an urge to press her napkin against his mouth to get rid of it, to push too hard until his lip split against the edge of his teeth, to separate the bread slices and smear the mayonnaise across his blank face. That's what it was. Blankness. The thin, empty voice. The uninhabited eyes. The sculpted jaw and sea-colored blue eyes—perfectly mundane.

"Hasn't there been one time?" she asked.

"One time . . . what?"

"Tell me about one time when you did something bad. Then maybe I'll believe you."

"I don't do bad things."

The waitress crossed the room, and Pia followed her with her eyes, noticing how different the woman looked from the women she knew back home, how everyone in the restaurant looked like they belonged to this place, this place with nothing much more than a block-long farmers market and uncrowded zoo. This place where Pia knew no one, where she could leave whenever she wished, where whatever ridiculous things she said or did would never follow once she'd gone.

"You must *think* of bad things," she said. "Tell me what bad things you think about."

He took a bite of the sandwich, chewing slowly.

"Have you ever wanted to say a bad word?"

"I've said bad words," he answered. "It's not so wrong."

"Have you ever wanted to punch someone?"

He didn't answer.

"Have you ever wanted to drink until you got sick? Haven't you ever needed to?"

"No, Pia," he said, slightly unsettled. "Have you?"

"God, yes. Almost every day."

He unlaced his fingers, picking at a blister on the inside of his thumb. "The hole inside you? God closes it up. Only God."

"Don't you mean He fills it?"

He motioned toward the waitress and asked her to bring the check and a box for the rest of his meal. The two of them sat in silence as they waited for the waitress to return. Pia watched as he tidily packaged up his dinner.

"God wants to talk to you," he said. "He wants you to find Him. He keeps stepping onto your path, but you keep walking around Him."

He took his wallet from inside his jacket, glanced at the check, and placed two crumpled bills beneath the ketchup bottle on the table.

"Dinner's on me," he said. "Good night, Pia."

She watched him walk through the restaurant toward the door, as much a part of this place as he was more beautiful than anyone else in the room. No one seemed to notice her sitting alone, hands in the air where Gilbert had just stood. But she sensed how far she'd drifted. What a stranger she'd become.

* * *

The front desk clerk hid the joint he'd been smoking behind his back when Pia found him huddled between the trash bins at the rear of the hotel where she'd gone to toss the slice of blueberry pie the waitress had given her on her way out of the restaurant.

"Are you gonna tell anyone?" he asked.

"Not if I can have some."

"You don't seem the type."

"I'm not." Pia extended her hand.

The clerk slid the joint between her fingers.

"Make another one for yourself," she said and brought it back to her room.

Dumping the contents of her purse onto the bed, she noticed a message on her phone as she reached for the pack of Pall Malls to slip the lighter from its sleeve. Circus.

Call me, the message read.

Pia hit the joint. Not since college had she smoked one, so the burn at the back of her throat made her cough a ball of spit into the toilet. She took another softer hit and held it in. Easing into the high, she watched funny videos of cats and babies on her phone, nibbling at the peanut butter candies left in her purse.

Then she swiped back to her messages.

Call me, Circus's text read.

Why? she typed.

Pia pitched her phone back into her empty purse and spread out across the bed, giving her eyes a rest. Circus, she knew from experience, wouldn't respond for hours.

But there he was again.

Finally, he'd typed. *Where the hell are you?*

None of your beeswax, she responded.

You gonna pick up if I call?

I don't know. Try me.

Seconds later her phone rang. Pia didn't answer, tittering as she imagined him grumbling on the other end of the line. The ringing stopped, then started again.

"You have one minute," she answered.

"What the hell are you doing, man? This is some serious drama you stirred up, Pia, even for you. You got our attention, if that's what you wanted. Koko showed me the note you wrote her, by the way. Why do you think you deserve a fresh start and the rest of us are supposed to sit back and applaud?"

"What do you want, Circus?"

"What do you think I want, goddamn it? Come back."

"Give me a reason why I should."

"You got a life to lead here."

"No," she said, lifting the joint to her lips. "I just have things to do."

"That's a life."

The smoke grazed her throat, so she muted the phone before Circus could hear her cough.

"Listen, I get it," he said. "I don't help out enough. I'll do more. Message received."

"This isn't about you."

"What are you gonna do? Who do you know anywhere else in the world? How are you gonna build something from nothing in some place you don't know? I get it, man, life can overwhelm you. But you really think you're just gonna turn your back on everything forever?"

Tears filled Pia's eyes. "You think you're so smart."

"No, no." His voice softened. "That's one thing I know I'm not."

"I'm out here. I made it this far."

"Where'd you make it, Pia? Where are you? Tell me all about your beautiful new life."

Pia looked around at the bland furniture and carpeting in the room where the scent of the fruit rotting in the bathroom finally hit her. She saw her clothes strung over the backs of chairs and heaped on the floor, saw the coffee-stained mugs and dirtied dinner plates from when she first arrived stacked on the desk across from the bed. Shame burned in her cheeks as she imagined confessing that she was less than six hours away from him.

"Don't you miss, Koko?" he asked. "Don't you miss your girl? She misses you."

In the empty space of the high, Pia floated inside his question. Clicking off the lights, she sat up in the bed in the dark so she could find the answer, so she could know with certainty. Taking a drag from the joint, she thought of Koko at three years old in a wading pool in the backyard, scooping water into a bucket, her forehead crumpling when the water spilled from her plastic shovel. She thought of an eight-year-old Koko mirroring her as she tried on a cocktail dress she couldn't afford at Bloomingdale's. Thought of a ten-year-old Koko proudly presenting her with a bouquet of flowers she'd pulled from the neighbor's garden. Thought of Koko in her lap beneath the blanket the three of them shivered under as Circus sang to them. Louis Armstrong. Otis Redding. But what made Pia's eyes water wasn't the memories but the absence of feeling. The lack of connection.

"She tells me all the time," Circus went on, seemingly pleased with how quickly he thought he was getting through to her. "'Mom knows how to cook my eggs.' 'Mom always gets me to school early,' she tells me. Man, I just can't get her out of the house on time."

"She never talks to me anymore," Pia said, haunted by the hollowness of her own voice. "Same with you. When was the last time you really talked to me? Really saw me?"

After an uncomfortable pause, Circus said flatly, "I see you all the time, buttercup. You're pretty as the day I met you."

A familiar silence passed between them, one Pia no longer needed to fill.

"You're coming back, aren't you?" he asked.

Before she could respond, she heard a knock at the door. Without saying goodbye, she hung up, flushing the rest of the joint. Gilbert stood in the hallway, wide-eyed, a layer of sweat on his pale skin as if in the brief time since she'd seen him, he'd come down with a flu. Her phone rang again, but she turned off the sound. Though Gilbert didn't speak, Pia understood that he wanted to come in, so she opened the door wider and let him pass. Quickly, she went around the room collecting her strewn-about clothes and piling the dirty dishes into the bathtub.

Gilbert was sitting on the bottom of the bed when she went back into the main room, his hands folded between his bouncing knees. Pia shoved the contents of her purse back into her bag, then sat on the opposite corner of the bed.

"It smells strange in here," he said.

"Oh," she said. "That's a perfume I have. There's a spice to it."

The obvious lie embarrassed her, though Gilbert seemed to take her word as he looked around the room like it wasn't, as Pia assumed, exactly like his own.

"There are a lot of things I haven't done." He steadied his gaze on a painting beside the television of a partridge standing in a snowy field.

"Like what?"

He shrugged, keeping his eyes on the painting. "Lots of things."

"There are lots of things in the world to do."

Gilbert glanced at her quickly from the corner of his eye, then stared back at the painting. "Doesn't it seem strange that God would put so many things in the world you aren't allowed to do? I mean, pretty much everything, you're not supposed to do. That doesn't seem fair."

"He wires us to do bad things."

"He makes it hard not to. He hurts you so much sometimes." He turned to her, and there was a flash, either a shift in the light of his eyes or a twitch of his lips, Pia wasn't sure, but something told her he'd touched a woman before, he'd come, he'd cursed and cried and screamed, he'd punched a wall or thought of it, at least. In an instant that came and went, Gilbert became obscenely, bloodily human.

"What do you have to drink? If you wanted to get"—he circled his fingers in the air around his ears—"loopy."

"You want to get loopy?" She eased back on the bed, crossing her legs on the mattress. "I'm sad you think I'm the type of woman who'd hide booze in her room."

"Are you?"

Pia grimaced and went to the room fridge, pulling out a half-empty bottle of Grey Goose. He moved toward the bottle as if it were a holy object before disappearing into the bathroom and coming back with the two paper cups left by housecleaning that morning.

"Why don't we get some orange juice downstairs?" she asked.

"Just give me some. I want to have at least one shot in my life."

Gilbert clacked the cups together, so Pia poured. Pacing the floor, he sloshed the vodka in the cup—sniffing it, cringing—then swallowed. He held out the cup again, so Pia poured another shot, taking only a short sip of her own. Gilbert gulped his down and sat at the edge of the bed waiting, it seemed, for the impact. He keeled briefly, winced.

"This isn't my fault, is it?" she asked.

"What's your fault?"

"You're a good person."

"I was born bad. Like everyone else." He tapped the edge of the cup, and Pia poured him a third shot. "I don't like that He sees everything I do. Y'know? Like I'm being followed."

He slithered off the bed and out the door. Pia grabbed the pack of cigarettes from her purse, stuffed them into her back pocket, and went after him.

Gilbert stumbled ahead of her down the corridor and went outside to a row of vending machines. Pia stood next to him as he contemplated his options. The brisk, wet air told her rain was coming, and she regretted not wearing her jacket. The service road stretched away from the hotel as far as Pia could see. Chain restaurants, gas stations, and more hotels lit the sky with a strange glow, and the smell of stale frying oil invaded the air. She had the distinct memory in her body of a moment like this one—following a boy around at nighttime, the oncoming rain settling into the roots of her hair. Was it high school? Younger? And who was that boy? Pia lit a cigarette just as she had done back then, sliding the rest of the pack in the back pocket of her blue jeans.

Gilbert glanced at her as she took a drag. "You need to get it out of you."

"Get what out?"

"The demon. Whatever's coming between you and God. Between you and freedom, that's what it is. God sets you free. You want to be free, don't you?"

Pia tossed the cigarette and kissed him.

Gilbert held his balled fist over his mouth as if she'd punched him. "You're drunk."

"Did you like it?"

Carefully, he dropped coins into the machines, pulling out bags of chips and cheese crackers and bubblegum. His eyes kept darting back to Pia, reminding her of little boys pretending not to hear their mothers.

"Hey," her voice grew louder, "this is what you want to do while I'm standing here? I'm standing right here. Haven't you noticed me?"

He placed the snacks on the ground. "I don't know you. Why are you making me feel like I owe you something?"

When Gilbert started back into the hotel, he didn't wait for Pia, just like that other boy and every boy after him, though they all still gave her a direction to go. She sensed an even greater lack than she'd felt before that night, even before Gilbert had arrived. No one cared about why she'd gone, no one cared about what had made her leave. Not Circus, not Koko, not her mother, all of whom seemed impatient rather than concerned in their messages to her. None of her friends had called, which made Pia realize how rarely she'd seen them and how unremarkable their time together must have been.

At the door of her room, she asked, "Does it really feel that good? God."

"Pia"—he beamed—"there's nothing like it."

She searched for the flash in his eye, a hint that the unholy self she'd seen in him earlier in her room was still there. But no flash came to his eyes, no twitch to his lips. Gilbert was gone, returned to a light and all-consuming emptiness, as if the content had been removed from his heart, and whatever hurt had been there was replaced by emptiness and peace.

"What do I have to do?" she asked.

* * *

The tub stood full, and Gilbert sat on its edge, his fingers nervously tapping his knees. Warm in her nightgown, Pia stood above him, nervous as she might have been on a first date.

"This is a special day," he said. "Your life's about to change."

He reached out his hand and helped her into the tub. The cool water rose to the backs of her calves.

"All the way," he said.

Slowly, Pia sank into the water, shivering as its coolness flowed up between her legs and swelled against the base of her spine. Gilbert slid from the tub to the floor, balancing on his knees.

"Now, I want you to think about our Lord and Savior, Jesus Christ," he said. "How He suffered for us, how He died for you.

He knew you were going to come into this world and not always make the right choices. He knew you'd have sin in your heart. But He died to wash those sins away so you could enter the kingdom of Heaven. Who do you know that would die for you, Pia? If you know someone, say his name. Say her name."

No one, she wanted to say but didn't think she could without crying. She fought the urge to continue sinking into the water until she was fully under and couldn't hear or see a thing.

"You can't stop Him from loving you," Gilbert went on, his face growing red, burning. "There's nothing you could do to lose His love. Even if you don't love Him back, He still loves you. How lucky we are, Pia. Don't you think?"

Tears bloomed in Gilbert's eyes, and so Pia let her own tears come. Finally she sensed a joining between them, even more so when Gilbert placed his hands on her shoulders.

"You're going to invite Jesus into your heart," he said. "And then we're going to cleanse you. Is that what you want, Pia?"

"Yes," she said, startled by the feeble sound of her own voice.

"Thank the Lord for sending His son to you," he instructed.

"Thank you for sending your son."

"Tell Him you believe Jesus died on the cross for you and rose on the third day."

"I believe Jesus died for me. I believe He rose." The words weren't quite cracking whatever surface needed to break, so Pia closed her eyes so the ordinariness of the hotel room—the pack of cigarettes on the lid of the toilet, the leaky shampoo bottle on the counter, the splat of hand soap she'd dropped on the floor that morning next to a heap of soiled towels, the speck of sand in the corner of Gilbert's eye—wouldn't keep her from the divine.

Gilbert said more things, and Pia repeated every word. A plop of water dropped from the faucet into the tub, and she briefly peeked, painfully aware of how silly she must have looked.

"Open your eyes," Gilbert finally said.

When she opened them, she saw tears streaming down Gilbert's cheeks. She waited. She took a breath. She scanned her body—her throat, her chest, her belly, seeking out the change. There was nothing.

"Are you ready to be cleansed?" he asked.

"Sure," she said.

Gently, he pushed her shoulders, and Pia went under. The watery silence swallowed her up, and she drifted within its coolness, overcome suddenly by the need to fall asleep. Cut off from her senses, everything that hurt, stopped. For a moment, she believed God had come, but when Gilbert lifted her by the shoulders and wiped her face in a scratchy hotel towel, she knew it was only the water.

"Praise Him," Gilbert said.

"Praise Him," Pia repeated to be kind.

"You see? You always have the Lord." Gilbert, eager as a boy, rolled the towel and hung it over his shoulders, reminding her of a photograph a pair of proud parents might have displayed of their athlete son.

"Imagine if I didn't have that," Pia said. "Where would I be then?"

* * *

Across the street at the diner, she found her favorite waitress wiping down menus behind the counter.

"You're back." The woman grinned.

"What's a good neighborhood around here to live?" Pia asked.

The waitress chuckled. "What, here?"

"That's right."

She shrugged. "Maybe you'd like Phoenixville. Just up the road."

"I'll check it out in the morning," Pia said. "Can I get a shift?"

The woman's brows arrowed upward, and she glanced over Pia's shoulder as if expecting someone to come into the restaurant to tell her she was part of a practical joke.

"Mikey?" The waitress called to the cook in the kitchen. "You need to fill a shift?"

The cook pulled back his cap, sizing Pia up. "Okay," he said and went back to his work.

"Well, there you go." The waitress nodded as if she weren't sure whether to congratulate Pia or pity her.

Pia took a seat at the counter and ordered her Reuben and creamed coffee with two sugar cubes. An older couple she'd seen sharing a slice of pecan pie earlier in the week came into the restaurant. Pia waved. The couple waved back. The waitress brought her coffee, then moved easily through the room with the pot, filling mugs that the customers held up or slid to the edges of their tables, all the while with a hum in her throat. Pia listened to the murmur of conversations, the gentle clank of spoons against teacups and forks against plates. Through the window, the service road stretched without end into the night, while inside the lights were dreary but warm. There was nothing here. She belonged.

Outro

*

Koko

Koko wanted balloons. Giant, confetti-filled balloons, gold foil balloons, balloons in pastel colors that spelled out her name. But she also wanted the boy selling them behind the counter, a stout comic book fan with a bushy goatee and a cracked name tag that read DAYTON.

"My father was born in Dayton," he explained after she asked. "It's in Ohio."

"It's a cool name," she said.

"I think so."

Not that the boy was especially handsome or intriguing. He had a hobble when he walked through the party store, not from an injury, he said, but from what seemed to be an innate slug-gishness in his personality, and he had blank and tired eyes like the kids in school she knew played video games all night. But he also had creamy brown skin, unlike the pockmarked boys in the neighborhood who liked her, and dimples in his cheeks she found cute. What fully inflamed Koko's new crush was the fact that she'd turned eighteen a month before, that in a week she would graduate high school and, two months later, drive with her father from Boston to Oakland to start college. She didn't want to arrive a virgin.

"What do you want the cake to say?" Dayton asked.

"Class of 2016. Do you decorate the cakes?"

He shook his head. "We can draw a diploma on it or one of those caps with the tassels. Or your school logo or, like, the mascot. Where do you go?"

"Watertown, but I live over here with my dad now. Who decorates them if you don't?"

"Mary. Why, you want to talk to her?"

"Just asking. Where do you go?"

"I'm not in high school anymore." He snickered as if countless years had gone by and tipped an imaginary beer bottle toward his mouth. "I'll be twenty-one in October."

"So you're in college?"

"Not at the moment." He pressed his fingertips together like the mad scientist on a cartoon she used to watch as a younger girl. "College would only hold me back right now. I'm saving up for a big trip because I plan on working for the CIA. They want people with travel experience. And I'm boning up on global geopolitics, you know, economy, government, warfare. I have every book ever written on those topics and two computers next to my bed simultaneously running international news. As soon as I wake up, I can turn over and see what's happening anywhere in the world."

"Wow, you have all that in your own apartment?"

"No, at my mom's."

Koko took a unicorn key chain from a basket on the counter, twirling it around her pinkie. "Where are you going on your trip?"

"Egypt. Jordan. Once I've got the cash, I'll go wherever the action is."

"That sounds dangerous."

"I like danger." He handed her a bag of orange kazoos from beside the register. "These come with your cake order if you spend more than fifty dollars."

She took a kazoo from the bag and blew through it. Dayton smiled bashfully and pushed his glasses up the bridge of his nose.

"I want this cake, but I have to check with my dad," she said. "He's paying."

"Well, it'll all be here if you come back."

"Do you want me to come back?"

Dayton stared back at her confused, knuckles tugging at the buckle of his Batman belt. Koko realized she'd said the wrong thing, because she had understood for a long time that whatever she said to boys was wrong. They always told her it was too much. She was too much.

"I'll talk to Mary if I come back," she said. "Unless you want to help me."

"I'll certainly do what I can."

The bell chimed over the door to the shop, and a couple walked in with two toddlers who ran to a stacked bin of candies and stuffed lollipops into their pockets. Dayton came out from behind the counter with paper bags for them to use instead, while the parents asked him to come with them to a second room to discuss birthday banners. Koko took an ink pen from her purse and, on the back of a slip of paper she pulled from a shelf, drew a fat heart with her name inside, then slipped it beside the register before she went out the door.

* * *

Circus had fallen asleep in front of the television—the Panos Antonopoulos disc he'd been playing on repeat for weeks whirling quietly in the player—by the time Koko got home just after sundown, her least favorite time of day in the cramped apartment, where the faint blue walls cast every room in a lightless haze. Neither of them had done much cleaning in the past week, so there was a rotting smell in the kitchen and a layer of dust on the shelves. Koko slipped on a pair of rubber gloves and started collecting dirty plates and silverware from the living room.

"I was watching that." Her father clambered awake when she turned off the television.

"Really?" She sorted through the mail in a bowl on the coffee table, then ripped open an envelope from her aunts in Louisville. "What's the last thing the guy said?"

"That guy is Steve McQueen. Know your history, kid."

"That was the news," she said, lowering the sound on the stereo.

"This kid was a student of mine. Panos."

"I know, Dad."

"Maybe I shoulda followed him out to Los Angeles. Big money in soundtracks."

"Maybe." Koko cleared a half-eaten banana from the coffee table. "How long have you been sleeping?"

"Last night was a long one." He yawned, pulling at his over-grown beard. After the slip in the shower cracked his tooth three years earlier, her father said his high notes had become flat when he played his trumpet, and his tone lacked shimmer. An infection had formed, a doctor told him, because he'd iced the wound too much. A surgery didn't do much to change things, so he stopped playing, then stopped teaching because he didn't like the pity he said he saw in his students' eyes. After months of barely leaving the house, he took a job managing a restaurant where he used to gig. It was there Koko learned that a woman, not a fall, had busted his mouth when she hit him with his own horn. She'd overheard his coworkers teasing him about it. For the first couple of years after her mother left, Circus checked in several times a night and came home at a decent hour. The work seemed to inspire him because it gave him time with musicians who could still play. But lately he was staying later at the restaurant and coming home some nights stinking of booze.

"You schedule the night off for my party?" she asked.

"Of course, darlin'." He ran his hands over his face. "You find a cake you like?"

"It's expensive."

"Don't make me no never mind."

Koko handed him the graduation card from his sisters with

a llama wearing a mortarboard on the front. "Mom hasn't sent anything."

Circus glanced at the card. Chuckled. "If she's got any sense left, she will."

"I keep thinking she'll show up unannounced at the party."

"And how'd you feel if she did?"

"Don't know. I feel nervous imagining it."

"It'd be just like Pia to make that kinda entrance. She'd stage her own funeral just to see people mourn."

Circus heaved his body off the sofa, then started toward the kitchen, his bare feet slapping the hard wood. "If it's my night to cook, we're ordering Chinese."

Koko folded into a chair, resting her head against a pillow. It had taken a while to get used to her mother's absence, though there were moments she thought she saw Pia in the streets or behind the wheel of a passing car. There were no calls, though Pia sent the occasional letter that included snapshots of misshapen skirts she'd sewn and the blue parakeet she'd bought. The letters offered descriptions of the weather, the tomato plants Pia had started growing, the roadside shop she wanted to open with a friend, updates on her own life, but she never asked about Koko. Her mother sent birthday and Christmas cards the first two years and an Easter basket once, but the last year had been mostly quiet. Her father and grandmother had kept phoning Pia and only sometimes got an answer. They pushed Koko to call, too, thinking it might make a difference. She couldn't. Koko understood her mother had issues that she had nothing to do with, because everyone told her so—her father, her grandmother, the school counselor, her friends. Still, she believed she was the reason Pia had gone, and she didn't need the added wound of her calls going unanswered.

"Hey." Circus leaned against the kitchen doorway. "Don't worry yourself. Everybody who matters is gonna be at your party next weekend."

"Does she just not care?" Koko asked. "Or is she just not think-ing about me?"

"Pia never was one to think much about other people. Although who am I to talk?"

He rubbed at the back of his neck and went to the kitchen to rifle through the drawer of restaurant menus. Koko propped up her aunts' graduation card on a shelf next to the ones sent from her friends, her grandmother, her cousin Cressida, and her aunt Pauline. She collected the last of the dirty dishes and went to the kitchen, where she found Circus hunched over the counter, head in his hands.

Koko had gotten used to walking in on him this way every once in a while. The two of them had moved together through a kind of fog after her mother's leaving, until Circus decided to occupy his time with the tasks of fatherhood, asking after Koko's grades and homework, and making sure her lunch money awaited her every morning on the kitchen table. He gave no rules or punishments, which made Koko less apt to do wrong, and she could tell him things—crushes she had on boys, fights she had with girls who were supposed to be her friends, dreams that scared her awake— and Circus would always listen and take her side if need be. They watched movies together, their feet up on the furniture, and ate breakfast at their favorite diner on weekends. There wasn't much music anymore, but he still filled rooms with magic when he walked into them, and he always made Koko laugh until her sides grew sore. He was a star in her eyes, if one that had lost its inner shine.

"Dad? You okay?"

Circus's smile fell tight on his lips as he helped her stack the dishes into the sink.

"Everything's gonna be all right, little lady." He gave an awk-ward squeeze to her shoulder. "We're gonna be fine."

* * *

Koko couldn't come up with an excuse fast enough to stop her father from following her into the party shop the next day, but

Dayton wasn't working anyway. She talked to an older woman she assumed was Mary and placed her order of marble sheet cake with chocolate buttercream shaped like an unfurled diploma, a dozen confetti-filled balloons, and three flower garlands made of crepe paper. Circus stood near the entrance slowly walking a circle into the floor, his hands shoved into his pockets. He hadn't said much on the walk over and had stuck close as Koko ordered party platters from the catering menu at the corner market and later tried on shoes at a boutique across the street. When she'd told him to wait on a bench outside while she asked about the cake, she saw hurt in his eyes, like a pet dog commanded to go home, and her heart twisted.

"Hey," her father called across the shop. "Get me a cupcake."

"He wants a cupcake," she told the woman who might have been Mary.

"Goody," Mary said, waggling her fingers in the air. "We have quite a selection. There's a red velvet cupcake that'll knock your socks off, and we just got a new one, a pineapple-upside-down cream cheese cupcake. Doesn't that sound yummy?"

"He likes chocolate."

"That," the woman chirped, tapping the air, "we can do."

Koko watched through the display case as Mary reached for a cupcake, then neatly folded a cardboard box around it. "Is Dayton working today?"

"Oh, do you know our Dayton?" Mary placed a tiny plastic fork and napkin into the box.

"He helped me out yesterday, so I wanted to say thanks."

"Dayton works later this week. I'm sure he'd appreciate a thank you."

Just as Koko reached for the box, something outside seemed to have caught her father's eye, and he rushed out of the shop, the bell above the door jangling.

"He knows everybody." Koko took a bite of the cupcake. "Wherever he goes."

"A lucky man has many friends," Mary said, teacher-like, then rinsed her hands in the sink behind her. Koko took another stroll through the shop to give her father time with whomever or whatever had his attention. At the back of the store, she found a display of wizard wands and pirate swords, rainbow wigs and tutus. She slipped a pair of furry rabbit ears over her head and a mask pasted with whiskers, primping in front of a mirror until she found her cutest smile, then snapped a photo and sent it to Bree.

On her way out the door, Mary handed her a free bite of vanilla fudge. "Congratulations on your graduation, my dear. The world's your oyster."

Koko folded the candy into a napkin in her purse. "That's what they tell me."

Outside, her father stood several paces up the block talking to a woman in a long ivory dress, her black hair in a loose knot atop her head, ringlets falling gracefully over her shoulders. Circus hadn't noticed Koko step out of the shop, his gaze fixed on the woman, so she slid her phone from her pocket and pretended to type a message. Secretly she strained to hear them.

"Me, too," the woman said. "Of course I do. I think about it."

"I'm different than when I met you," Circus rested his hand on the woman's shoulder, and she closed her eyes, softening against it. "Everything's changed."

"Same with me," the woman said.

Koko had never seen her father so carried away as the woman placed her hand over his. Then her gaze shifted, landing on Koko.

"Hi there," the woman said with a smile.

When Circus turned, Koko thought she saw tears in his eyes.

"Odessa, this is my girl," he said. "Koko, baby, this is Odessa. We met on a subway ages ago. Had an adventure together. We haven't seen each other for a long time."

Though her father had never mentioned the woman, Koko saw the two of them looking back at her as parts that already made a whole, a unit that felt more intimate than what she'd formed with him over the last three years. Before now, Koko had seen him with Maggie Swan and for the first time had understood that her father could feel love, though she also understood that Maggie was beyond him, that there was a plane on which she functioned that her father couldn't reach. After Maggie moved back to New York, visiting several times a year with the baby, Koko had never heard about other women. The fact that her father spent so much of his time outside work with her or at home alone suggested that any woman who was in his life didn't matter much. But this woman seemed to matter.

"Wonderful to meet you." Odessa folded her hands behind her back, graceful as a dancer. "I hear you're graduating."

"Yeah." Koko didn't know what to do with the moment.

"Are you excited about college?"

"Sure, it's cool." Koko glanced at her father, whose gaze was still fixed on Odessa. "Do you do music, too?"

"Odessa's an illustrator," her father said. "Isn't that something?"

"Cool," Koko answered.

"Well, congratulations. And good luck." Odessa quietly clapped her hands together. "It was good to see you."

"You're gonna call me," he said. "Tonight."

"I told you I would."

"You sure you got my number?"

"I'm sure." Odessa waved and walked away, Koko and her father watching after her as the hem of her white dress billowed, making her seem not of the world.

Circus moved through the rest of the day like he'd risen out of a long sleep, whistling as he made ham sandwiches for their lunch and singing with the Ray Charles record he let blast through the apartment. He trimmed his beard. He asked one of the neighbors, a hairdresser, to give him a cut. By the end of the afternoon, he seemed to have broken free of the gloom that had hovered during the last few years. So that afternoon, as they played their monthly game of chess, which he'd begun teaching her after she moved in, Koko hoped Odessa would phone.

Just before midnight, Koko found him on the front stoop with a beer.

"Maybe she got busy," she said.

"Maybe."

"Do you have her number? Why don't you call her?"

He shook his head. "I don't chase nobody no more."

"It seemed like she liked you. I bet she'd be glad you called."

"Why you so concerned?"

"Well, y'know." Koko sat beside him. "I'm going to be gone soon."

"And how's that matter?"

"You don't have to keep holding yourself back. You can find someone."

"You think you're the reason there's no woman in my life? Don't flatter yourself, kid."

He took a swig of the beer, tossed the empty bottle across the lawn toward a trash bin at the curb, missed. Koko got up to retrieve it from the grass and throw it into the bin. It clanked against something and shattered. She looked back at the building. Their apartment on the first floor, which she used to walk into as a younger girl with the same glee she stepped onto a playground, now seemed common and small.

"You should call her," Koko said.

Circus swiped the air.

"What's wrong, Dad?"

"Nothin', doll."

"I want to know."

He rubbed his knees, a move she'd come to recognize as the way he calmed himself. "You know you're gonna hit a moment in life when there's nowhere else for you to go, you're not going any farther. Everything you're gonna do and be is already in place, so you hit that plateau, right, and just coast until the end. That's okay if you like where you are, but if not . . ."

He let out a heavy sigh, took a cigarette from a pack Koko didn't realize he had in his shirt pocket, and slid it between his lips. "I guess I thought that moment would come later. And be easier. Or better."

After he lit the cigarette, she said, "I thought you quit."

He took a drag. "I did."

"Then what are you doing?"

"What's it look like?"

"I don't want you to smoke."

"One cigarette. Jesus, Koko, get off my back."

He rose from the steps and went past her through the yard onto the sidewalk, which he followed down the road, the streetlights and full moon covering him, his head drooped and shoulders slumped like an old man and no longer a king.

* * *

Monday after school, Koko went back to the party shop where she found Dayton stacking bundles of colored napkins onto a shelf.

"I need you," she said to his back.

He spun around quickly, and his glasses slipped down his nose.

"Can I come to your place?" she asked.

"Oh." Dayton stood, his limbs shrinking inward as if he wanted to disappear into the wall behind him. "But why?"

"I need your spy skills. I want to track someone down."

"Interesting." He glanced around as if they were planning a crime. "Who's the target?"

The seriousness with which he asked the question drew Koko to him less. He seemed younger now, boyish. She guessed he was a virgin, too, and perhaps not as ready as she was to change the fact. But each passing day brought her closer to the moment she would arrive on campus and closer to the night she would lie next to a boy she adored and not know what to do. Dayton was a last chance.

"I'll give you the details later." She lowered her voice. "Just tell me if you're in."

Dayton lived in a tiny house surrounded by gardens and tucked away from the street, its yellow facade and blue door reminding Koko of a fairy-tale cottage. His mother was working the late shift at the hospital and wouldn't be home until seven the next morning. The stuffy air in the basement smelled of dirty clothes, sweat, and a trace of lemon, which Koko assumed came from the can of disinfectant spray overturned on the floor. Samurai movie posters were taped to the walls, alongside prints of animated characters she imagined he'd drawn, and his unmade bed lay between two computer screens, the keyboard peeking out from beneath a pillow.

Dayton brought two cans of Sprite from a minifridge in the corner of the room and a bag of corn chips from a drawer. He tossed them onto a beanbag chair shaped like a sneaker and told Koko to have a seat while he went to an attached bathroom to change out of his work shirt. Pacing the room, she perused the posters and drawings on the walls and the comic books on the shelves, but she had trouble looking directly at the bed, knowing what she hoped would happen there before evening's end.

Dayton came back to the room in a sweatshirt with the solar system sewn into its front and clicked on the computers, reaching for a chair to sit on instead of the bed.

"Who do you hang out with?" she asked.

"What do you mean?"

She sank into the beanbag chair. "You're not in school, and it looks like the only other person you work with is an old lady."

Dayton pointed to the computer screens. "Oh, I got a lot of friends. Only way I get any alone time is when I turn these bad boys off."

"Do you have, like, a . . . girlfriend?"

Koko kept her eyes on the poster across from where she sat because she didn't know how to look at him without appearing like his answer mattered. But Dayton's silence made her take a glance, and she saw him arrange the possible responses in his mind, as if only some of them would he want her to hear.

"Kinda," he finally said. "She's in Singapore."

"You met her online?"

He nodded.

A twinge of jealousy nettled Koko's gut. "Have you ever seen her in real life?"

"Her dad travels for work. She says she might come with him if he ever flies this way."

"Cool," she said, pulling off her sweater so he could see her crop top in pink camouflage colors tightly cuddling her breasts. Dayton quickly turned back to his screens.

"Everyone has friends online," he said. "Don't you?"

"Yeah, but I like my friends here. I'll miss them when I'm in California."

"Why you going to school all the way out there?"

"It's got a good art program."

"Okay, but why so far?"

Koko lay back on the chair, dangling her legs over the edge as she thought about the question, realizing no one else had really asked. "I feel like I'm living in other people's lives, like I'm part of their lives but they're not part of mine. I want to live in my own life, and I can't do it here. You get what I mean?"

"I guess. And does this person you're looking for have anything to do with it?"

"I want her to take care of my dad after I leave."

"Is he sick?"

"No. He just needs someone loving him."

Dayton stretched out his fingers to let his knuckles crack. "All right, so tell me everything you know about this person."

"Her name's Odessa."

The buttons of the keyboard clattered under Dayton's busy fingers.

"She must live somewhere around here," Koko said. "And she's an illustrator."

The buttons clattered again, then Dayton turned to one of the screens. "Her?"

Odessa Keys grinned back from a photograph on the webpage

of a company called Dickerson Design. In a tailored black suit, she sat in a swivel chair, her legs stretched across the floor and hands folded over them gracefully as her gaze angled toward the camera.

"I guess there aren't a lot of illustrators around town named Odessa." Dayton zoomed in on the photograph. "What else do you want to know?"

"Nothing I can't find out on my own now, I guess." Koko reached into her purse for a pen and paper, jotting down the name of the company.

"All right then." Dayton opened a second window on the screen to a game Koko imagined he wanted to play. "What do we do now?"

So long had it been since she kissed a boy—a brief and disappointing kiss in eleventh grade with the Tower, at one of the only parties she ever went to—and so long had it been since Ian on Sanibel Island had run his hand up her shirt that Koko had withdrawn from encounters with boys as soon as they tried to kiss or touch her, for fear she'd do something wrong. Sophomore year, she'd fallen in with the group of girls she would spend her time with until high school was over, awkward girls who studied hard and played instruments and hung out in the art room to avoid the rest of the school. Some of those girls got awkward boyfriends, but never Koko, who boys called "pushy" even as they ogled her body, which they said was shaped like the number eight.

No one would ever know if Koko embarrassed herself with Dayton, who worked at a party shop in the neighborhood where she lived with her father, but not where Koko went to school. But she figured she would have to be pushy, because he was looking up at her like a boy who wanted to play a game and not like someone who wanted to touch her.

"I don't know," she answered. "What do you want to do?"

He held out one of the controllers from his game console. "I can teach you."

She strolled through the room, hands in the belt loops of her pants. "If you could be an animal, what animal would you be?"

"Easy." He smacked his palms together. "Eagle. It's an apex predator, nothing preys on it. Plus, you know, flying."

"If you had to lose one of your senses—"

"Taste, obviously. It's the only sense that exists more for our enjoyment than to keep us safe." He clicked his fingers. "But you didn't say which animal you'd be."

Koko took one last look at the posters on the wall, then sat on the bed. "A fox."

"Why?"

"They don't run with a pack, and they can see in the dark. You can never fool a fox." Koko rested her elbows on a pillow. "Do you mind if I take off my top? It's hot in here."

He wiped his mouth with the back of his hand, nodded. Koko pulled off the top, tossing it to the ground, then settled onto the mattress with a casual snap of the strap of her pink lace bra.

Dayton's knees bounced fiercely. "Did you know the spacesuits the astronauts wore for the moon landing were made from the same materials bras are made of? I bet no one told the astronauts before they went up there. They probably wouldn't have—"

"Next question." She rolled onto her side the way she saw pretty actresses do in sexy scenes on television. "If you were best in the world at something, what would it be?"

"Swordsmanship. Actually, I'm already pretty good." Dayton sounded out of breath even though he hadn't moved for almost an hour. "What about you?"

"A sailor," she said. "Can I get under the covers?"

"Wait, why a sailor?"

Koko lifted her chest so he would look while she came up with an answer. "If I was the best sailor, I could conquer the ocean. There's nothing in the world I wouldn't be able to get to."

His eyes widened, and his knees stopped their bounce. "Wow, you're cool."

He stared back at her with wonder, a clumsy grin hanging on his lips. The boy seemed ridiculous all of a sudden, and Koko felt sorry for him, which for some reason made her think of her father, and a slight shame flooded her chest as she realized she must have looked back at him many times in her younger days with the same hopeful smile. Koko knew what she wanted from the boy was brief and functional, so seeing his eyes fill with love made her doubt whether she should go on.

"You can get under the covers," he said. "Y'know, if you get cold."

She slid beneath the blankets, the sheets stiff on her skin as if they were brand new. "Do you want to get under here with me?"

He balled his fists and shoved them under the hem of his sweatshirt. Koko wondered if he was worrying about the girl in Singapore or his mother coming home, or whether he, like her, feared what might happen if their bodies came too close. He slipped out of the sweatshirt and crawled across the bed, reminding Koko of the clumsy way Bree's cat climbed over the mounds of her blankets to sit on Koko's chest whenever she spent the night. Dayton slid next to her, leaving enough space for another body to lie between them as they stared up at the ceiling.

"Have you ever been to Good Sugar Café, the Thai place on Centre?" he asked.

"Nope."

"They have a great *tod mun*."

Koko turned to face him. "Have you done this before?"

He kept his eyes on the ceiling. "Lie in a bed talking about food?"

"You know what I mean."

Dayton didn't reply, his lashes blinking. Koko took his silence as an answer. "Don't you want to get it over with?"

"Why do you think of it that way?" he asked.

"Because no one likes it the first time."

"That's not what I've heard."

"Should we try?"

Closing his eyes, he slid off his glasses and slowly folded them onto the headboard behind him. After several labored seconds, he turned, the stiff sheets crinkling around him.

Koko pushed through her nerves to kiss him quickly, and his puffy lips rose to meet hers. Dayton swallowed, his mouth sticky and moist, before kissing her back. She moved closer to him, happy to find that he smelled soapy and clean, despite the odor in the room, while his body, heavy beside her, seemed to bind them in a way that made her feel fastened to the world like she never had, like she imagined people in happy families felt.

"Do you want to take off your pants?" she asked.

"If you do."

"We'll do it at the same time."

Beneath the blankets, they slid out of their pants, kicking them to the edge of the bed.

"Okay," Dayton whispered as if to spur his own courage, then wrapped his hands around her waist. Their arms and legs lurched and tangled, while their mouths missed each other or came together too quickly, clattering their teeth. Her hair pulled accidentally when Dayton rolled onto it. The crown of his watch got stuck on a loose thread of her bra. They moved together in a mess, careful not to let their lower bodies graze against each other. Still, Koko sparked inside, just as she had the moment Ian placed his hand over her breast and flooded her body with warmth. She was eager to know what it would feel like to have Dayton between her legs where only she had ever touched.

As if he'd heard her thoughts, Dayton suddenly rose to his knees and hovered above her, lashes blinking in a frenzy. He dipped his hips so that his thing, hard beneath his boxer shorts, touched the top of her thigh. Her body stiffened.

"Wait," she said, sliding the pillow from behind her head, holding it over her chest. "You like me, right?"

He nodded. "Do you like me?"

"I guess so."

He frowned, covering his stomach with the sheet. "It'd be nice if you did."

"If you like me, you'll be nice when it hurts."

"Well," he said. "I don't want to hurt anyone."

Dayton slipped into his sweatshirt while Koko stayed under his blankets to get back into her top and sweater. They sat in silence, the night outside sending a murky hue into the room.

"Well, it was cool hanging out," he said.

"Yeah." Koko collected her bag. "For sure."

"When's your graduation party?"

"Saturday."

"Then you're gone, huh?"

"Not right away. Soon, though."

Dayton stood across from her, pulling at the tip of a tissue he'd pulled from his pocket. He seemed eager to say more but only told her, "I hope you get everything you want."

"Me, too."

* * *

Koko arrived home and found her father at the kitchen counter, an unlit cigarette hanging from his lips and his lighter in hand, as if he'd been about to strike it when his thoughts interrupted him.

"What up?" Circus pulled the cigarette from his mouth and stuffed it into a pack on the table. He ran a pot of water for coffee and pulled two bananas from a bunch, tossing one to Koko. His hair and beard looked unkempt, though he'd trimmed both only days before, while gray circles plumped beneath his eyes.

"Everything good?" she asked.

"Never better."

"You can tell me if something's wrong."

He scooped a teaspoon of sugar into a cup, then waited for the pot to boil.

"Did you make an appointment with your doctor about your knee?"

"It's fine. I'm just an old man now."

"You should get it checked," she said. "Work okay?"

"Jesus, Koko." He chucked the spoon into the sink. "Why you on my back lately?"

"Because you're moody. And you look like shit."

"Well, I got a right." He poured the coffee even though it hadn't boiled. "Go to bed or something, man. Get out of my hair."

"Is this how you want to spend our last days together?"

Circus groaned and went to his bedroom, slamming the door behind him.

Koko had a shower and set her hair. She sent a text to her friends to tell them about the encounter with Dayton, giggling when they all sent back messages demanding details the next morning. She read a chapter of Salinger so she could check him off the list she'd found online of books everyone should have read before the age of eighteen, another task she wanted to complete before she arrived at college. It was after one in the morning when she finally fell asleep and the dead of night when she woke up after dreaming of her teeth falling out. Koko went to the kitchen for a cup of chamomile tea.

"Make enough for me, will you?" her father called from the living room.

Circus was sprawled across the sofa, a glass of bourbon on the floor beside him and a wet washcloth folded over his eyes. He wore his old Conservatory T-shirt that she'd seen that morning at the bottom of a basket of dirty clothes, and there was a hole in the toe of one of his socks. Koko waited for the water to boil, then brought the two filled mugs to the living room.

"*Grazie.*" Circus sat up, tossed the washcloth onto the coffee table and sipped the bourbon instead of the tea. "You digging your last week as a senior?"

"It kinda feels like any other week."

"Maybe you need to get yourself into some good trouble."

"Like what?"

"Toilet paper the school. Put the principal's car in a tree. Whatever kids do these days."

"What'd you do?"

He scratched at his beard as the memory came back to him. "Come to think of it, I spent my senior week with my girl. Didn't have any classes. She was at the University of Louisville, I'd drive over whenever I could. Shanice Robinson. Prettiest eyes I've seen to this day."

"You've never talked about her."

"'Cause she's the only girl broke my heart. A man only lets that happen once."

"What about Maggie?"

"I knew going in I was never really gonna have her."

Koko blew the steam from her tea as she watched the light fade from her father's eyes.

"Did I do all right?" he asked.

"On what?"

He downed the last nip of bourbon, winced. "Never mind." He wrapped his hands around the warm mug of tea, holding it against his belly. "I thought I was finally getting the hang of being your dad and now you're leaving."

Koko tensed, feeling the need to defend herself. But as her father tightened the string of his teabag around his spoon and gently placed it in an ashtray, the simplest and most harmless of gestures, she knew this was no ploy to make her feel guilty. He was not her mother. What Koko had not yet grasped until this moment was that somewhere in the three years since her mother had gone away and her father had taken her in, Koko had become the one who had love, and he'd become the one who needed it. Crossing the room to sit beside him, she lifted his arm, draped it over her shoulders, and snuggled against his chest.

* * *

The next morning she took Tremont toward Cambridge instead of Pond Street toward school, searching her phone for the address to Dickerson Design. The offices were on the top floor of a building in Kendall Square. When Koko arrived, the security guard was asleep at the front desk, so she slipped by him to the elevators, stepping off at the top floor, where the walls and ceilings were orange, and the chairs in the lobby were pill-shaped and white, so that Koko imagined herself inside a fruit. Behind a glass wall, a group sat at an ivory desk, talking and typing into their laptops. Koko looked for but didn't see Odessa among them.

"Are you lost?" the receptionist asked from her desk at the side of the room.

"Oh," Koko said. "I'm here to see Odessa Keys."

"Odessa's offsite today. Can I relay a message?"

"When will she be back?"

The receptionist offered a strained smile. "Is there a message?"

Koko looked around, as if searching hard enough would bring Odessa into the room. "Tell her Circus's daughter came by."

"Circus?"

"Circus Palmer. She'll know who I mean."

"I'll be sure to let her know."

"Circus likes her," Koko went on. "Tell Odessa that Circus likes her, like, really, really likes her. And no matter what happened, she should give him a chance."

The receptionist capped the pen she'd been writing with. "This sounds like a personal matter. I'll let Odessa know you were here."

Koko slid one of the invitations to her graduation party from her backpack and handed it to the receptionist. "Odessa's invited. Tell her I really hope she comes. She'll see him there, and maybe, I don't know, something good can happen. I have no idea what went on between them, okay, like, maybe he was an asshole. I mean, probably he was an asshole. It's just . . ." Tears began to pool in Koko's eyes. "There's a lot of things he didn't know before. He knows now. But it's only making him sadder."

Koko covered her mouth as if she'd cursed, even though it was tears she wanted to stop. They came anyway, burning in her eyes. She sobbed in a way she hadn't since her mother left, and her cries seemed to reach down to a deeper wound so that she cried harder and fuller.

The receptionist stared up at her, eyes wide. Then she turned to her computer, opened a new message to Odessa, and started typing.

"Got it," she said. "What else?"

* * *

Koko could hear the music echoing through the neighborhood from the Swans' backyard in Brookline, as she and her father walked up to the front porch, where bouquets of balloons were tied to the handrails and a banner congratulated her above the door that stood open, letting free the scent of oven-fried chicken baking in the kitchen. Circus took a last drag from the cigarette he'd started smoking at the curb, mashed its end against one of the concrete steps, and slid it back into the pack in his pocket.

"You ready, baby girl?" he asked.

Before she could answer, Maggie rushed through the door and took Koko into her mighty arms. "There she is! Am I glad to see you, sugar, congratulations."

Koko thrilled the way she always had around Maggie Swan, whose arrival was like a burst of fireworks.

"Look at you, all grown now." Maggie hugged her again. "What took y'all so long? Everybody's here."

Koko nodded toward her father. "Someone needed cigarettes."

"Not in this house, boy," Maggie warned, kissing him on the cheek.

Circus stroked her chin. "Yes, ma'am."

Maggie grabbed Koko's hand and led her through the house into the backyard. Her grandmother sat at a picnic table with her boyfriend, while at the back of the yard, Koko's friends from her new neighborhood bumped a balloon like a volleyball to her girl-friends from school, some still in their graduation gowns, their siblings and parents watching from another table. Maggie's sister Belinda was the first to notice Koko and Circus come into the yard. She cheered and everyone followed her lead.

"Show us that diploma," Maggie told her. "Hold it high, girl."

Koko lifted it into the air, and the cheers grew louder. Through the tiny crowd ran Rosetta, Maggie and Circus's girl, a fiery three-year-old in overalls and braids. She wrapped her arms around Koko's knees and begged to be picked up. Koko held her as the child puckered her lips at their father. Circus kissed her, play-fully tugging her curls. Rosetta pointed toward the huge table in the center of the yard, so Koko walked her over, circling the buffet of grilled pork chops and steak, corncobs and French fries, baked beans and macaroni salad, fruit pies and cupcakes, soda for the kids and wine for the grown-ups. Rosetta asked for an olive, then retched after Koko handed her one and she took a bite.

"Congrats, lovely." Belinda gave her a hug. "Everything to your liking?"

Koko looked around at the banners and balloons, the two grills at the side of the yard cooking beef tips and scallops on skewers. Hung from trees were gold paper lanterns, one of which swayed in the breeze and caught Rosetta's eye. She wriggled out of Koko's arms and ran to it, her father chasing after.

"Everything's perfect," Koko said.

"Good," Belinda said. "We're proud of you, pumpkin."

"Can I tell you guys something?"

The sisters huddled close.

"I invited someone."

"It's your party," Maggie said. "Whoever you want is welcome."

"I'm nervous about it, though."

"Is it a boy?" Belinda asked eagerly.

Koko glanced across the lawn, where her father carried Rosetta on his shoulders so she could grab the blue string of a balloon. "The other day, we ran into a woman Dad used to know. I thought he was going to melt across the sidewalk when he saw her. So I kind of found her, and I kind of, asked her to come."

"Found her?" Belinda asked.

"Long story."

"Aren't you the sweetest?" Maggie glanced over her shoulder at Circus and Rosetta dancing in the yard. "Of course, she's welcome. What's there to be nervous about?"

"I don't know if she'll come. She was supposed to call him, and she never did."

Maggie bit her bottom lip as if this were a puzzle she needed to solve.

"The party's just getting started," Belinda said. "Give her time."

"Either way, you're an angel." Maggie kissed the air between them. "You're his angel. He's a lucky devil to have you."

Koko's grandmother ambled over arm in arm with her boyfriend, a retired dentist from the home, whose chin she always had to wipe. In the months after Pia left, the old woman had shown a greater cruelty than Koko had known her to be capable of. During the occasional meals she'd treat Koko to after school, she'd mocked Pia's vanity and lack of spine, the way she wore her hair, the way she'd tried to mother. Finally the old woman seemed to realize her daughter wasn't coming back, and she started to move with less vigor—not from age, Koko believed, but from shame.

"Congratulations, darling." Her grandmother kissed her forehead, leaving a trail of Chanel perfume. "You've come a long way."

"Thank you," Koko said, shaking Dr. Thompson's hand.

The corner of her grandmother's mouth twitched and her lashes fluttered as if she were on the verge of tears. "Things change so quickly."

"Yeah, they do."

Her grandmother grasped her hand. "I don't remember what

time felt like when I was a girl your age. Though even those years seem to have happened lifetimes ago." Her grandmother loosened her grip. "Did she . . ."

Koko knew she was asking about her mother. "I haven't heard from her."

"I'm sorry, dear," she said. "That's not right."

Koko escorted her grandmother and the dentist back to their seats, filling their plates with carrot sticks and stalks of celery. She spoke to the parents of her friends, who sat awkwardly around the next picnic table sipping cocktails and straining through conversation. She played badminton with her girlfriends and her old friends from the neighborhood at the net Belinda had set up at the back of the yard. She ate two chicken breasts and a scallop skewer, a spoonful of macaroni salad Bree's mother had made, and two slices of her graduation cake. But as the afternoon wore on, what Koko wanted was to be with her family—with her father, and with Maggie, Rosetta, and Belinda, who sat together on a blanket in a corner of the yard. She had a sense already that this was the kind of moment she would miss one day. She also found herself glancing at the back door of the house and realized it was Odessa Keys, not her mother, she hoped would walk through into the yard.

It was dusk when she finally came. Koko's friends had long ended their games and were lazing on the lawn, their parents and siblings gone home. Rosetta was napping in a bedroom upstairs, while Circus, Maggie, and Belinda passed around a flask on the blanket spread over the grass. Odessa, beautiful in a mint-green summer dress, lingered on the porch, a bottle of champagne in one hand and a wrapped gift in the other. Koko knew she should have greeted her, but she wanted to see her father's reaction. When he noticed Odessa, he went to her, wordlessly, took her hands in his, and kissed the inside of her palms.

Then he faced Koko and their eyes locked, his watery and injured but suddenly filling with light, hers steady and clear.

Everything else around them receded, so that Koko could feel she finally knew him completely and he knew her.

"Hey." Bree stepped up beside her. "We're going to Janey's to watch movies. You in?"

"Actually"—Koko dialed the number for a taxi—"there's somewhere I need to be."

* * *

It was clumsy. Bloody. But eventually they found their rhythm. She had knocked on his window, and Dayton had let her in through the back door. He'd cleaned his room since the last time Koko was in it, leaving behind a scent of bubblegum and pine. He'd had one light on in the room when she came in but clicked it off when Koko requested it. She didn't bother asking about his day. He didn't ask about the graduation or the party. He only took a condom from a fresh box in the drawer of his bedside table, hiding himself as he struggled to slip it on.

"Not yet," she said. "Do something to me first."

"What should I do?"

"Something you think will make me feel nice."

He hovered over her like homework that confused him. Koko laughed. He blushed, then ran his hand from her knees over her thighs down the hem of her panties. "I saw this once on—"

"Don't tell me," she said. "Don't ruin it."

He fumbled at first but then he found her. Koko tried to move against his hand the way she did her own.

"Touch me here." She nodded toward her chest. "Kiss me. Put your hands in my hair."

Dayton did as she asked, nuzzling her shoulders and holding her in a way that made her realize he was stronger than he looked.

"Do it now," she said and parted her knees.

Koko had tears in her eyes as he pushed into her, and they stayed as he drove his hips without quite knowing how. She placed her hands on his back to steady him and ease the strain. It hurt and burned until it moved into a strange numbness, though she could feel beneath the discomfort the possibility of something good.

"So what happens now?" Dayton asked once they'd settled back into their own skins.

"Nothing."

In the silence between them, Koko slid across the mattress so their bodies could touch. Beneath the sheets, she took his hand.

"Okay," he said.

A clock somewhere in the house chimed nine o'clock. Koko took a shower, watching her virgin's blood flow from her thighs against the porcelain tub into the drain. Already she felt years older, and her body looked more like a woman's than a girl's, weighed as it seemed now with a new sense of purpose and power. Back in the bedroom, she lay with Dayton as crickets chirped in the garden outside his window. Koko told him about the graduation ceremony, how the class valedictorian had cried after her notes scattered in the wind and the school band played off-key. Dayton told her the plot of his favorite samurai movie, acting out the fight scenes in the dark. Then her phone buzzed with a message from her father.

Come back, he'd typed. *We have to open your champagne.*

He'd sent a photograph Maggie had taken of herself next to Belinda with Rosetta asleep in her lap, Odessa and her father with their arms around each other on the blanket beside them. Circus held two champagne flutes, ready to toast.

"I have to go."

* * *

Outside the window of the taxi, the town appeared different to Koko's eyes, smaller somehow, and though this was her town, she felt like she was seeing it for the first time after having been away. *There's the spot I smoked my first and only cigarette,* she imagined telling whomever she'd one day bring home. *I broke my ankle on that corner.* The driver wished her well as she stepped out of the cab onto the main road, and it seemed a meaningful goodbye. The air was warm as she walked down the quiet street toward the Swans' house, and as she heard her own strong footsteps make a rhythm of the night, she decided it was possible to have a hand in the way her life played out. She walked slowly, knowing everyone would wait for her because they wanted to give her something solid that would always be there when she needed to come back to it.

As she neared the house, Koko heard it. The trumpet sounding in the air. The notes, major-keyed and plump, hopped from one to the next like a parade, while the melody fell easy and light. Koko assumed it was a tune her father had played when she was a girl, until he played the melody again and she heard it in a fuller, deeper way, recognizing it as the song they'd written together. Koko remembered that long-ago day in faint images—the backyard of the house they'd once shared with her mother, her father sitting on top of the rickety picnic bench he'd built himself, his feet bare, tapping the rhythm as Koko made up words to go with it. A zebra on a xylophone. An elephant on an oboe. A monkey on a trombone.

"'Jungle orchestra,'" Koko sang quietly as her father continued to play in the distance, the notes still flat because his mouth could hardly find them anymore. She liked hearing him search for them.

She listened as her father blew his horn, and her town—their town—seemed to fill with the sound. Something told her she would always remember this day, because it was the day she'd slept with someone for the first time, the day she'd graduated high school and left behind a universe, the day her father had rediscovered the woman he'd love for the rest of his life. But soon the years would pass, and she would forget the details. The class valedictorian's notes scattering across the schoolyard. What her father said to her when she walked off the stage with her diploma.

The color of Odessa's dress. What Dayton felt like on top of her. Koko would forget most of these details, save for one. That the wind shifted and sent a chill across her freshly cleaned skin so that she sensed her own solitude in a way that no longer frightened her as she walked bare and unhindered toward what was new.

Acknowledgments

*

My mother still has the first book I wrote around the time I started learning how to write letters. As a girl, I wanted to be a movie star, so I barely registered how routinely I was writing stories. It was as natural to me as walking. If you'd have told that little girl it would take decades before she published a book, I doubt she'd have stuck with it. These folks kept me going, and I am forever grateful to them.

To my rock star agent, Chad Luibl, whose every move—from our initial meeting to the moment we inked the deal—has been flawless. Chad, on our first Zoom you articulated my vision for the book in a way I never could, and it was clear that you got me as a writer. I dig your style and thank you for guiding me through this process with patience and aplomb. I'm convinced I have the smartest, kindest, hardest-working agent on my side, and I hope this is the start of a long professional relationship and friendship.

To my editors, Lisa Lucas and Deb Garrison, two supernovas whose brilliance and enthusiasm for literature electrified the Zoom screen during our introductory call. Barely a minute into it, I was already thinking, "I want to work with them!" Deb, you offered the most loving arms for my literary baby, and I am thankful for the care you took with each line. This is a better book because of you. Lisa, you were able to see things in my manuscript I hadn't seen and made me love it all the more. I am so honored to be among your roster of writers. To my hardworking publicity team—Julianne Clancy, Rose Cronin-Jackman, Josefine Kals McGehee, Kelly Blair, Rebecca Jozwiak, Michiko Clark, and Andreia Wardlaw. Thank you to Todd Portnowitz, Nora Reichard, Zuleima Ugalde, and everyone at Pantheon and Penguin Random House whose great talent made this book what it is today.

Alexandria Coe, seeing your image on a mock-up of my cover was one of the best moments of 2021. Thank you for your work. Thanks to you and Linda Huang for designing such a gorgeous book. Linda, I spent months–MONTHS–staring at the cover. It's breathtaking.

This book would not be in the world if not for the generosity of writer pals who read the manuscript, gave advice, or simply told me to hang in there. Thank you Edan Lepucki (a lifesaver a thousand times over), Chris Terry, Matthew Specktor, Caeli Wolfson Widger, Catherine Buni, Linda Rosenkrantz, Christopher Finch, and Chris Daley (who gets additional thanks for letting me text her incessantly on book auction day). More thanks to Melissa Chadburn, Amanda Fletcher, Andrea Rothman, Afia Atakora, Randy Susan Meyers, and Rachel Lyon for making connections.

I got through the bumpy journey to publication with support from the best friends a gal could have. Thank you for being there: Dan O'Brien (best joke texter, best unboxing video producer, best friend a gal could have), Charley Taylor, Eric Arnold, Rich Bradway, Chris Stagliola, Marco Lorenzetto, Mathieu Cailler, Maria McKee, and Rich Farrell.

Thank you to my mentors at Vermont College—Doug Glover, David Jauss, Abby Frucht, and Clint McCown—and at the Tin House Summer Workshop and Bread Loaf Writers' Conference—Dana Spiotta and Danzy Senna, respectively, for helping me see and address my blind spots as a writer. You all recognized what I was trying to achieve and helped me dig out of some messy drafts.

Thank you to all the musicians who provided details about their industry and craft so I could make Circus Palmer and Maggie Swan come to life, especially Owen Plant and Michael Alongi, who double-checked my drumming terminology, and all my Berklee students who had no idea how much of what they did in my classes (instead of paying attention to lectures) would end up in this book.

I am so lucky to have a family who has supported me from day one. Thanks eternally to the Warrells—Grandma and Grandpa, Mike, Kathy, Bill, Geoff, and the Ellises—Rick, Alex and Jesse, all of whom never stopped cheering me on.

Most of all, thank you to my mother who raised me on her own but still found time to read to me every night and give me whatever she could to nurture the person I might become: photography and drama classes, woodburning sets and paints, the list goes on. It was the books and typewriter that finally brought it all together. Mom, thank you for your unwavering belief in me. It gave me the courage to see this thing through.

A NOTE ABOUT THE AUTHOR

Laura Warrell is a contributor to the Bread Loaf Writers' Conference and the Tin House Summer Workshop, and is a graduate of the creative writing program at Vermont College of Fine Arts. Her work has appeared in *HuffPost*, *The Rumpus*, and the *Los Angeles Review of Books*, among other publications. She has taught creative writing and literature at the Berklee College of Music in Boston and through the Emerging Voices Fellowship at PEN America in Los Angeles, where she lives.

A NOTE ON THE TYPE

This book was set in a modern adaptation of
a type designed by the first William Caslon
(1692–1766). The Caslon face, an artistic, easily
read type, has enjoyed more than two centuries
of popularity in the English-speaking world.
This version, with its even balance and honest
letterforms, was designed by Carol Twombly for
the Adobe Corporation and released in 1990.

Typeset by Scribe Inc.
Philadelphia, Pennsylvania

Printed and bound by Berryville Graphics
Berryville, Virginia

Book design by Pei Loi Koay